Rave
The Best Child

MW01065544

"Trachtenberg took out the legwork—researching books, talking with librarians, etc.—so parents can get on to the most important thing, which is spreading a love of literature. This book is an essential resource for parents who want to share the joy of reading with their child."

—Donna Smith,
Senior Editor of *Baby Years* Magazine

"Exposing your children from tots to teens to books is the first step in turning them into bookworms. Ellen Trachtenberg has organized classic and modern children's books into a well-researched, easy-to-understand format to help parents select books. Remember, the right book can intrigue even reluctant readers."

—Marge Eberts, "Dear Teacher" Columnist and Education Author

"Ellen Trachtenberg has sifted through thousands of books to give parents a comprehensive, well-organized and practical guide to first-rate children's literature for all ages. *The Best Children's Literature* takes the mystery out of finding books kids—and their parents—will love."

—Laura Backes
Publisher of *Children's Book Inside*

"*The Parent's Guide to the Best Children's Literature* is a rich resource for all adult who wish to captivate children with books starting at a young age and nurture them to continue a love of reading into their teenage years and beyond This easy-to-use reference lists the best in nonfiction literature according to th wide spectrum of children's interests and issues, including such topics as anci civilizations, hobbies, grief and loss, dinosaurs, sign language, space, and volunteerism. More than 140 fiction titles are listed for the elementary school-aged reader. Historical fiction, chapter and series books are included, along v helpful explanations of the roles such books play in teaching and encouragin young readers."

—Ellen Toms
St. Paul Pioneer Pr

"This book is a great resource containing not only children's classics, but also many not-so-obvious selections that are sure to become children's favorites. It the perfect tool to help sort through the infinite number of children's book ti available. Unique parent/child reviews scattered throughout illustrate how excited children, even reluctant readers, can become with great books."

—Kelly Robson,
Free Spirit Publishing

"The guide is easy to use, well organized and sound in its description of the books —an almanac for parents hunting the best-read for their children."

—Leigh Woosley,
Tulsa World

"The research that went into compiling this guide is obvious. Any parent would be lucky to have this tool in their parenting toolbox. From birth to the teen years, this guide allows parents to help their children reach their intellectual potential. What I didn't expect was to find topics broken down, based on a child's specific interests. In just seconds you can find a list of books suited for your child's age and interests. It's long overdue!"

—Julie Henricks,
WTWO-TV

"To the point and knowledgeable, the author has written expertly to help parents choose books their children will enjoy. Parents will appreciate hearing what other parents think about a specific book. Of importance, I highly recommend *A Parent's Guide to the Best Children's Literature* by Ellen Trachtenberg."

—Alice R. McCarthy, Ph.D.,
Publisher of *Healthy Newsletters*

"Finally an all-in-one, age-by-age indispensable guide to children's literature. As my daughter grows, I will refer to this book often."

—Deb DiSandro,
Family Columnist and Author of
Tales of a Slightly Off Supermom

The Best Children's Literature

A Parent's Guide

Ellen Trachtenberg

los angeles, california
www.pgpress.com

parent's
guide
press

The Best
Children's Literature
A Parent's Guide

Edwin E. Steussy, CEO and Publisher
Dianne Tangel-Cate, Project Editor
Lars H. Peterson, Acquisitions Editor
Michael P. Duggan, Graphic Artist

PO Box 461730
Los Angeles CA 90046

parent's guide press

Contents

The Best Children's Literature
A Parent's Guide

Contents

Acknowledgments

I would like to extend my heartfelt thanks and deepest appreciation to everyone who helped in creating this book. These gracious givers include the staff at the main branch of the Free Library of Philadelphia, Lower Merion Library System, and Children's Book World in Haverford, Pa., who patiently allowed me to peruse their shelves for hours on end. I offer 400 pages worth of gratitude to Parent's Guide Press for giving this book a home in its infancy and treating it with the utmost respect. I'd also like to thank all of the parents, caregivers, and children who contributed to the Parent/Child Review segments included herein. My friends and family have always provided ample encouragement. They include Andy, Amy, and Phil Trachtenberg; Kent Anderson; Jen Lightner; Jim Dash; Gail and Michael Silver; Laura Schatz Lapin; the Heller family; Maggi; Pierce and E.J.; Gret Gentile; Jenny Feder; and Jill Dunbar. The loving memory of one amazing individual, Tracy O'Dwyer, gives me daily motivation to live life, love books, and write often. It is with the tenderest memories that I pay tribute to my grandparents, Ben and Sarah Segal and Henry Weiss. And with a lifetime full of gratitude, dating back to the earliest bedtime readings of *Madeline*, I want to express my thanks and love to Mom, Dad, Nan, and MomMom Honey for their unfailing support. I'd like to dedicate this book to them, as well as to young book lovers everywhere, and, of course, to Jeff and Maija. Any labor of love would be impossible without them. Here's to many years of happy reading!

Introduction

"I was thrilled when my daughter received books as baby gifts. I know she'll always treasure them. The only question is, where to begin?"
—Kristin, new mother, Portland, Oregon

How wonderful to be a child with an entire lifetime of stories ahead! How equally wonderful to be a parent or caregiver who can introduce a child to the amazing world that lies between the covers of great books.

Children's literature builds dazzling playgrounds in the minds of its young readers. Whether a child's early preference is for high-flying fantasy or contemporary realism, there is no substitute for great books when it comes to engaging children's imagination and mirroring their experiences. And while we live in a world of technological wizardry that every day replaces old devices with new and improved kid-tested gadgets, books will never be obsolete.

The publishing industry in America has witnessed fits and starts of growth and consolidation, yet children's books are being published in record numbers. What's more, their breadth and scope is ever expanding so that the books that now populate your favorite bookstore or library's shelves include not only the classics but also newer titles that reflect the diverse population and dynamic interests of today's kids. With different cultural heritages being recognized and celebrated, there is truly a book for every child. Now more than ever, books invite children to examine the wide world around them and their special place within it.

The Best Children's Literature
A Parent's Guide

Introduction

> *"I walk into the children's section at the bookstore and my eyes start to swim. I don't even know where to begin."*
> —Barbara, mother of three, Philadelphia, PA

While the selection of available children's books may seem overwhelming, you and your children are already experts, believe it or not. In other words, nobody knows better than your family what interests your kids most, and this knowledge provides a giant educated leap into book selection. Even parents who don't tend to read many adult books are able, when given the opportunity, to accurately assess what their children are to likely enjoy.

This guide is intended to work in conjunction with your intuition and to provide ample suggestions for quality literature that is targeted to your children's developmental stages and unique interests. And remember, your kids will serve as guides themselves, perusing the shelves and stacks for books that catch their eye, books they've heard about, books by authors and illustrators they already adore, and books about subject matter that fascinates them.

The idea is to give children ample access to books, and to make them vested participants in the selection process from a young age. Visits to the library, bookstore, or e-commerce Web site can be fruitful additions to your busy routine and will go a long way in helping your family remain informed about the best books to read while fostering a lifetime love of reading in your children.

Choosing the Best Books for Your Children

If you were to ask any reading specialist or children's book aficionado for recommendations, they would most likely ask a few questions first. Your answers to the following inquiries will help you select the best books for your children.

- The Basics (boy or girl, age, reading ability)?
- What are your child's interests?
- What books has he or she enjoyed in the past?
- What books has he or she not enjoyed?
- Is your child able to read by him- or herself?
- Does your child enjoy having books read aloud to him or her?
- What is your child studying in school?
- Does your child have siblings?

Introduction

"If you put two books about the same thing in front of me, I'm not sure I could decide which one was better."

–Peter, father of four, San Diego, CA

Okay, you've narrowed the process down quite a bit; at least you know which shelves to search, or, hopefully, a friendly bookseller or librarian has pointed you in the right direction. Now you'll want to evaluate the quality and suitability of individual books. Certainly this process involves some subjectivity based on your own preferences and those of your child. This guide includes a descriptive, indexed list of great books for children. But how do you personally judge each book's merits? Here are a few questions for you to consider:

- Are the illustrations clear, ample, and exciting (in picture books and story books)?
- Does the ratio of illustrations to text seem balanced and connected (in picture books, story books, and easy readers)?
- Is the story or concept engaging, thoughtful, and well written?
- Does the book address a set of ideas that are of interest to your child?
- Does the book address subject matter that you want your child to understand?
- Does the book include a multicultural cast of characters?
- Is the book written from an unbiased, unprejudiced point of view?
- Does the book seem appropriate to the age group for which it was intended? (See developmental guidelines below.)
- Do any elements of this book seem inappropriate in terms of your family's specific beliefs?
- Is the book cohesively organized (in nonfiction books)?
- What are other parents and kids saying about this book?
- Did it receive favorable professional reviews?

Now that you're equipped with a selection framework, you can more easily navigate through the colorful sea of children's books and get down to the happy business of reading. There's no time like the present, and it's never too early.

Introduction

Why Read? When? How?

You've heard educators talk about the importance of frequently reading to and with your child, beginning when they're babies. But what exactly makes reading so important? In other words, what are the tangible benefits of reading?

Language Learning: While some books intended for toddlers and preschoolers make extravagant claims about expanding your child's vocabulary and reading readiness through special formulas and methods, it's the simple act of reading in and of itself that will help in the gradual decoding of words and comprehension of grammatical forms. In other words, reading promotes the growth of reading.

Concept Learning: There's an astonishing array of concept or nonfiction books available for children of every age and developmental stage. For toddlers and preschoolers, the familiar concepts of home, family, food, animals, and neighborhood are introduced and reinforced through vibrant illustrations. Young children view items in books, then learn to recognize them in their surroundings and vice versa. For children in elementary school, this notion is taken a step further as concepts that reflect their natural curiosities and school curriculum—science, world cultures, health, art—appear in living color on the pages of books.

Growth of Imagination: The goblins, fairies, princes, wizards, barnyard animals, aliens, celebrities, and just plain kids that exist on the pages of great books can be the inspiration for flights of imaginative fancy. Children who read have a springier foundation from which to view the world and its possibilities. They're also more likely to appreciate the value of storytelling, humankind's oldest tradition.

Global Perspective: Children gain an ever-widening understanding of their place in the world and the cultural contributions of people around the globe.

Lifetime Skill: The understanding that comes from learning to read translates into skills that children and adults use every day. These include the ability to ask questions and access information, recognize patterns, decipher hidden meanings (read between the lines), identify different perspectives and points of view, and refine one's own preferences and dislikes.

Time Spent Together: If you're looking for ways to spend more quality time with your kids, look no further. Within our hectic schedules, setting aside daily time for reading is akin to investing in a great cause, for all of the above reasons. Besides, the last great reason for reading? The sheer enjoyment of wonderful stories.

*"I hope I'm not choosing books that are too babyish for my boys.
They're six years old, but they still love illustrated books and don't
really seem motivated to read by themselves."*
—Zora, mother of twin boys, Brooklyn, NY

Reading Readiness,
A Developmental Timeline

Is child development set in stone? Of course not. If you have more than one child, you've surely seen that children's physical, social, emotional, and intellectual growth varies in terms of its pacing. Maybe your eldest child began walking at one year, while your second only began to take tentative steps at 15 months. With that said, it's realistic to expect children to reach certain developmental milestones, but there's a lot of room for individual differences.

So how do the issues involved in child development relate to reading behavior? Well, language learning, social and emotional growth, and even fine motor skills are involved, among other factors. Again, each child will vary in terms of their pacing, so you can't expect all children to be self-sufficient readers by age six. However, within these differences in timing, the advancement of reading skills does tend to follow a general pattern. Take a look:

Infants: Babies love the sound of the human voice, so why not use it to tell a story that amuses both of you? Predictable, rhythmic language is especially soothing to babies, as they begin to gain their earliest understanding of what it means to open a book and listen to the stories that magically emerge.

Toddlers: Children's next understanding of the act of reading comes when, as toddlers, they begin to recognize that people read books by turning pages in sequence. If you hand a book to a toddler, it's likely that she will turn the pages by herself. This is where board books come in handy. Their sturdy cardboard pages are friendly to little fingers.

Preschoolers: Young children learn that the words and pictures on each page work together to tell a story. This is one of the reasons that dynamic illustrations in picture books are so vitally important. Toddlers and preschoolers may not be engaging in strict reading per se, but they begin to read stories through the pictures, while often memorizing words or entire pages of text.

Introduction

Early Elementary: Gradually, more text and more elaborate stories accompany the illustrations, and as children's reading ability grows, their reliance on the illustrations diminishes. This is not to say, of course, that picture books and story books are intended solely for the youngest readers. There are some lovely and rather sophisticated story books that will appeal to children in the early- to mid-elementary grades and beyond. In addition, children can refine their newfound ability to read independently by selecting Easy Readers, which are often categorized into reading levels based on vocabulary, words per page, and sentence length.

Middle Grades: Children who feel comfortable with their ability to decode words while naturally "getting the gist" of a story are ready to proceed to chapter books, juvenile fiction, and nonfiction. Again, there's a wide array of material intended for children of this age group, from simple close-to-home stories and whirlwind fantasies to more dramatic coming-of-age novels.

Adolescents: By early adolescence, kids have developed a strong sense of like and dislike, and this applies to their choice of reading material. Typically, with the mind-boggling questions that accompany puberty, young teens will discreetly seek answers. Adolescents will want to strike out on their own in terms of the selection of reading material, but it's important to provide encouragement and access to quality literature that addresses their concerns and curiosities.

Activities That Encourage Reading

Reading can be so much more than an isolated daily episode. In fact, reading can be incorporated into everyday events and special occasions. Here are a few suggestions:

- **Encourage young children to read street and store** signs that they see in the neighborhood. Work together to create a story based on what they've seen.

- **Implement a "book swap"** between your children and their pals. Kids love the negotiations involved in trading cards. Help them establish a similar system where books are traded according to a set of rules or criteria.

- **Host book-themed birthday parties.** This has been accomplished with great success using Harry Potter's ample wizardly inspiration (see "Why Harry Potter Is a Great Teacher" in "Chapter Books").

- **Participate in your local library's summer reading programs.** For children who need a motivational jumpstart, the awarding of points and prizes can spur interest all year long.

- **Attend story hours at your library or bookstore.** Check newspaper listings for events where authors will be signing their books. Kids who meet their favorite authors are likely to become starstruck and, in turn, more interested in finding additional books by that author.

- **Help your kids to keep lists** (or dog ear this guide!) of their favorite books. Establish a rating system and colorful wall chart. Use stars or stickers to denote the all-stars amongst the bunch.

- **Engage your child in discussions about the books** they like and those they dislike. Ask questions and read the books yourself to get a more complete picture of your child's preferences.

**The Best
Children's Literature**
A Parent's Guide

Introduction

How to Use This Guide

The more than 1,000 titles included in this guide were compiled over the course of several years. This process, of course, involved a great deal of reading! It also required dozens of conversations with librarians, booksellers, teachers, parents, and children about the best available children's books. Next, professional resources, including trade journals, bibliographies, curriculum guidelines, and Web site recommendations, were consulted. The lists of books and annotations included herein are the result of hundreds of hours of research as well as a bit of subjectivity that has culminated, one hopes, into the creation of a truly user-friendly, cross-referenced guide.

The vast majority of the books you're about to discover or rediscover are in print at the time of this guide's publication. The publishing of new books and reissues of classics is a tricky business, however, and retail sales are the bottom line. Unfortunately, as a result of this financial priority, some quiet favorites or "sleepers" are quickly made unavailable because they didn't pull their weight in dollar signs. You can employ out-of-print book searches, online or otherwise, to help locate cherished books from your childhood and introduce them to the next generation.

The books are categorized into chapters based on standards (possibly inadvertent) set by the publishing industry that tend to correlate to age/grade/developmental level. These categories are Infant/Toddler, Picture Books, Story Books, Easy Readers, Nonfiction, and Juvenile Fiction/Chapter Books.

Each entry includes the book's title, author and illustrator, publisher, price (if a paperback edition is available, it is listed), and number of pages. The year the book was first published is also noted. This date denotes the year the book first appeared in any form, usually hardcover. While reissues or different versions of the book may have been published since, including paperback editions, it's the year that the book was first introduced to the public that is indicated.

Next, a general age range guideline is provided. Remember, these recommendations are simply a broad suggestion. We've already discussed the variance between young readers' abilities and interests as it pertains to their developmental level. You and your child are most likely the best testers of their reading level, as children will not show a whole lot of interest in materials for which they are not prepared to understand. If you are experiencing difficulty in assessing your child's reading level, or if you feel her abilities are regressive or falling drastically behind those of her peers, consult her teacher or a reading specialist for evaluation.

Introduction

Art Dog
Written and Illustrated by Thacher Hurd
HarperCollins, $5.95, 32 pages
First published in 1996
Ages 4–7

parent's
guide
choice award

Arthur Dog could give Van Gogh a run for his money! While Arthur seems like a cool cat working days as a guard at the Dogopolis Museum of Art (where else?), he becomes one artful dogger at night, creating masterpiece murals while solving crimes. You'll recognize many of the museum's notable works, including a painting by none other than Henri Muttisse. Thacher's frantic brush strokes perfectly match the pace of this painterly pooch's story. Pair this title with *Norman the Doorman* by Don Freeman. Also by Hurd, *Mama Don't Allow* and *The Pea Patch Jig*.

The annotation of each book gives a brief plot or content summary. It also mentions other books by the same author and, often, books by different authors that address similar subject matter. The intention is to employ an "If you enjoyed this…then you may enjoy that" framework that continuously leads readers to additional literature.

If a book has received an award, that, too, is noted. Of the awards bestowed upon children's literature, the best known and most highly prized are the **Newbery Medal** and **Caldecott Medal**, both sponsored by the American Library Association. Each year a committee of librarians nominates and ultimately chooses a winner, as well as three **Newbery Honor** and **Caldecott Honor** recipients. The Newbery Medal is presented to authors of the best American children's books published during the previous year. The Caldecott Medal is awarded to the best illustrators of American picture books. You'll find books that have been recipients of these high honors marked by round gold or silver stickers on their front covers.

Other coveted prizes awarded to authors of children's literature include the **Coretta Scott King Award**, which is presented yearly to "authors and illustrators of African descent whose distinguished books promote an understanding and appreciation for 'The American Dream.'"

Introduction

Parent's Guide Choice Award

In addition, we at Parent's Guide Press have established our own children's book prize entitled the **Parent's Guide Choice Award**. The fine recipients of this award represent dynamic, contemporary, diverse and eclectic traditions, and innovations in children's literature. The award is given to books published within the last ten years, and you'll find recipients listed throughout the guide.

Bud, Not Buddy
Written by Christopher Paul Curtis
Yearling, $5.95, 245 pages
First published in 1999
Ages 10–14

After being shuffled through several unhappy foster home placements during the Great Depression, ten-year-old Bud Caldwell runs away to seek his long-absent father. Believing that his dad is a noted jazz musician and club owner, Bud heads for Grand Rapids, Michigan, encountering some shady characters and hazy truths along the way. As with his wonderful *The Watsons Go to Birmingham—1963* (detailed in this chapter), Curtis's story is a masterly mix of humor and pain, earning it a Newbery Medal and a great deal of deserved notoriety.

Finally, please consult the extensive cross-referenced index for titles, authors, and subjects. If your child is searching, for example, for a book about Benjamin Franklin, you'll find several, both fiction and nonfiction, listed under his name in the subject index.

If you're seeking books by an author whose previous work your family has enjoyed, please look in the author index for a listing of all titles that appear in this guide.

Most importantly, scribble in the margins, place check marks besides titles that your children have read, make notes about books your family has enjoyed, and take this book with you when you next visit the library or bookstore!

Happy Reading!

Chapter One

Books for Infants and Toddlers

Welcome to the wonderful array of books for babies and toddlers! This is the colorful collection of books that have been strategically placed within crawling reach in perusable floor baskets or low shelves at your favorite library or bookstore. Many of these titles are available in board book editions: a more sturdy, drool-proof version of their hardcover and paperback counterparts. With cardboard-backed pages that are turnable for even the tiniest of fingers, board books are an excellent choice for infants and toddlers. After withstanding repeated tossings from highchairs and cribs, board books are always ready for another reading.

If you're hoping to introduce your toddler to enduring picture book classics, you'll be pleased to learn that many titles are obtainable in a board book format. A wide variety of these perennial smile-makers is listed (in their paperback or hardcover incarnations) in the "Picture Books" and "Story Books" chapters, including *Goodnight Moon*, *The Very Hungry Caterpillar*, and sensational stories by Dr. Seuss. Ask your favorite librarian or bookseller if they have a board book selection, especially if you're trying to discourage your child's predilection for page ripping!

Chapter One

In this chapter, you'll find a selective list of lovely, funny, and touching stories, as well as concept books that address children's earliest curiosities. In addition to board books, there are touch-and-feel books, such as the charming *Pat the Bunny*, that appropriately address babies' and toddlers' need to make sense of the world through the ever-refined use of their hands and maturing fine motor skills. Beware of gimmicky series that make extravagant claims about increasing your toddler's vocabulary and reading abilities. It's the act of spending frequent time reading together that will most likely encourage further forays into the endless joys of books. In other words, reading, in and of itself, will promote the growth of reading skills. So pick up a great book and enjoy!

Baby Food
Written and Illustrated by Margaret Miller
Little Simon, $5.99, unpaged
First published in 2000
Ages 9 months–2 years

A savory choice for finicky eaters, Miller's photographs and simple text depict a culturally diverse group of babies enjoying an array of finger and spoon foods. A single word—cracker, yummy, bottle—is matched with each enticing picture. Other board books by this author include *Baby Faces*; *Get Ready, Baby*; *I Love Colors*; and *What's on My Head?*

Bear's Day
Written and Illustrated by Lisa Campbell Ernst
Viking, $5.99, 12 pages
First published in 2000
Ages 1–4

A young child and his teddy bear buddy engage in a day's worth of activities—marching, clapping, and snacking—that will be quite familiar to your toddler. The overall effect is cozy and inviting, and the extra sturdy construction of this board book will stand up to multiple readings. There's also *Cat's Play*.

Books for Infants and Toddlers

Bedtime for Bunny: A Book to Touch and Feel
Written by Jane Yolen, Illustrated by Lynn Norton Parker
Little Simon, $7.99, unpaged
First published in 2002
Ages 1–4

There are gentle rhymes, softly hued illustrations, and textured images in this bedtime board book. The sense of touch is of primary importance to babies and toddlers, and this book will withstand a lot of prodding by little fingers. Jane Yolen is the versatile author of many storybooks as well as novels for middle-grade readers.

Black on White
Written and Illustrated by Tana Hoban
Greenwillow, $5.95, unpaged
First published in 1993
Ages 1–4

Tana Hoban knows a great deal about child development. Here, she's working in accordance with a proven principle: babies are drawn to black and white images. There are artfully drawn figures—butterfly, spoon, leaf—to be examined, and the simplicity of this book's design is yet further proof of its author's talents. Also see the companion volume, *White on Black*, and look for *Baby Animals Black and White* by Phyllis Limbacher Tildes. Additional books by Hoban can be found in the "Picture Books" chapter, including *26 Letters and 99 Cents* and *Exactly the Opposite*.

But Not the Hippopotamus
Written and Illustrated by Sandra Boynton
Little Simon, $4.99, 12 pages
First published in 1982
Ages 2–5

Boynton's funny and winsome characters are immediately recognizable. You've seen them on countless greeting cards and calendars. Here, a shy hippo is reluctant to join in the other animals' games. They may be playing, eating, and generally having a good time, but "not the hippopotamus"…until the end. Also look for *The Going to Bed Book* and *Moo Baa La La La*.

Chapter One

Carl's Afternoon in the Park
Written and Illustrated by Alexandra Day
Farrar Straus Giroux, $5.95, unpaged
First published in 1992
Ages 1–4

Carl is the beloved family pet, a smiling rottweiler who keeps careful watch over baby. In this wordless board book, pooch and tot head for a frolic-filled romp in the park. Millions of toddlers and preschoolers have fallen head over heels for Carl, basking in his protective affection and creating their own personalized narration. Other titles include *Carl Goes Shopping*; *Carl Goes to Day Care*; *Carl's Birthday*; and *Good Dog, Carl!*

Count with Dora
Written by Phoebe Beinstein, Illustrated by the Thompson Bros.
Simon Spotlight, $4.99, unpaged
First published in 2002
Ages 1–4

With text in both Spanish and English, Dora engages in a bilingual counting celebration! She's going on a picnic and wants to be certain that she has enough fruit for everyone. Perfect for children living in multilingual homes or attending ethnically diverse day care. There's also *Dora's Opposites* and *Dora's Color Adventure*.

Does a Kangaroo Have a Mother, Too?
Written and Illustrated by Eric Carle
HarperFestival, $7.95, unpaged
First published in 2000
Ages 1–4

Carle's colorful cut-paper illustrations have set the standard for children's books with enduring appeal. This title is perfectly suited to the youngest readers in its new board book format. Twelve animals and their mommies are featured, demonstrating that parental affection is not exclusive to humans. Carle's emphatic response to the title question? "Yes, a kangaroo does have a mother! Just like me and you." Eric Carle has been bringing smiles to children's faces for thirty years with titles including *The Very Hungry Caterpillar* (see "Picture Books"); *The Grouchy Ladybug*; *Today Is Monday*; *Pancakes, Pancakes*; and *The Very Quiet Cricket*. Also see *Draw Me a Star* and *Papa, Please Get the Moon for Me* in "Picture Books."

Books for Infants and Toddlers

Everywhere Babies

Written by Susan Meyers, Illustrated by Marla Frazee
Harcourt, $16.00, 32 pages
First published in 2001
Ages 1–4

If there's one thing babies like to gaze upon it's other babies, and this book's got 'em. These are not the blond cherubs of old. Here we see a multicultural array of expressive infants and learn that "Every day, everywhere, babies are born." Also look for *Baby Faces* by Margaret Miller and *Big Book of Beautiful Babies Board Book* by David Ellwand.

Eyes, Nose, Fingers and Toes: A First Book All about You

Written by Judy Hindley, Illustrated by Brita Granstrom
Candlewick, $5.99, unpaged
First published in 1999
Ages 2–5

"Eyes are to wink" and, of course, for playing "peek-a-boo." Toddlers are invited to make joyful use of their hands, feet, nose, toes, and fingers through the lively rhyming text. With so much marvelous movement, this book is a perfect choice for morning, afternoon, and rainy day romps. Judy Hindley is the author of *The Best Thing about a Puppy* (see "Picture Books"), as well as *The Big Red Bus* and *Do Like a Duck Does!*

Guess How Much I Love You

Written by Sam McBratney, Illustrated by Anita Jeram
Candlewick, $6.99, 24 pages
First published in 1995
Ages 1–4

Little Nutbrown Hare expressively shows his love for daddy. "I love you as high as I can hop," he says. Daddy proves that his love is as ample, exclaiming at the end, "I love you right up to the moon…and back." Clearly, a perfect bedtime choice for toddlers and their adoring dads, this book is also available in Spanish and French. For more fatherly fun, look for *Baby Dance* by Ann Taylor. Also by McBratney, *I'll Always Be Your Friend*; *I'm Sorry*; and *Just You and Me*.

Chapter One

Here Are My Hands
Written by Bill Martin Jr. and John Archambault, Illustrated by Ted Rand
Henry Holt, $6.95, unpaged
First published in 1998
Ages 1–4

Clever collaborators Martin, Archambault, and Rand gently explore the similarities and differences between children of different cultural and ethnic groups. Initially, toddlers will love gazing upon Rand's quietly expressive illustrations. Preschoolers will begin to make increasing sense of the global concept. Martin is also the author of *Brown Bear, Brown Bear, What Do You See?*; *Chicka Chicka Boom Boom*; and *Fire! Fire! Said Mrs. McGuire* (all in "Picture Books," available in board book editions).

How a Baby Grows
Written by Nola Buck, Illustrated by Pamela Paparone
HarperFestival, $5.95, unpaged
First published in 1998
Ages 9 months–2 years

Babies will revel in recognizing all of the things they can do—and possibly add to their repertoire—while reading the bouncy, rhyming verse. The pictures are uncluttered, yet cozy, with a few familiar toys and nursery items displayed.

Hug
Written and Illustrated by Jez Alborough
Candlewick, $6.99, unpaged
First published in 2000
Ages 1–4

Bobo the chimp needs a bit of affection. He's looking for a big hug. His friends don't seem to understand, but it's Mama who comes through with the cozy comfort in the end. There's minimal text, but the warm, detailed illustrations speak volumes. Other books by Alborough include *Duck in the Truck*; *My Friend Bear*; and *Where's My Teddy?*

Books for Infants and Toddlers

Humpty Dumpty and Other Nursery Rhymes
Written and Illustrated by Lucy Cousins
Dutton, $6.99, unpaged
First published in 1996
Ages 1–4

Any thoughtful collection of nursery rhymes is a welcome addition to story time, but this board book is truly a gem. There are the familiar favorites, featuring a culturally inclusive cast of characters. The text is succinct and will engage toddlers, while older children will want to revisit this book during their early attempts at reading alone. Cousins is the author of the popular *Maisy* series (see *Happy Birthday, Maisy* in "Picture Books"), as well as *Flower in the Garden* (a cloth book) and *Bedtime*.

Max's Toys
Written and Illustrated by Rosemary Wells
Dial, $5.99, unpaged
First published in 1979
Ages 1–4

Now available in a board book, along with other favorites by Rosemary Wells, Max is likely to become one of your toddler's most adored characters. He's counting his toys from 1 to 10, and considering trading some of his prized possessions in exchange for his sister's doll. You'll find more Max in *Bunny Cakes* (see "Picture Books"). There's also *Max's Chocolate Chicken* and *Max Cleans Up.*

Mr. Brown Can Moo, Can You?
Written and Illustrated by Dr. Seuss
Random House, $4.99, unpaged
First published in 1970
Ages 1–4

Welcome to the whimsical world of Dr. Seuss. You'll become well acquainted with the wonderful word wizard over the next few years, and this title is a perfect place to begin. Mr. Brown is an aficionado of sound; he loves to imitate animal noises, and your child will, too! Other titles by Dr. Seuss are available in board book editions such as *Dr. Seuss's ABC*; *The Foot Book*; and *My Many Colored Days.* You'll find *The Cat in the Hat*; *Green Eggs and Ham*; and *One Fish Two Fish Red Fish Blue Fish* in "Picture Books" and additional titles, including *The Lorax* and *Oh, The Places You'll Go* in "Story Books" and "Easy Readers."

Chapter One

My First Farm Touch and Feel Book

Dorling Kindersley, $9.95, unpaged
First published in 2002
Ages 1–4

Dorling Kindersley (DK) is firmly established as a leader in children's publishing. It's no wonder, too. Its brand of illustration, using vivid color photography, is immensely appealing to children. This fun farm in a portable package has soft sheep, bouncy rubber tractor tires, and fuzzy peaches to feel, all evoking an ideal afternoon spent at a country farm. Objects are clearly identified by simple text in bold letters. A perfect choice before a springtime visit to the farm.

My First Learning Library

Dorling Kindersley, $19.95, unpaged
First published in 2000
Ages 6 months–3 years

Another exceptional offering from DK is this mini boxed set that's a well-rounded introduction to basic concepts. It includes *My First ABC Board Book*; *My First Number Board Book*; and *My First Word Board Book*, the latter being a beginner dictionary that helps toddlers and preschoolers group objects into easily understood categories such as "All About Me."

One Red Sun: A Counting Book

Written and Illustrated by Ezra Jack Keats
Viking, $5.99, 10 pages
First published in 1968
Ages 1–4

You'll find more of Keats's stunningly illustrated stories in "Picture Books" (see *Peter's Chair* and *The Snowy Day*), but this board book adaptation is perfectly suited to toddlers. Originally published as a number chart in 1968 by Scholastic, Keats's incredible cut-paper illustrations are given beautiful due, as toddlers will be drawn to the one glowing sun, two green stoplights, three children, and so on.

Books for Infants and Toddlers

Pat the Bunny

Written and Illustrated by Dorothy Kunhardt
Golden Books, $14.99, unpaged
First published in 1940
Ages 2–5

It's very likely that this sensory celebration will send you reeling with nostalgic glee back to your own toddlerhood. Possibly the best known, and certainly the forerunner, of the modern touch-and-feel books, its look has changed little. You'll still find soft pastels and innocent drawings that reflect the bygone days of the mid-20th century. And it's still Paul and Judy who invite young pre-readers to play peek-a-boo, smell the flowers, and, of course, pat the bunny. There's also *Pat the Cat* and *Pat the Puppy*.

Peek-A-Boo!

Written and Illustrated by Janet and Allan Ahlberg
Viking, $6.99, 32 pages
First published in 1997
Ages 1–4

The tried and true game of peek-a-boo is at the heart of this warm and inviting oversized board book. Encouraging participation throughout, toddlers are encouraged to play along while peeking through die-cut holes in each page.

Ten Little Ladybugs

Written by Melanie Gerth, Illustrated by Laura Huliska-Beith
Piggy Toes Press, $10.95, unpaged
First published in 2000
Ages 1–4

The cute critters playfully hide in the pages' die-cut holes, inspiring little ones to poke fingers, count to ten, and read this book over and over again. There's a touch-and-feel element to this dynamic book, too, as the three-dimensional ladybugs invite exploration by tiny fingers. Continue counting with *Thomas the Tank Engine Counts to Ten* by Rev. W. Awdry.

Chapter One

Where Is Baby's Mommy: A Lift-the-Flap Book

Written and Illustrated by Karen Katz
Little Simon, $5.99, unpaged
First published in 2001
Ages 1–3

Introduce a lift-the-flap book to your toddler and a whole new world seems to open up before her eyes. Of course, this book is especially well constructed and features the intriguing search by one playful toddler for his mommy. She must be there somewhere! Karen Katz is the author of the equally adorable *Counting Kisses* (in "Picture Books").

Your New Potty

Written by Joanna Cole, Photographs by Margaret Miller
Morrow, $5.95, 40 pages
First published in 1989
Ages 1–3

While there is certainly no exact baby science that determines when or where a child will wave bye-bye to diapers, this book will set families on the right track. The story advocates patience and consistent affirmation as important tools of the trade in the potty-training business. Toddlers will love peeking at their potty bound cohorts in the lively color photographs. Cole (author of the ever expanding *Magic School Bus* series, in "Easy Readers") has also written a gender-specific set of books, *My Big Boy Potty* and *My Big Girl Potty*. Other pleasing potty books include *I Want My Potty* by Tony Ross and *On Your Potty* by Virginia Miller.

Chapter Two
Picture Books

In picture books, illustrations are of primary importance. Toddlers and preschoolers often glean content by repetitively studying the pictures, which need not be elaborate. In fact, it is often the simplest of images that captures a child's attention. In most cases, text is rather minimal, ranging from one well-placed word to a brief descriptive sentence. Quiet moments spent between caregiver and child provide not only the opportunity for storytelling, but this is also the time when children begin to understand how a book is read—by turning its pages and reading in sequence—and this is an early milestone on the road to reading.

For the most part, picture books are intended for preschoolers. That's not to say that older children won't enjoy them. In fact, many picture books have sophisticated visual styles that appeal to children in the early- and middle-elementary grades.

Chapter Two

Family, neighborhood, school, alphabet, numbers, emotions, and animals are common themes. Generally, the topics addressed represent familiar and comforting notions for young children. There are also, of course, classic nursery rhymes and beguiling bedtime stories. The use of catchy rhythmic language with predictable patterns encourages children to participate in the reading and rereading of favorite books.

So, from the alphabetical tour of busy city streets in *ABCDrive!: A Car Trip Alphabet,* to the simply drawn imaginary adventures of *Harold and the Purple Crayon,* to the lovely sentiment and gentle morality of *Stellaluna* and *Swimmy,* your children will find ample opportunity to become enthralled by the world of children's literature. It's a world that reflects their own experiences, while opening the door to a wider landscape.

10 Minutes Till Bedtime
Written and Illustrated by Peggy Rathmann
Putnam, $7.99, unpaged
First published in 1998
Ages 2–6

Time may be an abstract concept to young children, but Rathmann shows how much fun can be squeezed into those all-important pre-bedtime moments. There will be lots of giggles at the frolicking hamsters and hilarious visual details as the minutes tick away. For more of Rathmann's antic illustrations, see *Officer Buckle and Gloria* (detailed in this chapter) and *Good Night, Gorilla.*

1,2,3 Go
Written and Illustrated by Huy Von Lee
Henry Holt, $16.00, 28 pages
First published in 2000
Ages 3–8

This is a joyous introduction to both basic counting skills and the beauty of Chinese symbols. Lee's vibrant cut-paper illustrations show Chinese children engaged in various activities. The text is simple, matching an action with a number ("one catches"). Reading this book aloud provides a perfect opportunity for discussion about the wide world of children and the different languages they speak. Other books by Lee include *In the Park; At the Beach;* and *In the Snow.*

Picture Books

26 Letters and 99 Cents
Written and Illustrated by Tana Hoban
Mulberry, $5.95, 18 pages
First published in 1995
Ages 3–8

First it's a colorful counting book, then flip it over and... surprise! It's an amazing alphabet book. Tana Hoban is highly regarded amongst teachers and librarians for creating uniquely crafted concept books, and this title is no exception. The math portion is especially clever, matching numbers with different combinations of coins. Also by Hoban, *A Children's Zoo*; *Colors Everywhere*; *Construction Zone*; *Exactly the Opposite* (detailed in this chapter); *I Read Signs*; *Look Book*; and *Shadows and Reflections*, among others.

Featured Author: Tana Hoban

A skilled photographer and illustrator by trade, Tana Hoban has a very clear understanding of child development. Beginning with books intended for toddlers (see **Black and White** in Chapter One), Hoban juxtaposes images that are inherently appealing to her youngest audience. Her vibrantly designed picture books feature objects and concepts that are familiar to preschoolers, depicting photographs or brightly colored drawn images of children engaging in age-appropriate activities and inquiries (see **Exactly the Opposite** in this chapter). Demonstrating her facility behind the camera, Hoban continues to illustrate her books with amusing, candid photos of children in urban settings that provide ample opportunities for the imaginative exploration of common experiences.

ABCDrive! A Car Trip Alphabet
Written and Illustrated by Naomi Howland
Clarion Books, $4.95, 32 pages
First published in 2000
Ages 2–5

parent's
guide
choice award

The busy streets are full of sights and sounds, and this engaging book has a picture for every letter of the alphabet... from ambulance to zoom! Each page presents a clear single image, but take a closer look. The lively background illustrations depict a widely diverse group of objects and people. This is a great title for reinforcing early word recognition that often starts from viewing neighborhood signs. For more along these colorful lines, see *I Read Signs* by Tana Hoban.

**The Best
Children's Literature**
A Parent's Guide

Chapter Two

The Adventures of Bert

Written by Allan Ahlberg, Illustrated by Raymond Briggs
Farrar Strauss Giroux, $16.00, 32 pages
First published in 2001
Ages 2–6

Introduce Bert to your preschooler and your household will never be the same. The product of two acclaimed storytellers, this wacky romp combines the best Ahlberg antics with Briggs's zooming color-pencil drawings. For more from these two smile-makers, see *Each Peach Pear Plum* and *The Jolly Postman* (Ahlberg), and *The Snowman* (Briggs), detailed in this chapter.

A-Hunting We Will Go!

Written and Illustrated by Steven Kellogg
HarperTrophy, $5.95, unpaged
First published in 1998
Ages 2–5

"A-reading we will go!" Kellogg's famously jubilant artwork gives a peppy new twist to the familiar chant, as two children and their animal friends engage in a lively spree of pre-bedtime activity. Other titles by Kellogg include *Can I Keep Him?*; *Chicken Little*; *Give the Dog a Bone*; *The Island of the Skog*; *Jack and the Beanstalk* (detailed in "Story Books"); *Pecos Bill* (detailed in "Story Books"); and the Pinkerton series, including *Pinkerton, Behave!*

Alfonse, Where Are You?

Written and Illustrated by Linda Wikler
Dragonfly Books, $6.99, 32 pages
First published in 1998
Ages 3–5

It may take a gaggle of geese to find one fluffy duck, but your child will have no trouble locating him on every page. This joyful hide-and-seek story is enlivened by its lovely watercolor illustrations. You'll also enjoy *Have You Seen My Duckling?* by Nancy Tafuri.

Picture Books

All Kinds of Children

Written by Norma Simon, Illustrated by Diane Paterson
Whitman, $15.95, 32 pages
First published in 1999
Ages 3–5

What do children all around the world have in common? Lots of things! This colorful look at world cultures opens a child's eyes to diversity, and the differences and similarities of children near and far. For one thing, Simon points out, all children have belly buttons! Other preschool-appropriate books that illuminate diversity include *All the Way to Morning* by Marc Harshman and *All in a Day* by Mitsumasa Anno.

Alphabatics

Written and Illustrated by Suse MacDonald
Aladdin, $6.95, 56 pages
First published in 1986
Ages 2–6

This fabulously creative **Caldecott Honor** book provides a one-of-a-kind introduction to the alphabet as it spins, twists, and flips each letter to make it resemble the object it represents. Did you know that an upside down "A" can become an ark? For additional clever alphabet picture books, ask your favorite librarian about *Alphabet Adventure* by Audrey and Bruce Wood; *A Is for Amos* by Deborah Chandra; and *Ape in a Cape: An Alphabet of Odd Animals* by Fritz Eichenberg. Other books by MacDonald include *Look Whooo's Counting*; *Once upon Another*; and *Sea Shapes*.

Alphabet City

Written and Illustrated by Stephen T. Johnson
Puffin, $6.99, unpaged
First published in 1995
Ages 4–9

New York City is home to 26 hidden letters in this glorious **Caldecott Honor** book. The startling photo-realism of Johnson's illustrations will compel older readers and children with an interest in visual arts. Also look for the urban amazement of *City by Numbers*.

Chapter Two

Alphabet Fiesta
Written and Illustrated by Anne Miranda
Turtle Books, $12.95, unpaged
First published in 2001
Ages 3–8

With text in both English and Spanish, this ingenious bilingual alphabet romp is a treat. Using word pairs beginning with the same letter in both languages—from A to Z—Miranda tells the story of Zelda Zebra and her birthday surprise. Also by Miranda, *To Market, To Market* and *Beep! Beep!*

And If the Moon Could Talk
Written by Kate Banks, Illustrated by Georg Hallensleben
Frances Foster Books, $15.00, 32 pages
First published in 1998
Ages 2–6

With illustrations reminiscent of Van Gogh and a story that's a cozy counterpart to *Goodnight Moon*, this poetic dream sequence will have children basking in its bedtime glow. Other stories by Kate Banks include *Baboon* and *The Bird, the Monkey, and the Snake in the Jungle*. More melodic moon stories include *Circle Song* by Diana Engel; *Dreaming: A Countdown to Sleep* (detailed in this chapter) by Elaine Greenstein; and *Can't Sleep* by Chris Raschka.

And the Dish Ran Away with the Spoon
Written by Janet Stevens and Susan Stevens Crummel, Illustrated by Janet Stevens
Harcourt, $17.00, unpaged
First published in 2001
Ages 3–7

The familiar nursery rhyme employs a host of equally familiar characters, borrowed from other Mother Goose tales, to search for the errant Dish and Spoon. Using a wildly funny map, Cat, Dog, and Cow seek assistance from Little Boy Blue and Jack (of the famous beanstalk), amongst others, in an entertaining race to restore the ending intended by Ms. Goose. For more mirth, look for Stevens's *Cook-A-Doodle-Doo!*

Picture Books

Parent/Child Review: And the Dish Ran Away with the Spoon

The Parent: Sharon, Age 33, Pediatric Nurse
The Child: Michael, Age 4, Future Construction Worker

Michael says: I know this book! This is... this is with the dish running. Dishes don't run. You put them in the sink after you eat lasagna. My sister read this book with me before we went to visit my grandma. It's funny and the pictures are like the ones in grandma's kitchen. I think we have this book at home. Mom, can we read this book when we get home?

Sharon says: Sure! Well, there's an endorsement for you. My older daughter who's eleven read this to Michael and he really liked it and pointed to the funny pictures. Then Michael and I read it together and he told me the story. I've actually never seen him do that before. This was a nice change for us, since he has mostly been into **Blue's Clues**... which we love, too... but I liked the way they changed a familiar nursery tale.

Andy (That's My Name)

Written and Illustrated by Tomie de Paola
Aladdin, $5.95, 30 pages
First published in 1973
Ages 3–6

The incomparable de Paola is certain to become a favorite (you'll find more of his titles in the "Story Books" chapter). This simply illustrated tale is well-suited to preschoolers as Andy's friends—and the older kids on the block—explore the words and sounds they can make from his name. If your children are intrigued by this concept, they may also want to look for *There's an Ant in Anthony* by Bernard Most.

Angelina Ballerina

Written by Katharine Holabird, Illustrated by Helen Craig
Pleasant Company, $9.95, 26 pages
First published in 1983
Ages 4–8

A delightful young mouse dreams of becoming a prima ballerina, and with steadfast determination, she's headed for stardom! You'll follow Angelina's rise to fame with *Angelina's Birthday*; *Angelina on Stage*; and *Angelina and Alice*, among others.

Chapter Two

Animals Should Definitely Not Wear Clothing
Written by Judi Barrett, Illustrated by Ron Barrett
Macmillan, $5.99, 31 pages
First published in 1970
Ages 3–6

With enough good-hearted silliness to last through early-elementary school, this thirty-year-old classic has become a favorite for many families. You'll also enjoy the Barretts' *Animals Should Definitely Not Act Like People*. And see *Cloudy with a Chance of Meatballs* (detailed in this chapter).

Annie, Bea, and Chi Chi Dolores: A School Day Alphabet
Written by Donna Maurer, Illustrated by Denys Cazet
Orchard, $6.95, 32 pages
First published in 1993
Ages 3–6

Three animal friends ride the bus to kindergarten ("all aboard") and proceed through a hilarious romp during the school day. This clever story—with a focus on both language learning and an introduction to school—has minimal text and large lettering.

Anno's Journey
Written and Illustrated by Mitsumasa Anno
Putnam, $7.99, 48 pages
First published in 1997
Ages 4–8

Noted Japanese artist and author Anno has created an elegant story without words. Documenting his travels through Europe, Anno captures his impressions of the cultures, land, art, and architecture he encountered. The absence of text allows for endless creative interpretations. Other titles include *Anno's Counting Book*; *Anno's Hat Tricks*; *Anno's Magic Seeds*; and *Anno's U.S.A.*

Are We There Yet, Daddy?
Written by Virginia Walters, Illustrated by S. D. Schindler
Viking, $6.99, unpaged
First published in 1999
Ages 4–7

You've heard that question before. During the 100-mile trip to Grandma's house, a young boy is given a map to chart their progress. This inviting story is cleverly positioned to teach basic counting and map-reading skills.

Picture Books

Are You a Butterfly?
Written by Judy Allen, Illustrated by Tudor Humphries
Kingfisher, $9.95, 28 pages
First published in 2000
Ages 2–5

The life cycle of a butterfly is deftly explained to small children by encouraging them to imagine themselves as a caterpillar, a chrysalis, and a beautiful Painted Lady. *Are You a Butterfly?* is a wonderful invitation to creative playacting. Other introductions to insect life by Allen include *Are You a Spider?*; *Are You a Snail?*; and *Are You a Ladybug?*

As the Crow Flies: A First Book of Maps
Written by Gail Hartman, Illustrated by Harvey Stevenson
Aladdin, $6.99, 32 pages
First published in 1993
Ages 4–8

A triumphant introduction to maps, with various animals—an eagle, rabbit, and horse, among others—describing the terrain they roam. Within this context, the notions of distance, topography, and other geographical concepts are enlivened as the final pages link all of the animals' "neighborhoods" together.

Astro Bunnies
Written by Christine Loomis, Illustrated by Ora Eitan
Putnam, $15.99, 28 pages
First published in 2001
Ages 3–6

Sing this to the tune of "Twinkle, Twinkle Little Star": "Astro bunnies... See a Star... Think they'd like to... Go that far." You're off on a space race with some rollicking rabbits. The familiar rhythm, joyful adventure, and soothing ending will elicit soaring responses from every preschooler. Also look for *Zoom! Zoom! Zoom! I'm Off to the Moon* by Dan Yaccarino. Other stories by Loomis include *Across America, I Love You* (see "Story Books"); *Cowboy Bunnies*; and *Rush Hour*.

Chapter Two

Baby Duck and the Bad Eyeglasses

Written by Amy Hest, Illustrated by Jill Barton
Candlewick, $5.99, 26 pages
First published in 1996
Ages 3–7

Baby Duck is not happy with her new red eyeglasses. She's afraid they'll fall off when she's playing and is not at all convinced that they flatter her. It takes a conversation with Grandpa for her to finally see the light. Realistic family interaction and child-centered sentiment provide a fine focus for this ducky tale. Also by Hest, *In the Rain with Baby Duck*; *The Friday Nights of Nana*; and *Mabel Dancing*, among others.

Bam Bam Bam

Written by Eve Merriam, Illustrated by Dan Yaccarino
Henry Holt, $5.95, 26 pages
First published in 1994
Ages 2–5

Does your preschooler's bedroom resemble a demolition site? Read this book and have some fun putting it back together! Kids are fascinated by all things related to construction—machines, big hats, big noise—and the big, bold illustrations will inspire some constructive playacting. Also look for *Construction Zone* by Tana Hoban.

Bark, George

Written and Illustrated by Jules Feiffer
HarperCollins, $15.95, 32 pages
First published in 1999
Ages 3–6

parent's
guide
choice award

This is the hilarious tale of a puppy who could say everything—meow, quack, oink—except "arf." A trip to the vet uncovers the cause of George's woes and just when we think George is cured, he utters an enthusiastic "Hello!" Feiffer's simple, uncluttered images and spare text combine to create a book that will have the whole household howling with laughter. If you enjoy Feiffer's comic stylings, you'll also want to read *I Lost My Bear* and *Meanwhile* (ages 5–9).

Picture Books

Barnyard Banter
Written and Illustrated by Denise Fleming
Owlet, $6.95, 32 pages
First published in 1994
Ages 2–6

All the animals are in their beds, but where's the goose? A lively and cheerful glimpse inside a barn with familiar animal sounds that will please young children as their vocabularies are enriched by words like "wallow," set in big bold print. Also available as a board book. And don't miss Fleming's *In the Small, Small Pond*, a 1993 **Caldecott Honor** book and *Count!* (both detailed in this chapter) as well as *In the Tall, Tall Grass*; *The Everything Book*; *Mama Cat Has Three Kittens*; and *Where Once There Was a World* (detailed in "Story Books").

Be Gentle
Written and Illustrated by Virginia Miller
Candlewick, $5.99, 32 pages
First published in 1997
Ages 2–5

When Bartholomew gets a kitten of his very own, he must learn to be gentle and take care of him. That's an important—and age-appropriate—lesson! Follow his adventures with *I Love You Just the Way You Are* and *In a Minute!*

Bedtime
Written by Ruth Freeman Swain, Illustrated by Cat Bowman Smith
Holiday House, $15.95, 30 pages
First published in 1999
Ages 3–7

There are plenty of swell bedtime stories, but how many focus on the actual beds? A cozy look at beds around the world—from Ancient Egypt to the Space Age. Swain covers a lot of cultural ground in this unique picture book.

Chapter Two

The Beastly Feast
Written and Illustrated by Bruce Goldstone
Henry Holt, $6.95, unpaged
First published in 2001
Ages 3–7

The beasts are planning a feast—and what a feast!—in this colorful collection of images and rhymes. Each beast brings a tasty treat so intriguing that young children will want to share in the festivities.

Benjamin Comes Back/Benjamin Regresa
Written and Illustrated by Amy Brandt
Redleaf, $11.95, 32 pages
First published in 2000
Ages 2–5

At day care, Benjamin misses his mother so much that he can't enjoy the toys or the company of the other children. With text in English and Spanish, this title acknowledges the apprehensions that children feel during their earliest school days. Also look for *Bernard Goes to School* by Joan Elizabeth Goodman (detailed in this chapter).

Benny's Pennies
Written and Illustrated by Pat Brisson
Bantam, $6.99, 32 pages
First published in 1995
Ages 3–5

Benny sets off with five pennies and returns home with gifts for every member of his family, including his dog and cat. Featuring torn-paper collage illustrations, this carefully crafted story touches on the theme of generosity, without being preachy. And look for the eloquence of Brisson's *The Summer My Father Was Ten*.

Picture Books

Bernard Goes to School

Written and Illustrated by Joan Elizabeth Goodman
Boyds Mill Press, $15.95, unpaged
First published in 2001
Ages 2–5

The endearing elephant from *Bernard's Bath* and *Bernard's Nap* has returned. This time he's tackling his fear of starting preschool. Will he make friends? Will he miss his mom and dad? Goodman's gentle illustrations and text will help your pre-preschooler face similar concerns. Also look for the enduring charm of *Will I Have a Friend?* by Miriam Cohen.

Bertie and Small and the Brave Sea Journey

Written and Illustrated by Vanessa Caban
Candlewick, $12.99, 17 pages
First published in 1999
Ages 3–6

With his faithful toy bunny at his side, Bertie sets sail for an imaginary adventure on the high seas. Fashioning a boat from a wooden crate, the dynamic duo bravely face scary creatures and treacherous weather conditions. Like *Harold and the Purple Crayon*, this excellent adventure is certain to inspire creative playacting in your household. Also see *Bertie and Small and the Fast Bike Ride*.

The Best Thing about a Puppy

Written by Judy Hindley, Illustrated by Patricia Casey
Candlewick, $3.29, 18 pages
First published in 1998
Ages 3–6

Having a new puppy is fun, but young pets need a lot of attention. Patricia Casey's color ink drawings vividly capture the energy of the young pup, while the simple text makes this a great choice for beginning readers. Also by Hindley, *Eyes, Nose, Fingers and Toes: A First Book All about You* (detailed in Chapter One).

Chapter Two

Big Bad Bunny
Written by Alan Durant, Illustrated by Guy Parker-Rees
Dutton, $15.99, 26 pages
First published in 2001
Ages 3–6

Big Bad Bunny is... well... funny, but he's one mean dude. This Wild West winner follows his misadventures as his heists and hijinks are sabotaged by a couple of wise citizens. Will Big Bad Bunny turn good?

The Big Green Pocketbook
Written by Candice F. Ransom, Illustrated by Felicia Bond
HarperCollins, $6.95, 32 pages
First published in 1993
Ages 4–7

Riding the bus into town with her mama, a young girl is anxious to fill her pocketbook with enough treasures to match the dimensions of mama's bag. One lollipop, two punched tickets and several crayons later, she's collected a day's worth of special mementos and added some satisfying weight to her purse. This is a loving tribute to mamas everywhere and the endless possibilities for special time spent together.

Blueberries for Sal
Written and Illustrated by Robert McCloskey
Puffin, $5.95, 54 pages
First published by Viking in 1948
Ages 3–6

Truly a classic of children's literature, this lovely **Caldecott Honor** book evokes the timeless pleasures of a warm day in Maine and will likely be as enchanting to your children as it was to you. Young Sal and her mother set out to pick blueberries, as do a mother bear and her cub. The two youths become a bit lost but are happily found by story's end. See featured author Robert McCloskey below. Also, look for *Make Way for Ducklings*, detailed in this chapter, and *One Morning in Maine*.

Picture Books

Featured Author: Robert McCloskey
As a child, Robert McCloskey hoped to become a professional musician. Much to the good fortune of young readers around the world, McCloskey became interested in illustration after earning a scholarship to Boston's Vesper George School of Art in 1932. Spending several years back in his native Ohio, he drew upon his own childhood experiences and immediate surroundings to create the famous **Lentil**. A professional venture in Boston allowed McCloskey to spend time in the lovely Public Garden, where inspiration for his **Caldecott Medal**–winning book **Make Way for Ducklings** (in this chapter) was realized. Time spent in coastal Maine with his wife and young daughter, Sally, resulted in the celebrated **Blueberries for Sal** (see above) and **One Morning in Maine**, while **Journey Cake, Ho!** and **Time of Wonder** (another Caldecott winner) followed shortly after. Robert McCloskey has claimed that his books begin with "an idea/ideas inside my head. I imagine a lot of pictures."* On behalf of millions of fans, here's three cheers for the power of imagination.

*Lolly Robinson, "Robert McCloskey," Children's Books and Their Creators. Ed. Anita Silvey, Houghton Mifflin, 1995. 443.

Blueberry Shoe

Written and Illustrated by Ann Dixon
Graphic Arts Center, $15.95, 30 pages
First published in 1999
Ages 3–7

When Baby loses a shoe during a blueberry picking expedition with his family, it takes on a variety of uses throughout the seasons—nest, plaything, even a possible snack—for the animals that reside on the mountain. The illustrations are stunningly atmospheric, adding to the warmth of this family tale. Fans of Robert McCloskey will certainly be pleased.

Boomer Goes to School

Written by Constance W. McGeorge, Illustrated by Mary Whyte
Chronicle Books, $6.95, 26 pages
First published in 1996
Ages 3–5

Boomer, the playful golden retriever from *Boomer's Big Day*, becomes the center of attention at show-and-tell. Featuring convincing kid-centered text and illustrations, this title is also available in Spanish as *Boomer Va a la Escuela* and would be a great show-and-tell contribution in itself!

Chapter Two

A Boy, a Dog and a Frog

Written and Illustrated by Mercer Mayer
Dial, $4.99, 32 pages
First published in 1967
Ages 3–6

Mercer Mayer relies on his famously expressive illustrations to tell the tale of a boy's persistence in catching a frog. Books without words encourage young children to use their own vocabulary to relay a story. Other titles in this series include *A Boy, a Dog, a Frog and a Friend*; *Frog on His Own*; *Frog, Where Are You?*; and *One Frog Too Many*. Also by Mercer Mayer: *All by Myself* (part of the *Little Critters* series).

Brave Bear

Written and Illustrated by Kathy Mallat
Walker, $15.95, 22 pages
First published in 1999
Ages 3–6

With the same endearing persistence as *The Little Engine That Could*, a bear cub helps a baby bird that has fallen from his nest. Delightful ingenuity and gentle morality make this a great story about trying one's hardest to be a helpful friend. Also by Mallat, *The Picture That Mom Drew* and the clever bedtime book *Seven Stars, More!*

Brown Bear, Brown Bear, What Do You See?

Written by Bill Martin Jr., Illustrated by Eric Carle
Henry Holt, $17.00, 26 pages
First published in 1962
Ages 3–6

A favorite with preschool teachers and parents alike, Bill Martin's rhythmic text paired with Eric Carle's trademark collages makes this title a must-read. Interestingly, this book was revamped in 1992 with clearer illustrations and minor updates. The effect is dazzling and memorable. Also by Bill Martin, *Chicka, Chicka, Boom, Boom* (detailed in this chapter); *The Maestro Plays*; *Polar Bear, Polar Bear, What Do You Hear?*; and *Fire! Fire! Said Mrs. McGuire* (also in this chapter). Carle's famous favorites include *The Very Hungry Caterpillar* and *Draw Me a Star* (both detailed in this chapter).

Picture Books

Bunny Cakes

Written and Illustrated by Rosemary Wells
Puffin, $5.99, 25 pages
First published in 1997
Ages 3–6

One of the more prolific children's authors, Wells has whipped up a tasty tale that simply takes the cake! Familiar characters, Max and Ruby, each have their own ideas about the perfect birthday cake for Grandma. But will they make Max's earthworm cake or Ruby's angel surprise with raspberry fluff icing? Wells's warm and wonderful illustrations will whet your preschoolers' appetites for other stories such as *Max's Chocolate Chicken*; *Noisy Nora*; and *Shy Charles*.

Can You Count Ten Toes?
Count to 10 in 10 Different Languages

Written by Lezlie Evans, Illustrated by Denis Roche
Houghton Mifflin, $16.00, 26 pages
First published in 1999
Ages 3–8

This multilingual counting extravaganza playfully demonstrates cultural differences while introducing basic number skills. A dog points to each object to be counted with the help of children from Japan, Russia, Korea, Israel, and Africa, among others. Children with a culturally diverse group of preschool classmates will be especially appreciative. Also by Evans, the meteorologically musical *Rain Song* (detailed in this chapter) and *Snow Dance*.

Can't You Sleep, Little Bear?

Written by Martin Waddell, Illustrated by Barbara Firth
Candlewick, $5.95, 32 pages
First published in 1992
Ages 2–5

Afraid of "the dark all around us," Little Bear has a hard time falling asleep. Cuddles from Big Bear provide loving reassurance. Certain to become a bedtime favorite, this title is a **Kate Greenaway Medal** winner. With the same cozy comfort as Else Minarek's *Little Bear*, Waddell has also penned *Good Job, Little Bear*; *Let's Go Home, Little Bear*; and *You and Me, Little Bear* as well as *A Kitten Named Moonlight* (detailed in this chapter); *Mimi and the Dream House*; and *Owl Babies*.

Chapter Two

Caps for Sale

Written and Illustrated by Esphyr Slobodkina
HarperTrophy, $5.95, 43 pages
First published in 1947
Ages 3–7

Immediately recognizable and adored by several generations, this is the amusing story of some mischievous monkeys who steal the caps off a feckless peddler's head as he naps under a tree. This enduring monkey business is also available in hardcover and in English and Spanish audio packages from Live Oak Media. Based on the same African folktale, you may also want to introduce *The Hatseller and the Monkeys* by Baba Wague Diakite.

Car Wash

Written by Sandra Steen and Susan Steen, Illustrated by G. Brian Karas
Putnam, $15.95, 32 pages
First published in 2001
Ages 3–7

Washing the car becomes an unforgettable, underwater adventure in this unique story. With poetic text and dazzling collage illustrations, this book encourages a visit to the outer boundaries of imagination. It may also be useful to children—and there are many—who are afraid of going through the car wash.

The Carrot Seed

Written by Ruth Krauss, Illustrated by Crockett Johnson
HarperTrophy, $5.95, 27 pages
First published in 1945
Ages 3–7

While nobody seems to have much faith in the little boy's plans, he is marvelously certain that the carrot seed he plants will grow. The illustrations may be simple, but the timeless message—persistence, confidence, and patience—is abundantly clear. Also by Krauss, *A Hole Is to Dig: A First Book of Definitions* (in this chapter).

Picture Books

The Cat in the Hat

Written and Illustrated by Dr. Seuss
Random House, $7.99, 61 pages
First published in 1957
Ages 3–8

Oh, the marvelous mind of Dr. Seuss! In this familiar tale, a clever cat pays a visit and creates a merrily rhymed mess. Dr. Seuss's books are published under the Beginner Books imprint at Random House and are thus intended as Easy Readers. But as the parents of millions of pre-reading preschoolers know, there are few things more enjoyable than time spent with Dr. Seuss's fictional friends. Look for *One Fish Two Fish Red Fish Blue Fish* and *Green Eggs and Ham* (also in this chapter).

Featured Author: Dr. Seuss

As the beloved creator of wonderfully whimsical stories for children, Dr. Seuss has set many publishing records. Born Theodore Seuss Geisel in Springfield, Massachusetts, our favorite doctor spent a great deal of time with his father, a zookeeper. An early fascination with animals translated into the creation of the veritable feast of beasts that would appear in his many books, including the ever-popular Proo a Nerkle a Nerds, Seersuckers, Ooblecks, and one grouchy Grinch. Amazingly, twenty-eight publishers rejected Dr. Seuss's first book, **And to Think I Saw It on Mulberry Street**, before it found a happy home at Random House. What followed was a remarkable career that included a silly string of hits including **Horton Hatches the Egg; Horton Hears a Who!; The Lorax** (see "Story Books"); **The Butter Battle Book; If I Ran the Zoo; The Cat in the Hat** (see above); **Green Eggs and Ham** (in this chapter); and **Oh, the Places You'll Go** (see "Story Books"). At the time of his death in 1991, Dr. Seuss had sold more than two hundred million copies of his books and earned numerous awards and a permanent spot in the hearts of countless kids of all ages.

Cats, Cats, Cats!

Written by Leslea Newman, Illustrated by Erika Oller
Simon & Schuster, $16.00, 27 pages
First published in 2001
Ages 3–7

Cats and more cats comprise this feline fiesta. Sixty cats make their home with Mrs. Brown. They doze in the sunshine during the day, but the real fun begins after dark when "as soon as she began to snore, the fun began with cats galore." The watercolor illustrations of cats engaging in various humorous activities will tickle your cat fancy. Newman is known for the sensitive and timely *Heather Has Two Mommies* (in "Story Books") as well as the thoughtful *Too Far Away to Touch*, a story that deals with the loss of a loved one to AIDS.

Chapter Two

Chicka Chicka Boom Boom

Written by Bill Martin Jr. and John Archambault, Illustrated by Lois Ehlert
Aladdin, $4.99, 38 pages
First published in 1989
Ages 3–6

A spirited adventure ensues as the letters of the alphabet race up a coconut tree. Lois Ehlert's bold colors provide a perfect accompaniment to this clever rhyming story. Also by Martin, *Fire! Fire! Said Mrs. McGuire* and *Brown Bear, Brown Bear, What Do You See?* (both in this chapter). Lois Ehlert's picture books include *Circus*; *Color Zoo* (detailed in this chapter); *Eating the Alphabet* (detailed in this chapter); *Feathers for Lunch*; *Fish Eyes: A Book You Can Count On*; and *Market Day* (detailed in this chapter).

Chugga-Chugga Choo-Choo

Written by Kevin Lewis, Illustrated by Daniel Kirk
Hyperion, $6.99, unpaged (board book edition)
First published in 1999
Ages 2–5

Trains are big sources of wonder for small children. With rhyming text, bold colors, and computer-aided illustration, this modern choo-choo celebration provides mesmerizing entertainment. Other train titles include *Here Comes the Train* by Charlotte Voake and *Freight Train* by Donald Crews (detailed in this chapter).

Circle Dogs

Written by Kevin Henkes, Illustrated by Dan Yaccarino
HarperTrophy, $5.95, 32 pages
First published in 2001
Ages 3–7

Cute canines abound in this circular tale of two dachshunds and their humans. Household objects take the form of simple shapes that can be easily identified by preschoolers. The retro style illustrations are appealingly clean and uncluttered, and the fun language is in perfect pitch with the pet pooches. Also by Henkes: *The Biggest Boy*; *Julius, the Baby of the World* (detailed in "Story Books"); *Chester's Way*; and *Chrysanthemum* (also in "Story Books").

Picture Books

Circus 1-2-3
Written and Illustrated by Megan Halsey
HarperCollins, $14.95, 24 pages
First published in 2000
Ages 3–6

Step right up and count the clowns, ponies, seals, and other attractions you'll find under the big top. There's a festive "seek-and-find" element to this swinging story, and preschoolers who have recently been to the circus will delight in spotting the familiar animals and performers. Pair this picture book with *Circus Shapes* by Stuart J. Murphy

Clifford the Big Red Dog
Written and Illustrated by Norman Bridwell
Scholastic, $3.50, 32 pages
First published in 1985
Ages 3–6

This is the big dog that launched a small cottage industry. There are dozens of titles about Clifford's adventures, from playful puppy to overgrown pooch. In this sweet introduction, Amy Elizabeth describes how she takes care of Clifford... and how Clifford returns the favor. Other titles include *Clifford and the Big Parade*; *Clifford and the Big Storm*; *Clifford at the Circus*; *Clifford Counts 1-2-3*; *Clifford Grows Up*; and *Clifford the Small Red Puppy*. There is also an Easy Reader series of books for beginning readers who can't get enough of Clifford.

Cloudy with a Chance of Meatballs
Written by Judi Barrett, Illustrated by Ron Barrett
Aladdin, $5.99, 32 pages
First published in 1978
Ages 3–8

In the town of Chewandswallow, life is deliciously unpredictable. It rains soup and hails hamburgers, and those are just the appetizers. The Barretts' tasty tale has become a staple of children's collections and is available in a variety of editions, including hardcover and audio. Its salty sequel is *Pickles to Pittsburgh*.

Chapter Two

Clown

Written and Illustrated by Quentin Blake
Henry Holt, $6.95, 32 pages
First published in 1996
Ages 3–8

A discarded toy clown climbs out of a trash bin and into the life of a loving family. The sadness of the forgotten toys is made imminently clear and will lead children to take a more appreciative look at their own stuffed companions. Also by Blake, the zany *Zagazoo*. You'll also recognize his illustrations from Roald Dahl's books.

Cock a Doodle Moo

Written and Illustrated by Bernard Most
Harcourt, $13.00, 33 pages
First published in 1996
Ages 3–7

When the rooster loses his voice, the farm's schedule is thrown off kilter. A helpful cow is willing to pitch in, but after many attempts, is only able to muster "cock a doodle moo." For more barnyard ballyhoo, look for *The Cow That Went Oink*. Also by Most, *Catbirds and Dogfish*, and dinosaurs aplenty in *A Dinosaur Named After Me*; *How Big Were the Dinosaurs*; *If the Dinosaurs Came Back*; and *The Littlest Dinosaurs*.

Cold Little Duck, Duck, Duck

Written by Lisa Westberg Peters, Illustrated by Sam Williams
Greenwillow, $15.95, 32 pages
First published in 2000
Ages 3–6

A lovely choice for the last days of winter, this is the story of an optimistic little duck that wishes for spring. The terrific rhyming text will cause contagious chanting as the wonder of the changing seasons is introduced to preschoolers. The forecast is good for Peters's *The Sun, the Wind and the Rain*.

Picture Books

Color Zoo
Written and Illustrated by Lois Ehlert
Lippincott, $16.95, 32 pages
First published in 1989
Ages 3–6

An ingenious menagerie of transforming images, as a tiger becomes a mouse with the turn of a page. Ehlert's colorful configurations earned her a place on the esteemed **Caldecott Honor** list. Also, see listing for *Market Day* in this chapter. Other titles by Ehlert include *Color Farm; Feathers for Lunch; Fish Eyes: A Book You Can Count On*; and *Eating the Alphabet: Fruits and Vegetables from A to Z* (detailed in this chapter).

Come on, Rain!
Written by Karen Hesse, Illustrated by Jon J. Muth
Scholastic, $15.95, 32 pages
First published in 1999
Ages 3–6

Children can look forward to years of literary enjoyment from **Newbery Award**–winning author Karen Hesse, beginning with this beautiful rain dance. Muth's glistening watercolor illustrations combined with Hesse's entrancing text provide a cooling sensory delight for the hottest summer days.

Corduroy
Written and Illustrated by Don Freeman
Puffin, $5.99, 30 pages
First published in 1968
Ages 3–7

You'd be hard pressed to find anyone under thirty-five years old who hasn't fallen in love with this adorable stuffed bear. Today's preschoolers carry on the affectionate tradition, as Corduroy and Lisa (the little girl who brought him home from the store) enjoy high adventure. Also available in Spanish. There are several sequels and related novelty items available, but the original version will most assuredly capture the heart and imagination of your children. Also by Freeman, *Gregory's Shadow* and *Norman the Doorman* (both in "Story Books").

Chapter Two

Count!
Written and Illustrated by Denise Fleming
Henry Holt, $6.95, 32 pages
First published in 1995
Ages 3–6

Frisky and friendly animals help your preschooler learn basic number skills. For more colorful counting, look for *Each Orange Had Eight Slices* by Paul Giganti, with illustrations by Donald Crews.

Counting Kisses
Written and Illustrated by Karen Katz
McElderry, $14.00, 28 pages
First published in 2001
Ages 2–5

The kissing is contagious as a whole family offers loving busses to baby in this affectionate picture book. There are "ten little kisses on teeny tiny toes," all the way up to a final smooch on a baby's adorable nose. The kissing and counting will surely become a part of your toddler or preschooler's bedtime rituals. Also by Katz, *The Colors of Us* (detailed in "Story Books") and *Over the Moon: An Adoption Tale*.

Curious George
Written and Illustrated by H. A. Rey
Houghton Mifflin, $5.95, 46 pages
First published in 1942
Ages 3–6

Curiosity may have killed the cat, but it certainly hasn't dampened the popularity of this mischievous monkey. Curious George's foibles and the perpetual chagrin of the "man in the yellow hat" have entertained preschoolers for decades. There are more than a dozen sequels available including *Curious George at the Fire Station*; *Curious George Flies a Kite*; and *Curious George Gets a Medal*.

Picture Books

Daddy Is a Doodlebug
Written and Illustrated by Bruce Degan
HarperTrophy, $5.95, unpaged
First published in 2000
Ages 3–7

"We walk our poodlebug down the lane. We ride the caboodle car on the train." With its cast of fantastic Doodletown characters, realistic Daddy-and-child sentiment, and raucously imaginative language, this is a sweet story that's full of whimsy. Degan's bright and contemporary illustrations are fresh and appealing, as is his talent for catchy, rhythmic storytelling.

Parent/Child Review: Daddy Is a Doodlebug
The Parent: Tomas, Age 42, Horse Trainer
The Child: Carla, Age 5, Kindergartner
Carla says: "We read this book for story hour and we all asked questions. I don't know where they live in the book but it seems like New York. I took it home from the library to read with my dad and we were laughing a lot... especially my dad."
Tomas says: "That's true, actually. I think I laughed more than Carla but she loved it, too, and keeps talking about it. Now we call our younger daughter Reboodle instead of Rebecca. We borrowed the book from the library twice then Carla and her mom bought it for me for Father's Day. It's definitely become a favorite."

The Day Jimmy's Boa Ate the Wash
Written by Trinka Hakes Noble, Illustrated by Steven Kellogg
Dial Books, $6.99, 32 pages
First published in 1980
Ages 3–8

What happens when Jimmy's snake joins the class on a field trip to a farm? A hilarious and frantic adventure! Further havoc is wreaked in *Jimmy's Boa Bounces Back* and *Jimmy's Boa and the Big Splash Birthday Bash*.

Dear Daisy, Get Well Soon!
Written and Illustrated by Maggie Smith
Dell Dragonfly, $6.99, 38 pages
First published in 2000
Ages 3–7

With good-natured cheer in abundance, this simple tale of friendship will become a read-again favorite... especially for children stuck in bed with chicken pox. Another fantastic friendship book is *My Best Friend* by Pat Hutchins.

Chapter Two

DiDi and Daddy on the Promenade
Written by Marilyn Singer, Illustrated by Marie-Louise Gay
Clarion, $14.00, 32 pages
First published in 2001
Ages 4–7

The scenic Brooklyn Promenade is the setting for this delightful story of a little girl's quality time with her daddy. New York pride is evident with the Manhattan skyline looming majestically across the river. The text echoes the staccato rhythms of preschoolers' verbal interactions as well as the city's rapid pace. Also by Singer, *Fred's Bed*; *Monster Museum*; *Nine O'Clock Lullaby* (in "Story Books"); and *On the Same Day in March: A Tour of the World's Weather*.

Different Just Like Me
Written and Illustrated by Lori Mitchell
Talewinds, $6.95, 32 pages
First published in 1999
Ages 3–7

While acceptance of the unfamiliar may be a difficult concept for small children, this story gently addresses various differences and disabilities through the eyes of a young girl who notices a blind woman and a person in a wheelchair during a trip to the market.

Dinosaurs, Dinosaurs
Written and Illustrated by Byron Barton
HarperTrophy, $5.95, 36 pages
First published in 1989
Ages 3–6

With simple text and bold blocks of color, Barton provides the dino-details that preschoolers crave. Additional scientific information is included in the endpapers, allowing for the expansion of children's curiosity, vocabulary skills, and knowledge base as they grow. Young dinosaur connoisseurs and budding paleontologists will also want to read Byron's sequel, *Bones, Bones, Dinosaur Bones* as well as Aliki's *Digging Up Dinosaurs*.

Picture Books

Do You See a Mouse?
Written and Illustrated by Bernard Waber
Sanpiper, $5.95, 32 pages
First published in 1995
Ages 3–6

The guests at the Park Snoot Hotel are... well... snooty. They cannot bear the idea that a mouse has taken up residence there. Your preschooler will be happy to point him out as the mouse-catchers are called in to "look into this beastly matter." Waber is the author of the perennial favorite *Lyle, Lyle Crocodile* and its sequels, as well as *Ira Sleeps Over* (see "Story Books").

Dog's Day
Written and Illustrated by Jane Cabrera
Orchard, $12.95, 26 pages
First published in 2000
Ages 2–5

The illustrations that portray this day in the life of a playful pup practically leap off the page with exuberance. What does the puppy like to do at the end of the day? "Play with Daddy," of course. Little dog lovers will also adore *Little Dog Poems* by Kristine O'Connell George.

Don't Forget the Bacon
Written and Illustrated by Pat Hutchins
Mulberry, $5.95, 32 pages
First published in 1989
Ages 3–7

A little boy is sent to the grocery store by his mom, but will he remember all of the items on her list? A great rhythmic read-aloud story—and beginning readers may want to give it a whirl as well. Also by Hutchins, *The Doorbell Rang* (detailed in this chapter); *Good-Night Owl!*; *Rosie's Walk* (in this chapter); and *Ten Red Apples*.

Chapter Two

Don't Wake the Baby: An Interactive Book with Sounds

Written and Illustrated by Jonathan Allen

Candlewick Press, $19.99, 18 pages

First published in 2000

Ages 3–7

While you won't find many novelty items listed in this guide, this is an interactive book you don't want to miss. Cleverly conceived in the integration of technology with a story that is familiar and naturally compelling to preschoolers (especially those who often hear a similar warning about waking their younger sibling), your child will reach for the sound-activating pull tabs in this dynamic book again and again. Also look (and listen!) for *Wake Up, Sleeping Beauty: An Interactive Book with Sounds*.

The Doorbell Rang

Written and Illustrated by Pat Hutchins

Mulberry, $5.95, 24 pages

First published in 1986

Ages 4–8

The children love Ma's delicious cookies but must decide how to equally divide them amongst their many unexpected visitors. There's a hidden math lesson in this delightfully simple story, which is also available in hardcover and as an audio adaptation from Live Oak Media. Other books by Hutchins include *Don't Forget the Bacon* (detailed in this chapter); *It's My Birthday*; *My Best Friend*; *Rosie's Walk* (in this chapter); and the wonderfully wordless *Changes, Changes*.

Draw Me a Star

Written and Illustrated by Eric Carle

Penguin Putnam, $6.99, 36 pages

First published in 1998

Ages 3–7

Simplicity of design and verse, as well as his influential cut-paper illustration style, are the hallmarks of Carle's wildly popular picture books. Here, the lovely pictures come to life as an artist creates an expanding universe, with each drawn object asking for additional drawings. Of course, Carle is the author of the always-adored *The Very Hungry Caterpillar* (detailed in this chapter); *The Very Busy Spider*; *Today Is Monday*; *Pancakes, Pancakes*; *The Grouchy Ladybug*; *The Very Quiet Cricket*; *Papa, Please Get the Moon for Me* (detailed in this chapter), and many others.

Picture Books

Dreaming: A Countdown to Sleep
Written and Illustrated by Elaine Greenstein
Arthur A. Levine, $15.95, 32 pages
First published in 2000
Ages 2–5

A gentle fantasy sequence sets this bedtime book apart from the crowd. With radiant drawings, objects are counted in a swirling send-off to sleep. Follow this nifty nocturne with *Counting Kisses* by Karen Katz (detailed in this chapter). Your toddler or preschooler will love marking her growth with *As Big as You!* also by Greenstein.

Duncan the Dancing Duck
Written and Illustrated by Syd Hoff
Clarion, $5.95, 32 pages
First published in 1994
Ages 3–7

Duncan loves to move his dancing feet, even though his mother repeatedly tells him to "stay in line." Everyone else enjoys Duncan's dancing, and he eventually gains international fame. Being a world-renowned dancing duck has its drawbacks though, and Duncan soon longs for the quiet life back on the farm. Hoff's humor has earned him legions of fans throughout his lengthy career. Also look for *Danny and the Dinosaur* (detailed in "Story Books"); *Bernard on His Own*; and *Sammy the Seal*.

Each Peach, Pear, Plum: An "I Spy" Story
Written by Janet Ahlberg, Illustrations by Allan Ahlberg
Puffin Books, $4.99, 31 pages
First published in 1978
Ages 3–6

Children will love searching for familiar nursery rhyme characters— Cinderella, Mother Hubbard, Little Bo Peep—hidden in the charming illustrations. With its memorable rhymes and delightful story, this title is a recipient of the **Kate Greenaway Medal** for illustrated children's books. Also by the amazing Ahlbergs, *The Adventures of Bert* and *The Jolly Postman* (both detailed in this chapter).

Chapter Two

Parent/Child Review: Each Peach, Pear, Plum: An "I Spy" Story
The Parent: Claire Anne, Age 39, Librarian
The Child: Julia, Age 6, Tap Dancer
Julia says: "My brother had this book in his room and one of the pages was ripped out. My mom said we could tape it back in and so we did that. Then (sigh) we read it a lot and a lot. I took it to school because my mom said that it's a famous book and kids would like it who haven't seen it. My teacher said, um, we would read it after lunch 'cause it was raining. Then we drew pictures with plums, and someone drew a picture of Humpty Dumpty sitting on an apple. I can find all of the hidden stuff in the pages."
Claire Anne says: "Well, that sums it up, doesn't it? I used to be a children's librarian and this was always a favorite. It's a great book to give to kids who are wanting to begin to read by themselves because there's so much to look at and the story is so absorbing."

Eating the Alphabet: Fruits and Vegetables from A to Z
Written and Illustrated by Lois Ehlert
Voyager, $7.00, 34 pages
First published in 1989
Ages 3–7

Ehlert has created a bold and beautiful alphabet book with gourmet appeal. She's found a delicious food for each letter of the alphabet, from the familiar apple and zucchini to the more exotic jicama and kohlrabi. Your preschooler's vocabulary will be expanded as well as his palate. Also by Ehlert, *Color Zoo* (detailed in this chapter); *Feathers for Lunch, Fish Eyes: A Book You Can Count On*; and *Market Day* (in this chapter).

The Egg Tree
Written and Illustrated by Katherine Milhous
Aladdin, $5.99, 32 pages
First published in 1950
Ages 3–7

With boldly stylized illustrations reminiscent of Amish hex signs, this longtime favorite and **Caldecott Medal** winner focuses on young Katy, who wakes on Easter morning to a special surprise.

Picture Books

Emily's First Hundred Days of School

Written and Illustrated by Rosemary Wells
Hyperion, $16.99, 58 pages
First published in 2000
Ages 4–7

The 100th day of school is quite a milestone in a young life and usually one that is marked by classroom celebration. This count-up to that special day, by celebrated author Rosemary Wells, is perfectly suited to preschoolers and their daily activities. Preschool and early-elementary–aged children will also enjoy the counting games in *100 Days of School* by Trudy Harris. For more of Wells's many tales, see *Bunny Cakes* in this chapter.

Estelle and Lucy

Written and Illustrated by Anna Alter
Greenwillow, $14.95, 23 pages
First published in 2001
Ages 3–6

Estelle is a kitten and Lucy is a little mouse, but they're sisters, nonetheless! Despite their occasional episodes of realistic rivalry, there is a subtle, yet consistent, display of love, admiration, and friendship between the two in this special debut. Further family ties can be found in *Big Sister and Little Sister* by Charlotte Zolotow. Also by Alter, a new take on *The Three Little Kittens*.

Everyone Poops

Written and Illustrated by Taro Gomi
Kane/Miller, $6.95, 27 pages
First published in 1977
Ages 3–7

Ain't it the truth. While some critics turned up their nose at this Japanese import, it has clearly gained an American following. And why shouldn't it? Kids are fascinated by bodily functions, especially post-potty training, and this book describes the poopy predilections of a number of animals. Bottoms up! Um... and then there's *The Gas We Pass* by Shinta Cho.

Chapter Two

Everything to Spend the Night: From A to Z
Written by Ann Whitford Paul, Illustrated by Maggie Smith
Dorling Kindersley, $6.95, unpaged
First published in 1999
Ages 3–6

This unusual alphabet introduction acknowledges a child's excitement at the prospect of an overnight trip. There are the usual packables—toothbrush and slippers—but is there room in the bag for a favorite quilt? Also by Ann Whitford Paul, the jubilant *Hello Toes! Hello Feet!* and *Eight Hands Round: A Patchwork Alphabet* (detailed in "Story Books").

Exactly the Opposite
Written and Illustrated by Tana Hoban
Mulberry, $5.95, 32 pages
First published in 1997
Ages 2–5

Demonstrating once again her talent for crafting exceptional concept books, Hoban uses vivid photography to illuminate the notion of opposites, from open/closed to front/back and hot/cold. Preschoolers as well as older children with different learning needs will benefit. Also by Hoban, *26 Letters and 99 Cents* (detailed in this chapter); *A Children's Zoo*; *Colors Everywhere*; *Construction Zone*; *I Read Signs*; *Look Book*; and *Shadows and Reflections*.

Fall Leaves Fall!
Written by Zoe Hall, Illustrated by Shari Halpern
Scholastic, $15.95, 32 pages
First published in 2000
Ages 3–6

A lively look at the beautiful colors of fall and a perfect accompaniment to preschool curriculum. This book crisply captures the boundless energy that the autumn air inspires. Designed to be followed by a hearty romp in the fallen leaves and a rousing reading of *Apples and Pumpkins* by Anne Rockwell, *Autumn Leaves* by Ken Robbins, or *Red Leaf, Yellow Leaf* by Lois Ehlert.

Picture Books

Feelings

Written and Illustrated by Aliki
Greenwillow, $5.95, 32 pages
First published in 1984
Ages 3–6

With its companion books, *Manners* and *Communication*, Aliki humorously, yet pointedly, addresses important childhood lessons. These titles also work quite well for slightly older children in special education settings. Young Aliki fans will also enjoy *All By Myself*.

Finders Keepers

Written and Illustrated by Will and Nicholas
Harcourt, $7.00, 32 pages
First published in 1951
Ages 3–7

An old-fashioned picture book with timeless appeal, its illustrations won a **Caldecott Medal** for its authors in the 1950s. Your family will howl as two doggies duke it out over the rightful ownership of a bone.

Finger Rhymes

Written and Illustrated by Marc Brown
Puffin, $5.99, 32 pages
First published in 1996
Ages 2–6

This is a perfect invitation to joyful parent/child together time, presenting fourteen rhymes and fun finger-games, from the familiar refrains to newer play-along favorites. Further fun can be found in Joanna Cole's *The Eentsy Weentsy Spider: Fingerplays and Action Rhymes*; and Maud Fuller Petersham's *The Rooster Crows: A Book of American Rhymes and Jingles*.

Fire Fighters

Written and Illustrated by Paulette Bourgeois
Kids Can Press, $5.95, 32 pages
First published in 1998
Ages 3–7

From the friendly and informative *In My Neighborhood Series* comes this look at the lives of everyday heroes, community fire fighters. The book also includes important fire prevention and safety lessons. Preschool and kindergarten curriculum often explores children's immediate surroundings, and this valuable series includes *Garbage Collectors*; *Police Officers*; and *Postal Workers*.

Chapter Two

Fire! Fire! Said Mrs. McGuire

Written by Bill Martin Jr., Illustrated by Richard Egielski
Harcourt Brace, $6.95, 32 pages
First published in 1996
Ages 4–8

The city is on high alert as the report of a fire sparks action amongst its residents. As everyone races to action (notice that women are in the fire-fighting forefront), the text races and zooms until the source of the blaze is discovered: the candles on old Mrs. Wear's birthday cake. Egielski's illustrations are drolly urban and frenzied, yet cozy. Also by Bill Martin Jr., *Brown Bear, Brown Bear, What Do You See?* and *Chicka Chicka Boom Boom* (both in this chapter).

Fire Truck

Written and Illustrated by Peter Sis
Greenwillow, $15.95, 24 pages
First published in 1999
Ages 3–6

To say that Matt has a fondness for fire trucks would be a vast understatement. When he wakes up in the morning, his first words are "fire truck." When he goes to sleep, his last words are... well, you get the picture. Clear and bright illustrations make this a perfect title for similarly fascinated youngsters. Other titles by Sis include *Trucks, Trucks, Trucks*; *An Ocean World*; and *Dinosaur*.

Five Creatures

Written by Emily Jenkins, Illustrated by Tomek Bogacki
Farrar Straus Giroux, $16.00, 26 pages
First published in 2001
Ages 4–8

parent's guide choice award

There are "three humans and two cats" in the young narrator's family, and many similarities and differences to be noted between them. The author is remarkably in tune with some very charming childhood ideas. Relationships are cleverly indicated through Venn diagrams that are likely to elicit some cozy family investigations of your very own. A future classic!

Picture Books

Follow the Leader

Written by Erica Silverman, Illustrated by G. Brian Karas
Farrar Straus Giroux, $15.00, 32 pages
First published in 2000
Ages 3–6

At this book's conclusion, your kids will be off and running to start a rousing round of this classic game. The story centers on two young brothers who, stuck inside on a snowy day, let their imaginations soar as they do handstands, imitate wild animals, and pretend to be acrobats. Also by Silverman, *Mrs. Peachtree's Bicycle* and *Big Pumpkin*, among others.

Freight Train

Written and Illustrated by Donald Crews
Mulberry, $5.95, 24 pages
First published in 1978
Ages 3–7

This **Caldecott Honor** book is awash in brilliant colors, as a freight train speeds through tunnels, cities, and countryside before disappearing into the final pages. Young aspiring engineers will be especially pleased and may also want to read *I Love Trains!* by Philemon Sturges. Also by Crews, *Bigmama's* (see "Story Books"); *Flying*; *Night at the Fair*; and *Inside Freight Train*, a board book adaptation for toddlers.

Ginger

Written and Illustrated by Charlotte Voake
Candlewick, $6.99, unpaged
First published in 1997
Ages 3–7

Ginger is a tabby that rules the roost. He feasts on delicious treats and snoozes contentedly in his basket. When a cuddly kitten becomes the newest member of the household, Ginger must set aside his solitude and make room for the kitty. Voake is the author of *Here Comes the Train* and *Mr. Davies and the Baby*.

Chapter Two

Giving

Written and Illustrated by Shirley Hughes
Candlewick, $3.99, 24 pages
First published in 1993
Ages 3–6

Wonderfully adept at portraying real childhood emotions and ideas, Hughes explores a child's concept of giving and the notion that gifts need not be material objects. Using sensible and simple situations, the message is abundantly clear. Give Hughes's other picture books your undivided attention, including *Abel's Moon*; *Alfie and the Birthday Surprise*; *Helping*; and *Out and About*.

Goodbye House

Written and Illustrated by Frank Asch
Simon & Schuster, $5.99, 32 pages
First published in 1986
Ages 2–5

Moving to a new house can be both sad and exciting. Here, Little Bear deals with his feelings by saying goodbye to each room of his old abode. The author of the Moonbear series, Asch also wrote *Happy Birthday, Moon* and *Moonbear's Dream*. And see *The Sun Is My Favorite Star* (detailed in this chapter).

Goodnight Moon

Written by Margaret Wise Brown, Illustrated by Clement Hurd
HarperCollins, $5.95, 32 pages
First published in 1947
Ages 2–5

How does one begin to describe the joys of this book? While the little rabbit prepares for bed, he bids goodnight to all his favorite possessions and beloved creatures. As the story progresses, the illustrations grow dimmer and dreamier. A favorite bedtime tradition for generations, this lovely story is available in several different languages and in a variety of editions, including a board book and a paperback/audio cassette package. Other classics by Brown include *The Runaway Bunny* (detailed in this chapter); *The Big Red Barn*; and *Little Fur Family*. See Featured Author, Margaret Wise Brown below.

Picture Books

Featured Author: Margaret Wise Brown
Born in Brooklyn, N.Y., in 1910, Margaret Wise Brown spent her childhood in a Long Island suburb. She began writing while a student in New York Bureau of Educational Experiments, later known as Bank Street College of Education. It was Lucy Sprague Mitchell, Bank Street's founder, who most influenced Brown's early literary career. The young writer learned the importance of creating developmentally appropriate stories for young children and began to craft the cozy, child–centered fiction that would become her hallmark. Beginning in the late 1930s, Brown penned children's books that were destined to become classics including **The Quiet Noisy Book**; **The Runaway Bunny** (in this chapter); **Night and Day**; **Little Fur Family**; and, of course, **Goodnight Moon**. Margaret Wise Brown died suddenly at the age of forty–two, leaving behind some of the most treasured children's literature ever written.

Green Eggs and Ham

Written and Illustrated by Dr. Seuss

Random House, $7.99, 62 pages

First published in 1960

Ages 3–8

Sam-I-Am is the champion of green cuisine, trying to convince a fellow Seussian character (and readers) to sample the delectable dish. The adamant refusal to eat green eggs and ham anywhere—in a house, with a mouse, in a box, with a fox—becomes the centerpiece of memorable verse, until he is finally coerced. Chances are, you know the rest. Also in this chapter are *The Cat in the Hat* and *One Fish Two Fish Red Fish Blue Fish*. In "Story Books," you'll find *The Lorax* and *Oh, the Places You'll Go*. There are additional titles in "Easy Readers," under "Beginner Books."

The Grey Lady and the Strawberry Snatcher

Written and Illustrated by Molly Bang

Aladdin, $6.99, 48 pages

First published in 1996

Ages 4–8

This book has entrancing illustrations and no text, allowing for antic narration by its readers. The mildly sinister plot involves a shady creature who stalks an unsuspecting woman, lured by her basket of succulent strawberries... until he becomes sidetracked by blueberries. Bang is the author of *The Paper Crane*; *Ten, Nine, Eight*; and *When Sophie Gets Angry, Really, Really Angry* (in this chapter).

Chapter Two

Half a Moon and One Whole Star

Written by Crescent Dragonwagon, Illustrated by Jerry Pinkney
Aladdin, $6.99, 32 pages
First published in 1986
Ages 3–7

This recipient of the **Coretta Scott King Award** is truly a sensory delight and a visual masterpiece. Young Susan listens to the sounds as she falls asleep on a warm summer night. Also by Dragonwagon, *Alligator Arrived with Apples: A Potluck Alphabet Feast* and *Annie Flies the Birthday Bike*.

Happy Birthday, Maisy

Written and Illustrated by Lucy Cousins
Candlewick, $13.99, 18 pages
First published in 1998
Ages 2–5

Maisy mania has arrived and is well deserved! This appealing lift-the-flap book shows all of the exciting rituals surrounding a child's birthday including a rousing rendition of "Happy Birthday to You." Other titles in the Maisy series include *Count with Maisy*; *Bathtime, Maisy*; *Doctor Maisy*; *Maisy at the Farm*; and *Maisy Drives the Bus*, to name a few.

Harold and the Purple Crayon

Written and Illustrated by Crockett Johnson
HarperCollins, $5.95, 62 pages
First published in 1955
Ages 3–7

With his trusty crayon, Harold draws himself in and out of trouble, creating an adventure that takes him over land and sea. This poignant illustration of the power of imagination has captured the hearts of children of all ages for nearly fifty years. Harold's travels continue in *Harold's ABC*; *Harold's Circus*; and *Harold's Trip to the Sky*. Also available in Spanish.

Picture Books

Harry the Dirty Dog
Written by Gene Zion, Illustrated by Margaret Bloy Graham
HarperTrophy, $6.95, unpaged
First published in 1956
Ages 3–7

Harry will do anything to avoid a bath. After running away, he gets so dirty that nobody recognizes him when he returns. Everybody loves Harry and his messy ways. Hey, what kid doesn't wish for a few days of bath skipping? Also available in Spanish. For more adventures with the crusty canine, look for *Harry and the Lady Next Door* and *Harry by the Sea*.

Hello, Shoes!
Written by Joan W. Blos, Illustrated by Ann Boyajian
Simon & Schuster, $13.00, 24 pages
First published in 1999
Ages 3–6

A boy and his grandpa search for his favorite pair of shoes, the red sandals with the buckle on the side. In the process they find forgotten treasures and enjoy their special together time. Preschoolers will certainly enjoy reading this story with their grandpas. Also look for *Grandpa* by Debbie Bailey.

Here Comes Mother Goose
Edited by Iona Opie, Illustrated by Rosemary Wells
Candlewick, $21.99, 107 pages
First published in 1999
Ages 2–8

An irresistibly charming collection of your family's favorite nursery rhymes and a few new ones. With a decidedly more modern feel than its predecessors and a good dose of visual humor, this volume will become a favorite childhood companion. And see *My Very First Mother Goose* (detailed in this chapter). You'll also enjoy *Animal Crackers* by Jane Dyer.

Chapter Two

Here Comes Spring... and Summer and Fall and Winter
Written and Illustrated by Mary Murphy
DK Ink, $9.95, 30 pages
First published in 1999
Ages 3–6

A group of playful puppies engage in preschool-appropriate activities throughout the seasons. With help from their mom, they plant seeds in spring and throw snowballs in winter. Their boundless energy is captured by lively, colorful illustrations. A perfect introduction to the seasons! Murphy has written a delightful grouping of topical picture books including, *Here Comes the Rain!*; *I Am an Artist*; *I Feel Happy and Sad and Angry and Glad*; *I Like It When*; and *Some Things Change*.

A Hole Is to Dig: A First Book of Definitions
Written by Ruth Krauss, Illustrated by Maurice Sendak
HarperCollins, $5.95, 48 pages
First published in 1952
Ages 3–6

"Toes are to wiggle" and "Arms are to hug" are among the sweet and hilarious definitions by the author of *The Carrot Seed* (in this chapter). The collection is enlivened by early illustrations by Maurice Sendak.

Hooway for Wodney Wat
Written by Helen Lester, Illustrated by Lynn Munsinger
Houghton Mifflin, $16.00, 32 pages
First published in 1999
Ages 3–7

Rodney Rat has a difficult time pronouncing his own name, thus the title. It's a common issue for preschoolers, children in the early-elementary grades, as well as children with developmental delays. Though the children tease him, he becomes a hero after foiling a bully. Other amusing, yet instructive, tales by Lester include *Listen, Buddy*; *Me First*; *Tacky the Penguin*; and *A Porcupine Named Fluffy* (detailed in this chapter).

Picture Books

Hurray for Pre-K!
Written by Ellen B. Senisi
HarperCollins, $12.95, 36 pages
First published in 2000
Ages 3–5

"Hurray" is the word of the day in this exuberant book about starting school. Every child has hopes, fears, and a lot of excitement about beginning preschool, and this book covers all of the bases. Basic activities such as playing, singing, reading, and snack time are featured. Minimal text—one summary sentence per page—allows the children to focus on the visual details and match their own new school experiences with those in the book. Next year, you'll want to look for *Kindergarten Kids*, also by Senisi. By then, your kids will be preschool pros!

I Am a Bunny
Written by Ole Risom, Illustrated by Richard Scarry
Golden Books, $4.99, unpaged
First published in 1967
Ages 2–5

Little bunny Nicholas gives children a glimpse into his life throughout the seasons. Richard Scarry's sweet and familiar illustrations (less busy than his typical style) contribute to the timeless charm of this lovely book. The opening refrain, "I am a bunny. I live in a hollow tree," presents a wonderful invitation to toddler and preschooler play-acting. Also look for *I am a Kitten* and *I am a Puppy*.

I Love Trucks!
Written and Illustrated by Philemon Sturges
HarperTrophy, $5.95, 26 pages
First published in 1999
Ages 2–5

Can't get enough of trucks? This picture book features a variety of vrrroooming vehicles—cement mixers, garbage trucks, and bulldozers included—described with simple rhyming text. There's also *I Love Trains!* and *The Little Red Hen Makes a Pizza* (detailed in this chapter).

Chapter Two

I Went Walking
Written by Sue Williams, Illustrated by Julie Vivas
Harcourt, $7.00, 32 pages
First published in 1989
Ages 3–6

In this engaging rhythmic story that invites participation, Williams features a little boy who goes walking and meets a wide variety of creatures, creating a veritable animal parade. *Sali de Paseo* is the Spanish version. Follow this with *Let's Go Visiting*, also by Williams and Vivas.

If You Give a Mouse a Cookie
Written by Laura Joffe Numeroff, Illustrated by Felicia Bond
HarperCollins, $15.95, 32 pages
First published in 1985
Ages 3–6

Wisdom about generosity and greed moves beyond the standard "give him an inch and he'll take a mile" metaphor in this hilarious tale. After all, if you give a mouse a cookie, he'll ask for a glass of milk. And what comes next? A sequel, of course: The equally gluttonous *If You Give a Moose a Muffin*, followed by *If You Take a Mouse to the Movies*.

In the Night Kitchen
Written and Illustrated by Maurice Sendak
HarperTrophy, $6.95, 37 pages
First published in 1970
Ages 4–8

Sendak is a master of children's fantasy, writing enchanting text accompanied by intriguing, almost otherworldly, illustrations. In this **Caldecott Honor** recipient, we follow a young boy through a memorable dream sequence, as he helps three enormous bakers find milk for their cake. This is destined to become a favorite in your household. And no discussion of children's books would be complete without *Where the Wild Things Are* (in this chapter). *The Nutshell Library* is a charming collection of Sendak's stories.

Picture Books

Featured Author: Maurice Sendak

Hailing from Brooklyn, New York, Maurice Sendak was the child of Jewish immigrants from Poland. Suffering from frequent debilitating illness as a young boy, Sendak called upon the sustaining force of his own imagination and began to sow the seeds of his prolific career in children's book illustration. In fact, Sendak would lend his drawings to nearly fifty children's books by other authors before writing such unforgettable classics as **In the Night Kitchen** (see above), **Where the Wild Things Are** (in this chapter), **The Sign on Rosie's Door**, and **We Are All in the Dumps with Jack and Guy**. It's the inner life of a child that seems to compel Maurice Sendak, who believes that children devise fantasies in order "to combat an awful fact of childhood." Because, according to the acclaimed author, "it is through fantasy that children achieve catharsis."* Sendak has led his considerable talents to the stage and screen and continues to champion young dreamers like Max (from **Where the Wild Things Are**) and his mind-monsters, who represent the best of children's secret fantasy worlds.

*John Cech, "Maurice Sendak," Children's Books and Their Creators, Ed. Anita Silvey, Houghton Mifflin. 1995.

In the Small, Small Pond

Written and Illustrated by Denise Fleming
Owlet, $6.95, 32 pages
First published in 1993
Ages 3–7

A glorious follow-up to *In the Tall, Tall Grass*, Fleming invites readers to examine the seasonal changes that affect the animal and plant life of the pond. The collage illustrations, made from dyed paper pulp, are breathtaking, earning a **Caldecott Honor** for the author. Fleming's talent is in abundant evidence in *Barnyard Banter* and *Count!* (both detailed in this chapter) as well as in *Where Once There Was a World* (detailed in "Story Books").

Is Your Mama a Llama?

Written by Deborah Guarino, Illustrated by Steven Kellogg
Scholastic, $5.99, 32 pages
First published in 1989
Ages 3–6

Lloyd, a baby llama, asks the magical title question to a variety of adorable animal friends. The rhyming responses and Kellogg's expressive illustrations make this a worthwhile accompaniment to any discussion about different animals and their special mommies.

Chapter Two

Jake Baked the Cake
Written by Barbara Hennessy, Illustrated by Mary Morgan
Puffin, $5.99, 32 pages
First published in 1992
Ages 3–7

Everybody is getting ready for the wedding! "Sally Price buys the rice... Mr. Fine paints a sign" and Jake? Well, he's baking a cake that's worth its weight in gold. The fluid rhymes and illustrations have true old-fashioned charm. Also by Hennessy, *School Days*.

Jesse Bear, What Will You Wear?
Written by Nancy White Carlstrom, Illustrated by Bruce Degen
Aladdin, $5.99, 32 pages
First published in 1986
Ages 3–6

Preschoolers will certainly relate to the important decisions that Jesse Bear makes during the day, as well as the daily wonders he encounters. You can find more of this endearing character in *Better Not Get Wet, Jesse Bear*; *Happy Birthday, Jesse Bear*; *What a Scare, Jesse Bear*; *It's About Time, Jesse Bear and Other Rhymes*; and the newly published *Climb the Family Tree, Jesse Bear*.

The Jolly Postman
Written by Janet and Allan Ahlberg
Little Brown, $17.95, 29 pages
First published in 1986
Ages 3–7

You'll find a playful narrative in the form of a group of letters, which will be read and reread by your preschoolers. The novelty of examining these parcels won't soon be diminished, and your early-elementary–aged children will revisit this inventive picture book with nostalgic glee. Also by the Ahlbergs, *Each Peach, Pear, Plum* and *The Adventures of Bert* (both detailed in this chapter).

Kipper's A to Z: An Alphabet Adventure
Written and Illustrated by Mick Inkpen
Red Wagon Books, $16.95, 57 pages
First published in 2001
Ages 3–7

Chances are, your preschooler has become well acquainted with the cheerful British canine chap, Kipper. In this delightful volume, Kipper introduces the alphabet in fine fashion—both capital letters and lowercase—making it a perfect read-aloud book for preschoolers or read-alone book for early readers. Other Kipper tales include *Kipper Has a Party*; *Kipper's Book of Colors*; *Kipper's Book of Weather*; *Kipper's Rainy Day*; and *Kipper's Toy Box*, among others.

A Kitten Called Moonlight
Written and Illustrated by Martin Waddell
Candlewick, $15.99, 32 pages
First published in 2001
Ages 3–7

After Charlotte convinces her mother that she spotted a small creature scampering in the darkness, they set off to find it... an adorable white kitten that Charlotte names Moonlight. The story is told as a recollection, the young girl's favorite story; it's likely to become one of yours as well. Waddell is the author of the updated Little Bear stories—see *Can't You Sleep, Little Bear?* in this chapter, as well as *Mimi and the Dream House* and *Owl Babies*, among others.

A Kitten's Year
Written by Nancy Raines Day, Illustrated by Anne Mortimer
HarperTrophy, $5.95, unpaged
First published in 2000
Ages 3–8

They sure grow up fast... kittens, I mean. This sweet little picture book examines the first year of a cat's life with simple text and lifelike illustrations. If you're bringing a kitty home, bring this book as well. The author shows her versatility in *The Lion's Whiskers: An Ethiopian Folktale*.

Chapter Two

The Last Chocolate Cookie

Written by Jamie Rix, Illustrated by Arthur Robins
Candlewick, $4.99, 32 pages
First published in 1998
Ages 4–7

Maurice takes a lesson about sharing to heart... and to extremes. After he reaches for the last chocolate cookie, his mother reminds him that he must first offer it to everyone else. Maurice then puts the cookie in his pocket and offers it to just about everyone he meets, including an alien who would rather eat him! A hilarious mannerly twist that will have everyone in your household politely requesting seconds. More on manners? Try *The Berenstain Bears Forget Their Manners* by Stan and Jan Berenstain; *Manners* by Aliki; *Monster Manners* by Bethany Roberts; and *It's a Spoon, Not a Shovel* by Caralyn Buehner.

Parent/Child Review: The Last Chocolate Cookie

The Parent: Erika, Age 36, Attorney in Philadelphia, PA
The Kids: India, Age 4, Loves Bill Cosby
    Charles, Age 6, Future Pro–Basketball Player
India says: "It's not really nice when those people are selfish and take the last cookie or pretzel. That happens at school and people are mad. I like this book because it tells you not to be selfish 'cause it's nice to give cookies to people."
Charles says: "After we all read this book, now we talk about sharing a lot. I think the alien is funny. That's what you get if you do something bad... you have to go to outer space."
Erika says: "We did talk a lot about sharing after we read the book but I think the kids just thought it was cute and funny. Sharing is definitely an issue at home with these two... so, I guess we'll read this book again to make the point!"

Leo the Late Bloomer

Written by Robert Kraus, Illustrated by Jose Aruego
HarperTrophy, $6.95, 32 pages
First published in 1971
Ages 3–7

You'll love the energetic illustrations in this touching tale of a tiger cub whose abilities are a bit behind his buddies'. Leo's fellow late bloomers will be reassured by the end results. Catch up with Kraus' sequel, *Little Louie the Baby Bloomer*.

Picture Books

"Let's Get a Pup!" Said Kate

parent's
guide
choice award

Written and Illustrated by Bob Graham
Candlewick, $14.99, 32 pages
First published in 2001
Ages 3–8

Truly in tune with the rhythms of today's families, here is a story with characters that are realistic and modern. Young Kate convinces her parents that a dog would make the perfect addition to their family. After a visit to the local shelter, they spring a pup named Dave and return the next day to adopt an older dog named Rosie. Graham is an excellent recorder of contemporary detail, rendering Mom with a tattoo and Dad with two earrings. Also look for *Benny: An Adventure Story*; *Max*; and *Queenie, One of the Family*.

Listen to the City

Written and Illustrated by Rachel Isadora
Putnam, $15.99, 32 pages
First published in 2000
Ages 3–7

With her jaunty Pop Art inspired illustrations, this is a joyful study in sound. The toots and clomps and clinks of urban life are given center stage, enlivening the sensory stimulation of the big city. Isadora is also the author of *Ben's Trumpet* (in "Story Books") and *ABC Pop!*

The Little Engine That Could

Written by Wally Piper, Illustrated by George and Doris Hauman
Platt & Munk, $7.99, 40 pages
First published in 1930
Ages 4–8

"I think I can, I think I can" is the enduring message of this classic. Often cited by motivational speakers and self-help gurus, this book holds the same sweet appeal to children as it did when it was first published: the engaging story of a little train that is determined to bring toys to the children on the other side of the mountain. This title is available in several different editions including a board book.

Chapter Two

The Little House
Written and Illustrated by Virginia Lee Burton
Houghton Mifflin, $5.95, 40 pages
First published in 1942
Ages 3–7

A venerated favorite and **Caldecott Medal** winner, this is a story with an old-fashioned sentimentality that continues to appeal to children and adults. A little house on a hill sees big changes as a city sprouts up around it, until it is finally returned to country serenity. Also by Burton, see *Mike Mulligan and His Steam Shovel* (detailed in this chapter) as well as *Maybelle, the Cable Car*.

The Little Island
Written by Golden MacDonald, Illustrated by Leonard Weisgard
Yearling, $6.99, 56 pages
First published in 1946
Ages 4–8

A little island witnesses changes as the seasons pass. It also sees many visitors, from the birds and sea life that live nearby to a wayward kitten that somehow finds its way to the island. Children will be lulled by the gentle verse and surprise ending in this **Caldecott Medal** winner that was actually written by Margaret Wise Brown, using a pseudonym.

The Little Mouse, the Red Ripe Strawberry, and the Big Hungry Bear
Written by Don and Audrey Wood, Illustrated by Don Wood
Child's Play, $6.99, unpaged
First published in 1990
Ages 2–5

Its amusing narrative style immediately captures the attention of readers as an unseen interviewer asks pointed questions about the succulent strawberries that our little mouse is preparing to savor. Could the questioner have less than innocent intentions toward those strawberries? Also available in Spanish.

Picture Books

The Little Red Hen Makes a Pizza
Written by Philemon Sturges, Illustrated by Amy Walrod
Dutton, $15.99, 32 pages
First published in 1999
Ages 4–8

Sturges cooks up an uproarious retelling of the classic tale. This time our heroine develops a sudden, irresistible craving for homemade pizza. First she must run some preparatory errands but can't seem to find anyone willing to help... until it's time to eat. Also by Sturges, *I Love Trucks* (detailed in this chapter).

Look-Alikes
Written by Joan Steiner, Photography by Thomas Lindley
Little Brown, $13.95, 32 pages
First published in 1998
Ages 3–8

Steiner creates a world built of easily recognizable household objects in this amazing visual treat. Children who enjoy the popular *I Spy* series will adore the amazing collage construction of this artful enterprise, as well as its sequel *Look-Alikes Jr.*

Lunch Bunnies
Written and Illustrated by Kathryn Lasky
Little Brown, $5.95, 32 pages
First published in 1996
Ages 3–6

Will Clyde's fears about lunchtime at school be realized? After his brother, Jefferson, scares him with stories about nasty lunch ladies and belligerent bullies, Clyde survives his first day in the lunchroom and makes a new friend in the process. Rabbits abound in *Science Fair Bunnies* and *Show and Tell Bunnies*. Lasky's other picture books include *Starring Lucille* and *Sophie and Rose*. She has also penned an array of dynamic nonfiction for older readers including *The Most Beautiful Roof in the World: Exploring the Rainforest Canopy* (see Nonfiction, Ecology).

Chapter Two

Madeline
Written and Illustrated by Ludwig Bemelmans
Puffin, $6.99, 56 pages
First published in 1939
Ages 3–8

"In an old house in Paris that was covered with vines...." Chances are you're able to complete the verse, as Madeline has captured the hearts of millions of readers since her birth more than 60 years ago. A **Caldecott Honor** recipient, Bemelman's wit and wisdom, instantly recognizable black on yellow illustrations, and obvious affection for his clever characters have made Madeline a cottage industry... a French cottage, that is. Look for *Madeline and the Bad Hat*; *Madeline and the Gypsies*; *Madeline in London*; and *Madeline's Rescue*.

Featured Author: Ludwig Bemelmans
A difficult childhood in Austria and a rather unsuccessful school career led Ludwig Bemelmans to immigrate to America in 1914. After toiling in the restaurant business for many years, Bemelmans tried his hand at writing for children, resulting in his first book, entitled **Hansi**. Of course, it's his mischievous and loveable literary offspring **Madeline** that garnered the most attention after her publication in 1938. A sequel, **Madeline's Rescue**, earned a Caldecott Medal and Ludwig Bemelmans' influence on 20th century children's literature was set in stone. Becoming a dapper man about town, Bemelmans also gained a reputation as a talented painter. He lived in New York until his death in 1962.

Make Way for Ducklings
Written and Illustrated by Robert McCloskey
Puffin, $5.99, 70 pages
First published in 1941
Ages 3–7

A very genteel Boston is the setting for this **Caldecott Medal** winning story of a mother duck's attempt to find a home for her family. You'll recognize the famous swan boat of the Boston Common and be touched by the gentle illustrations and perfect pace of this timeless tale. See Robert McCloskey, Featured Author in this chapter under the darling *Blueberries for Sal*.

May I Bring a Friend?

Written by Beatrice Schenk de Regniers, Illustrated by Beni Montresor
Aladdin, $5.99, 48 pages
First published in 1964
Ages 3–8

A **Caldecott Medal** winner, this is a tale of generosity and manners as a young boy is granted permission to visit the king and queen with his animal friends in tow. The rhyming text puts this title amongst the high royalty of children's literature.

Mike Mulligan and His Steam Shovel

Written and Illustrated by Virginia Lee Burton
Houghton Mifflin..
First published in 1939
Ages 3–8

Burton once again demonstrates a fond nostalgia (see *The Little House* in this chapter) in this story of a steam shovel that seems outdated compared to the newer, faster, and stronger models. It's the good folks of Popperville who help Mike keep his beloved machine running like a dream. Also look for *Maybelle the Cable Car*.

Millions of Cats

Written and Illustrated by Wanda Gag
Penguin Putnam, $5.99, 30 pages
First published in 1928
Ages 3–7

When the little old man sets out to find a cat for his wife, he returns with... well... lots of cats and just as many surprises. A standout in children's literature, this story earned a **Newbery Honor**, an acclamation typically reserved for chapter books.

Chapter Two

Mooses Come Walking
Written by Arlo Guthrie, Illustrated by Alice M. Brock
Chronicle, $11.95, 26 pages
First published in 1995
Ages 3–7

The meandering moose in question are gentle, friendly, and curious. They'll walk right up to your window! Comical, contagious nonsense verse is the appeal of this short tale from an illustrious member of the famous folk-singing family.

Mouse Paint
Written and Illustrated by Ellen Stoll Walsh
Harcourt Brace, $5.00, 32 pages
First published in 1989
Ages 2–6

Red! Yellow! Blue! As three squeaky clean white mice jump gleefully into pots of brightly colored paint, toddlers and preschoolers learn about mixing colors. The mousecapades continue with *Mouse Count* and *Mouse Magic*.

My Car
Written and Illustrated by Byron Barton
Greenwillow, $14.95, 35 pages
First published in 2001
Ages 2–5

"I love my car. I keep it clean." And your children will love Byron Barton's use of simple illustrations and text. Young car connoisseurs will be especially intrigued by the explanations of how a car works, from engine to windshield wipers. Look for other books by Barton including *I Want to Be an Astronaut*; *Airplanes*; and *Machines at Work*; as well as the fantastic *Dinosaurs, Dinosaurs* (detailed in this chapter).

Picture Books

My Daddy
Written and Illustrated by Susan Paradis
Front Street, $15.95, 32 pages
First Published in 1998
Ages 3–6

A terrific depiction of a child's enchantment with his father. The beautiful, bordered illustrations portray the love, trust, and enchantment in this relationship, culminating in a heartwarming hug. Daddies and their children will love reading this book together. A board book edition is also available.

My Very First Mother Goose
Written by Iona Opie, Illustrated by Rosemary Wells
Candlewick, $21.99, 107 pages
First published in 1996
Ages 2–8

An essential introduction to the enduring legacy of Mother Goose, this substantial collection will provide many happy lap readings. Small children will delight to the tune of "Star Light, Star Bright" and "Hey Diddle Diddle" and their hilarious watercolor interpretations. Opie and Wells' obvious affinity for storytelling will capture the attention and imagination of toddlers and preschoolers. Nursery rhymes also abound in *Here Comes Mother Goose* (detailed in this chapter).

My Visit to the Aquarium
Written and Illustrated by Aliki
HarperCollins, $6.95, 30 pages
First published in 1993
Ages 3–7

Aliki e-fish-ently captures the sights and sounds of a modern aquarium in this readable field trip. There are sharks, coral reefs, and a tide pool where children can gently touch the fish. All of these watery wonders are depicted in marvelously refreshing aqua tones. For more fun sightseeing, look for Aliki's *My Visit to the Dinosaurs* and *My Visit to the Zoo*.

Chapter Two

Nutshell Library

Written and Illustrated by Maurice Sendak
HarperCollins, $15.95, 4 Volumes
First published in 1962
Ages 4–7

Available as a set of four books, Sendak's wonderful wit is omnipresent. Included are *Alligators All Around: An Alphabet*; *Chicken Soup with Rice*; *One Was Johnny*; and *Pierre*. Other wise tales by Sendak include *Where the Wild Things Are* and *In the Night Kitchen* (both detailed in this chapter).

Officer Buckle and Gloria

Written and Illustrated by Peggy Rathmann
Putnam, $16.99, 34 pages
First published in 1995
Ages 4–8

Officer Buckle loves to teach children about safety. If only the children would pay attention! When police dog, Gloria, joins him on stage, performing an amusing mime of the ardent officer's lessons, the kids perk up. But is Officer Buckle being upstaged? This **Caldecott Medal** winner is a safe bet for giggles and guffaws, as well as some safety lessons. Also look for Rathmann's *10 Minutes Till Bedtime* (detailed in this chapter) and *Good Night, Gorilla*.

Olivia

Written and Illustrated by Ian Falconer
Atheneum, $16.00, 36 pages
First published in 2000
Ages 3–6

parent's
guide
choice award

Rarely has a new character in children's literature sparked so much excitement. It's no wonder, too, because Olivia knows how to make an entrance! A pig with a penchant for performance... and perfectionism, we first meet Olivia as she tries to find just the right thing to wear. Will Olivia become a big star? If the thousands of preschoolers who have already made her acquaintance have anything to say about it, the answer is a resounding "yes!" Also available in Spanish. You'll want to look for the high flying adventure of *Olivia Saves the Circus*.

Picture Books

On Market Street

Written by Arnold Lobel, Illustrated by Anita Lobel
Mulberry, $6.95, 40 pages
First published in 1981
Ages 4–8

Arnold Lobel, creator of the famous *Frog and Toad* series (in Easy Readers), makes the alphabet come alive in this dear **Caldecott Honor** story of a young boy who sets out to buy presents for his friend, selecting an item for each letter. Also by Arnold Lobel, *Ming Lo Moves the Mountain* (detailed in "Story Books").

On the Day You Were Born

Written and Illustrated by Debra Frasier
Harcourt, $16.00, 32 pages
First published in 1991
Ages 3–8

If you're searching for the perfect gift for new parents, look no further. This is a truly special book, written as a poetic tribute to the world—moon, sun, oceans, animals, people—and a new baby's place in it. Its eloquent intelligence has earned a loyal following for Frasier. Also look for *Miss Alaineus: A Vocabulary Disaster* and *Out of the Ocean*.

Once a Mouse: A Fable Cut in Wood

Written and Illustrated by Marcia Brown
Macmillan, $6.99, 32 pages
First published in 1961
Ages 3–7

This **Caldecott Medal** winner is based on an ancient Indian folktale and features elaborate woodcut illustrations. Other stories by Marcia Brown include *Stone Soup: An Old Tale*.

Chapter Two

One Fish Two Fish Red Fish Blue Fish
Written and Illustrated by Dr. Seuss
Random House, $7.99. 62 pages
First published in 1960
Ages 3–7

The sensational Dr. Seuss created a whimsical world of multi-hued fish, pets called Zeds, and a one-humped Wump, ready to be counted. For millions of preschoolers, this book represents their first attempt at reading independently, as the contagious verse naturally lends itself to repeated perusal. The equally reader-friendly *The Cat in the Hat* and *Green Eggs and Ham* are both detailed in this chapter. Also see *The Lorax* and *Oh, the Places You'll Go* in "Story Books" as well as additional titles in Easy Readers.

One Gorilla: A Counting Book
Written and Illustrated by Atsuko Morozumi
Farrar, Straus & Giroux, $4.95, 28 pages
First published in 1990
Ages 3–7

The gorgeous illustrations and playful animal personalities make this story a winner, as a gentle gorilla counts his way through fields, forests, and the sea. Another fun story that incorporates counting is *Splash!* by Ann Jonas.

Our Granny
Written by Margaret Wild, Illustrated by Julie Vivas
Sandpiper, $5.95, 32 pages
First published in 1998
Ages 3–8

A loving tribute to modern grandmas everywhere—from those who wear "baggy underwear" to the grannies that "march in demonstrations." This affectionate book encourages discussion about diverse families and personalities. You'll also enjoy Margaret Wild's antic bedtime story, *Nighty Night!* featuring illustrations by Kerry Argent.

Picture Books

Over in the Meadow
Written by John Langstaff, Illustrated by Feodor Rojankovsky
Voyager, $7.00, 32 pages
First published in 1957
Ages 3–7

There are colorful and countable objects set to a familiar tune in this long-standing favorite, featuring lovely folk-art illustrations.

Owly
Written by Mike Thaler, Illustrated by David Wiesner
Walker, $5.95, 32 pages
First published in 1982
Ages 3–7

Owly is curious about the ways of the world, posing endless questions to his mother. She encourages him to seek answers on his own, while offering patient support. Aside from being a wonderful story, there is gentle wisdom about setting off on one's own to make sense of the wide world and its mysteries.

Pete's a Pizza
Written and Illustrated by William Steig
HarperCollins, $15.95, 32 pages
First published in 1998
Ages 3–8

William Steig knows how to have a good time. This author of many family favorites (see Featured Author, William Steig, page TK) has written a story designed to cheer-up the crankiest of characters. Dad tries to help Pete out of a funk by turning him into a delicious pretend pizza, complete with red checker tomatoes and paper scrap cheese. After baking on the sofa, Pete finds that his bad mood has melted away. Steig is the author of *The Amazing Bone*; *Brave Irene*; *Doctor DeSoto*; *Sylvester and the Magic Pebble* (all in "Story Books"), and other tremendous tales including *Abel's Island*; *Amos and Boris*; and *Dominic*.

Chapter Two

Peter Spier's Circus
Written and Illustrated by Peter Spier
Bantam, Doubleday, Dell, $7.50, 48 pages
First published in 1992
Ages 3–7

The high-flying wonders of the circus are beautifully presented in this visual extravaganza. Spier won the **Caldecott Medal** for his astounding illustrations in *Noah's Ark* (detailed in "Story Books"). Other titles include *People* (also in "Story Books") and *Peter Spier's Rain*.

Peter's Chair
Written and Illustrated by Ezra Jack Keats
Puffin, $6.99, 33 pages
First published in 1967
Ages 4–8

Peter's comfortable and familiar blue furniture is being painted pink for his baby sister. After he tries to keep a chair for his very own, he realizes that he has grown too big to sit comfortably in it, and decides to pass it along to his new sister. Once again, Keats' glorious illustrations provide the perfect accompaniment to this sensitive, child-centered story about confronting change in one's own special way. You won't want to miss Keats' *The Snowy Day* (detailed in this chapter) as well as *Apt. 3*; *Goggles!*; *Kitten for a Day*; *A Letter to Amy*; *Over in the Meadow*; and *Whistle for Willie*.

A Porcupine Named Fluffy
Written by Helen Lester, Illustrated by Lynn Munsinger
Houghton Mifflin, $6.95, 32 pages
First published in 1986
Ages 3–7

Fluffy isn't very happy with his name. After all, it's a rather unusual title for a porcupine. After he meets a rhinoceros named Hippo, the two become gleefully inseparable playmates, discovering the truth behind the age-old question, "What's in a name?" Lester keeps us cheering with *Hooway for Wodney Wat* (detailed in this chapter); *Listen, Buddy*; and *Me First*.

Picture Books

Rachel Fister's Blister

Written by Amy MacDonald, Illustrated by Marjorie Priceman
Houghton Mifflin, $5.95, 32 pages
First published in 1990
Ages 3–8

The experts are summoned to attend to Rachel's terrible ailment—a small blister on her little toe. After the doctor, pastor, rabbi, and vicar are consulted, it is Queen Alice who delivers the delightful diagnosis and cure. Of course, it's a kiss from Rachel's mom that provides the happy healing. The manic illustrations and contagious rhymes make this is a terrific read-aloud book.

Rain Song

Written by Lezlie Evans, Illustrated by Cynthia Jabar
Houghton Mifflin, $5.95, 32 pages
First published in 1995
Ages 3–6

A celebration of wet weather in jubilant rhymed verse marks this wonderful debut from Evans. Two little girls make the most of a rainy day, splashing in puddles, watching the raindrops, and listening to distant thunder. Preschoolers will be choreographing their own rain dances in anticipation for another opportunity to read this book. Also by the clever Evans, *Can You Count Ten Toes? Count to 10 in 10 Different Languages* (detailed in this chapter), and for more of the wet stuff, look for *Snow Dance*.

Rainbow Fish

Written and Illustrated by Marcus Pfister
North–South, $8.95, 28 pages
First published in 1992
Ages 3–7

This book quickly became a publishing phenomenon after its release in 1992. Now available in multiple editions and languages, this charming story teaches about generosity as a small fish decides to give away his beautiful scales. There is a message about the meaning of friendship, but young *Fish* fans seem primarily captivated by the shiny, iridescent scales and luminous illustrations. Sequels include *Rainbow Fish and the Big Blue Whale*; *Rainbow Fish and the Sea Monster's Cave*; and *Rainbow Fish to the Rescue!*

Chapter Two

The Red Balloon
Written and Illustrated by Albert Lamorisse
Delacorte, $12.95, 48 pages
First published in 1956
Ages 3–8

Photographs from the beloved film perfectly capture the wonder of a young boy as he is followed through the streets of Paris by a large red balloon that seems to have a mind of its own. Classic and understated, the minimal text allows for imaginative interpretation.

The Relatives Came
Written by Cynthia Rylant, Illustrated by Stephen Gammell
Aladdin, $6.99, 32 pages
First published in 1985
Ages 4–8

This gleeful celebration of family gatherings earned a **Caldecott Honor** citation. Rylant masterfully captures the sense of a fond childhood memory in the making. An excellent audio version, complete with spirited musical accompaniment, is available from Live Oak Media. Older readers will enjoy Cynthia Rylant's chapter book series, *Henry and Mudge* (detailed in the Easy Readers chapter).

Richard Scarry's What Do People Do All Day?
Written and Illustrated by Richard Scarry
Random House, $14.00, 95 pages
First published in 1968
Ages 3–6

Scarry's trademark "busy" illustrations provide hours of fascination for preschoolers. Here, the resident animals of Busytown are hard at work, showing the different jobs that compose a community, from policemen and firemen to doctors and nurses. You'll also want to keep an eye out for other Scarry favorites such as *Richard Scarry's Best Word Book Ever*; *Richard Scarry's Best Picture Dictionary Ever*; and *Mr. Frumble's ABC*.

Picture Books

Rosie's Walk

Written and Illustrated by Pat Hutchins
Aladdin, $5.99, unpaged
First published in 1971
Ages 4–7

Rosie is a hen who enjoys taking leisurely walks around the barnyard. She's blissfully unaware that a fox is pursuing her and unwittingly foils his gluttonous intentions. Make room in your household for *The Doorbell Rang* and *Don't Forget the Bacon* (both detailed in this chapter) also by Hutchins.

Rotten Ralph

Written by Jack Gantos, Illustrated by Nicole Rubel
Houghton Mifflin, $6.95, 46 pages
First published in 1980
Ages 4–8

Ralph is pretty darn rotten and that's what makes him so entertaining. This is the first in a series of Ralph's ruckuses. Other titles include *Back to School for Rotten Ralph*; *Happy Birthday Rotten Ralph*; and *Not So Rotten Ralph*. Children in the early elementary grades will also love Gantos' *Joey Pigza Swallowed the Key* (detailed in "Story Books").

Chapter Two

The Runaway Bunny
Written by Margaret Wise Brown, Illustrated by Clement Hurd
HarperCollins, $5.95, 38 pages
First published in 1970
Ages 2–6

Another perennial favorite from the much-loved author of *Goodnight Moon*. A little bunny tries to escape his mother's watchful eye, but she's always one step ahead of him. A perfect springtime treasure. Other wise tales by Brown include *The Big Red Barn* and *The Little Fur Family*. See Featured Author, Margaret Wise Brown, page TK.

Sheep in a Jeep
Written by Nancy Shaw, Illustrated by Margot Apple
Houghton Mifflin, $4.95, 32 pages
First published in 1986
Ages 3–6

"Beep! Beep! Sheep in a jeep on a hill that's steep" is but a sample of the rhyming verse that will cause contagious giggles amongst your preschool-aged children. Still feeling sheepish? Ewe will also adore *Sheep on a Ship*; *Sheep in a Shop*; *Sheep Out to Eat*; *Sheep Take a Hike*; and *Sheep Trick or Treat*.

Snow
Written and Illustrated by Uri Shulevitz
Farrar Straus Giroux, $16.00, 32 pages
First published in 1998
Ages 3–7

The enchantment of a snowy day is wonderfully depicted in this luminously illustrated story that earned a **Caldecott Honor**. While parents and weather forecasters are skeptical, a young boy celebrates as the snow begins to fall. More frosty fun can be found in Barbara Joosse's *Snow Day!* and *White Snow, Bright Snow* by Alvin Tresselt. Other titles by Shulevitz include *Dawn* and *Rain Rain Rivers*.

Picture Books

The Snowman
Written and Illustrated by Raymond Briggs
Random House, $7.99, 32 pages
First published in 1978
Ages 3–7

What happens when a snowman comes to life? Briggs' deftly expressive images make this charming story a favorite for all seasons. Briggs followed up this wordless winter tale with *Walking On Air*. Fans of Raymond Briggs will also want to look for *The Bear*.

The Snowy Day
Written and Illustrated by Ezra Jack Keats
Puffin, $5.99, 32 pages
First published in 1962
Ages 3–7

It's hard to imagine more beautiful illustrations, and Keats' famous collage style has inspired a great deal of literary art since this wonderful story was published 40 years ago. A **Caldecott Medal** winner, the crisp colors perfectly match the urban tone of the poetic text as Peter makes his way through the snow-covered city streets. Truly a masterpiece of children's literature. Also by Keats, *Peter's Chair* (detailed in this chapter); *Over in the Meadow*; and *Whistle for Willie*.

Featured Author: Ezra Jack Keats

Growing up in Brooklyn in the 1920s and '30s, Ezra Jack Keats dreamed of becoming an artist. Though he never attended art school, his natural talents were apparent from a young age. After spending many years honing his craft through public mural projects, Keats wrote **The Snowy Day**, which won the Caldecott Medal and was universally praised. Drawing inspiration from the inner-city life of African–American children, Keats used his stunning collage technique to great effect and continued to examine the lives of minority children in subsequent works. **Peter's Chair** and **A Whistle For Willie** also received great acclaim, as Keats' reputation as a remarkable artist and storyteller was cemented. More stories followed including **Hi Cat!**; **Apt. 3**; and **Regards to the Man in the Moon**, with Keats turning to painted illustration, until his death in 1983.

Chapter Two

Stellaluna
Written and Illustrated by Janell Cannon
Harcourt, $16.00, 48 pages
First published in 1993
Ages 3–7

Sweet baby bat, Stellaluna, becomes separated from her mother and is adopted by a family of birds. She tries to fit in with her new family, sleeping at night and eating insects, but is relieved upon being reunited with her mother. This wonderful debut from Janell Cannon is an affectionate and funny story that sheds light on bat behavior. Also look for *Verdi* and *Crickwing* for more amusing and demystifying animal stories.

The Story about Ping
Written by Marjorie Flack, Illustrated by Kurt Wiese
Puffin, $5.99, 32 pages
First published in 1933
Ages 3–7

A young duck loses his way on the Yangtze River and can't find his way back to his home on the beautiful houseboat. Kurt Wiese's lithographs are a radiant counterpart to this special story. Interestingly, it was Flack's research of Peking ducks during the writing of her popular book *Angus and the Ducks* (and its sequels) that led to Ping's creation.

The Story of Ferdinand
Written by Munro Leaf, Illustrated by Robert Lawson
Puffin, $6.99, 72 pages
First published in 1936
Ages 3–7

It's likely you've met someone who cites this beautiful story as one of their childhood favorites. Children feel immediate sympathy for the gentle bull who is content to sit under his favorite tree and smell the flowers. When Ferdinand leaps impressively into the air after sitting on a bee, a group of toreadors decide he has bullfighting potential. Available in hardcover and as an audio adaptation from Live Oak Media. This book is also available, most appropriately, in Spanish as *El Cuento de Ferdinando*.

Picture Books

The Stray Dog

Written and Illustrated by Marc Simont
HarperCollins, $15.95, 32 pages
First published in 2001
Ages 3–8

Simont's story crafting is in top form in this waggish tale that's bound to become a sentimental favorite. A family spends a fine afternoon picnicking in the park when they become acquainted with a delightful pup that they name Willy. Certain that the dog is missed by his owners, the family leaves him in the park, but thinks of him constantly in the days that follow. A joyful reunion the following weekend allows Willy to become an official member of the fine family.

Parent/Child Review: The Stray Dog

The Parent: Margie, Age 40, Musician
The Child: Simon, Age 5, Dog Lover
Simon says: "This is my favorite book and I love dogs. We used to have a dog named Puck but he died. Now we just got a puppy named Lucy. In the book, Willy reminds me of peanut butter."
Margie says: "Okay, to clarify, Peanut Butter was the name of our neighbor's dog who was a stray and who ran away a bunch of times. But Simon really loves this book. We went a couple of weeks before we could get him to read anything else."

The Sun Is My Favorite Star

Written and Illustrated by Frank Asch
Gulliver, $15.00, 32 pages
First published in 2000
Ages 3–7

The author of the warm and wonderful *Moonbear* books, Asch uses simple language and powerfully vivid illustrations to depict a young child's fascination with the sun and the feeling of safety and security he derives from its presence... even at night when the sun hides and the moon "sends some light to keep me company." Other books by Frank Asch include *Happy Birthday, Moon*; *Bear Shadow*; and *The Earth and I*.

Chapter Two

Swimmy
Written and Illustrated by Leo Lionni
Knopf, $5.99, 29 pages
First published in 1963
Ages 3–6

Swimmy, an adorable little fish, demonstrates his ingenuity and selfless-ness by dreaming up a way to protect his friends from the hungry big fish in the sea. Lioni earned a **Caldecott Honor** for his graceful watercolor col-lages. Also available in Spanish. Other titles by Leo Lionni include *A Color of His Own*; *An Extraordinary Egg*; *Frederick*; *Inch by Inch*; *It's Mine*; and *On My Beach There Are Many Pebbles*.

The Tale of Peter Rabbit
Written and Illustrated by Beatrix Potter
Frederick Warne, $6.99
First published in 1902
Ages 3–7

Potter's legacy has been preserved in the publisher's lovely reproductions of her original series. The lure of goodies in Mr. MacGregor's garden is a big temptation for Peter Rabbit, even after his mother strictly forbids him to visit. There are dozens of editions and slick packages available, but these small versions are reminiscent of the beloved editions you read as a child. Following Peter are *The Tale of Benjamin Bunny*; *The Tale of Tom Kitten*; *The Tale of Jemima Puddle-Duck*; *The Tale of Mrs. Tiggy-Winkle*; *The Tale of Pigling Bland*; *The Tale of the Flopsy Bunnies*; and *The Tale of Squirrel Nutkin*. Frederick Warne has also published *The Complete Tales of Beatrix Potter*. If this delightful foray into Potter's work creates a spark of interest about her life, you may also enjoy *Beatrix Potter* by Alexandria Wallner, an easy-to-read biography of the famed author.

Picture Books

A Teeny Tiny Baby

Written and Illustrated by Amy Schwartz
Orchard, $6.95, unpaged
First published in 1994
Ages 2–6

There are few things that fascinate a preschooler more than stories of her babyhood, and this baby bonanza is a laugh riot. The babbling narrator gives readers an insider's view of the wonderful world of infancy, including the fun of being tickled, fed, held, and the joys of having one's diaper frequently changed. The expressions of baby's rapt yet exhausted parents bring this story very close to home for many moms and dads who'll want to turn to their preschoolers and exclaim, "You've come a long way, baby!" Also by the savvy Schwartz, *Annabelle Swift, Kindergartner* (detailed in "Story Books"); *How to Catch an Elephant*; and *Old MacDonald*.

Parent/Child Review: A Teeny Tiny Baby

The Parent: Marc, Age 51, Accountant
The Kid: Madison, Age 5, Aspiring artist

Madison says: "Well, we tried to read this to our baby but she's too little, I think. She cries a lot 'cause of the noise from the workers in our kitchen. It's noisy. I'm five and I don't sleep in the same room as Lola but I help change her diaper. I like babies and I think the lady who wrote this book here must have a baby."

Marc says: "All true. This book came along at just the right time, since Madison is newly a big sister. I think it makes her feel important and helps her understand that babies cry a lot and she did, too. Maybe once we finish fixing the kitchen, the crying will subside."

Tell Me a Story, Mama

Written by Angela Johnson, Illustrated by David Soman
Orchard, $6.95, 32 pages
First published in 1989
Ages 3–6

Children find comfort in the re-telling of familiar family stories. It is but one of the ways they begin to make sense of the special place in the world into which they fit. This darling story takes the form of a cozy bedtime conversation between a mother and young daughter. It might just encourage a new tradition of family storytelling in your home. Other family favorites by Angela Johnson: *Julius, One of Three; The Wedding*; and *Down the Winding Road*, a beautiful story of young boy's feelings about visiting his aging grandparents.

Chapter Two

Tell Me Again about the Night I Was Born
Written by Jamie Lee Curtis, Illustrated by Laura Cornell
HarperTrophy, $5.95, 36 pages
First published in 1996
Ages 3–8

Don't be skeptical about actress Jamie Lee Curtis's ability to write an engaging story for children. This is a wonderfully told tale of an adopted child's curiosity about her arrival into the world. All children love to hear stories about their birth, and Curtis adeptly addresses the questions that children commonly ask about adoption, while focusing on the affection of a close-knit family. The illustrations are funny and fantastic. Also by Curtis, *When I Was Little: A Four Year-Old's Memoir of Her Youth;* and *Today I Feel Silly and Other Moods That Make My Day.* Other picture or story books that address adoption include *Did My First Mother Love Me? A Story for an Adopted Child* by Kathryn Ann Miller; *Over the Moon: An Adoption Tale* by Karen Katz; and *How I Was Adopted: Samantha's Story* by Joanna Cole.

Telling Time: How to Tell Time on Digital and Analog Clocks
Written by Jules Older, Illustrated by Megan Halsey
Charlesbridge, $6.95, 32 pages
First published in 2000
Ages 4–8

While time telling is likely to be introduced in kindergarten and reinforced in the early elementary grades, this visually intriguing book will be enjoyed by preschoolers as well. It begins with a lighthearted discussion about different classifications of time—seconds to hours, days to centuries—before moving onto reading digital and, ultimately, good old-fashioned analog clocks.

There Was an Old Lady Who Swallowed a Fly
Written and Illustrated by Simms Taback
Viking, $15.99, 32 pages
First published in 1997
Ages 3–8

The refrains of this familiar and delightfully gruesome song are irresistible to children. Here, the punchy illustrations feature a die-cut hole in the old lady's belly, making for easier viewing of the creatures that find themselves fatefully swallowed. There's a lot of cleverly inserted visual detail to amuse older children. This glorious gluttony earned a **Caldecott Honor** for Taback who is also the author of *Joseph Had a Little Overcoat* (detailed in Story Books).

Picture Books

A Tree Is Nice

Written by Janice May Udry, Illustrated by Marc Simont
Harper & Row, $6.95, 32 pages
First published in 1956
Ages 4–8

This **Caldecott Medal** winner pays an eloquent tribute to trees, illustrating their significant qualities and the simple pleasures they provide. Published nearly 50 years ago, this lovely picture book remains a timelessly effective way to impart the importance of respecting and protecting nature's treasures.

The Very Hungry Caterpillar

Written and illustrated by Eric Carle
Philomel, $19.99, 26 pages
First published in 1969
Ages 2–5

This is a wonderful book in many ways. It is first and foremost the story of a little caterpillar who nibbles on various fruits while eating through the book's pages. The story also incorporates basic number learning and days of the week. While board books and smaller paperback editions are available, this larger hardcover is best suited to the finger poking that is naturally elicited by the holes in each page. Carle's trademark technique of layering colored tissue paper also creates stunning effects in *The Very Busy Spider*; *The Grouchy Ladybug*; *Today Is Monday*; *Pancakes, Pancakes*; and *The Very Quiet Cricket*. Also see *Draw Me a Star* and *Papa, Please Get the Moon for Me* in this chapter.

Featured Author: Eric Carle

It's clear that Eric Carle loves animals and knows a lot about children. He spent much of his childhood in Germany but longed to return to America. Upon doing so, he was approached by writer Bill Martin who wanted Carle to illustrate **Brown Bear, Brown Bear, What Do You See?** (in this chapter). Their agreement about color, scope and creating illustrations that intrinsically appeal to children set Carle on a path toward stardom. He proceeded to create the much-adored classic **The Very Hungry Caterpillar** (see above), followed by a string of equally loveable stories. His talent with tissue paper collage not only sets him apart from the crowd, but has also greatly influenced an entire generation of illustrators. He continues to craft exceptional children's literature from his home in Massachusetts.

Chapter Two

The Wheels on the Bus

Written and Illustrated by Paul O. Zelinsky
Dutton Books, $17.99, 14 pages
First published in 1990
Ages 3–6

The popular tune is given ingenious treatment in this lift-the-flap book. The sturdy and artful construction of the book itself is a marvel, and you'll be singing along to the familiar refrain—one more time! Also by Zelinsky, *Rapunzel* (in "Story Books") and *Rumpelstiltskin*.

When Sophie Gets Angry, Really, Really Angry

Written and Illustrated by Molly Bang
Blue Sky Press, $15.95, 36 pages
First published in 1999
Ages 3–7

Molly Bang masterfully conveys a child's frustration at having to share a favorite toy. Sophie roars, runs, and cries until she is comforted by the "wide world." This is an exploration of emotions that rings true. Bang is a two-time **Caldecott Honor** recipient for *The Grey Lady and the Strawberry Snatcher* (detailed in this chapter) and *Ten, Nine, Eight*. But if it's more foot-stomping exasperation you're looking for, try *Angry Arthur* by Hiawyn Oram and *The Chocolate-Covered Cookie Tantrum* by Deborah Blumenthal.

Where the Wild Things Are

Written and Illustrated by Maurice Sendak
HarperTrophy, $7.95, 40 pages
First published in 1963
Ages 4–8

There's no doubt that this **Caldecott Medal** winner will become a prized favorite amongst your preschoolers. There's an enduring allure to Max, who after behaving like a "wild thing" is sent to his room. Of course, his parents couldn't have imagined the world that would be created in Max's mind as he dreams of a strange land where real wild things reside. Sendak is the immensely popular author of *In the Night Kitchen*; *The Nutshell Library* (both detailed in this chapter); and *Outside Over There*.

Picture Books

Where's Spot?
Written and Illustrated by Eric Hill
Puffin, $6.99, 22 pages
First published in 1980
Ages 2–5

Somewhere along the way, *Spot* set the standard for minimalist yet highly effective picture book illustration. This particular episode in the life of the curious yellow pup features lift-the-flap construction, and children will delight in uncovering his hiding place. There's also *Goodnight Spot*; *Spot Bakes a Cake*; *Spot Counts from 1 to 10*; *Spot Goes to School*; *Spot Goes to the Circus*; *Spot Goes to the Farm*; and *Spot Looks at Opposites*, among a couple of dozen others by Hill.

Will's Mammoth
Written by Rafe Martin, Illustrated by Stephen Gammell
PaperStar, $5.95, 32 pages
First published in 1989
Ages 3–7

"Will loved mammoths," begins this joyous celebration of one boy's imagination. When Will's parents tell him that mammoths don't exist, he finds a woolly world in his own backyard. Martin's cultural explorations include *The Rough-Face Girl* and *The Shark God*.

William's Doll
Written by Charlotte Zolotow, Illustrated by William Pene du Bois
HarperTrophy, $5.95, 32 pages
First published in 1972
Ages 3–7

William has his heart set on a doll, much to the chagrin of his brother and friends. Try as they may to lure him with basketball and toy trains, young Will stands firm. While the idea of a boy preferring "girl's toys" seemed somewhat provocative at the time of this book's publication in the early 1970s, much of that controversial edge has fortunately been lifted. It's a good thing, too, because it's wonderful to encourage playacting that inspires nurturing behavior, in children of either gender. Other family favorites by Zolotow are *My Grandson Lew* and *Mr. Rabbit and the Lovely Present*.

Chapter Two

Yo! Yes?

Written and Illustrated by Chris Raschka
Orchard, $6.95, unpaged
First published in 1994
Ages 4–8

If there's one thing to be said for Raschka, it's that he's got a contagious sense of rhythm. This book, posing one-worded questions and responses, captures the staccato beat of urban-speak. It reads like the best modern poetry or hip-hop song! The author's inspiration was rewarded with a **Caldecott Honor** and followed up by *Ring! Yo?* Also look for the dreamy *Can't Sleep*; *Charlie Parker Played Be Bop* (in Story Books); *Like Likes Like*; and *Mysterious Thelonius*.

Zoom

Written and Illustrated by Istvan Banyai
Puffin, $6.99, 64 pages
First published in 1995
Ages 4–9

A fascinating look at the world of close-up and far away. Banyai begins by examining a rooster's comb and pans away to wind up in outer space. This conceptually sophisticated title will be compelling to older children, while younger readers will enjoy the elaborate drawings. Also look for its equally alluring sequel, *Re-Zoom*.

Chapter Three

Story Books

In this chapter, you'll find enchanting folk tales alongside comedic jaunts and realistic child centered stories. Beloved fairy tales receive inspired updates as authors and illustrators work together, and flights of literary fancy reach new heights. The talents of children's authors and illustrators are in prominent evidence here and recent award-winning efforts have truly raised the bar for quality literature. While illustrations remain abundant, text becomes more extensive and elaborate. These are perfect read-aloud selections, and story books will mark children's first forays into reading alone.

Whereas picture books tend to address themes that are "close to home" for preschoolers, story books expand ever outwards, introducing other cultures, foreign lands and far flung fictional landscapes. Because of the wide range of subject matter and style, these books will suit children well into the early and middle elementary school grades.

Chapter Three

The 12 Days of Christmas: A Pop-Up Celebration

Written and Illustrated by Robert Sabuda
Little Simon, $19.95, 12 pages
First published in 1996
Ages 3–8

Oh come all ye faithful and admire the artistry of this spectacular book. The familiar countdown of the 12 days is rendered in glorious three dimensional paper cuts, transforming French hens into tree ornaments and dancing ladies into jewelry box ballerinas. You'll treasure this fantastic feat of bookmaking for years to come. The festivities continue with *B is for Bethlehem: A Christmas Alphabet* by Isabel Wilner.

Abiyoyo

Written by Pete Seeger, Illustrated by Michael Hays
Aladdin, $6.95, 48 pages
First published in 1994
Ages 4–9

A boy and his father are sent into exile, charged with making things mysteriously disappear. After encountering a monster, the banished pair work their magic and are welcomed back into the village. Folksinger Seeger infuses this South African folktale with wit and charm and follows the story with *Abiyoyo Returns.*

The Acrobat and the Angel

Written by Mark Shannon, Illustrated by David Shannon
G.P. Putnam's Sons, $15.99, 30 pages
First published in 1999
Ages 5–12

With majestic enchantment, the Shannons breathe life into an elaborate French folktale. An orphan clings to his dearest possession, a statuette of an angel made by his mother long ago. He is permitted to reside at a monastery, but is asked to make sacrifices that threaten to diminish his faith. Glimpses of medieval society are given glorious treatment by the acrylic illustrations.

Story Books

Across America, I Love You
Written by Christine Loomis, Illustrated by Kate Kiesler
Hyperion, $15.99, 26 pages
First published in 2000
Ages 4–8

A mother pays lyrical tribute to the vast land and diverse people of America while acknowledging her daughter's impending maturity and independence. This touching duality is enhanced by charming metaphors and clear affection. On a quite different note, Loomis is also the author of the hilarious *Astro Bunnies* (detailed in Picture Books).

Across the Big Blue Sea
Written and Illustrated by Jakki Wood
National Geographic Society, $14.95, 28 pages
First published in 1998
Ages 4–8

An informative and enchanting look at ocean life, as a small boat sets sail for a journey around the world. With stops in California, Australia, and Africa, this is a great story for young sailors as well as primary grade students studying marine life and ocean travel. For more seaworthy tales, see *Hello Ocean* by Pamela Muñoz Ryan and *Neptune's Nursery* by Kim Michelle Toft.

The Adventures of Taxi Dog
Written by Debra and Sol Barracca, Illustrated by Mark Buehner
Puffin, $5.99, 30 pages
First published in 1990
Ages 4–7

"My name is Maxi, I ride in a taxi" begins the kindhearted and ebullient story of a homeless dog who is rescued by a taxi driver named Jim. Maxi loves riding through the New York City streets, and your young children will love accompanying him through his sequels *Maxi the Hero* and *Maxi the Star*.

Chapter Three

Aesop's Fables

Selected and Illustrated by Michael Hague
Henry Holt, $6.95, 27 pages
First published in 1985
Ages 4–9

Using his celebrated style of detailed illustration, Hague has assembled 13 fine fables from Aesop. Hague also lent his artistry to *The Book of Dragons*, an anthology of stories about the famous fire breathers, as well as *The Book of Fairies*.

Africa Calling, Nighttime Falling

Written by David Adlerman, Illustrated by Kimberly M. Adlerman
Charlesbridge, $6.95, 24 pages
First published in 1996
Ages 4–8

A unique style of collage artistry—using an array of textured photo images and cut paper designs—marks this powerful debut from the Adlermans. After opening the book, we find a mysterious multitude of animals cloaked in blue shadow. Readers are then drawn into the descriptive text that rhythmically evokes the beating of a distant tribal drum. Children studying African animals will want to embark on their own safari to locate this distinguished book.

Parent/Child Review: Africa Calling, Nighttime Falling
The Parent: George, Age 40, High School Science Teacher
The Child: George Jr., Age 5, Future Scientist
George Jr. says: "My dad's favorite animal is a giraffe. He has a picture of giraffes in the bathroom. He saw the giraffes in the book and he said 'Wow, giraffes!' My dad wants to go to Africa and visit his friend. I want to see elephants."
George says: "We have been talking a lot about going to Kenya. I wonder how he pictures Africa in his mind. This is really a beautiful book and I think my son will read it many times."

Story Books

After the Flood
Written and Illustrated by Arthur Geisert
Houghton Mifflin, $16.95, 32 pages
First published in 1994
Ages 4–8

An unusual perspective on the biblical epic of Noah's Ark, this story takes place after the waters recede. As the ark is moved to a fertile valley, Noah's family and the paired animals work together to grow crops and repopulate the earth. While younger children will enjoy counting the animals, this story will also serve as a great extension for primary grade Bible studies. Geisert also provides a dynamic treatment of the original Bible story in *The Ark*. The youngest readers will want to seek *Aardvarks, Disembark* by Ann Jonas for an amazing ark animal alphabet.

Alejandro's Gift
Written by Richard E. Albert, Illustrations by Sylvia Long
Chronicle Books, $6.95, 30 pages
First published in 1994
Ages 4–8

Alejandro is lonely until various desert dwellers—jackrabbits, coyotes, roadrunners—begin to visit his garden oasis. The illustrations' muted colors perfectly evoke life in the desert. A wonderful modern folk tale and introduction to desert animals that can be paired with *The Desert Is Theirs* by Byrd Baylor.

Alexander and the Terrible, Horrible, No Good, Very Bad Day
Written by Judith Viorst, Illustrated by Ray Cruz
Aladdin, $4.99, 32 pages
First published in 1972
Ages 4–7

In a bad mood? Feeling frustrated? Want to move to Australia? You're not alone. Alexander learns that he's not the only one who has an occasional terrible day. You'll want to follow Alexander's emotional adventures in *Alexander, Who Used to be Rich Last Sunday* and *Alexander, Who's Not (Do You Hear Me? I Mean It!) Going to Move*.

97

Chapter Three

Alice Nizzy Nazzy, The Witch of Santa Fe
Written by Tony Johnston, Illustrated by Tomie de Paola
Putnam, $6.99, 32 pages
First published in 1995
Ages 4–8

Manuela's sheep have mysteriously disappeared. Have they been stolen? She must bravely face Alice Nizzy Nazzy to plead for the return of her flock. Also by Johnston, *Amber on the Mountain*; *The Barn Owls*; *The Ghost of Nicholas Greebe*; and *The Iguana Brothers: A Tale of Two Lizards*, among other enticing tales.

Alice Ramsey's Grand Adventure
Written and Illustrated by Don Brown
Sandpiper, $5.95, 32 pages
First published in 1997
Ages 4–9

Alice Ramsey was the first woman to drive a car across the U.S.A., no small feat in 1909! Her story is enlivened by roadside views of early 20th century America, including a grand reception upon arriving at her destination, San Francisco. Brown has penned a number of picture book biographies that illuminate the lives of colorful, yet lesser-known, historical figures including *Rare Treasure: Mary Anning and her Remarkable Discoveries*; *Ruth Law Thrills a Nation*; and *Uncommon Traveler: Mary Kingsley in Africa*.

Alison's Zinnia
Written and Illustrated by Anita Lobel
Mulberry Books, $6.95, 30 pages
First published in 1996
Ages 3–7

Lively alliteration and playful use of language marks this alphabetical adventure. Children's names and the names of flowers provide a botanical tour of the alphabet as "Alison acquired an amaryllis for Beryl" and so on. Older children will want to look for Lobel's *No Pretty Pictures: A Child of War*, an account of Holocaust imprisonment.

Story Books

All I See

Written by Cynthia Rylant, Illustrated by Peter Catalanotto
Orchard, $6.95, 32 pages
First published in 1994
Ages 4–8

The eloquent and tender story of a growing friendship. Gregory paints pictures by the side of a lake and is quietly observed by Charlie. When Charlie gently expresses his admiration for Gregory's work, a special friendship begins. Softly hued illustrations capture the glowing summer days as a message about the power of creativity is addressed. Rylant is the author of *The Relatives Came* (detailed in Picture Books); the *Henry and Mudge* series (see Easy Readers); the *Mr. Putter and Tabby* series; *Night in the Country*; and *Tulip Sees America* among many others.

Featured Author: Cynthia Rylant

A former children's librarian, Cynthia Rylant's stories show a clear affection for her young audience as well as nostalgia for her own childhood. Themes of family and friendship emerge in each of her books and she has, perhaps, become best known for delightful series such as **Henry and Mudge** (in Easy Readers) and **Poppleton.** A two time Caldecott Honor recipient, for **The Relatives Came** and **When I Was Young in the Mountains**, Rylant's ability to evoke warm sentiment and youthful wonder is always evident. In her books for older readers such as **Missing May**, Rylant adeptly tackles difficult childhood experiences, such as the death of a beloved relative, with skilled sensitivity.

All the Colors of the Earth

Written and Illustrated by Sheila Hamanaka
Mulberry, $5.95, 32 pages
First published in 1994
Ages 4–9

The comparison of children's cultural diversity to the colors found in nature is at the heart of this artful endeavor. Because, as Hamanaka poetically expresses, "love comes in cinnamon, walnut, and wheat." Also by this author, *I Look Like a Girl*; *Peace Crane*; and *Screen of Frogs: An Old Tale*.

Chapter Three

All Those Secrets of the World
Written by Jane Yolen, Illustrated by Leslie A. Baker
Little Brown, $5.95, 32 pages
First published in 1991
Ages 4–9

Yolen's versatility is quite apparent in this affecting story of a young girl's attempts to make sense of the world at war. Based on Yolen's own childhood experiences, Janie begins to understand the "secrets of the world" as she gazes out at the ships that resemble tiny specks on the sea's horizon, and wonders if her father is aboard one of them. Jane Yolen is a prolific author whose work will enchant your children through adolescence. Her other story books include *Beneath the Ghost Moon: A Halloween Tale*; *Mz Berlin Walks*; and *Moon Ball*.

The Alphabet from Z to A
(With Much Confusion on the Way)
Written by Judith Viorst, Illustrated by Richard Hull
Atheneum, $15.00, 32 pages
First published in 1994
Ages 4–8

A cleverly inverted look at the alphabet for children who are already quite familiar with their ABCs, this letter romp includes silent letters, homophones and other wacky wordplay, demonstrating that rules—especially linguistic ones—can sometimes be broken. Viorst is the author of the enormously popular *Alexander and the Terrible, Horrible, No Good, Very Bad Day* and its sequels (in this chapter) as well as *The Good-Bye Book*, and *The Tenth Good Thing about Barney* (also in this chapter).

Always Room for One More
Written by Sophie Nic Leodhas, Illustrated by Nonny Hogrogian
Henry Holt, $5.95, 31 pages
First published in 1965
Ages 4–9

Versions of this instructive folk tale are told by many different cultures and this **Caldecott Medal** winning rendition is based on a Scottish folk song. It tells the story of a loving family who welcomes all passersby into their home with amusing—and very crowded—results. On a similar note, make room for *It Could Always Be Worse* by Margot Zemach, a Yiddish tale.

Story Books

Amahl and the Night Visitors

Written by Carlo Menotti, Illustrated by Michelle Lemieux
Morrow, $22.95, 64 pages
First published in 1986
Ages 5–12

Noted composer Menotti reveals the story behind his famous opera of the same name, giving us an enlightening perspective on the journey of the three kings as they travel to Bethlehem. Truly an elegant book, Lemieux's watercolors vividly capture the spirit of the first Christmas.

The Amazing Bone

Written and Illustrated by William Steig
Sunburst, $5.95, 30 pages
First published in 1976
Ages 4–8

The author of *Shrek* and *Abel's Island* brings us another endearingly offbeat and memorable story. Here, a piglet finds a magical bone on her way home from school. Also by the sensational Steig, *Amos and Boris*; *Brave Irene*; *Doctor De Soto* (in this chapter); and *Pete's a Pizza* (in "Picture Books").

Featured Author: William Steig

Grimm's Fairy Tales, Charlie Chaplin and **Pinocchio** are among William Steig's greatest creative influences. As a young man, Steig helped support his family through the dark days of the Depression by selling cartoons to magazines. A successful career as a wood sculptor followed and, amazingly, Steig did not begin to write books for children until he was sixty!

A self-described doodler, the celebrated author/illustrator tends to build his beguiling stories around a central character—Shrek, Doctor DeSoto, Sylvester—who is often an animal, but always with real child–centered emotions. It's his affinity for enlivening dramatic plots with humorous and poignant moments that has elevated Steig's books to the status of all-time favorites.

Chapter Three

parent's
guide
choice award

Amazing Grace

Written by Mary Hoffman,
Illustrations by Caroline Binch
Dial, $16.99, 26 pages
First published in 1991
Ages 4–8

Grace loves to act, dance, and tell stories. She's thrilled to learn that *Peter Pan* has been chosen as the school play, but disheartened when some of her classmates try to convince her that she can't play the lead role. You see, Peter Pan is not black, nor is he a girl. Grace looks to her effervescent family for support and gains the confidence to win the part. A truly triumphant debut from Hoffman with jubilant illustrations by Binch, this book will earn a highly sought spot on your child's bookshelves. Grace's amazing antics continue in *Boundless Grace*.

Amazing Graces: Prayers and Poems for Morning, Mealtime, Bedtime, or Anytime

Compiled by June Cotner, Illustrated by Jan Palmer
HarperCollins, $12.95, 59 pages
First published in 2001
Ages 3–9

Stemming from a variety of religious and secular traditions, this collection is rooted in children's everyday experiences. While many of the illustrations represent blond, angelic looking toddlers, the collection itself is charming and useful.

Amelia and Eleanor Go for a Ride

Written by Pamela Muñoz Ryan, Illustrated by Brian Selznick
Scholastic, $16.95, 44 pages
First published in 1999
Ages 5–10

When Amelia Earhart visited the White House in 1933, she asked Eleanor Roosevelt to accompany her on a short flight to Baltimore. What the two famous women talked about and saw during their time together is the subject of speculation in this terrific story. With graphite illustrations and an archival photograph at the end of the book, this adventure provides an imaginative invitation to exploring history from alternative viewpoints. Also by this author, the happy birthday adventure of *Mice and Beans* as well as *Hello Ocean*.

Story Books

Amy Elizabeth Explores Bloomingdales

Written and Illustrated by E.L. Konigsburg
Aladdin, $5.99, 29 pages
First published in 1992
Ages 4–8

With a street-smart knack for painting a bustling picture of the Big Apple, Konigsburg invites us on a modern urban adventure. The title character, based on the author's granddaughter, sees the Empire State Building, Chinatown, and the lights of Broadway, but will she arrive home with Big Brown Bags from Bloomingdales? E.L. Konigsburg is the Newbery Medal winning author of *From the Mixed Up Files of Mrs. Basil E. Frankweiler* and *The View From Saturday* (both detailed in Chapter Books).

Anansi and the Talking Melon

Written by Eric A. Kimmel, Illustrated by Janet Stevens
Holiday House, $6.95, 32 pages
First published in 1994
Ages 4–8

"Talking melons are nothing but trouble," sums up this lively retelling of the famous African folk tale. Always one to pull a prank, clever spider Anansi convinces all of the animals that a melon can talk. Of course, it's Anansi who's providing the biting narration from his cozy inner-melon hiding place. This is a perfect story for repeated read-alouds and is the third in Kimmel's series. The other titles include *Anansi and the Moss-Covered Rock* and *Anansi Goes Fishing*.

And Still the Turtle Watched

Written by Sheila MacGill–Callahan, Illustrated by Barry Moser
Puffin Pied Piper Books, $6.99, 32 pages
First published in 1991
Ages 5–9

A subtle, yet effective, tale that underscores the danger of pollution, this book is a wonderful supplement to non-fiction ecology materials. After an Indian carves a turtle into a stone, it bears witness to devastating changes in its surroundings. Share this story with your child on Earth Day and everyday. Also look for *A River Ran Wild* by Lynne Cherry (in this chapter).

Chapter Three

Andrew's Loose Tooth
Written by Robert Munsch, Illustrated by Michael Martchenko
Scholastic, $4.99, 29 pages
First published in 1998
Ages 4–8

Perfect for beginning readers who are expecting a visit from the tooth fairy. Here's the biting account of Andrew, who can't quite coax a loose tooth from his sore gums. It takes a close pal to render a cure, and Andrew is once again able to partake in his favorite treat, delicious apples. More Munsch: *Angela's Airplane*; *Get Out of Bed!*; *The Paper Bag Princess*; and the popular sentiment of *Love You Forever*.

Annabelle Swift, Kindergartner
Written and Illustrated by Amy Schwartz
Orchard, $6.95, 32 pages
First published in 1988
Ages 4–7

With the best of intentions, big sister Lucy tries to ensure that Annabelle is well prepared for her first day of kindergarten. Some of Lucy's advice causes momentary embarrassment, but when young Annabelle is named milk money monitor, she is quite thankful to her sister for the counting lessons. For an entertaining identity swap, look for Schwartz' *Bea and Mr. Jones*. Also by Schwartz, *A Teeny Tiny Baby* (in Picture Books).

Annie and the Old One
Written by Miska Miles, Illustrated by Peter Parnell
Little, Brown, $7.95, 44 pages
First published in 1971
Ages 4–9

This lovely and graceful **Newbery Honor** recipient addresses a child's concern about the impending loss of a grandparent. With beliefs stemming from the Navajo tradition, Annie is told that her grandmother will die upon the completion of a woven rug that the young girl is helping to create, causing her to take great pains to delay the project.

Story Books

Apple Picking Time
Written by Michele Benoit Slawson, Illustrated by Deborah Kogan Ray
Dragonfly, $6.99, 32 pages
First published in 1994
Ages 4–8

The golden days of autumn are crisply captured in this charming story of a young girl who accompanies her family on an apple picking expedition. She's determined to fill up an entire bin of her own for the first time. Younger children will want to pair this story with *Apples and Pumpkins* by Anne Rockwell.

Arrow to the Sun: A Pueblo Indian Tale
Written and Illustrated by Gerald Mcdermott
Puffin, $6.99, 40 pages
First published in 1975
Ages 4–9

Steeped in Pueblo traditions, this vivid depiction of an Indian myth centers on the Lord of the Sun's origin. Most stunning are the **Caldecott Medal** winning illustrations, incorporating the oranges, blues, reds, and yellows of Pueblo motifs. Mcdermott demonstrates his keen knack for vivid native storytelling with *Anansi the Spider* and its sequels, as well as *Coyote: A Trickster Tale from the American Southwest* and *Musicians of the Sun*.

Arroz Con Leche:
Popular Songs and Rhymes from Latin America
Selected and Illustrated by Lulu Delacre
Scholastic, $4.99, 32 pages
First published in 1992
Ages 4–9

A festive bilingual celebration that features songs, games, and nursery rhymes from an array of Hispanic traditions. The book includes fingerplay instructions and watercolor illustrations that seem to dance along with the musical selections.

Chapter Three

Art Dog

Written and Illustrated by Thacher Hurd
HarperCollins, $5.95, 32 pages
First published in 1996
Ages 4–7

Arthur Dog could have given Van Gogh a run for his money! While Arthur seems like a cool cat working his day job as a guard at the Dogopolis Museum of Art (where else?), he becomes one artful dogger at night, creating masterpiece murals while solving crimes. You'll recognize many of the museum's notable works, including a painting by none other than Henri Muttisse. Thacher's frantic brush strokes perfectly match the pace of this painterly pooch's story. Pair this title with *Norman the Doorman* by Don Freeman. Also by Hurd, *Mama Don't Allow* and *The Pea Patch Jig.*

> *Parent/Child Review: Art Dog*
> The Parent: Jen, Age 32, Stay-at-home Mom
> The Child: Ethan, Age 5, Car Enthusiast
> Ethan says: "Okay, we went to the museum and it was really big. I got tired but we had some cookies... Arthur Dog has a really hard job but he's an artist. The best part is when he paints on the walls."
> Jen says: "Ethan isn't usually a museum fan, so I wondered if he would like this book. I think it's for all kids though 'cause there's so much action. He's a clever guy, the author, with all those spoofy paintings... that must have been to get the parents' attention."

Aunt Flossie's Hats and Crab Cakes Later

Written by Elizabeth Fitzgerald Howard, Illustrated by James Ransome
Clarion Books, $6.95, 31 pages
First published in 1991
Ages 4–8

This is a wonderfully evocative story of sweet childhood memories. Aunt Flossie has quite a collection of hats that Susan and Sarah love to admire. And, of course, there's always Aunt Flossie's special crab cakes to savor afterwards. The vivid illustrations glowingly portray the close-knit African-American family in this warm treasure of a book.

Story Books

Babushka Baba Yaga

Written and Illustrated by Patricia Polacco
Penguin Putnam, $6.99, 32 pages
First published in 1999
Ages 4–9

Polacco gives a painterly approach to the retelling of folk tales. Everyone in the village is frightened of old Baba Yaga so she dons a disguise in order to experience being a grandmother. Other books by Polacco include *Aunt Chip and the Great Triple Creek Dam Affair*; *The Bee Tree*; *Chicken Sunday*; *The Keeping Quilt*; *Mrs. Katz and Tush*; *Pink and Say*; and *Thunder Cake*.

Featured Author: Patricia Polacco

Drawing upon her Russian ancestry and childhood memories, Patricia Polacco has fashioned some of the most unique and affecting children's literature of the twentieth century. Her immediately recognizable books, with their lovely pastel and acrylic illustrations, address cross-cultural relationships and are often based on the experiences of her family (see **Pink and Say** in this chapter). Other stories are autobiographical, like in **Meteor!**, when Polacco recounts an episode from her own childhood when she witnessed a meteor land behind her grandparents' house. Perhaps best known for her Russian tales such as **Babushka Baba Yaga**, it's clear that Patricia Polacco has a knack for gracefully interpreting oral tradition while adding a flavor to her stories that evokes memories of favorite family tales.

Back Home

Written by Gloria Jean Pinkney, Illustrated by Jerry Pinkney
Puffin, $6.99, 40 pages
First published in 1992
Ages 4–8

Young Ernestine, an eight-year-old African-American girl, eagerly anticipates a trip to visit relatives on the North Carolina farm where she was born. There's ample charm and affection in this nostalgic story from the Pinkneys. Set just prior to this story is *The Sunday Outing*.

Badger's Parting Gifts

Written and Illustrated by Susan Varley
Mulberry, $6.95, 25 pages
First published in 1992
Ages 4–8

The woodland animals adore Badger and are deeply saddened by his death. When they begin to share fond memories of their friend, they realize the many gifts he has given them. A fine and sensitive portrayal, certain to be useful in helping young children come to terms with loss.

Chapter Three

A Band of Angels:
A Story Inspired by the Jubilee Singers
Written by Deborah Hopkinson, Illustrated by Raul Colon
Atheneum, $16.00, 33 pages
First published in 1999
Ages 5–9

A heartwarming episode arises from the most shameful of American eras, as Ella becomes a proud member of an African-American chorus comprised of freed slaves. The distinguished watercolor illustrations resemble sepia tone photography and lend the feeling of gaining a glimpse into a treasured family album. Told from the perspective of Ella's great-great granddaughter, there is a pervasive message of learning not to take for granted one's freedoms and opportunities. Also by Hopkinson, *Birdie's Lighthouse*; *Maria's Comet*; and *Sweet Clara and the Freedom Quilt*.

Barefoot: Escape on the Underground Railroad
Written by Pamela Duncan Edwards, Illustrated by Henry Cole
HarperTrophy, $5.95, 32 pages
First published in 1999
Ages 4–9

A group of vigilant forest creatures guide an escaped slave to freedom in this glorious story. While younger children won't have a sense of the historical context, this is an excellent introduction to the topic of slavery. For children in the early elementary grades, the story can serve as a supplement to classroom discussions of slavery and the Underground Railroad.

Baseball Saved Us
Written by Ken Mochizuki, Illustrated by Dom Lee
Lee & Low, $6.95, 32 pages
First published in 1993
Ages 5–9

Subject matter that is not often addressed in the classroom provides the setting for this compelling drama. A young Japanese-American boy is interned with his family at a labor camp during World War II where they build a baseball diamond to raise spirits. Also available in Spanish. Other affecting stories by Mochizuki include *Heroes* and *Passage to Freedom*.

Story Books

Beautiful

Written by Susi Gregg Fowler
Greenwillow Books, $15.00, 32 pages
First published in 1998
Ages 5–9

A boy is given a lasting gift from his terminally ill uncle, who teaches the youngster about the bountiful joys of gardening. As his uncle's condition worsens, their shared hobby takes on additional meaning. Fowler is also the author of *Circle of Thanks*.

A Beautiful Feast for a Big King Cat

Written by John Archambault and Bill Martin Jr.,
Illustrations by Bruce Degen
HarperTrophy, $6.95, 32 pages
First published in 1994
Ages 4–8

A mischievous young mouse narrowly escapes capture as he repeatedly teases the resident cat. When he is finally taken hostage by the feisty feline, he must use the power of savory suggestion to distract his captor before scampering to safety. Archambault co-authored several stories with Bill Martin Jr. including *Chicka Chicka Boom Boom* (in Picture Books); *Here Are My Hands*; and *Knots on a Counting Rope*.

Ben's Trumpet

Written and Illustrated by Rachel Isadora
Mulberry, $6.95, 32 pages
First published in 1991
Ages 4–9

Effective black and white illustrations mark this **Caldecott Honor** recipient's story of a boy who aspires to play the trumpet. At first, Ben must suffice with an imaginary instrument until a local jazz musician becomes impressed by the boy's ambition. Isadora shows her penchant for the performing arts in *Lili at Ballet* and its sequels, as well as *Listen to the City* (in Picture Books), and *Over the Green Hills*.

**The Best
Children's Literature**
A Parent's Guide

Chapter Three

Big Boy
Written by Tololwa M. Mollel, Illustrated by E. B. Lewis
Clarion Books, $5.95, 27 pages
First published in 1995
Ages 4–7

From Tanzanian lore springs this cautionary tale of wishful thinking. When Oli expresses his wish to be a big boy, he becomes larger than life... or does he? Lewis is a gifted illustrator whose entrancing watercolor landscapes will captivate readers. Also by Mollel, *Kitoto the Mighty*; *My Rows and Piles of Coins*; and *Orphan Boy: A Maasai Story*, among others.

Big Rain Coming
Written by Katrina Germein, Illustrated by Bronwyn Bancroft
Clarion Books, $15.00, 33 pages
First published in 2000
Ages 4–8

In this tale that builds like the most rewarding suspense story, the inhabitants of a parched Australian landscape await an overdue rainstorm. When it finally happens, readers are vicariously cooled as the animals and people engage in a wet and wonderful celebration. The illustrations are inspired by aboriginal art, lending a truly authentic air to this refreshing tale.

Bigmama's
Written and Illustrated by Donald Crews
Mulberry, $5.95, 32 pages
First published in 1998
Ages 4–8

With joyful nostalgia, Crews recalls a childhood trip to his Grandma's farm. The children run gleefully through the house and yard, as the family prepares a delicious supper. The effervescent illustrations, in summery earth tones, convincingly portray the special significance of this treasured childhood episode. You'll also enjoy *Back Home* by Gloria Jean Pinkney. Also by Crews, *Freight Train* (in "Picture Books"); *Night at the Fair*; and *Shortcut*.

Story Books

Bird Talk

Written and Illustrated by Ann Jonas
Greenwillow, $15.00, 32 pages
First published in 1999
Ages 4–9

Jonas jovially narrates the conversation between our feathery friends in this one-of-a-kind introduction to birdcalls. While much of what the birds discuss is given a comical human perspective, the author also provides factual information about bird species and their special songs. This imaginative book will have your children grabbing their binoculars and whispering "tweet" nothings in no time. Jonas is the author of the ever-innovative *The 13th Clue*; *Aardvarks Disembark*; *Color Dance*; and *The Quilt*.

Black Is Brown Is Tan

Written by Arnold Adoff, Illustrated by Emily Arnold McCully
HarperTrophy, $5.95, 31 pages
First published in 1973
Ages 4–8

Unfolding in colorful verse, this influential cultural celebration employs a multi-racial family to explore the wide variety of people's skin tones and the connection of the human spirit, regardless of race. For further discussion of ethnic diversity, pair this title with *The Colors of Us* by Karen Katz. Also by Adoff, *In for Winter, Out for Spring*; and *Touch the Poem*.

Booby Hatch

Written and Illustrated by Betsy Lewin
Clarion Books, $4.95, 32 pages
First published in 1995
Ages 4–8

Pepe is a blue-footed booby who emerges from an egg on the Galapagos Islands. His parents help him learn all of the important lessons—how to fly, fish, and eventually choose a mate, bringing the story full circle so that "a little white egg will sit in a circle of stones, on a tiny island, in a vast blue sea." This is an engaging story that illuminates the life cycle of birds while shedding light on the importance of protecting endangered species and preserving fragile ecosystems. Lewin is also the author of *Chubbo's Pool* and *What's the Matter, Habibi?*

Chapter Three

Boodil, My Dog
Written by Gabrielle Charbonnet, Illustrated by Pija Lindenbaum
Henry Holt, $5.95, 48 pages
First published in 1995
Ages 4–8

Boodil is the perfect pet in the eyes of his young owner (a narrator who remains faceless throughout the story), but upon examining some of Boodil's habits, it becomes clear to the reader that he's more of a timid terrier than a courageous canine. All of Boodil's less-than-perfect qualities are happily and hilariously overlooked in this story that dog owners will adore.

Parent/Child Review: Boodil, My Dog
The Parent: Hildy, Age 44, Jewelry Maker
The Child: Loren, Age 6, Animal Aficionado
Loren says: "Ohmygod... this is the best book and it's so, so funny. It's about a dog that's not really brave but it kinda tricks its owners about stuff. We have two dogs and two fish. My dogs aren't brave either and they bark every time our neighbor's phone rings. I love my dogs."
Hildy says: "What's funny here is that we are so guilty of exaggerating our dogs' best qualities. But, I think that's a nice human tendency, to become so attached to our pets. My daughter clearly agrees and I think this book definitely reminded her of our family."

Book! Book! Book!
Written and Illustrated by Deborah Bruss
Scholastic, $15.95, unpaged
First published in 2001
Ages 4–7

When the kids return to school, the barnyard animals become bored and lonely... until they hatch a plan! They venture into town and find the local library, with the appropriately verbose hen leading the pack, calling out her request (the book's title gives a clue). Satisfied with their endeavor, they head back to the barn for an afternoon of quiet reading time.

Story Books

The Boy of the Three Year Nap
Written by Dianne Snyder, Illustrated by Allen Say
Houghton Mifflin, $6.95, 32 pages
First published in 1988
Ages 4–8

Taro loves to sleep, much to the dismay of his hardworking mother. He emerges from his slumbers long enough to devise a scheme to marry into a wealthy family, thus ensuring a life of ease. Will his mother foil his plans? This elegantly crafted **Caldecott Honor** recipient features illustrations that resemble Asian woodcuts, adding to the charm of this Japanese folktale. Also available in Spanish.

Brave Irene
Written and Illustrated by William Steig
Farrar Straus Giroux, $5.95, 32 pages
First published in 1986
Ages 4–8

Not rain, nor sleet, nor snow will deter Irene from coming to the rescue after her mother, a dressmaker, becomes ill. Irene sets off in a fierce winter storm to deliver a gown for the duchess's gala. Once again, Steig reigns as the king of spunk. Also available in Spanish. Other stories by Steig include *The Amazing Bone*; *Doctor DeSoto*; and *Sylvester and the Magic Pebble* (all detailed in this chapter), as well as *Pete's a Pizza* (in Picture Books).

Bringing the Rain to Kapiti Plain: A Nandi Tale
Written by Verna Aardema, Illustrated by Beatriz Vidal
Puffin, $6.99, 32 pages
First published in 1992
Ages 4–7

An East African tale told in lively rhythmic verse that gains joyous momentum, this book has become a favorite of kindergarten teachers everywhere. The mesmerizing illustrations add to the appeal of this accessible, yet exotic, story. Pair this one with *Jambo Means Hello: Swahili Alphabet Book* (detailed in Non-Fiction, see under Africa) by Muriel and Tom Feelings.

Chapter Three

Brown Honey in Broomwheat Tea

Written by Joyce Carol Thomas, Illustrated by Floyd Cooper

HarperTrophy, $5.95, 32 pages

First published in 1996

Ages 5–9

The diverse and proud experiences of African-Americans are elegantly examined in this collection of sweet poems. The text and illustrations are a sensory delight, overflowing with metaphoric verse that underscores both beautifully fragrant and bittersweet notions. Taylor is the author of *The Bowlegged Rooster and Other Tales that Signify* as well as *I Have Heard of a Land*.

The Bus Ride

Written by William Miller, Illustrated by John Ward

Lee & Low, $6.95, 32 pages

First published in 1998

Ages 5–9

Featuring an eloquent introduction by Rosa Parks, this story is based on her barrier-breaking role in the civil rights movement. Young Sara wanted to catch the view from the front of the bus, curious about "what was so special." After being arrested, she becomes a celebrated symbol of fortitude. With realistic illustrations, this book is a perfect accompaniment to elementary grade discussions about civil rights and a must-read for Black History Month. Also by Miller, *The Piano* and *Richard Wright and the Library Card* (see Nonfiction, African American). For more on the valiant efforts of Ms. Parks, look for *If a Bus Could Talk: The Story of Rosa Parks* by Faith Ringgold.

Butterfly House

Written by Eve Bunting, Illustrated by Greg Shed

Scholastic, $15.95, 32 pages

First published in 1999

Ages 4–8

A young girl rescues a caterpillar and turns an empty box into a lovingly constructed faux garden for the creature. After metamorphosis, a beautiful Painted Lady butterfly emerges and is set free. Told as an elderly woman's cherished memory, this story will instantly inspire an appreciation for nature's glorious treasures. You'll also want to read *Becoming Butterflies* by Anne Rockwell. Eve Bunting is the prolific author of *A Day's Work*; *Flower Garden*; *Fly Away Home* (in this chapter); *Going Home*; *Night of the Gargoyles*; and *Red Fox Running* (in this chapter), among many others.

Story Books

Career Day
Written and Illustrated by Anne Rockwell
HarperCollins, $15.95, 32 pages
First published in 2000
Ages 4–8

Part of a series that focuses on lessons learned in Mrs. Madoff's cheerful multicultural classroom, this volume invites us to meet the parents. Holding an array of occupations from nurse, carpenter, paleontologist, writer, and musician, it's clear that there is a wide world of careers for the children to someday pursue. The story also makes it perfectly plain that one's aspirations need not be restricted by gender. Also in this series, *Halloween Day*; *Thanksgiving Day*; and *Valentine's Day*. Other books by Rockwell include *Apples and Pumpkins*; *Becoming Butterflies*; *One Bean*; and *Welcome to Kindergarten*.

Carmine the Crow
Written and Illustrated by Heidi Holder
Farrar Straus & Giroux, $5.95, 32 pages
First published in 1992
Ages 4–9

Carmine is granted a box of stardust, and as many wishes, after performing a heroic act. But on his way home, he gives it all away to animals in need. All is not lost in the karma department, though. Carmine finds one last grain of magic dust and wishes to be young again. Holder's illustrations are astonishing, and her virtuous story has a great deal of lasting appeal.

A Chair for My Mother
Written and Illustrated by Vera B. Williams
Mulberry Books, $5.95, 32 pages
First published in 1982
Ages 4–7

After a fire destroys their home and possessions, a young girl and her family save money to purchase an armchair in this touching tale. Also available in Spanish. Other books by the divinely inspired Williams include, *Amber Was Brave, Essie Was Smart* (detailed in Chapter Books); *Cherries and Cherry Pits*; *More, More, More Said the Baby*; and *Music, Music for Everyone*.

Chapter Three

Charlie Parker Played Be Bop
Written and Illustrated by Christopher Raschka
Orchard Books, $5.95, 32 pages
First published in 1992
Ages 4–9

While young children are most likely unfamiliar with the jazz master, this story, based on Parker's fast and furious be-bop innovation, is a glorious study in sound, with verse mimicking the zooming and halting rhythms of the music. Also by Raschka, *Like Likes Like*, the tuneful tale of *Mysterious Thelonious* as well as *Yo! Yes* (detailed in Picture Books).

Chato's Kitchen
Written by Gary Soto, Illustrated by Susan Guevera
Paperstar, $6.99, 32 pages
First published in 1997
Ages 4–7

Soto is a gifted and groovy word wizard, giving authentic attitude to his characters in their East Los Angeles setting. The effect is hilarious, as Chato the cat hatches a plan to devour the mice that live next door. All is well until he becomes daunted by a dachshund. Pair this one with *Hip Cat* by Jonathan London. There's more from Soto in *Chato and the Party Animals* as well as *The Old Man and His Door* and *Too Many Tamales*. Older readers will adore *Baseball in April and Other Stories* (detailed in Chapter Books).

Chestnut Cove
Written and Illustrated by Tim Egan
Houghton Mifflin, $5.95, 32 pages
First published in 1995
Ages 4–8

The hippo king issues a challenge to the residents of Chestnut Cove. Whoever grows the biggest, juiciest watermelon will inherit the kingdom. While the competition begins on friendly footing, greed soon sets in, until a rescue mission unites the plump peasants. There's a lot to laugh about, and a gentle moral missive to consider, in this terrific story. Other books by Egan include *Friday Night at Hodges Café* and *Metropolitan Cow*.

Story Books

Chibi: A True Story from Japan

Written by Barbara Brenner and Julia Takaya, Illustrated by June Otani
Clarion Books, $5.95, 63 pages
First published in 1996
Ages 4–7

Based on a true story, Brenner and Takaya relate the story of a mother duck who chooses a pool beside a Tokyo office building to raise her ducklings. Crowds gather and urban lore is created, especially when an elderly photographer nearly risks his life to escort the family of ducks to a new location. Admirers of *Make Way for Ducklings* by Robert McCloskey will surely relish this tale. Brenner has contributed several volumes to the *Bank Street Ready-to-Read* Series and the *Hide & Seek Science* Series.

Chrysanthemum

Written and Illustrated by Kevin Henkes
Mulberry, $5.95, 32 pages
First published in 1996
Ages 4–8

When her blossomy name becomes the subject of school ridicule, Chrysanthemum the mouse turns to her doting parents for support. It's her beloved music teacher, Delphinium, who enlightens the children that a rose by any other name... well, you know. Henkes' champion comic style and perceptive wit are also evident in *Circle Dogs* (in Picture Books); *Julius, the Baby of the World*; and *Lily's Purple Plastic Purse* (both in this chapter); as well as *The Biggest Boy*; *Owen*; and *Sheila Rae, the Brave*.

Cinderella

Written by Charles Perrault, Illustrated by Marcia Brown
Aladdin, $6.99, 32 pages
First published in 1954
Ages 4–8

This **Caldecott Medal** winning rendition of the celebrated story is not to be missed. All of the drama and enchantment of the famous tale are magically captured by Brown's elegant translation and illustrations. Look for *Puss in Boots* (in this chapter) and the grand collection of *Perrault's Complete Fairy Tales*.

Chapter Three

Clever Beatrice: An Upper Peninsula Conte

Written and Illustrated by Margaret Willey
Atheneum, $16.00, unpaged
First published in 2001
Ages 4–9

Beatrice must outwit a giant in order to return home with food for her poor family. The dialect is terrific, and the woodsy multi-media illustrations are simply perfect. With her perseverance and determination, young Beatrice is certain to become a folk hero in your household.

Click, Clack Moo: Cows That Type

parent's
guide
choice award

Written by Doreen Cronin,
Illustrated by Betsy Lewin
Simon & Schuster, $15.00, 32 pages
First published in 2000
Ages 4–8

You'd be hard pressed to find a funnier story so run, don't walk, to look for a copy of this book! Farmer Brown's cows become quite communicative and downright chatty in this hilarious tale. When the cows find an old type-writer, they quickly begin to request items—an electric blanket is at the top of their wish list. After a perplexed Farmer Brown ignores their messages, a strike ensues with a bold bovine declaration: "Sorry, we're closed. No milk today." Good-natured mayhem ensues as the hens join the picket line and a neutral duck is called in to preside over the negotiations. Catchy prose and splashy illustrations of the barnyard animals pecking typewriter keys adds to the fun of this story, which will appeal to preschool protesters while light-heartedly imparting the importance of cooperation. *Giggle, Giggle, Quack* is the wacky and wonderful sequel.

A Collection for Kate

Written and Illustrated by Barbara Derubertis
Kane Press, $4.95, 30 pages
First published in 1999
Ages 4–9

During "Collection Week" at school, the children bring in the fruits of their labors—coins, shells, postcards—for a show-and-tell rap session. Kate is per-plexed about her own contribution, eventually settling on a clever collection of collections. There's a bit of math and a lot of realism in this appealing story. Also by Derubertis, *Count on Pablo* and *Deena's Lucky Penny* among others.

Story Books

The Cow Who Wouldn't Come Down

Written and Illustrated by Paul Brett Johnson
Orchard, $6.95, 32 pages
First published in 1997
Ages 4–7

Gertrude the cow has developed a sudden fondness for flying, and even Miss Rosemary's most innovative schemes and tempting offers won't lure the airborne bovine down to the ground. There's a look of pure delight on the cow's face as her keeper worries about what the neighbors will think because, after all, "It's a known fact cows don't fly." You'll also enjoy Johnson's *The Pig Who Ran a Red Light*.

Cowboy Country

Written by Ann Herbert Scott, Illustrated by Ted Lewin
Clarion, $6.95, 42 pages
First published in 1993
Ages 4–8

Saddle up, buckaroos! You're in for a good old-fashioned cowboy story and glimpse into the workings of the rural American west. Within this genial yarn is a lot of information about the lives of cowboys from yesterday and today. You'll get a real sense of jargon and drawl from Scott's colorful verse, and Lewin's atmospheric illustrations will open your child's eyes to the beautiful landscape of the southwest.

Dear Juno

Written by Soyung Pak, Illustrated by Susan Kathleen Hartung
Puffin, $5.99, unpaged
First published in 1999
Ages 3–7

Juno receives letters and small gifts from his beloved grandmother in Korea. His parents help to translate his grandmother's sentiments. An affectionate story, realistically expressed by its warm illustrations, this book will encourage discussion about languages, cultures, and the devotion of family. For similar subject matter, you'll also enjoy *Grandfather Counts* by Andrea Cheng.

Chapter Three

Dinner at Aunt Connie's House
Written and Illustrated by Faith Ringgold
Hyperion, $4.95, 32 pages
First published in 1996
Ages 4–8

The walls of Aunt Connie's house are lined with portraits of twelve divinely influential African-American women—including Rosa Parks and Zora Neale Hurston—that magically come to life, informing nine-year-old Melody about their legacy. The remarkable Ringgold is the author of *Tar Beach* (in this chapter) and its sequel *Aunt Harriet's Underground Railroad in the Sky* as well as *If a Bus Could Talk: The Story of Rosa Parks.*

Doctor De Soto
Written and Illustrated by William Steig
Sunburst, $5.95, 30 pages
First published in 1982
Ages 4–8

While Doctor De Soto is a caring dental practitioner, he is also, quite frankly, a mouse. As such, he has taken care not to accept dangerous animals as patients. When a fox appears at his office, begging for medical attention, the Doc puts aside his principles and outwits the sly fox in the process. The adventures continue in *Doctor De Soto Goes to Africa*. There's a slew of Steig in this guide, including *The Amazing Bone*; *Brave Irene* (both in this chapter); as well as *Pete's a Pizza* (in Picture Books).

Drummer Hoff
Written by Barbara Emberley, Illustrated by Ed Emberley
Aladdin, $5.95, 32 pages
First published in 1972
Ages 4–8

The escalating rhythm of this cumulative story/song (think "house that Jack built") centers on several soldiers as they prepare a cannon. It's the title character who is granted the ultimate honor of firing it off. The imperially droll illustrations earned a **Caldecott Medal** for this beloved book. Ed Emberley is the creator of a popular series of instructional books about drawing including *Ed Emberley's Fingerprint Drawing Book.*

Story Books

Earth Tales from Around the World

Written by Michael Caduto, Illustrated by Adelaide Murphy Tyrol
Fulcrum, $17.95, 192 pages
First published in 1997
Ages 5–12

Truly a book for all ages, this collection centers on stories that provoke thought about our relationship to the world we share. Beautiful and contemplative, these are tales to revisit throughout the years, especially as accompaniment to classroom discussions about environmental protection and natural resources.

Edward and the Pirates

Written and Illustrated by David McPhail
Little, Brown, $15.95, 32 pages
First published in 1997
Ages 4–8

Celebrating the creative power of reading, this rollicking adventure centers on Edward who "loves to read books—all kinds of books." Edward becomes so immersed in his favorite stories that he finds himself involved in a brave battle with some errant pirates that have leapt from the pages right into his bedroom. McPhail has been a frequent contributor to several Easy Reader series with titles including *Big Brown Bear*; *A Bug, a Bear, and a Boy*; and *The Great Race*. He is also the author of *Mole Music*; *The Puddle*; and *Santa's Book of Names*.

Eight Hands Round: A Patchwork Alphabet

Written by Ann Whitford Paul, Illustrated by Jeanette Winter
HarperCollins, $5.95, 31 pages
First published in 1991
Ages 4–9

Pairing each letter of the alphabet with a patchwork pattern, this lovingly crafted book also explores early American life. With an object or pioneer activity featured on each page, kids will gain a unique perspective on history, as well as the rich tradition of quilting. Pair this title with *The Log Cabin Quilt* by Ellen Howard. Also by this author, *All By Herself: 14 Girls Who Made a Difference* (see Nonfiction, Women); *Everything to Spend the Night: From A to Z* (in Picture Books); and *Hello Toes! Hello Feet!*

Chapter Three

The Eleventh Hour: A Curious Mystery
Written and Illustrated by Graeme Base
Puffin, $7.99, 34 pages
First published in 1997
Ages 5–9

You'd think nobody would be brazen enough to steal an elephant's birthday feast, but that's precisely the premise for this interactive mystery. Readers are invited to join in the search for the thief. Hidden clues and clever text add to the excitement of this story. Also by Base, the artful alphabet of *Animalia*, as well as *The Water Hole* and *The Worst Band in the Universe*.

Eloise
Written by Kay Thompson, Illustrated by Hilary Knight
Simon and Schuster, $18.00, 65 pages
First published in 1955
Ages 4–9

Having become the campy champion of uptown excess since her mid-20th century birth, Eloise truly knows how to work a room. She lives in the posh Plaza Hotel where her every whim is catered to. Her chatty narration is told in long, un-punctuated phrasing, echoing the frantic way young children sometimes express themselves. Follow her indulgent travels in *Eloise in Paris*.

Emeline at the Circus
Written and Illustrated by Marjorie Priceman
Dragonfly, $6.99, 33 pages
First published in 1999
Ages 4–8

A field trip to the circus is supposed to be great fun, right? Well, Mrs. Splinter's multitude of rules threatens to turn the big top into a big flop. That's until Emeline sets off on her own adventure, dismissing her teacher's warnings and becoming an unwitting performer. She encounters elephants, cavorts with clowns, and twirls on the trapeze before returning nonchalantly to her seat. The explosion of color is in perfect pitch with the high-flying pace of this story, which is surely a familiar childhood fantasy. Also by Priceman, *Froggie Went A-Courting*; *How to Make an Apple Pie and See the World*; and *My Nine Lives, By Clio*.

Story Books

The Emperor's New Clothes
Written by Hans Christian Anderson, Translated by Naomi Lewis,
Illustrated by Angela Barrett
Candlewick, $5.99, unpaged
First published in 1837
Ages 4–9

   The naked truth about an emperor's foolhardy flair for fashion is enlivened here by humorous illustrations. Two mischievous weavers convince the ruler that his prêt-a-porter ensemble is so fine, it can only be viewed by the most worthy citizens. Little does the emperor realize he is about to march through the streets in his birthday suit.

Everybody Bakes Bread
Written by Norah Dooley, Illustrated by Peter Thornton
Carolrhoda Books, $6.95, 40 pages
First published in 1996
Ages 5–8

   When her mother sends Carrie out to run an errand on a rainy day, the young girl samples a bountiful array of bread from her ethnically diverse neighbors. There's cornbread, challah, pita, and coconut bread. She returns home in time to catch the aroma of her mother's own Italian rolls. Recipes included! For more culinary commonalities, look for *Everybody Serves Soup* and *Everybody Cooks Rice*.

Fables
Written and Illustrated by Arnold Lobel
HarperTrophy, $6.95, 40 pages
First published in 1980
Ages 4–9

   This **Caldecott Medal** winning collection includes 20 enchanting and instructive fables, featuring a bevy of animals. Also available in Spanish as *Fabulas*. Lobel is the author of *Ming Lo Moves the Mountain* (in this chapter) and the *Frog and Toad* series (in "Easy Readers").

Chapter Three

The Five Dog Night
Written and Illustrated by Eileen Christelow
Clarion, $6.95, 36 pages
First published in 1993
Ages 4–8

The bitter chill of a New England winter is the setting for this amusing story of Betty and her somewhat cantankerous neighbor, Ezra. Betty treks through the snow and ice to deliver cookies, and admonishes Ezra about protecting himself from the cold. Ezra befuddles his neighbor by replying sardonically, it's only a "two-dog night," until we discover that he measures the weather by the amount of dogs he needs to use as blankets! Christelow is the author of *Five Little Monkeys Jumping on the Bed* and its sequels, as well as *The Great Pig Escape* and *What Do Authors Do?* (see "Nonfiction, Writing").

Fly Away Home
Written by Eve Bunting, Illustrated by Ronald Himler
Clarion, $5.95, 32 pages
First published in 1993
Ages 5–8

This story of a young homeless boy and his father is startling and effective. The child, as narrator, describes the hardships of making a home in an airport, including washing in the restroom and keeping out of sight of the security guards. The muted colors match the bleak outlook of this tale that, quite realistically, does not have an easy ending. When your children begin to ask questions about the people they notice living on the street, it's time to introduce this exceptional book. Bunting is the versatile author of *Dreaming of America: An Ellis Island Story*; *Flower Garden*; *Night of the Gargoyles*; and *Red Fox Running* (in this chapter), among many others.

Parent/Child Review: Fly Away Home
The Grandpa: Charles, Age 63, Retired Detective
The Child: Sammy, Age 6, Future Detective
Sammy says: "It's a sad book because these people don't have a place to go and they live in the airport chairs. I saw a man and a dog in Philadelphia on the corner and my mom said they didn't have houses. Some people gave them quarters, though."
Charles says: "Yeah, it's a tough topic for kids but they definitely see it on the streets. Don't think they don't. It's best to talk about these things and answer questions."

Story Books

The Fool of the World and the Flying Ship

Written by Arthur Ransome, Illustrated by Uri Shulevitz

Farrar, Straus and Giroux, $6.95, 48 pages

First published in 1968

Ages 4–9

The Fool of the World rises to a challenge set by the Czar: whoever can deliver a flying ship will win his daughter's hand in marriage. It's a bit risky, but The Fool learns by carefully studying the best qualities of his compatriots, including The Swift-Goer and The Listener. This **Caldecott Medal** winner will certainly raise spirits in your household.

A Frog Prince

Written and Illustrated by Alix Berenzy

Henry Holt, $6.95, 32 pages

First published in 1991

Ages 4–9

Some frogs need not be kissed in order to show their princely proclivities. The hero of Berenzy's updated fairy tale is brave and true. He must face an arduous journey and daunting tests of courage before winning the love of his perfect mate. With deeply textured, rich illustrations, this is a fairy tale worth its weight in gold. You'll also want to reach for Berenzy's *Rapunzel*.

The Frog Prince, Continued

Written by Jon Scieszka, Illustrated by Steve Johnson

Puffin, $6.99, 32 pages

First published in 1994

Ages 4–9

Scieszka reigns supreme as the king of the droll spoof, and this far-out fairy tale is amusing proof. While the frog in question becomes a prince, "happily-ever-after" seems out of the question for him and his intended princess. There are guaranteed guffaws to be found in *The Book That Jack Wrote*; *The Stinky Cheese Man and Other Fairly Stupid Tales* (in this chapter); and *The True Story of the Three Little Pigs*. Older readers will want to indulge in *The Time Warp Trio* series (in "Chapter Books").

Chapter Three

From Here to There
Written by Margery Cuyler, Illustrated by Ya Cha Pak
Henry Holt, $16.95, 29 pages
First published in 1999
Ages 4–9

A child's place in the world is explored and made meaningful as young Maria stakes out her unique cosmic territory. It's a common ritual amongst children: to name the street, town, state, and country of one's origin. Maria expands upon this theme, reaching out to the solar system, galaxy, universe and beyond, making sense of her seemingly small, yet abundantly significant mark on the map. Pair this title with *Me on the Map* by Joan Sweeney (see "Nonfiction, Geography"). Also by Cuyler, *The Biggest, Best Snowman* and *That's Good! That's Bad!*

Galimoto
Written by Karen Lynn Williams, Illustrated by Catherine Stock
Mulberry, $5.95, 32 pages
First published in 1990
Ages 4–8

A lack of playthings does not deter an African boy from realizing his creative potential. He gathers scraps to make a toy car, a galimoto. There's much to learn from his efforts and a great deal to enjoy from his inherent rewards. This is an intriguing entry into discussion about materialism and the satisfaction that comes from making the most of what we're given. There's more along these instructive lines in *Painted Dreams* and *Tap-Tap*.

The Gardener
Written by Sarah Stewart, Illustrated by David Small
Sunburst, $5.95, 39 pages
First published in 1998
Ages 4–8

When her father loses his job, Lydia Grace is sent to live with her rather somber Uncle Jim in the city, bringing with her a love of gardening and boundless good cheer. As we read the letters she sends home and witness the gradual brightening of her urban surroundings, it becomes clear that one individual is capable of changing the lives of many. Set during the Great Depression, this lovely and graceful story, a **Caldecott Honor** recipient, is poised to take its place amongst the classics. Stewart is also the author of *The Journey*; *The Library*; and *The Money Tree*.

Story Books

George and Martha
Written and Illustrated by James Marshall
Houghton Mifflin, $6.95, 46 pages
First published in 1972
Ages 4–8

The two title characters are happy hippos and best friends. Their cheerful antics and comical misadventures teach readers a lot about the meaning of true friendship. Their many fans include Maurice Sendak, who writes in the foreword, "Those dear, ditzy, down-to-earth hippos bring serious pleasure to everybody, not only to children." You'll find smiles in the sequels, *George and Martha Encore*; *George and Martha Rise and Shine*; *George and Martha One Fine Day*; *George and Martha Tons of Fun*; *George and Martha Back in Town*; and *George and Martha Round and Round*.

Gila Monsters Meet You at the Airport
Written by Marjorie Weinman Sharmat, Illustrated by Byron Barton
Aladdin, $5.99, 32 pages
First published in 1980
Ages 4–8

A young boy's anxiety about moving from Manhattan to the West is manifested in some outrageous fears about his new life. With all those roaming buffalo, how does a boy play baseball? How will he travel to and from school when he doesn't know how to ride a horse? It's only upon his arrival in the strange and foreign land of the West that he realizes that it isn't quite as strange and foreign as he thought. This perceptive story explores children's fears without an ounce of condescension. Marjorie Weinman Sharmat is the author of the *Nate the Great* series (see "Chapter Books").

The Girl Who Loved Wild Horses
Written and Illustrated by Paul Goble
Aladdin, $5.99, 30 pages
First published in 1978
Ages 4–9

A Native American girl feels a deep affinity for the wild horses that roam her homeland. While she has great respect for her people, she can only feel truly free amongst her equine friends. This astonishing story of following one's dreams is a **Caldecott Medal** winner. Paul Goble is the author of a number of native tales, including *Adopted by the Eagles*; *Crow Chief: A Plains Indian Story*; *Death of the Iron Horse*; and *Iktomi and the Boulder: A Plains Indian Story* (detailed in this chapter).

The Best Children's Literature
A Parent's Guide

Chapter Three

The Giving Tree
Written and Illustrated by Shel Silverstein
HarperCollins, $15.95, 57 pages
First published in 1964
Ages 5–12 (and beyond!)

The lasting joys of this touching parable are measured by the number of grown-ups who vividly recall its story, in which a tree extends repeated acts of generosity to a young boy as he grows into adulthood. The illustrations are simple, and couldn't be more effective. The look of the book, in its signature green hardcover, hasn't changed much since its publication nearly 40 years ago. Also by Silverstein, *Falling Up*; *A Giraffe and a Half*; *A Light in the Attic* (see "Nonfiction, Poetry"); *The Missing Piece*; and *Where the Sidewalk Ends*.

Featured Author: Shel Silverstein
The late Shel Silverstein was a man of many talents. A poet, songwriter, author and illustrator, his work has a quiet insistence that has left an indelible mark on children's literature and popular culture. His first book, **The Giving Tree**, was rejected by several publishers who felt that it was a bit too subtle to appeal to children. After its release in 1964, Silverstein proved his editors wrong, selling thousands of copies worldwide. Collections of poetry such as **A Light in the Attic** and **Where the Sidewalk Ends** demonstrate Silverstein's facility with realism and silly rhyme. The funny, and sometimes scary, parts of being a child are reflected in his jubilant verse.

Glasses: Who Needs 'Em?
Written and Illustrated by Lane Smith
Puffin, $5.99, 32 pages
First published in 1991
Ages 4–8

Visiting the eye doctor can be daunting, and the little boy in this story insists that he doesn't need glasses. The comically blurry illustrations betray his adamant stance, until the doctor points out all of the famous people—inventors, actors, stunt people—who have donned specs. In the end everything, including the illustrations, becomes clear. Children who need glasses will find that this witty tale puts matters into focus. Smith is the author of *Flying Jake* and *The Happy Hocky Family*.

Story Books

The Glorious Flight:
Across the Channel with Louis Blériot

Written and Illustrated by Alice and Martin Provensen
Puffin, $6.99, 39 pages
First published in 1987
Ages 5–9

Louis Blériot was a man with a mission. Fascinated by flying machines, he designed the first flyer able to withstand a trip across the English Channel. This **Caldecott Medal**–winning book describes his plan and recreates his exciting journey in vivid detail that will please the science-minded, especially those with an eye on aviation. Alice Provensen is the author of *The Buck Stops Here: The Presidents of the United States* and *The Year at Maple Hill Farm*.

Goin' Someplace Special

Written by Patricia McKissack,
Illustrated by Jerry Pinkney
Atheneum, $16.00, 34 pages
First published in 2001
Ages 4–9

parent's guide choice award

Compelling scenes from McKissack's own childhood comprise this stunning story of a young girl who, after gaining permission to travel downtown unaccompanied, witnesses the pervasive injustice of the segregated south. She arrives "someplace special"—the racially integrated public library—with weighty matters to consider, but a newfound freedom. Also look for *Richard Wright and the Library Card* by William Miller (see "Nonfiction, African American").

The Golden Sandal: A Middle Eastern Cinderella Story

Written by Rebecca Hickox, Illustrated by Will Hillenbrand
Holiday House, $6.95, 32 pages
First published in 1998
Ages 5–9

Set in Iraq, this version has many of the same motifs as Perrault's familiar fairy tale, in slightly different forms. In place of a fairy godmother is a red fish that Maha, our Cinderella, rescues and from whom she receives gifts and advice. While the props may be different, kids will recognize the enchanting story. Also look for *The Egyptian Cinderella* by Shirley Climo, illustrated by Ruth Heller.

Chapter Three

Golem

Written and Illustrated by David Wisniewski
Clarion, $16.00, 32 pages
First published in 1996
Ages 5–10

In 16th century Prague, Rabbi Judah Loew created a clay giant, a golem. He was trying to protect the Jewish people from certain punishment due to a widespread fabrication known as "the blood lie" (the myth that Jews mixed the blood of Christian children into their matzoh). The story that follows is immensely powerful and suspenseful, made more awesome by Wisniewski's elaborate cut-paper illustrations. This is a story that has all the qualities of the best folk tales, while making a strong statement about the dangers of religious persecution. Wisniewski is the author of *Elfwyn's Saga*; *Rain Player* (in this chapter); and *Sundiati: Lion King of Mali*.

Grandfather Tang's Story

Written by Ann Tompert, Illustrated by Robert Andrew Parker
Crown, $6.99, 32 pages
First published in 1990
Ages 4–9

A tangram is a square that can be divided into seven shapes. The resulting patterns are used as part of a traditional form of Chinese storytelling. In this episode a young girl and her grandfather devise a story using tangrams that eventually take the form of an old man and girl resting under a tree.

Grandfather's Journey

Written and Illustrated by Allen Say
Houghton Mifflin, $16.95, 32 pages
First published in 1993
Ages 4–9

This exquisite tribute follows the author's grandfather from his early adulthood in Japan through his arrival in America. After reaching his destination, he travels throughout the states, marrying and raising a child in California, before revisiting his homeland. The author makes a journey of his own toward the end of the book, mirroring his grandfather's restless search for home. Allen Say is also the author of *El Chino*, the story of a Chinese-American bullfighter, as well as *Home of the Brave* and *Stranger in the Mirror*, among others.

Story Books

Grandmother Bryant's Pocket

Written by Jacqueline Briggs Martin, Illustrated by Petra Mathers
Sandpiper, $5.95, 48 pages
First published in 1996
Ages 5–9

Sarah is grief stricken after her adored dog dies in a barn fire. After suffering nightmares, she is sent to visit her grandparents for a rest cure. Grandmother Bryant presents Sarah with a "pocket" (a small purse) filled with herbs, bandages, and two gold buttons, but it's her grandfather's wisdom, "There are no quick cures," that resonates. Sarah takes comfort in a one-eyed cat that comes to sleep on her pillow at night. Her own act of bravery, in retrieving the purse after it is stolen, further restores her spirits. This is a loving, soothing, and wise story that will echo in reader's hearts for many years. Also by this author, *Good Times on Grandfather Mountain* and *Snowflake Bentley*.

Grandpa's Corner Store

Written by DyAnne DiSalvo-Ryan
HarperCollins, $15.95, 36 pages
First published in 2000
Ages 4–8

When a big supermarket moves into town and threatens to put Grandpa out of business, Lucy and her neighbors rally to protect the cozy corner store. It's a familiar scenario these days as superstores devour their smaller, independent competitors. There's a moving spirit of community pride in this lovely story that will inspire your family to support local business. DiSalvo-Ryan is also the civic-minded author of *City Green* and *Uncle Willie and the Soup Kitchen*.

The Great Kapok Tree: A Tale of the Amazon Rain Forest

Written and Illustrated by Lynne Cherry
Voyager, $7.00, 39 pages
First published in 1990
Ages 4–8

The kapok tree becomes a beleaguered symbol of environmental devastation in this beautifully rendered tale. A man falls asleep while attempting to cut down a kapok. The rainforest residents—snakes, a jaguar, a child—whisper in his ear about the danger of eliminating trees until the man awakens and departs from the forest with a newfound respect, leaving his ax behind. Cherry is the enchanting author of *The Armadillo from Amarillo* as well as the ecologically-inspired, *The Dragon and the Unicorn* and *A River Ran Wild* (in this chapter).

Chapter Three

Gregory's Shadow

Written and Illustrated by Don Freeman
Viking, $15.99, 32 pages
First published in 2000
Ages 4–7

Published posthumously, the author of the beloved *Corduroy* (see "Picture Books") and *Norman the Doorman* (in this chapter) created another character with the same potential for enduring childhood adoration. Gregory is a groundhog who derives courage from his shadow, a lively figure that sticks close by his side. One day, Gregory accidentally leaves his shadow behind, but they are joyfully reunited in time for Groundhog Day. An excellent introduction to the February 2nd festivities for preschoolers and children in the early elementary grades.

Gulliver in Lilliput

Retold by Margaret Hodges from **Gulliver's Travels** by Jonathan Swift,
Illustrated by Kimberly Bulcken Root
Holiday House, $6.95, 32 pages
First published in 1995
Ages 5–9

Swift's famous tale of *Gulliver's Travels*—complete with Lilliputians—is made accessible for the youngest readers in this storybook adaptation. There's a lot of humor and wit in the meticulously detailed illustrations.

Hansel and Gretel

Written by Rika Lesser, Illustrated by Paul O. Zelinsky
Putnam, $6.99, 40 pages
First published in 1984
Ages 4–9

With a vision that is true to the original Grimm tale, Lesser and Zelinsky have fashioned an entrancing, woodsy, and brilliantly executed story book. A **Caldecott Honor** recipient, the famous lost siblings are not given the gentler treatment of latter day versions but, rather, a rich drama that befits the enduring lore.

Story Books

Harvey Potter's Balloon Farm

Written by Jerdine Nolan, Illustrated by Mark Buehner
Mulberry, $5.95, 32 pages
First published in 1994
Ages 4–9

Harvey (no relation to Harry, Harvey came first!) is the proprietor of a balloon farm where he grows 'em made-to-order, in all shapes and colors. What's his secret? That's what the young narrator, a little girl who lives in Harvey's neighborhood, stays up late to find out.

Hattie and the Wild Waves: A Story from Brooklyn

Written and Illustrated by Barbara Cooney
Puffin, $6.99, 40 pages
First published in 1990
Ages 4–8

With old-fashioned charm, Cooney relates the story of her mother who, as a young girl, dreamed of becoming a painter. Set in the early 20th century, Hattie's wealthy and mannered, yet affectionate, family moves between their Brooklyn home and seaside summer retreats. Hattie looks to the wide ocean for inspiration, determined to pursue her unconventional goals. Cooney is the author of *Chanticleer and the Fox* and *Eleanor* (see "Nonfiction, Biography"), as well as *Island Boy* and *Miss Rumphius* (in this chapter).

Heather Has Two Mommies

Written by Leslea Newman, Illustrated by Diana Souza
Alyson Wonderland, $8.95, 36 pages
First published in 1989
Ages 4–9

While it created a bit of a stir upon its release, the simple fact is that this book addresses a need, and it does it with sensitivity, realism, and affection. Heather's parents are two women, and as the little girl examines her friends' families, she notices the difference. Her mommies provide age-appropriate explanations about Heather's conception and birth. Most importantly, they provide a framework for Heather's understanding of different types of families. Also by Newman, *Too Far Away to Touch* (in this chapter), and *Gloria Goes to Gay Pride*. Along similar inclusive lines are *Daddy's Roommate* by Michael Willhoite; *Lucy Goes to the Country* by Joe Kennedy; and *Anna Day and the O-Ring* by Elaine Wickens.

Chapter Three

Henry's First-Moon Birthday
Written by Lenore Look, Illustrated by Yumi Heo
Atheneum, $16.00, 40 pages
First published in 2001
Ages 3–7

It's time for Jen's baby brother's one-month birthday party, with all of the customary Chinese rituals that surround it. Jen enthusiastically tells readers about the decorations, foods, and presents that are part of the celebration. Buoyed by her special role as "older sister," Jen takes special pride in the preparations. A sensitive, unique portrayal of a cultural tradition, this story will be savored by all preschoolers, particularly those with baby siblings. Also by Lenore Look, *Love as Strong as Ginger*.

Hey, Al
Written by Arthur Yorinks, Illustrated by Richard Egielski
Farrar, Straus and Giroux, $5.95, 32 pages
First published in 1986
Ages 4–8

Al is a janitor who lives with his dog, Eddie, in a tiny Manhattan apartment. It's hard to make ends meet, so when a mysterious bird appears at their window, offering the chance to visit a place where there are "no worries," Al gratefully accepts. However, upon close inspection of paradise, Al realizes that home is where the heart is. The depiction of Al's cluttered quarters in contrast with the lush island landscape is superb and earned a **Caldecott Medal** for Egielski. Other books by Arthur Yorinks include *Company's Coming* and its apt sequel *Company's Going*, as well as *Oh, Brother*.

If You Should Hear a Honey Guide
Written by April Pulley Sayre,
Illustrated by S.D. Schindler
Sandpiper, $5.95, 32 pages
First published in 1995
Ages 5–9

parent's guide
choice award

A honey guide is a small East African bird with a big appetite for honeycombs. When it is unable to gain access to its favorite sweet treat, it emits a special call that honey badgers and humans have come to recognize as a way to locate sources of honey. This amazing adaptive behavior is the subject of this wonderful book, with muted, earthy illustrations that perfectly capture the vast African landscape. Also by this author, *Home at Last: A Song of Migration* (see "Nonfiction, Animals"); *Shadows*; and *Splash! Splash! Animal Baths* among other informative and entertaining titles for budding naturalists.

Story Books

Iktomi and the Boulder
Written and Illustrated by Paul Goble
Orchard Books, $6.95, 32 pages
First published in 1991
Ages 4–8

Iktomi gives new meaning to the term, "fair weather friend," and this Plains Indians trickster tale is one of Goble's finest. After shedding his blanket on a hot day, Iktomi rather ungraciously gives it to a boulder. When the nights turn cold, however, Iktomi asks for the return of the blanket, incurring the boulder's wrath. You'll find more about this Indian giver in *Iktomi and the Buffalo Skull*; *Iktomi and the Buzzard*; and *Iktomi and the Coyote*. Goble is also the author of *The Girl Who Loved Wild Horses* (in this chapter).

Ira Sleeps Over
Written and Illustrated by Bernard Waber
Houghton Mifflin, $5.95, 48 pages
First published in 1972
Ages 4–9

Waber, with his keen wit and wisdom, has created some unforgettable characters. Here, he has fashioned a story that is deeply rooted in a child's feelings. Ira is everychild, excited by the prospect of spending the night at his friend Reggie's house, but also wanting to bring a bit of home with him—his adored teddy bear—even though Reggie lives just next door. Also look for *Ira Says Goodbye*. Other books by Waber include *Do You See a Mouse?* (in Picture Books); *A Firefly Named Torchy*; *Lyle, Lyle, Crocodile* and its sequels (in this chapter); and *The Mouse That Snored*.

Is This a House for Hermit Crab?
Written by Megan McDonald, Illustrated by S. D. Schindler
Orchard Books, $6.95, 32 pages
First published in 1990
Ages 3–7

With playful alliteration and simple uncluttered illustrations, the hermit crab's search for shelter is adeptly explored. The text is rhythmic, inviting young readers to repeatedly ask the title question, and the ending is appropriately comforting. A wonderful story that introduces an intriguing concept, which early elementary-aged children engaged in marine life curriculum will want to share with their classmates. McDonald is also the author of *The Bone Keeper*; *Insects Are My Life*; and *The Night Iguana Left Home*.

Chapter Three

Jack and the Beanstalk
Written and Illustrated by Steven Kellogg
Mulberry, $6.95, 40 pages
First published in 1991
Ages 4–9

Kellogg's wildly elaborate illustrations put a new spin on Joseph Jacob's classic tale. The giant takes the form of a grotesque ogre, and Jack must face him down in order to carry home the riches. There's plenty to admire, gasp, and giggle about in this raucous retelling. Also by Kellogg, *Chicken Little*; *Give the Dog a Bone*; *The Island of the Skog*; *Johnny Appleseed*; and *Pecos Bill: A Tall Tale* (in this chapter).

Jamela's Dress
Written and Illustrated by Niki Daly
Farrar Straus & Giroux, $16.00, 31 pages
First published in 1999
Ages 4–8

Jamela cannot resist parading through the South African streets swathed in the beautiful fabric her mother has purchased to make herself a dress for an upcoming wedding. The young girl struts her stuff as the children chant, "Kwela Jamela African Queen!" When she notices that her makeshift cloak has become torn and dirty, she fears an altercation with Mama is imminent. All is well, however, in an ending that befits the young queen-for-a-day. This irresistible character reappears in *What's Cooking, Jamela?* Niki Daly is the author of other enchanting stories set in his native South Africa, including *The Boy on the Beach*; *Not So Fast Songololo*; and *Papa's Lucky Shadow*.

Jocasta Carr, Movie Star
Written and Illustrated by Roy Gerrard
Farrar Straus & Giroux, $4.95, 32 pages
First published in 1992
Ages 4–9

Surrounded by a droll vision of old Hollywood, Jocasta Carr, the celebrated movie starlet, sets forth on a mission to rescue her kidnapped dog. The adventure takes her over land and sea, until she and her companion are joyfully reunited. Jocasta is a spunky superstar—a winning combination of Little Orphan Annie and Shirley Temple—and is bound to become a legendary figure in your household. Also by Roy Gerrard, the ingenious *Croco'nile*; *Mik's Mammoth*; and *The Roman Twins*.

Story Books

John Henry
Written by Julius Lester, Illustrated by Jerry Pinkney
Puffin, $6.99, 40 pages
First published in 1994
Ages 5–9

John Henry is a larger than life mythical figure whose battle with a steam drill sealed his legendary status. Lester and Pinkney portray him with awe and respect, while imparting a message about determination and the value of making the most of every moment. Lester is the author of *The Blues Singers: Ten Who Rocked the World* and *From Slave Ship to Freedom Road* (both in Nonfiction, African-American) as well as the important updated tale of *Sam and the Tigers: A New Telling of Little Black Sambo* and *To Be a Slave*.

Joseph Had a Little Overcoat
Written and Illustrated by Simms Taback
Viking, $15.99, 36 pages
First published in 1999
Ages 4–8

A Yiddish folk song is given effusive due through Taback's extraordinary die-cut artwork and energetic text. When Joseph's coat of many colors becomes tattered, he spins the material into a sequential array of smaller garments. Also see Taback's irrepressible *There Was an Old Lady Who Swallowed a Fly* (detailed in "Picture Books").

Julius, the Baby of the World
Written and Illustrated by Kevin Henkes
Mulberry, $5.95, 32 pages
First published in 1995
Ages 3–7

The arrival of a new baby is a source of wonder and, sometimes, dismay for a young child. Henkes' story runs the gamut of emotions with great humor and sensitivity. Ask the stork to deliver this bundle of joy. Also by the hilarious Henkes, *The Biggest Boy*; *Chester's Way*; *Circle Dogs* (detailed in Picture Books); as well as *Lilly's Purple Plastic Purse* and *Chrysanthemum* (both in this chapter).

Chapter Three

Jumanji

Written and Illustrated by Chris Van Allsburg
Houghton Mifflin, $17.95, 31 pages
First published in 1981
Ages 5–9

In this **Caldecott Medal** winner, two children bring home a mysterious board game they find in the park. When the game's jungle animal characters spring to life, the kids must account for the sudden appearance of mischievous monkeys, stampeding rhinoceros, and a marauding lion. Van Allsburg's finely detailed illustrations and nail-biting narrative contribute to his ability to create stories that straddle the fine line between fantasy and reality. He is also the author of the beloved winter tale, *The Polar Express* (in this chapter); as well as *Just a Dream*; *Two Bad Ants*; and *The Widow's Broom*.

June 29, 1999

Written and Illustrated by David Wiesner
Clarion, $5.95, 32 pages
First published in 1992
Ages 5–9

While the title date may have come and gone, Wiesner's world of perfect absurdity lives on! Here, a young girl named Holly Evans launches weather balloons carrying vegetable seedlings into the sky. When, at the end of the following month, people across America begin spotting giant hovering vegetables—calamitous cucumbers and amazing artichokes—Holly wonders how her innocent experiment took on such epic proportions. Other must-reads by Wiesner include *The Three Pigs* and *Tuesday* (both in this chapter), as well as *Free Fall* and *Sector 7*.

Featured Author: David Wiesner

Creating a fantastic splash in children's literature, David Wiesner has earned critical acclaim—he's received three Caldecott Medals—as well as a loyal following. Wiesner's fans are thrilled by his ingenious stories of fantasy and his droll spin on familiar fairy tales. Sometimes spooky, often funny, and always incredibly imaginative, it's likely that this author/illustrator will find millions of new fans in the new millennium.

Story Books

Kate and the Beanstalk
Written by Mary Pope Osborne, Illustrated by Giselle Potter
Atheneum, $16.00, 35 pages
First published in 2000
Ages 4–8

Here's a version of a famous fairy tale with a feminist twist. In this retelling, it's Kate, not Jack, who must foil the giant in order to bring treasures home to her poor mother and avenge her father's death. By the end of the vividly reconstructed tale, Kate will have earned favorite action hero status in your children's eyes. Students in the early elementary grades will become quite familiar with Mary Pope Osborne, as she is the author of the immensely popular *Magic Tree House* series (see Easy Readers) and a contributor to the *My America* series. She has also penned several compelling nonfiction titles for older children. Other spunky heroines like Kate can be found in *Princess Furball* by Charlotte Huck (in this chapter); *The Good Little Girl* by Lawrence David; and *The Twelve Dancing Princesses* by Jane Ray.

King Midas and the Golden Touch
Written by Charlotte Craft, Illustrated by K. Y. Craft
Morrow, $15.95, 32 pages
First published in 1999
Ages 4–9

A lavish medieval kingdom is the setting for the cautionary tale of a king who wishes for gold at his fingertips. The moral is useful and often cited, but it's the mother and daughter Craft team that brings special nuances to this version, which is truly a sensory delight. Pair this title with *A Medieval Feast* by Aliki.

Lilly's Purple Plastic Purse
Written and Illustrated by Kevin Henkes
Greenwillow, $15.95, 32 pages
First published in 1996
Ages 4–8

Little fashion plate Lilly arrives at school decked out in red cowboy boots, glamorous sunglasses, and a purple purse that plays music when opened. She gets into trouble with her revered teacher Mr. Slinger, who takes away the tuneful tote. Lilly's plan for revenge backfires, and she must devise a plan to set things straight. Once again, Henkes gets high marks for creating adorable, yet quite realistic, characters and plot lines. His other books include *Chester's Way*; *Circle Dogs* (in "Picture Books"); *Chrysanthemum*; and *Julius, the Baby of the World* (both in this chapter).

Chapter Three

Linnea in Monet's Garden
Written by Christina Bjork, Illustrated by Lena Anderson
Farrar Straus Giroux, $14.00, 52 pages
First published in 1987
Ages 4–8

Linnea visits Paris and sees many of Claude Monet's glorious paintings in a museum. When she has the opportunity to visit Giverny, Monet's house and gardens, she begins to understand the source of his inspiration as the most famous of Impressionist painters. A lovely introduction to art for young children. You'll also want to look for *Linnea's Almanac* and *Linnea's Windowsill Garden*.

Lon Po Po: A Red Riding Hood Story from China
Written and Illustrated by Ed Young
Paper Star, $6.99, 30 pages
First published in 1989
Ages 4–8

Three young girls must match wits with a wicked wolf who arrives at the door dressed as dear PoPo, their grandmother. There's drama and mystique in this page-turner by Ed Young, whose story should ring familiar fairy tale bells with young children. The **Caldecott Medal** winning illustrations are astonishingly beautiful. Young is the author of other enchanting Chinese tales such as *Cat and Rat: The Legend of the Chinese Zodiac* and *Monkey King*, as well as *Seven Blind Mice* (in this chapter).

The Lorax
Written and Illustrated by Dr. Seuss
Random House, $14.95, 64 pages
First published in 1971
Ages 4–9

Long a staple of curriculum that raises environmental awareness, Dr. Seuss's masterfully fashioned story uses his famously capricious characters and rhymes to raise a red flag about pollution. The once villainous, now repentant, Once-ler, tells of a world he used to greedily pillage, chopping down Truffula Trees at a whim. The Lorax was the trees' appointed spokes-creature, warning Once-ler about the devastation he was causing. Ultimately, the Lorax throws his hands up in dismay, leaving behind only a rock, engraved with the warning "UNLESS." Clearly, environmental concerns were on Dr. Seuss's mind in the early 1970s but, true to form, the story ends with a glimmer of hope.

Story Books

The famous books by the good Dr. typically defy classification, but you'll find *The Cat in the Hat*; *Green Eggs and Ham*; and *One Fish Two Fish Red Fish Blue Fish* in Picture Books. *Oh, the Places You'll Go* is detailed in this chapter. Look in the "Easy Readers" chapter, under "Beginner Books," for additional titles.

Lucy's Summer
Written by Donald Hall, Illustrated by Michael McCurdy
Browndeer Press, $6.00, 40 pages
First published in 1995
Ages 5–9

As refreshing as a cool breeze, this slice of life story takes place in 1910 when Lucy and her family spend the summer on a New Hampshire farm. Each day's experiences are joyful revelations, told with a fond nostalgia that will cause young readers to wonder at the simple pleasures of these bygone days. Hall is also the author of *I am the Dog, I am the Cat*; *The Milkman's Boy*; and *The Ox-Cart Man* (in this chapter).

Lyle, Lyle Crocodile
Written and Illustrated by Bernard Waber
Houghton Mifflin, $5.95, 48 pages
First published in 1965
Ages 4–8

Lyle lives with the Primms on Manhattan's Upper East Side and is a welcome addition to the household. Things become a bit rocky when Lyle accidentally angers their aptly named neighbor, Mr. Grumps, who then sends the crying crocodile to the Central Park Zoo. Lyle eventually becomes a hero and his winning ways make him the most respected reptile in New York, even in the eyes of the Grumps' cantankerous cat, Loretta. The story started with *The House on East 88th Street* and continues with *Lovable Lyle*; *Lyle at the Office*; *Lyle Finds His Mother*; and *Funny, Funny Lyle*. Waber is also the author of the irresistible *Ira Sleeps Over* (in this chapter); *Do You See a Mouse* (in "Picture Books"); and *A Firefly Named Torchy*.

Chapter Three

Mama, Do You Love Me?
Written and Illustrated by Barbara M. Joosse
Chronicle, $14.95, 26 pages
First published in 1991
Ages 4–8

A young Inuit girl asks for words of reassurance from her Mama, testing the limitless boundaries of her love. The simple text subtly informs readers about Inuit customs, and there's a glossary in the back, providing further explanations. A wonderful choice for snuggling on a cold winter night, or anytime. Also look for *Snow Day!*; *The Morning Chair*; and *Nugget and Darling*.

Mama Zooms
Written and Illustrated by Jane Cowen-Fletcher
Scholastic, $4.95, 32 pages
First published in 1993
Ages 4–8

A loving look at time well spent between a mother with physical disabilities and her son. It's Mama's lively wheelchair maneuvering that entertains the boy as they zip, dart, and dash through a series of adventures. There are few stories that treat the subject of a family member's disabilities with such a positive spirit. You may also want to look for *The Views from Our Shoes: Growing Up with a Brother or Sister with Special Needs* by Donald J. Meyer. Cowen-Fletcher is also the author of *Farmer Will* and *It Takes a Village*.

Many Moons
Written by James Thurber, Illustrated by Louis Slobodkin
Harcourt, $7.00, 48 pages
First published in 1943
Ages 4–9

Princess Lenore sets her sights quite high. She wants the moon, literally. Many royal attendants try to fulfill the princess's lofty dreams, but it is the court jester who finally succeeds. Slobodkin employs the same swirling sky-blues as in *The Hundred Dresses* (see "Easy Readers"), with mesmerizing results. Thurber is the celebrated and witty author of *The Great Quillow*. A selection of his stories can be found in *The Thurber Carnival*.

Martha Speaks

Written and Illustrated by Susan Meddaugh
Hougton Mifflin, $5.95, 32 pages
First published in 1995
Ages 4–9

parent's
guide
choice award

This book has been known to send both children and adults into fits of uncontrollable giggles (this adult is no exception). After Martha, the pet dog, chows down on a bowl of alphabet soup, she becomes suddenly loquacious, uttering every thought that pops into her head. The results are hilarious, as Meddaugh offers a stream of canine consciousness that will leave you howling for more. But will Martha's humans tire of their pontificating pup? You'll find out in *Martha Calling*; *Martha Blah Blah*; *Martha Walks the Dog*; and *Martha and Skits*. Meddaugh is also the author of *The Best Place* and *Hog-Eye*.

A Million Fish, More or Less

Written by Patricia McKissack, Illustrated by Dena Schutzer
Dragonfly, $6.99, 32 pages
First published in 1996
Ages 4–8

While fishing in Louisiana's Bayou Clapateaux with Papa-Daddy and Elder Abbajon, Hugh hears some of the tallest tales around. The storytelling inspires him to create his own legend after his companions depart. He'll claim that he caught a million fish, but the alligators and pirate raccoons demanded their share... and then there was the 20-foot snake! A colorful ode to the oral tradition with a regional flair, McKissack's brand of storytelling is heartily enjoyable. She's also the author of *Goin' Someplace Special* (in this chapter); *Flossie & the Fox*; *The Honest-to-Goodness Truth*; *Ma Dear's Aprons*; *Messy Bessy*; and *Mirandy and Brother Wind* (in this chapter), as well several intriguing biographies of notable African-American figures.

Milo's Hat Trick

Written and Illustrated by Jon Agee
Hyperion Books for Children, $15.95, 32 pages
First published in 2001
Ages 4–8

Milo loves magic but, unfortunately, he's no Houdini. If he doesn't clean up his act, he runs the risk of being ousted from his stage show. An unlikely, and quite accidental, pairing with a friendly bear puts Milo back on the magic track, and Agee's droll drawings perfectly capture the hocus-pocus. Agee is also the author of *The Incredible Painting of Felix Clousseau*.

Chapter Three

Ming Lo Moves the Mountain
Written and Illustrated by Arnold Lobel
Mulberry Books, $5.95, 32 pages
First published in 1993
Ages 4–9

It's not easy living in the shadow of a mountain. Rocks fall on your roof and a giant thundercloud looms above. But when Ming Lo's wife pleads with him to move the next-door-mountain, he decides to consult the village wise man, with ingenious results. Arnold Lobel is the author of *Fables* (in this chapter); *Mouse Soup*; *On Market Street*; *Owl at Home*; and the *Frog and Toad series* (see Easy Readers).

Mirandy and Brother Wind
Written by Patricia McKissack, Illustrated by Jerry Pinkney
Dragonfly, $6.99, 32 pages
First published in 1988
Ages 4–9

Mirandy believes that if she can enlist the help of Brother Wind, she'll be a sure winner in the junior cakewalk. The story is set in the first decade of the 20th century, and Pinkney's gentle watercolors evoke the quiet post-emancipation pride of Mirandy's rural community. This lovely, breezy story is a **Caldecott Honor** and **Coretta Scott King Award** recipient. Also by McKissack, *Goin' Someplace Special* and *A Million Fish, More or Less* (both in this chapter), as well as *Flossie & the Fox*; *The Honest-to-Goodness Truth*; *Ma Dear's Aprons*; and *Messy Bessy*.

Mirette on the High Wire
Written and Illustrated by Emily Arnold McCully
Paperstar, $5.99, 32 pages
First published in 1996
Ages 4–8

parent's
guide
choice award

When a mysterious guest takes a room at the Parisian boarding house that Mirette's mother runs, a whole new world of adventure is opened for the young girl. You see, the elusive Bellini was once a famous tightrope walker, until he lost his nerve. Mirette begins practicing on a backyard high wire, and when Bellini decides to make a daring comeback, it is Mirette who inspires his courage. Elegant and evocative, the **Caldecott Medal** winning illustrations bring to mind the paintings of Toulouse-Latrec. The stunning sequels are *Mirette and Bellini Cross Niagara Falls* and *Starring Mirette and Bellini*. Emily Arnold McCully is also the author of *The Ballot Box Battle*; *The Orphan Singer*; and *Popcorn at the Palace*.

Story Books

Miss Nelson Is Missing!
Written by Harry Allard, Illustrated by James Marshall
Houghton Mifflin, $5.95, 32 pages
First published in 1977
Ages 5–9

The children in Room 207 are fond of Miss Nelson, but take advantage of her kind disposition. When she disappears, they are faced with a nasty substitute, the super-sadistic Miss Viola Swamp. It's only then that they realize just how much they had been taking for granted. But where has Miss Nelson gone? Find out in *Miss Nelson is Back* and *Miss Nelson Has a Field Day*.

Miss Rumphius
Written and Illustrated by Barbara Cooney
Puffin, $6.99, 32 pages
First published in 1982
Ages 4–8

With a painterly knack for portraying bygone eras and worthwhile aspirations (see *Hattie and the Wild Waves* in this chapter), Cooney brings us the story of Alice Rumphius who, as a young girl, receives an important message from her grandfather: "Do something to make the world more beautiful." After living a life of travel and adventure, Miss Rumphius, now an elderly woman, remembers her grandfather's words of wisdom and sets about scattering lupine seeds wherever she goes. Cooney is also the author of the similarly inspired *Island Boy*.

Molly's Pilgrim
Written by Barbara Cohen, Illustrated by Michael Deraney
Beechtree, $3.95, 32 pages
First published in 1983
Ages 5–9

A Jewish-Russian immigrant, Molly has a difficult time making friends as a new student in an American school. As Thanksgiving approaches, Molly's teacher gives her class a special assignment; she asks them to make a Pilgrim doll. Molly fashions a doll that resembles herself, revealing her affinity to the 14th century immigrants that are typically the focus of Thanksgiving curriculum. Her work illuminates the true meaning of the holiday—expanding upon the notion of what it means to be a pilgrim—and earns the awed respect of her classmates. Also look for *Make a Wish, Molly*. Cohen has written a number of stories that reflect the diverse experiences of children in America including *The Carp in the Bathtub* and *213 Valentines*.

Chapter Three

Mufaro's Beautiful Daughters: An African Tale
Written and Illustrated by John Steptoe
Morrow, $16.95, 32 pages
First published in 1987
Ages 4–9

From a Kaffir folk tale springs this lovely Cinderella-esque story. Mufaro has two daughters that differ greatly in temperament. Mean-spirited Manyara taunts Nyasha behind her back, but Nyasha takes the high road and eventually weds the king. Of course, it's Manyara who is sentenced to work as her sister's servant. A noble, beautifully rendered tale.

Nana Upstairs and Nana Downstairs
Written and Illustrated by Tomie de Paola
Puffin, $6.99, 32 pages
First published in 1973
Ages 4–8

The two title nanas are Tommy's grandmother and great-grandmother. The little boy loves to visit both of them, although the elder upstairs nana spends much of her time in bed. When she passes away, Tommy is deeply saddened and turns to his parents for comfort and explanation. This is a lovely personal story, based on de Paola's own childhood, that will help young children come to terms with the death of a loved one. Also look for *Saying Goodbye to Grandma* by Jane Thomas. Other books by the delightful de Paola include *26 Fairmount Avenue* (see "Easy Readers"); *Jamie O'Rourke and the Pooka*; *The Lady of Guadalupe*; *Oliver Button Is a Sissy*; *Pancakes for Breakfast*; and *Strega Nona* (in this chapter), among many others.

Nine O'Clock Lullaby
Written by Marilyn Singer, Illustrated by Frane Lessac
HarperCollins, $6.95, 32 pages
First published in 1991
Ages 4–8

An intriguing look at world cultures that spins around the globe like the hands of a clock. In fact, the story itself is based on the concept of time. Beginning in New York at 9 p.m., readers travel to Puerto Rico, London, Zaire, India, and Switzerland to see what's happening at the very same moment. It's a great concept and while younger children may need some time to gradually grasp it, they'll adore the splashy pictures. Singer is the author of *DiDi and Daddy on the Promenade* (in "Picture Books") and *On the Same Day in March: A Tour of the World's Weather*.

Noah's Ark
Written and Illustrated by Peter Spier
Bantam, Doubleday, Dell, $7.99, 46 pages
First published in 1977
Ages 4–8

This exceptional adaptation of the biblical story earned a **Caldecott Medal** for Spier. There's little text, other than a Dutch ode to the deluge. The ample illustrations speak volumes, however, inviting readers to create their own narration. From the construction of the ark, to lavish sequences portraying the long, harrowing flood, children and adults will marvel at this epic tribute. Spier is the author of *People* (in this chapter) and *Peter Spier's Circus* (in "Picture Books").

Norman the Doorman
Written and Illustrated by Don Freeman
Viking, $5.99, 64 pages
First published in 1987
Ages 4–8

Norman is a dormouse like no other. He guards a mouse hole at the Majestic Museum of Art. In his spare time, he creates his own unique works of art, trying to avoid the cheese-laden traps that are set by the human guards. There's a lot of visual humor and puns, including some masterfully reproduced, and very recognizable, paintings. Freeman is the author of the beloved *Corduroy* (in "Picture Books"), as well as *Gregory's Shadow* (in this chapter).

Now Everybody Really Hates Me
Written by Jane Read Martin and Patricia Marx, Illustrated by Roz Chast
HarperTrophy, $6.95, 32 pages
First published in 1993
Ages 5–8

Patty Jane has sequestered herself in her bedroom, announcing that she'll never come out! She's been banished for bopping her brother, but insists she didn't hit him; she "touched him hard." While she plots sweet revenge, we are treated to a sequence of hilarious illustrations from Chast, a frequent and funny contributor to *The New Yorker*. Martin and Marx are both former *Saturday Night Live* writers, and their comedic savvy is in full evidence here. See their sequel, *Now I Will Never Leave the Dinner Table*.

Chapter Three

Now Let Me Fly: The Story of a Slave Family
Written and Illustrated by Dolores Johnson
Aladdin, $5.99, 32 pages
First published in 1997
Ages 5–9

Minna's life has never been easy. As a child, she was kidnapped and sold into slavery, spending her youth picking cotton. She grows up under the cruelest of circumstances only to witness her husband and children suffer the same imprisonment. The story is haunting, and while Minna is a fictional character, her family represents the thousands of African Americans who endured the brutality of life as slaves. This is an excellent introduction to the topic of slavery for children in the early elementary grades and can be effectively paired with *Tar Beach* by Faith Ringgold, as well as Johnson's own *Seminole Diary: Remembrance of a Slave*.

Oh, the Places You'll Go
Written and Illustrated by Dr. Seuss
Random House, $17.00, 48 pages
First published in 1990
Ages 4 and up (really!)

A favorite gift for graduates, from kindergarten through college, it's no wonder this latter day Seuss story has earned a steady spot on the New York Times bestseller list. With his trademark brand of whimsy, Dr. Seuss offers a commencement speech for the ages, advising readers about the pleasures and pitfalls of life. Most importantly, he decrees in the end, "You're off to Great Places!.. Get on your way!" Look for *The Lorax* (in this chapter); *The Cat in the Hat*; *Green Eggs and Ham*; and *One Fish Two Fish Red Fish Blue Fish* (all in Picture Books). Additional titles are listed in Easy Readers under "Beginner Books."

Story Books

The Other Side

Written by Jacqueline Woodson,
Illustrated by E. B. Lewis
Putnam, $16.99, 32 pages
First published in 2001
Ages 5–9

parent's guide choice award

While a fence stands between them, there is little that can deter the eventual friendship of a young African-American girl and her white neighbor. While each girl's parents forbid them to climb over the barrier, they soon discover that a fence is a perfect place to sit and share thoughts on a hot summer day. Lewis's watercolors are as lovely as Woodson's story, one that offers an important message without weighing the story down in heavy morality. Woodson is the author of *Sweet, Sweet Memory* and *We Had a Picnic This Sunday Past*. Books illustrated by E.B. Lewis include *Big Boy* by Tololwa Mollel (in this chapter) and *I Love My Hair!* by Natasha Anastasia Tarpley.

Owl Moon

Written by Jane Yolen, Illustrated by John Schoenherr
Putnam, $16.99, 32 pages
First published in 1987
Ages 4–8

It's a moment that a child never forgets. One evening, past bedtime, a man asks his young daughter to accompany him on a trek through the snow. They're looking for the Great Horned Owl and together they listen, in the still cold night, for the call of the elusive bird. The ethereal watercolor illustrations earned a **Caldecott Medal** and are so convincing you can fairly feel the chill of the winter night and the warmth of the shared experience. Yolen is the author of *All Those Secrets of the World* (in this chapter); *Beneath the Ghost Moon*; *The Emperor and the Kite*; *The Firebird*; and *How Do Dinosaurs Say Goodnight?* among other story books and dozens of chapter books.

Chapter Three

The Ox-Cart Man

Written by Donald Hall, Illustrated by Barbara Cooney
Puffin, $6.99, 40 pages
First published in 1979
Ages 4–8

This collaboration between acclaimed poet Donald Hall and award-winning illustrator Barbara Cooney is truly a treasure. Set in the early 19th century, this immensely appealing book follows the life of a New England family throughout the seasons. Cooney earned a **Caldecott Medal** for her folk-art illustrations and is best known for *Miss Rumphius* (in this chapter) and *Island Boy*. Hall is the author of *Lucy's Summer* (in this chapter).

Paper John

Written and Illustrated by David Small
Farrar Straus Giroux, $5.95, 32 pages
First published in 1987
Ages 4–8

He's a curious chap, a unique individual. Paper John spends his days in a paper house, crafting paper boats for the village children. A life or death situation puts him in a close encounter with the devil. Will Paper John use his extraordinary skills to ward off further evil? Small is the inventive author of *George Washington's Cows* and *Imogene's Antlers*.

Pecos Bill: A Tall Tale

Written and Illustrated by Steven Kellogg
Morrow, $6.95, 40 pages
First published in 1986
Ages 4–9

The legend of the wild Texan is alive and well in Kellogg's action packed depiction. As a young 'un, Bill is raised by coyotes. He battles rattlesnakes and meets his match in Slewfoot Sue, who becomes his wife. Pair this tall tale with *Bill Pickett: Rodeo-Ridin' Cowboy* by Andrea Pinkney. Kellogg is the author of *A-Hunting We Will Go* (in "Picture Books"); *Chicken Little*; *The Island of the Skog*; *Jack and the Beanstalk* (in this chapter); and *Pinkerton, Behave!* (and its several sequels).

Story Books

Peeping Beauty

Written and Illustrated by Mary Jane Auch
Holiday House, $6.95, 32 pages
First published in 1993
Ages 4–8

A chicken versus fox plot with a refreshing reversal, Auch brings us the story of a little hen named Poulette who dreams of becoming a prima ballerina. A fox passes himself off as a talent scout, and Poulette, lured by the image of her name in lights, follows him to New York. When his ravenous intentions are finally revealed, Poulette pitches a fit, delivering a swift kick worthy of a karate master. Adults and children alike will be charmed and bemused by their favorite new hero-hen. Watch her dance into the sunset in *Hen Lake*. Also by Auch, *Bird Dogs Can't Fly*; *The Easter Egg Farm*; and *The Nutquacker*.

People

Written and Illustrated by Peter Spier
Doubleday, $12.95, 44 pages
First published in 1980
Ages 4–10

The colorful crowd on the front cover speaks volumes about this distinguished book. Acknowledging the differences between the billions of people in the world, the straightforward text and finely detailed pictures examine our varied skin colors, food preferences, clothing, and lifestyles. The message is clear: diversity is what makes the world go round. Along similar (but different!) lines, look for *The Colors of Us* by Karen Katz and *All Kinds of Children* by Norma Simon (in "Picture Books"). Spier is the gifted author and illustrator of *Noah's Ark* (in this chapter); *Peter Spier's Circus* (in "Picture Books"); and *Peter Spier's Rain*.

Chapter Three

The People Could Fly: American Black Folktales
Written by Virginia Hamilton, Illustrated by Leo and Diane Dillon
Knopf, $13.00, 178 pages
First published in 1985
Ages 5–9

A collection to grace any child's bookshelves, the highly acclaimed Hamilton has assembled an astonishing array of lively, vibrant, and provocative stories from rich and varied African-American experiences. Electric illustrations by the Dillons provide a powerful dimension to the proud tales. This book was a recipient of the **Coretta Scott King Award**. Hamilton perpetuates oral tradition in *Her Stories: African-American Folk Tales; Fairy Tales and True Tales* (see "Nonfiction, African-American"). Her other books include *The House of Dies Drear; M.C. Higgins the Great*; and *The Planet of Junior Brown* (all in "Chapter Books"), as well as *Sweet Whispers, Brother Rush*.

Peppe the Lamplighter
Written by Elisa Bartone, Illustrated by Ted Lewin
Mulberry, $5.95, 32 pages
First published in 1997
Ages 5–9

With illustrations that give new meaning to the word "luminous," here's a unique story with wide appeal. Peppe is an immigrant who lives in Manhattan's Little Italy at the turn of the 20th century. His family is poor, and he takes a job lighting the lampposts in his neighborhood. Although his Papa is ill, he is disappointed and ashamed that his son should have such a menial vocation. It becomes clear, however, that Peppe's hard work is deeply appreciated. Ted Lewin received a **Caldecott Honor** for his radiant art.

The Philharmonic Gets Dressed
Written by Karla Kuskin, Illustrated by Marc Simont
Harper & Row, $5.95, 46 pages
First published in 1982
Ages 4–9

The 105 members of the philharmonic are gearing up for a performance! It's a Friday evening and the musicians (92 men and 13 women) are bathing, shaving, dressing, and departing for the concert hall. At 8:30 pm, after all of their preparation, they finally begin to play, and readers can nearly hear the beautiful sounds. Also by Kuskin, *The Animals and the Ark; City Dog*; and *I Am Me*. Simont has lent his artistry to *A Tree Is Nice* by Janice Udry (in Picture Books) and the *Nate the Great* series by Marjorie Weinman Sharmat (in Easy Readers).

Story Books

Pink and Say

Written and Illustrated by Patricia Polacco
Philomel, $16.99, 48 pages
First published in 1994
Ages 4–9

An interracial friendship between two teenaged soldiers in the Civil War is at the heart of this moving story. Pink's family were slaves in Georgia, and after saving young Say's life, he brings the injured boy home to be cared for by Pink's mother. Their bond deepens as Say teaches Pink to read but is cut tragically short when the boys are hauled off to Andersonville Prison. Say survived, and as Polacco's great-great-grandfather, handed down the inspiration for a story with the brand of quiet, insistent power that has earned the reverence of her many readers. See Featured Author, Patricia Polacco, under *Babushka Baba Yaga,* page TK. Other stories by Polacco include *Appelemando's Dreams; Aunt Chip and the Great Triple Creek Dam Affair; Chicken Sunday; Mrs. Katz and Tush; Rechenka's Eggs;* and *Thank You, Mr. Falker.*

The Polar Express

Written and Illustrated by Chris Van Allsburg
Houghton Mifflin, $18.95, 32 pages
First published in 1985
Ages 4–8

A mystical steam engine takes children on a Christmas Eve journey to meet Santa Claus and his devoted staff in this **Caldecott Medal** winning tale. Having become a standard of holiday storytelling, its sense of magic and wonder are of perennial appeal to children and adults. Also by Van Allsburg, *Bad Day at Riverbend; Ben's Dream; The Garden of Abdul Gasazi; Jumanji* (in this chapter); *Just a Dream; Two Bad Ants;* and *The Z Was Zapped.*

Princess Furball

Written by Charlotte Huck, Illustrated by Anita Lobel
Mulberry, $6.95, unpaged
First published in 1989
Ages 4–8

Putting a spunky spin on the classic Cinderella story, Huck has crafted a feisty and clever heroine who takes steps to shape her own destiny. After learning that her father, the King, promised her hand in marriage to an ogre in exchange for fifty wagons full of silver, the Princess plots her escape and seeks true love. Also by this author, *The Black Bull of Norroway: A Scottish Tale* (see "Chapter Books"), and *Toads and Diamonds.*

Chapter Three

Puss in Boots
Written by Charles Perrault, Illustrated by Fred Marcellino
Farrar Straus Giroux, $8.95, 27 pages
First published in 1990
Ages 4–9

Grand paintings and faithful narrative mark this **Caldecott Honor** recipient's version of the French fairy tale. The youngest son of a poor miller is not thrilled to learn that he has inherited a cat, until the clever pet proves his mettle, turning the young man into a prince who wins the hand of the King's daughter. It's a glorious treatment of a story first told three centuries ago. Also in this chapter, Perrault's *Cinderella*, illustrated by Marcia Brown.

Rain Player
Written and Illustrated by David Wisniewski
Clarion, $6.95, 32 pages
First published in 1991
Ages 4–9

Mixing Mayan folklore with cultural tradition, Wisniewski shares the story of a boy named Pik who challenged the god of rain to a soccer-like game called pok-a-tok in order to spare his village from a potentially devastating drought. This is a truly original tale, enhanced by the fine cut-paper collages in earthy hues, echoing the mystique of nature that inspires the story. Also look for *Elfwyn's Saga*; *The Golem* (in this chapter); *Sundiati: Lion King of Mali*; and *The Wave of the Sea Wolf*.

Rapunzel
Written and Illustrated by Paul O. Zelinsky
Dutton, $16.99, 40 pages
First published in 1997
Ages 4–8

Zelinsky's astounding paintings, in the style of the Italian Renaissance masters, transport readers to an intricately detailed fairy tale world. Imprisoned in a tower for many years, it is Rapunzel's lengthy locks that enable a brave prince to free her. You won't want to miss this **Caldecott Medal** winning interpretation. Also by Zelinsky, *Rumpelstiltskin* and *The Wheels on the Bus* (see Picture Books).

Story Books

Red Fox Running

Written by Eve Bunting, Illustrated by Wendell Minor
Clarion, $5.95, 32 pages
First published in 1993
Ages 4–7

Bunting's rhythmic verse and Minor's haunting illustrations capture the frozen landscape through which a fox must travel in order to feed his family. It's a masterful portrayal of life in the wild, chilling and uncompromising, and thoroughly intriguing. Eve Bunting is the author of many fine works, including *Butterfly House* (in this chapter); *A Day's Work*; *December*; *Flower Garden*; *Fly Away Home* (in this chapter); *How Many Days to America: A Thanksgiving Story*; *Mother's Day Mice*; and *Night of the Gargoyles*.

Rikki-Tikki-Tavi

Written by Rudyard Kipling, Illustrated by Jerry Pinkney
Morrow, $16.95, 48 pages
First published in 1997
Ages 5–9

Set in India, a fearless and loyal mongoose is adopted by a British family. He protects their son from an attack by a savage cobra, and his unflagging bravery is ultimately rewarded. While some of the animal battle scenes can be frightening to young children, Pinkney's treatment of Kipling's cherished story is warm and alluring. Jerry Pinkney has provided illustrations for *Back Home* by Gloria Jean Pinkney; *Goin' Someplace Special* by Patricia McKissack; *Half a Moon and One Whole Star* by Crescent Dragonwagon; *John Henry* by Julius Lester; and *Mirandy and Brother Wind* (all detailed in this chapter), among many others.

A River Ran Wild

parent's guide
choice award

Written and Illustrated by Lynne Cherry
Voyager, $7.00, unpaged
First published in 1992
Ages 4–9

New Hampshire's Nashua River becomes a symbol of bounty, ecological damage, and eventual preservation. Cherry takes readers on a tour through the river's long life, portraying early native peoples by its bank, the deadly effects of 18th and 19th century industrialization, through present day clean-up efforts. Each spread features a detailed border depicting elements of life during the era being portrayed. This is an essential tool for helping children understand the dangers of pollution. Lynne Cherry is the author of *The Armadillo from Amarillo*; *The Dragon and the Unicorn*; *The Great Kapok Tree: A Tale of the Amazon Rain Forest* (in this chapter); and *The Shaman's Apprentice*.

Chapter Three

Sadako

Written and Illustrated by Eleanor Coerr
Putnam, $6.99, 48 pages
First published in 1993
Ages 4–9

This thoughtful picture book adaptation of the esteemed chapter book is truly a gift, and a story to be shared with children of all ages. It's based on the life of a young girl hospitalized in Hiroshima, with "atomic bomb sickness." Her name is Sadako. When she learns that origami cranes are a symbol of long life, she begins an endeavor to fold the requisite amount, 1,000 paper cranes.

Seven Blind Mice

Written and Illustrated by Ed Young
Puffin, $6.99, unpaged
First published in 1992
Ages 4–8

In this clever and thoughtful twist on an Indian folktale, the mice in question use their heightened senses to decipher the identity of a new creature in their midst. This **Caldecott Honor** recipient represents the best in conceptual storytelling, and parents will be delighted by their children's energetic participation as the mystery unfolds. Young is the author of *Lon Po Po: A Red Riding Hood Story from China.*

Snowflake Bentley

Written by Jacqueline Briggs Martin, Illustrated by Mary Azarian
Houghton Mifflin, $16.00, 32 pages
First published in 1998
Ages 4–9

It's hard to capture a snowflake, as young Wilson Bentley discovers, but that doesn't deter a growing fascination with their shapes and sizes. He parlayed this interest into a life's work, becoming a renowned photographer of nature's wonder. In this **Caldecott Medal** winner, there's a subtle message that the most beautiful objects are not always the most permanent.

Story Books

The Stinky Cheese Man and Other Fairly Stupid Tales
Written by Jon Scieszka, Illustrated by Lane Smith
Viking, $16.99, 51 pages
First published in 1992
Ages 5–9

If you're up for the distinctive brand of puckish revelry that Jon Scieszka provides so gloriously well, take a gander at this offbeat collection of fractured fairy tales. Even the book's cover and title pages do not escape sardonic squawking, as the Little Red Hen ponders the eternal question: "Who is this ISBN guy?" Awarded a **Caldecott Honor** for the sight gags and giggles, you'll quickly find an adoring audience in your family. Look to Scieszka for further folly in *The Frog Prince, Continued* (in this chapter); *The True Story of the Three Little Pigs*; *The Math Curse*; and *The Time Warp Trio* series (in "Juvenile Fiction/Chapter Books").

A Story, a Story: An African Tale
Written and Illustrated by Gail E. Haley
Aladdin, $6.99, 36 pages
First published in 1970
Ages 4–9

This African folktale earned a **Caldecott Medal** for its alluring and authentic introduction to the Sky God Nyame and his role in creating all the stories in the world. He kept them locked in a box next to his throne, until the determined Ananse took great pains to gain ownership.

The Story of Babar
Written and Illustrated by Jean De Brunhoff
Random House, $14.95, 48 pages
First published in 1933
Ages 4–9

It's an eloquent, touching tale that has been adored by millions since its publication in 1933. After he escapes the clutches of the hunter who killed his mother, Babar travels to the city where he meets a kind old woman who becomes his benefactor. Truly, Babar is an elephant you'll always remember. Several sequels follow, including *The Travels of Babar*; *Babar and His Children*; *Babar and Father Christmas*; and *Babar the King*.

Chapter Three

Strega Nona

Written and Illustrated by Tomie de Paola
Aladdin, $6.95, 32 pages
First published in 1975
Ages 4–8

Set in an enchanted medieval village, de Paola's story introduces Strega Nona and her faithful friend, Big Anthony. Strega Nona, the witch, has a knack for stirring up some very tantalizing culinary spells. The outstanding prequel is *Strega Nona: Her Story*. Other titles include *Strega Nona Meets Her Match* and *Merry Christmas, Strega Nona*, as well as *Big Anthony: His Story*.

Sylvester and the Magic Pebble

Written and Illustrated by William Steig
Simon & Schuster, $6.99, 32 pages
First published in 1969
Ages 4–8

There's heartbreak and humor, enlivened by Steig's masterful storytelling skills, in this **Caldecott Medal** winning tale. Sylvester is a young donkey who, despite his happy home life, searches for a magic pebble with the power to grant wishes. A series of rather unfortunate consequences leaves Sylvester immobilized in the form of a rock. His distraught parents, meanwhile, search frantically for their son as Sylvester, in stony silence, ponders his fate. The effervescent William Steig is the author of *The Amazing Bone*; *Amos & Boris*; *Doctor DeSoto*; and, of course, that famous ogre of page and screen, *Shrek*.

The Tale of the Mandarin Ducks

Written by Katherine Paterson, Illustrated by Leo and Diane Dillon
Puffin, $6.99, 40 pages
First published in 1990
Ages 4–8

A majestic fable unfolds as Shozo, a Samurai servant and a kitchen maid named Yasuko make the acquaintance of a mandarin duck living in captivity under the rule of a fierce lord. The friends risk their lives to free the drake and come to realize that the power of friendship can overcome trouble. The Dillons' illustrations, resembling Japanese woodcuts, are fantastic.

Story Books

Tar Beach
Written and Illustrated by Faith Ringgold
Dragonfly, $6.99, 32 pages
First published in 1996
Ages 4–9

Cassie picnics with friends on the roof—the tar beach—of her Harlem home and lets her imagination soar as she flies over the city skyline. Ringgold's marvelous story quilts are the star of the literary show, featuring glorious painterly scenes of the young girl's mind journey. Rising high above Manhattan, Cassie gives readers a tour of her family's proud history as we view the awesome George Washington Bridge, which her dad helped build. We also become privy to disappointments and discrimination, as she shows us the union that denied her father membership due to race. It's a poignant journey, rendered by Faith Ringgold's artful signature style.

The Tenth Good Thing about Barney
Written by Judith Viorst, Illustrated by Erik Blegvad
Aladdin, $4.95, 25 pages
First published in 1971
Ages 4–8

After his beloved cat dies, a young boy tries to make sense of his loss by listing the ten best things about his adored pet. It's a lovely, touching story that is also quite useful in terms explaining death, a difficult concept for young children. More tales of love and loss in *The Old Dog* by Charlotte Zolotow.

This Land Is Your Land
Written by Woody Guthrie, Illustrated by Kathy Jakobsen
Little Brown, $15.95, 34 pages
First published in 1998
Ages 4–9

A fitting tribute to the American folk song and landscape as envisioned by Woody Guthrie, there's a lot to admire and consider in this handsome collection. Focusing primarily on the Depression era, Jakobsen's double page folk-art illustrations are uplifting and impressively detailed. The whole package is an excellent celebration of Americana and a unique supplement to studies of the Great Depression.

Chapter Three

The Three Pigs
Written and Illustrated by David Wiesner
Clarion, $16.00, 40 pages
First published in 2001
Ages 4–9

Wiesner puts an ingenious new spin on the huffing and puffing tale of three porcine pals and the wolf who wants to have them for dinner. It's his amazing visual antics that steal the show, as the poor pigs are whisked in and out of the reader's view. At the same time, the familiar story book characters are treated with different styles of illustration as they meander through the pages. It's a true winner and the recipient of a **Caldecott Medal**. Wiesner is also the author of *Tuesday* and *June 29, 1999* (both in this chapter).

Tikki Tikki Tembo
Written by Arlene Mosel, Illustrated by Blair Lent
Henry Holt, $6.95, 42 pages
First published in 1968
Ages 4–8

The famous story of the boy with a proud, unwieldy and, ultimately dangerous name is a rhythmic treat for all ages. The law of the land dictates that his name must always be spoken completely, but when he becomes trapped after falling into a well, help seems unlikely. By the time his would-be rescuers can utter his name, it may too late for Tikki.

Tuesday
Written and Illustrated by David Wiesner
Clarion, $6.95, 32 pages
First published in 1991
Ages 4–9

Would you like to see some fantastic flying frogs? One Tuesday, a group of amphibians find themselves airborne, perched upon their levitating lily pads, much to the surprise of eyewitnesses below. Once again, David Wiesner has crafted a masterful fantasy tale that earned a **Caldecott Medal**. His other titles include *June 29, 1999* and *The Three Pigs* (both in this chapter), as well as *Sector 7*; *Free Fall*; and *Hurricane*.

Story Books

Uptown

Written and Illustrated by Bryan Collier
Henry Holt, $16.95, 32 pages
First published in 2000
Ages 5–9

parent's
guide
choice award

The sights and sounds of Harlem spring to life in this gloriously illustrated book. Using vibrant photographic collages, readers are given an authentic tour of one boy's famous neighborhood. Stops along the way include the Apollo Theater, the Metro-North train, a local basketball game, and shopping on 125th Street. Fans of Ezra Jack Keats will be especially pleased.

Who's Who In My Family

Written and Illustrated by Loreen Leedy
Holiday House, $6.95, 32 pages
First published in 1995
Ages 4–9

Your great grandmother's brother? Your cousin twice removed? Children learn about the members of an extended family in this lovingly rendered book. Family relationships can be a bit confusing to children (and many adults) and Leedy's book examines the family tree with tenderness and clarity. It's a must-read introduction to ancestry, genealogy and heredity. Fine nonfiction from this author includes *Messages in a Mailbox: How to Write a Letter*; *Blast Off to Earth! A Look at Geography*; and *Postcards From Pluto: A Tour of the Solar System*.

Why Mosquitoes Buzz in People's Ears: A West African Tale

Written by Verna Aardema, Illustrated by Leo and Diane Dillon
Puffin, $6.99, 32 pages
First published in 1975
Ages 5–9

A **Caldecott Medal** recipient, this is the cautionary tale of a mosquito who tells a lie that prevents the sun from rising. How the fibbing critter got his buzz is the moral of the story. It's a wonderful introduction to folk legends, featuring the winning illustrations of the dynamic Dillons.

Chapter Three

Zella, Zack and Zodiac
Written and Illustrated by Bill Peet
Houghton Mifflin, $7.95, 32 pages
First published in 1986
Ages 4–8

Baby ostrich Zack, is adopted by Zella, a generous and devoted zebra. Zella's own baby, Zodiac, is a bit lacking in the running department, an important ability for zebras. Zack repays his foster mother by protecting young Zodiac from predators. Clever use of adages and a gentle moral ending add to the story's charm.

Zin! Zin! Zin! A Violin
Written by Lloyd Moss, Illustrated by Marjorie Priceman
Aladdin, $6.99, 32 pages
First published in 1995
Ages 4–8

A booming, stirring, humming and zinging introduction to the orchestra, children see the glorious instruments as the conductor strikes up the band. One by one, we hear the trombone, trumpet and French horn as the sounds of each combine to create a harmonic trio. There's nothing stuffy about classical music here and Marjorie Priceman's illustrations add ample charm.

Chapter Four

Easy Readers

This chapter is organized a bit differently than the others, largely due to a longstanding tradition in the publishing industry: Series titles! Here you'll find many books grouped under their series name (*Magic School Bus, DK Readers*), as well as individual books listed alone (*You Want Women to Vote, Lizzie Stanton?*). There are hundreds of titles to choose from, and you'll find them merchandised in spinning racks or special shelves at your local bookstore or library. The content and quality of these highly accessible books varies greatly, and there are different schools of thought regarding their use. So, what's the real story with Easy Readers?

Easy Readers serve several related purposes. Many are specially designed with controlled vocabulary and grammatical structure, and are intended to boost reading skills according to a set of standards based on national curriculum for language arts. Working within this formula, many of the series are categorized into different reading levels and some even include a glossary. In fact, many teachers use Easy Readers as an integrative part of instruction and assessment. But remember, these are not the "primers" or "Dick and Jane" books that parents remember from their childhoods, but rather a much more contemporary set of stories and concept books that reflect the needs and experiences of today's kids. In other words, Easy Readers provide age-appropriate content—both fiction and nonfiction—that is entertaining, while employing language that is targeted to specific developmental stages.

Chapter Four

During the early- to mid-elementary school years, children's reading skills become generally advanced enough to decode words relatively smoothly so that they are able to comprehend content without repeatedly "getting stuck" on vocabulary. Easy Readers, then, serve as an important transition between story books and chapter books, the latter of which require more advanced reading skills. Because of their specific emphasis on the balance between content and developmental level, Easy Readers can be especially useful for children with special learning needs.

Most importantly, Easy Readers are quite often the first books that your child will read independently, so they need to capture his or her attention. Many of the titles described in this chapter were not necessarily written to fit the Easy Reader mold, but just happen to have the right recipe of age-appropriate content and language usage for early reading success.

26 Fairmount Avenue Series
Written by Tomie de Paola
Puffin, $5.99, 56 pages
First published in 1999
Ages 6–9

The marvelous de Paola takes readers on a sentimental journey back to his childhood home. Both joyful and difficult childhood memories are gently recounted, including young Tomie's first day of kindergarten, their new home's ongoing construction problems, and the hurricane of '38. Perfect for new readers and all fans of Tomie de Paola. Also by this author, *Nana Upstairs and Nana Downstairs* and *Strega Nona* (both in "Story Books"), as well as the continuation of the *26 Fairmount Avenue* series that includes:

- *Here We All Are*
- *On My Way*
- *What a Year!*

Easy Readers

The Adventures of Benny and Watch Series

Written by Gertrude Chandler Warner, Illustrated by Daniel Mark Duffy
Albert Whitman, $3.95 per volume, 40–50 pages each
First published in 1998
Ages 6–10

The popularity of *The Boxcar Children* series led to the creation of these Easy Reader books that focus on the same characters, but are intended for younger readers. Beginning the series with *Meet the Boxcar Children*, young fans follow the antics of Benny and his dog, Watch. Other titles in the series include:

- *Benny Goes into Business*
- *Benny's New Friend*
- *Benny's Saturday Surprise*
- *The Magic Show Mystery*
- *A Present for Grandfather*
- *The Secret under the Tree*
- *Watch Runs Away*

All Aboard Reading Series

Various authors
Grosset & Dunlap, $3.99 per title, 47 pages
First published in 1997
Ages 5–9

With an ever-growing array of titles, this series has something for every reader! Featuring nature studies, history, biography, and fun fiction, the books are grouped into three reading levels that are based on national curriculum standards for vocabulary. Outstanding titles include the following:

- *Bats: Creatures of the Night* by Joyce Milton
- *Butterflies* by Emily Neye
- *Egyptian Gods and Goddesses* by Henry Barker
- *Gargoyles: Monsters in Stone* by Jennifer Dussling, Illustrated by Peter Church
- *Hoop Stars* by S.A. Kramer, Illustrated by Mitchell Heinze
- *Martin Luther King Jr. and the March on Washington* by Frances E. Ruffin, Illustrated by Stephen Marchesi
- *Totem Poles* by Jennifer Frantz, Illustrated by Allan Eitzen

Chapter Four

Amber Brown Is Not a Crayon

Written by Paula Danziger
Apple, $3.99, 80 pages
First published in 1995
Ages 8–11

It looks as though third grade will be another exciting school year for Amber, until she learns that her best friend, Justin, will be moving away. With realistic sentiment and dialogue, Amber and Justin try to come to terms with their sadness, but must first settle an argument that threatens to end their friendship. The series continues with:

- *Amber Brown Goes Fourth*
- *Amber Brown Is Feeling Blue*
- *Amber Brown Sees Red*
- *Amber Brown Wants Extra Credit*

Amelia Bedelia

Written by Peggy Parish, Illustrated by Fritz Seibel
HarperCollins, $3.99, 63 pages
First published in 1963
Ages 5–9

She's clumsy, a bit foolish, and kids love her. As a housekeeper, Amelia tends to take her instructions rather literally, so when her employers instruct her to "draw the drapes," she actually provides a sketch. Amelia's perpetual misunderstandings and close calls make her a long shot in the "employee of the year" category, but her loveable disposition ensures her favored status amongst new readers. Kids really get a kick out of spotting her preposterous errors and deciphering the contextual meanings of various idioms. Also look for:

- *Amelia Bedelia and the Baby*
- *Amelia Bedelia Goes Camping*
- *Amelia Bedelia Helps Out*
- *Amelia Bedelia's Family Album*
- *Teach Us, Amelia Bedelia*

Peggy Parish's nephew, Herman Parish, has extended the series with:

- *Amelia Bedelia 4 Mayor*
- *Bravo, Amelia Bedelia!*
- *Calling Doctor Amelia Bedelia*
- *Good Driving, Amelia Bedelia*

Easy Readers

Parent/Child Review: Amelia Bedelia

The Parent: Anna, Age 44, Social Worker

The Child: Aimee, Age 7, Loves Will Smith

Aimee says: "We've read all of the Amelia Bedelia books like three times. She's funny but she's not as dumb as people think. Or else, why wouldn't she get fired?"

Anna says: "Yep, I read the first book to Aimee when she was four. Now she reads them alone. I'm sure when she's an adult, she'll say that these were some of her favorite kid books. We especially love when she invites everyone on the street to the family party."

Arthur Chapter Books Series

Written and Illustrated by Marc Brown

Little Brown, $3.95 per volume, 58 pages

First published in 1998

Ages 5–9

Stories about the much-adored aardvark have now been extended into an Easy Reader format. Preschoolers become acquainted with Arthur and his sister, D.W., through his ample storybook selections, as well as his popular TV program. Here, new readers can continue to faithfully follow the folly and foibles of their favorite character while honing their newly acquired independent reading skills. Have you read the following?

- *Arthur Accused*
- *Arthur and the Best Coach Ever*
- *Arthur and the Big Blow-Up*
- *Arthur and the Crunch Cereal Contest*
- *Arthur and the Double Dare*
- *Arthur and the Popularity Test*
- *Arthur and the Scare-Your-Pants-Off Club*

Chapter Four

A Word about... Television

Whether you are adamantly anti–TV or a big fan of the tube, children's television can be so much more than just an "electronic babysitter." In fact, combining a healthy diet of quality TV programming with abundantly available book tie–ins is a great way to reach reluctant readers and children with different learning needs. The idea here is balance. Look for programs that invite participation and thought, then encourage children to read books that feature their favorite TV characters. Try watching an episode of **Blue's Clues** with your preschooler, then spend time together reading a volume from its book series. Or tune in to LeVar Burton's wonderful **Reading Rainbow** series or PBS's **Between the Lions** to hear children and familiar characters read aloud from a wide array of lively and diverse stories. Older children should mix video versions of classic literature like **Shiloh** and **James and the Giant Peach** (see "Juvenile Fiction/Chapter Books") into their mix of cartoons and other Nickelodeon favorites. Television, for better or worse, is a big part of kid culture, as are other technological distractions like the Internet and video games. While you may often be tempted to entirely ban TV watching, it will probably be easier to set reasonable limits and to provide your children with easy access to the book versions of these favorites:

- Arthur
- Barney
- Bear in the Big Blue House
- Between the Lions
- Blue's Clues
- Bob the Builder
- Bookworm Bunch
- Caillou

- Clifford
- Dragon Tales
- Franklin
- Little Bear
- Little Bill
- Madeline
- Magic School Bus
- Maisy
- Noddy

- Reading Rainbow
- Redwall
- Sesame Street
- Teletubbies
- Thomas the Tank Engine
- Wishbone
- Zooboomafoo

Easy Readers

A Bear Called Paddington
Written by Michael Bond
Sandpiper, $4.95, 132 pages
First published in 1958
Ages 5–9

The Brown family finds young Paddington in a London train station, donning the now famous sign "Please look after this bear. Thank you." The Browns take these instructions quite seriously, bringing home the bear from "Darkest Peru," and inviting him into the fold with open arms. That's when the fun starts, because Paddington is no ordinary errant bear. His fantastic adventures and offbeat sense of humor (fans of *Amelia Bedelia* will be especially pleased) has charmed the yellow hat off millions of children.

- *More about Paddington*
- *Paddington Abroad*
- *Paddington at Large*
- *Paddington at Work*
- *Paddington Goes to Town*
- *Paddington Helps Out*
- *Paddington on Top*
- *Paddington Takes the Air*

Beginner Books
Various authors and featuring Dr. Seuss!
Random House, $8.99 per volume, 30 pages
First published in 1964
Ages 4–8

You'll find a lot of comforting favorites (hardly altered since your childhood) and more word wizardry from Dr. Seuss and his cohorts in this classic collection. These titles are encouragingly labeled "I Can Read All By Myself," and indeed they will account for some of your children's earliest forays into independent reading. The contagious rhythm guarantees it! For additional Seussian silliness, check the "Picture Book" chapter for *The Cat in the Hat*; *Green Eggs and Ham*; and *One Fish Two Fish Red Fish Blue Fish*. *The Lorax* and *Oh, the Places You'll Go* are featured in "Story Books." *Beginner Books* titles include:

- *Are You My Mother?* Written and Illustrated by P.D. Eastman
- *Dr. Seuss' ABC* Written and Illustrated by Dr. Seuss
- *Hop on Pop* Written and Illustrated by Dr. Seuss
- *I Want to Be Somebody New* Written and Illustrated by Robert Lopshire
- *Ten Apples Up on Top!* by Theo LeSieg, Illustrated by Roy McKie

The Best
Children's Literature
A Parent's Guide

Chapter Four

Berenstain Bears First Time Books

Written by Stan and Jan Berenstain
Random House, $3.25 per volume, 32 pages
First published in 1987
Ages 5–8

The famous bear family is instantly recognizable and has been entertaining children for many years. This Story Book/Easy Reader series bestows the bears with a variety of different dilemmas and, in the process, introduces young children to an assortment of age-appropriate concepts and experiences. Titles include:

- *The Berenstain Bears and Baby Makes Five*
- *The Berenstain Bears and Mama's New Job*
- *The Berenstain Bears and the Bad Habit*
- *The Berenstain Bears and the Homework Hassle*
- *The Berenstain Bears and the Messy Room*
- *The Berenstain Bears and the Trouble with Grown-Ups*
- *The Berenstain Bears and Too Much TV*

Bunnicula: A Rabbit Tale of Mystery

Written by Deborah and James Howe
Aladdin, $3.99, 98 pages
First published in 1979
Ages 7–10

Harold is the Monroe family's dog. He's also the narrator of this winning story in which the family finds a baby bunny while watching Dracula at the movie theater. They name him Bunnicula, of course. Chester the cat becomes immediately suspicious of Bunnicula, accusing him of being a vampire, and goes to great lengths to expel him from the household. You'll also howl for:

- *Bunnicula Strikes Again*
- *The Celery Stalks at Midnight*
- *Howliday Inn*
- *Nightly Nightmare*

Easy Readers

Cam Jansen Mysteries

Written by David A. Adler
Puffin, $3.99 per volume, 50–60 pages each
First published in 1980
Ages 7–10

Here's a series that young mystery buffs will enjoy. Each volume places Cam in the middle of a lively whodunit, as she calls upon her photographic memory to solve crimes. This series is part of the *Puffin Easy-to-Read* series (see additional titles in this chapter). Pick up your magnifying glass and look for the following titles:

- *Cam Jansen and the Library Mystery*
- *Cam Jansen and the Mystery of the Dinosaur Bones*
- *Cam Jansen and the Mystery of the Stolen Diamonds*
- *Cam Jansen and the Mystery of the U.F.O.*
- *Cam Jansen and the Scary Snake Mystery*

Captain Underpants Series

Written by Dav Pilkey
Scholastic, $4.99 per volume, 100–140 pages
First published in 1997
Ages 7–11

Two fourth grade mischief-makers hypnotize their unsuspecting principal, Mr. Krupps, into believing he is a superhero. After he flies out the window, clad only in briefs and a cape, the fun begins. The good-natured slapstick and natural kid appeal have made this series a bestselling phenomenon. After all, when a book cleanly combines potty jokes with clever comic style, it's sure to be a hit. Look for:

- *The Adventures of Captain Underpants*
- *Captain Underpants and the Attack of the Talking Toilets*
- *Captain Underpants and the Invasion of the Incredibly Naughty Cafeteria Ladies from Outer Space*
- *Captain Underpants and the Perilous Plot of Professor Poopypants*
- *Captain Underpants and the Wrath of the Wicked Wedgie Woman*

Chapter Four

Childhood of Famous Americans Ready-to-Read Series

Various authors
Aladdin, $3.99 per volume, 30 pages each (approximately)
First published in 2002
Ages 6–10

Singular moments in the lives of history's brightest stars are revealed in this excellent new series. This is an intriguing entry into biography, made kid-friendly by focusing on the younger years of famous history makers. The books invite readers to examine how important childhood events (or even everyday occurrences) can alter one's destiny. The vocabulary is simple and each book includes a useful timeline. There's also a series for slightly more advanced readers (ages 8-12), entitled *Childhood of Famous Americans*. Titles in the series include:

- *Abe Lincoln and the Muddy Pig* by Stephen Krensky
- *Ben Franklin and His First Kite* by Stephen Krensky
- *Betsy Ross and the Silver Thimble* by Stephanie Greene
- *Sacagawea and the Bravest Deed* by Stephen Krensky

Danny and the Dinosaur

Written and Illustrated by Syd Hoff
HarperCollins, $3.95, 64 pages
First published in 1958
Ages 4–8

Syd Hoff has a clear knack for tickling the funny bone of young readers. This story, written more than 40 years ago, continues to amuse and delight. Young Danny visits the museum and leaves with an unlikely new friend... a dinosaur! Together they parade through the city streets and even play hide-and-seek. No small task for a giant prehistoric animal. Other Easy Readers by Hoff include:

- *Chester*
- *Danny and the Dinosaur Go to Camp*
- *Happy Birthday, Danny and the Dinosaur*
- *The Lighthouse Children*
- *Oliver*
- *Sammy the Seal*

Easy Readers

Dial Easy-to-Read

Various authors
Dial Books for Young Readers, $13.99 per volume, 30–40 pages each
First published in 1992
Ages 6–10

Riddles, fun facts, and spooky stories abound in this eclectic series. The books often use easily remembered poems to impart science and social studies concepts. The nonfiction titles tend to employ appealing photo illustrations and all of the books are lighthearted, thoughtful, and well-suited to children in the early- to mid-elementary grades.

- *The Bookstore Ghost* by Barbara Maitland
- *Breakout at the Bug Lab* by Ruth Horowitz
- *I Am Rosa Parks* by Rosa Parks
- *Sam's Wild West Show* by Nancy Antle
- *Why Do Dogs Bark?* by Joan Holub

DK Readers

Various authors
Dorling Kindersley, $3.95 per volume, 30–50 pages each
First published in 2000
Ages 7–11

You won't find a more inclusive, dynamic collection of Easy Readers anywhere, and DK uses its trademark blend of crisp photography and clear text to great effect in this series. They are divided into different reading levels, and the wide variety of topics will appeal to all mid-elementary grade kids.

- *A Day in the Life of a TV Reporter* by Linda Hayward
- *Bermuda Triangle* by Andrew Donkin
- *Dinosaur Detectives* by Peter Chrisp
- *George Washington: Soldier, Hero, President* by Justine Fontes
- *Horse Show* by Kate Hayden
- *The Story of Muhammad Ali* by Leslie Garrett
- *The Story of Spider-Man* by Michael Teitelbaum
- *Time Traveler: Children Through Time* by Angela Bull
- *Titanic! The Disaster That Shocked the World* by Mark Dubowski

Chapter Four

Frog and Toad Together

Written and Illustrated by Arnold Lobel
HarperTrophy, $3.99, 64 pages
First published in 1973
Ages 6–10

This **Newbery Honor** recipient has all the makings of a classic children's story, and it's no wonder its popularity has endured. It's a heartwarming tale of friendship complete with cozy illustrations. Readers follow Frog and his pal Toad through a series of domestic adventures. Together they bake cookies (and try not to eat all of them), fly kites, and generally spend quality time together. These amiable amphibians will be kept close to your child's heart for many years. Also look for:

- *Days with Frog and Toad*
- *Frog and Toad All Year*
- *Frog and Toad Are Friends*

The Great Brain

Written by John Fitzgerald, Illustrated by Mercer Mayer
Dell, $4.99, 175 pages
First published in 1967
Ages 7–10

With contagious nostalgia and affection, Fitzgerald relates the intellectual adventures of The Great Brain, a memorable character based on the author's older brother. Set in Adenville, Utah, just before the turn of the 20th century, the gentle spirit and simple setting are refreshing and timelessly appealing. Sequels include:

- *The Great Brain at the Academy*
- *The Great Brain Does It Again*
- *The Great Brain Reforms*
- *Me and My Little Brain*
- *More Adventures of the Great Brain*
- *The Return of the Great Brain*

Easy Readers

Green Light Readers

Various authors
Harcourt, $3.95 per volume, unpaged
First published in 1999
Ages 6–10

Populated with exciting stories and diverse nonfiction, the books in this series are written by a talented group of children's authors. It's clear that a lot of research was involved in the development of these books, as their vocabulary levels and subject matter are perfectly matched. You'll find:

- *A Bed Full of Cats* by Holly Keller
- *The Big, Big Wall* by Reginald Howard
- *Big Pig and Little Pig* by David McPhail
- *The Fox and the Stork* by Gerald McDermott
- *The Very Boastful Kangaroo* by Bernard Most
- *What Day Is It?* by Patti Trimble
- *Where Do Frogs Come From?* by Alex Vern

Half Magic

Written by Edward Eager, Illustrated by N. M. Bodecker
Harcourt, $6.00, 192 pages
First published in 1954
Ages 7–11

A wonderful lead-in to *Harry Potter and the Sorcerer's Stone* and *Ella Enchanted* (see "Juvenile Fiction/Chapter Books"), beginning readers will be swept away into this story of a brother and sister who find a magic coin that grants half wishes. The children try to harness the powers of their treasure before making one final wish. The story continues with *Magic by the Lake* and *Knight's Castle*.

Harley

Written by Star Livingstone, Illustrated by Molly Bang
Seastar, $14.95, unpaged
First published in 2001
Ages 6–9

Molly Bang's **Caldecott Award**–winning illustration style and Livingstone's peppy prose lend a lot of cheer to this story of a llama who is training to be a guard, but has his own ideas about his future. After all, it's okay to be different. A must for llama lovers!

Chapter Four

Hello Reader Series

Various authors
Scholastic, $3.99 per volume, unpaged
First published in 1992
Ages 6–9

Developed with vocabulary and sentence length in mind, this series includes tips from language arts specialist on teaching children to read. The content is very targeted to the varied interests of children in the early-elementary grades, and the series is broken into several thematic units, including the integration of math, phonics, science, and Spanish lessons into lively stories. You'll find:

- *The Case of the Shrunken Allowance* by Joanne Rocklin
- *George Washington: Our First President* by Garnet Jackson
- *Germs! Germs! Germs!* by Bobbi Katz
- *Helping Paws: Dogs That Serve* by Melinda Luke
- *Hiccups for Elephant (Elefante Tiene Hipo)* by James Preller
- *I Am Planet Earth* by Jean Marzollo
- *Screech! A Book about Bats* by Melvin Berger

Henry and Mudge Series

Written by Cynthia Rylant, Illustrated by Suçie Stevenson
Aladdin, $3.99 per volume, 40 pages each
First published in 1987
Ages 7–10

Henry and his loveable mutt, Mudge, engage readers in a series of close-to-home adventures. The same brand of warmth, humor, and comforting affection that Rylant demonstrates in her many story books (see *The Relatives Came* in "Story Books") pervades these Easy Reader offerings. Her facility with linguistic nuances lends a more poetic feeling to her work than is found in other books of this genre. There are more than 20 volumes currently available. Look for:

- *Henry and Mudge in Puddle Troubles: The Second Book of Their Adventures*
- *Henry and Mudge in the Green Time: The Third Book of Their Adventures*
- *Henry and Mudge in the Sparkle Days: The Fifth Book of Their Adventures*
- *Henry and Mudge: The First Book of Their Adventures*
- *Henry and Mudge under the Yellow Moon: The Fourth Book of Their Adventures*

Easy Readers

The Hoboken Chicken Emergency
Written by Daniel Pinkwater, Illustrated by Jill Pinkwater
Aladdin, $4.99, 108 pages
First published in 1977
Ages 6–10

This "tall chicken tale" seems to elicit gleeful guffaws in all its readers. It features a rather oversized chicken named Henrietta who will do nearly anything to avoid becoming the main course at Thanksgiving dinner. With help from a young boy named Arthur, Henrietta becomes assured that her goose won't be cooked. Admirers of Pinkwater's fantastic sense of humor won't be disappointed by *Blue Moose*; *Roger's Umbrella*; and *Pickle Creature*.

The Hundred Dresses
Written by Eleanor Estes, Illustrated by Louis Slobodkin
Voyager, $6.00, 80 pages
First published in 1944
Ages 6–10

With its picture-book appearance and lovely illustrations, young readers often mistake this book as being intended for a preschool audience. On closer examination, however, Eleanor Estes' tale is a serious depiction of the painful consequences of childhood alienation. It recounts the story of a poor young girl who, after enduring persistent teasing by her classmates, becomes a scapegoat. The effects are haunting and unforgettable. The story's message of tolerance, understanding, and kindness truly resonates.

Parent/Child Review: The Hundred Dresses
The Parent: Gwen, Age 33, Restaurant Manager
The Child: Mandy, Age 8, Soccer Goalie
Mandy says: "This is a sad book. It's horrible when kids are mean and say things that hurt your feelings. I think they probably feel bad the next day but some don't. They're just mean again."
Gwen says: "Mandy and I were talking about some bullies at her school after we read this book. It's amazing how the same basic problems exist decade after decade. I know my daughter would never hurt anyone's feelings on purpose and this book is a good topic of discussion."

Chapter Four

I Can Read Series
Various authors
HarperTrophy, $3.99 per volume, 30–65 pages each
First published in 1957
Ages 5–10

With hundreds of titles to its credit, the terrific books that comprise this winning series can certainly stand alone based on their individual merits. The books are grouped into three reading levels, measured by vocabulary and sentence length. Here you'll find beloved series characters such as *Amelia Bedelia*; *Minnie and Moo*; *The High-Rise Private Eyes*; and Syd Hoff's *Harry*. With so many great books to choose from, newly independent readers have plenty of options!

- *The Adventures of Snail at School* by John Stadler
- *Bootsie Barker Ballerina* by Barbara Bottner
- *Buffalo Bill and the Pony Express* by Eleanor Coerr
- *Captain and Matey Set Sail* by Daniel Pinkwater
- *Emma's Yucky Brother* by Jean Hill
- *The High-Rise Private Eyes: The Case of the Sleepy Sloth* by Cynthia Rylant
- *Hooray for the Golly Sisters!* by Betsy Byars
- *The Horse in Harry's Room* by Syd Hoff
- *Marvin One Too Many* by Katherine Paterson
- *Minnie and Moo Meet Frankenswine* by Denys Cazet
- *Stuart Hides Out* by Susan Hill

Kids in the Polk Street School Series
Written by Patricia Reilly Giff, Illustrated by Blanche Sims
Dell, $4.50 per volume, 70–80 pages each
First published in 1984
Ages 7–10

Richard Best, also known as Beast, is the star of this entertaining series. There's real kid sentiment, fears, and dialogue as Beast and his classmates invite readers into the wonders of their everyday world. The experiences of the Polk Street Kids mirror the common occurrences of millions of elementary aged children, and it's this realism that continues to draw legions of new readers. Some of the titles in this fifteen-book series include:

- *The Beast in Ms. Rooney's Room*
- *The Candy Corn Contest*
- *December Secrets*
- *Fish Face*
- *In the Dinosaur's Paw*
- *The Valentine Star*

Easy Readers

Let's Read and Find Out Science Series
Various authors
HarperTrophy, $4.95 per volume, 32 pages
First published in 1972
Ages 5–9

With enough titles to satisfy all types of scientific inquiry, this series explores a multitude of concepts including germs, pets, space, bugs, dinosaurs... even hiccups! The strength of this series lies in its thoughtful execution, with vocabulary that is age-appropriate and ideas that are of great interest to early- and mid-elementary–aged children. It's no wonder teachers have been integrating these books into curriculum for years! Titles include:

- *How Animal Babies Stay Safe* by Mary Ann Fraser
- *Let's Go Rock Collecting* by Roma Gans
- *Milk: From Cow to Carton* by Aliki
- *The Moon Seems to Change* by Franklyn M. Branley
- *A Safe Home for Manatees* by Pricilla Belz Jenkins
- *Sleep Is for Everyone* by Paul Showers
- *A Tree Is a Plant* by Clyde Robert Bulla
- *Where Does the Garbage Go?* by Paul Showers
- *Who Eats What? Food Chains and Food Webs* by Patricia Lauber
- *Why I Sneeze, Shiver, Hiccup and Yawn* by Melvin Berger

Little Bear
Written by Else Minarik, Illustrated by Maurice Sendak
HarperCollins, $3.99, 63 pages
First published in 1957
Ages 5–9

The coziest of stories with language that can be easily deciphered by new readers, this adorable book (and its companions) are part of the above-mentioned *I Can Read Series*. The pairing of Minarik's homey, warm sentiment and Sendak's expressive illustrations make the Little Bear stories a steady favorite of classic children's literature. Look for:

- *A Kiss for Little Bear*
- *Father Bear Comes Home*
- *Little Bear's Friend*
- *Little Bear's Visit*

Chapter Four

Little Bill Series

Written by Bill Cosby, Illustrated by Varnette P. Honeywood
Cartwheel, $3.99 per volume, 32–40 pages each
First published in 1997
Ages 4–8

You need not be a Cosby fan to find these books completely irresistible. While many preschool-aged Nickelodeon viewers are well-acquainted with Bill Cosby's child self, their book adaptations are worth equal attention. The stories are truly contemporary, urban, and child-centered, focusing on the day-to-day experiences of an African-American family. The books work well as read-to's for preschoolers and kindergartners as well as read-alones for newly independent readers. Titles in this series include:

- *The Best Way to Play*
- *The Meanest Thing to Say*
- *Money Troubles*
- *One Dark and Scary Night*
- *Super-Fine Valentine*
- *The Worst Day of My Life*

Magic School Bus Series

Written by Joanna Cole, Illustrated by Bruce Degan
Scholastic, $4.99 each, 40 pages each
First published in 1987
Ages 5–9

For those parents who have yet to be initiated into the dazzling travels of Ms. Frizzle and her student cohorts, the time will surely come. This is a series that has seen unparalleled popularity, due to Joanna Cole's talent for combining exciting stories with intriguing scientific or historical concepts. There's a slew of titles available, and it's likely that you'll be boarding the bus for a magical ride in the near future. Recent titles are by various authors. Look for:

- *The Magic School Bus at the Waterworks*
- *The Magic School Bus Explores the Senses*
- *The Magic School Bus Gets Programmed: A Book about Computers*
    by Nancy White
- *The Magic School Bus in the Rainforest* by Eva Moore
- *The Magic School Bus in the Time of Dinosaurs*
- *The Magic School Bus inside Ralphie: A Book about Germs* by Beth Nadler
- *The Magic School Bus inside the Earth*
- *The Magic School Bus inside the Human Body*
- *The Magic School Bus Lost in the Solar System*

Easy Readers

Magic Tree House Series

Written by Mary Pope Osborne, Illustrated by Sal Murdocca
Random House, $3.99 per volume, 60–70 pages each
First published in 1992
Ages 7–10

What's more entertaining than a team of curious kids who are magically transported through time to witness crucial historical eras and events? Not much, according to the children's bestseller lists, on which the titles from this fantastic series repeatedly appear. Of course, this is once again proof that a perfect blend of fantasy and reality is a tried and true recipe for popularity amongst elementary school–aged children. Once they begin climbing through the titles that comprise this series, they'll be hooked! Titles include:

- *Dinosaurs before Dark*
- *Midnight on the Moon*
- *Mummies in the Morning*
- *Night of the Ninjas*
- *Pirates Past Noon*
- *Vacation under the Volcano*
- *Viking Ships at Sunrise*

The Mouse and the Motorcycle

Written by Beverly Cleary, Illustrated by Louis Darling
Avon, $5.99, 158 pages
First published in 1965
Ages 7–10

Residing in a hotel room knothole, Ralph the mouse dreams of escaping its confines. When a boy named Keith and his family check into the hotel, opportunity presents itself. He succumbs to temptation and takes off on Keith's toy motorcycle. After discovering the joys of cruising, there's no stopping Ralph! Beverly Cleary has a masterful way of writing stories with natural kid appeal. You'll find *Dear Mr. Henshaw* and *Ramona the Pest* in "Juvenile Fiction/Chapter Books." Other stories include:

- *Ellen Tebbits*
- *Henry Huggins*
- *Muggie Maggie*
- *Ralph S. Mouse*
- *Runaway Ralph*
- *Strider*

Chapter Four

My Father's Dragon

Written by Ruth Stiles Gannett, Illustrated by Ruth Chrisman Gannett
Random House, $5.99, 86 pages
First published in 1948
Ages 6–10

   This **Newbery Honor** recipient crosses the line into fabulous fantasy while retaining a great deal of child-centered emotion. As the story begins, Elmer Elevator embarks on a mission to rescue a baby dragon that's being held captive on the Wild Island. Armed with some chewing gum, a handful of lollipops, and a fine-toothed comb, Elmer prepares for battle. The fact that he is the narrator's father lends a warm feeling of proud family lore, albeit fictional. Also look for *Elmer and the Dragon* and *The Dragons of Blueland.*

Nate the Great Series

Written by Marjorie Weinman Sharmat, Illustrated by Marc Simont
Dell, $4.50 per volume, 60 pages each
First published in 1977
Ages 7–11

   Nate loves solving mysteries almost as much as he loves eating pancakes. He takes his job seriously, too, donning a trench coat and cap while relentlessly pursuing pesky perpetrators. No crime is too small and no enigma too complicated for Nate. Look for:

- *Nate the Great*
- *Nate the Great and the Big Sniff*
- *Nate the Great and the Lost List*
- *Nate the Great and the Missing Key*
- *Nate the Great and the Monster Mess*
- *Nate the Great and the Sticky Case*
- *Nate the Great Goes down in the Dumps*
- *Nate the Great Goes Undercover*

Easy Readers

Puffin Easy-to-Read Series
Various authors
Puffin, $3.99 per volume, 30–50 pages each
First published in 1992
Ages 5–9

With highly regarded titles to its credit, Puffin has collected a great assort-ment of pleasing stories (see *Cam Jansen* in this chapter), wacky riddles, and updated fairy tales. The series is divided into two reading levels, so kids can choose titles that best suit their interests and reading ability. Titles include:

- *Amanda Pig and Her Best Friend Lollipop* (and others in this series) by Jean Van Leeuwen
- *April Fool!* by Harriet Ziefert
- *Creepy Riddles* by Katy Hall
- *Fox and His Friends* (and others from this series) by Edward Marshall
- *Lionel in the Summer* (and others from this series) by Stephen Krensky
- *On the Go with Pirate Pete and Pirate Joe* by A. E. Cannon
- *The Pizza That We Made* by Joan Holub
- *Pooh Goes Visiting* (and other Winnie the Pooh titles) by A.A. Milne

Step into Reading Series
Various authors
Random House, $3.99 per volume, 32–50 pages each
First published in 1982
Ages 4–9

Categorized into four reading levels, you'll find books intended for preschoolers through the middle-elementary grades. This is one of the most venerated and extensive Easy Reader series with an eclectic list of titles, both fiction and nonfiction. Take a look at:

- *Great Women Athletes* by Darice Bailer
- *Johnny Appleseed: My Story* by David L. Harrison
- *Moonwalk: The First Trip to the Moon* by Judy Donnelly
- *Polar Babies* by Susan Ring
- *Pompeii... Buried Alive!* by Edith Kunhardt
- *Sir Small and the Dragonfly* by Jane O'Connor
- *The Titanic, Lost and Found* by Judy Donnelly
- *Whales: The Gentle Giants* by Joyce Milton

The Best
Children's Literature
A Parent's Guide

Chapter Four

You Want Women to Vote, Lizzie Stanton?

Written by Jean Fritz, Illustrated by DyAnne DiSalvo-Ryan
Paperstar, $6.99, 88 pages
First published in 1995
Ages 6–10

Jean Fritz has a marvelous way of making history come alive for young children. With humor and insight, she captures remarkable historical moments in a way that young children understand and remember. Here, the cause is women's suffrage, and Fritz underscores the importance of equality and portrays Stanton and her friend Susan B. Anthony as strong, outspoken women with an eye on the future. You won't want to miss Jean Fritz's other books, including:

- *Harriet Beecher Stowe and the Beecher Preachers*
- *Just a Few Words, Mr. Lincoln: The Story of the Gettysburg Address*
- *Shhh! We're Writing the Constitution*
- *What's the Big Idea, Ben Franklin?*
- *Where Do You Think You're Going, Christopher Columbus?*
- *Who's That Stepping on Plymouth Rock?*
- *Why Don't You Get a Horse, Sam Adams?*
- *Will You Sign Here, John Hancock?*

Chapter Five
Nonfiction

A book about dinosaurs? A biography of Hellen Keller or Muhammad Ali? A guide to the planets? Ideas for kid-friendly craft projects? The vast array of children's nonfiction leaves no stone unturned. Whether your child needs information to support curricular themes or just wants to satisfy their growing curiosity, there is truly a book for every child and every interest.

Most of the titles listed here are intended for children across the elementary school grades, with additional titles for middle school students. Nonfiction for children is perhaps the fastest growing genre, with scientific explorations being facilitated by the remarkably inclusive *Eyewitness* series. Biographies of remarkable history makers and influential folks abound, and these titles often appeal to kids who are reluctant fiction readers. In fact, parents who recognize and encourage their children's interests and abilities by exposing them to quality nonfiction are not only furthering kids' knowledge about these subjects, they are also fostering a love of reading. Additionally, as children become comfortable with the notion of "reading to learn," they will become increasingly adept at accessing information through books and other written materials, an important scholastic skill.

From astronomy to archaeology, insects to inventions, music to mythology, your family is on their way to becoming experts on objects of interest while finding new favorite topics of discussion.

Chapter Five

Africa

Ashanti to Zulu: African Traditions
Written by Margaret Musgrove, Illustrated by Leo and Diane Dillon
Puffin, $6.95, 32 pages
First published in 1976
Ages 5–10

The customs of 26 African tribes, from Ashanti to Zulu, are vibrantly described within the pages of this **Caldecott Medal** winning book, the second consecutive prize won for the talented Dillons.

Jambo Means Hello: Swahili Alphabet Book
Written by Muriel Feelings, Illustrated by Tom Feelings
Pied Piper, $6.99, 56 pages
First published in 1974
Ages 5–10

This sophisticated picture book presents a rare glimpse into various East African tribal rituals as it pairs a Swahili word with its English translation. Children studying African cultures will want to share this **Caldecott Honor** recipient, as well as *Moja Means One: Swahili Counting Book*, with their classmates

Mandela: From the Life of the South African Statesman
Written by Floyd Cooper
Philomel, $15.99, 40 pages
First published in 1996
Ages 5–12

With an intriguing focus on his happy childhood and early adulthood, readers see the evolution of Mandela's commitment to eradicating the injustice of apartheid in South Africa. As a result of his anti-establishment indignation, Mandela was imprisoned for 27 years, but his work was certainly rewarded. Older readers will want to seek *Long Walk to Freedom: The Autobiography of Nelson Mandela* and *No More Strangers Now: Young Voices from a New South Africa* by Tim Mckee.

Nonfiction • African-American

African American

The Blues Singers: Ten Who Rocked the World
Written by Julius Lester, Illustrated by Lisa Cohen
Jump at the Sun, $15.99, 47 pages
First published in 2001
Ages 7–12

The tuneful contributions of B.B. King, Little Richard, Billie Holiday, and other African-American blues and soul musicians are highlighted in this highly entertaining collective biography. Older children shouldn't be fooled by the picture book format... this book rocks! Also look for *I See the Rhythm* by Toyomi Igus.

Bound for the North Star: True Stories of Fugitive Slaves
Written by Dennis Brindell Fradin
Clarion, $20.00, 206 pages
First published in 2000
Ages 11 and up

The heroic and startling stories of twelve escaped slaves are told through testimonials and first-hand accounts. The selfless deeds of those working on the Underground Railroad are also detailed. Middle school-aged readers will be as drawn into these stories as they would with the most compelling novel. Pair this book with *Amos Fortune: Free Man* by Elizabeth Yates (in "Chapter Books"); *Escape From Slavery: Five Journeys to Freedom* by Doreen Rappaport; *Juneteenth: Freedom Day* by Muriel Mille Branch; and *The Underground Railroad* by Raymond Bial.

Celebrating Kwanzaa
Written by Diane Hoyt-Goldsmith
Holiday House, $6.95, 32 pages
First published in 1993
Ages 5–9

One family's observance of the rituals of Kwanzaa is featured in this photo essay. Symbols and celebratory elements of the Seven Principles of Kwanzaa are explained. Moreover, this is an affectionate glimpse into the life of one contemporary African-American family sharing a significant tradition. You'll find lively facts and stories about the holiday in *Children's Book of Kwanzaa* by Dolores Johnson and *Seven Spools of Thread: A Kwanzaa Story* by Angela Shelf Medearis.

Chapter Five

Cracking the Wall: The Struggles of the Little Rock Nine
Written by Eileen Lucas, Illustrated by Marc Anthony
Carolrhoda Books, $6.95, 48 pages
First published in 1997
Ages 6–10

The 1953 Supreme Court ruling against school segregation set the stage for a dramatic series of events for the first black students to enter Central High in Little Rock, Arkansas. Through firsthand accounts, each of their experiences and perceptions of the event are vividly recalled, and information about their lives as adults is appended. This is an essential document about the issues surrounding desegregation, and can be effectively paired with *Going to School During the Civil Rights Movement* by Rachel A. Koestler.

Frederick Douglass: The Last Days of Slavery
Written by William Miller, Illustrated by Cedric Lucas
Lee & Low, $6.95, 32 pages
First published in 1995
Ages 6–10

When a young Douglass decided to fight a slave overseer, he took his place amongst the bravest battlers of racial injustice. This picture book biography centers on this pivotal moment in Douglass' young life, while also illuminating his compassion and determination.

From Slave Ship to Freedom Road
Written by Julius Lester, Illustrated by Rod Brown
Puffin, $6.99, 40 pages
First published in 1998
Ages 11–15

The author features twenty paintings by artist Rod Brown as visual stimulus for meditation on slavery and eventual freedom. Lester includes powerful "imagination exercises" that invite readers to explore their own fears, prejudices, and misconceptions about America's shameful history of slavery and civil injustice. Also look for *Many Thousand Gone: African Americans from Slavery to Freedom* by the acclaimed Virginia Hamilton.

Nonfiction • African-American

Harlem
Written by Walter Dean Myers, Illustrated by Christopher Myers
Scholastic, $16.95, 32 pages
First published in 1997
Ages 11–15

This father/son collaboration employs jazzy poetry and striking images to evoke the spirit of the cultural mecca for African-American artists, authors, and musicians from the heyday of the Harlem Renaissance and forward. Middle readers will enjoy a fictional rendering of the famous New York neighborhood as seen by Gail Carson Levine in *Dave at Night* (see "Chapter Books"). Also look for *The Harlem Renaissance* by Veronica Chambers. Younger readers (and all grown-ups) should set their sights on *Uptown* by Bryan Collier (in "Story Books").

Her Stories:
African-American Folktales, Fairy Tales and True Tales
Written by Virginia Hamilton
Blue Sky, $19.95, 112 pages
First published in 1995
Ages 4–14

Between the covers of this unique collection reside 19 stories about African-American girls and women. These telling tales earned a **Coretta Scott King** Award for Virginia Hamilton. Also by Hamilton, *The People Could Fly: American Black Folktales* (in "Story Books").

I Have a Dream
Written by Martin Luther King Jr.
Scholastic, $16.95, 40 pages
First published in 1997
Ages 6–14

Accompanied by dazzling illustrations from 15 Coretta Scott King Award winning artists, Martin Luther King, Jr.'s monumental speech really hits home. Also look for *Martin's Big Words: The Life of Dr. Martin Luther King Jr.* (see under Biographies).

Chapter Five

Ida B. Wells: Mother of the Civil Rights Movement
Written by Dennis Brindell Fradin
Clarion, $18.00, 178 pages
First published in 2000
Ages 10–14

Wells was Rosa Parks' fervent civil rights forbearer, suing a railroad company for forcing her out of a "whites only" seat in the early 20th century. Born a slave, Wells eventually became a journalist and activist who demanded the end of institutional racial inequality. This is a perfect supplement to Civil Rights studies and important material for children who seek information on female leaders of the movement.

Love to Langston
Written by Tony Medina, Illustrated by R. Gregory Christie
Lee & Low, $16.95, 34 pages
First published in 2002
Ages 5–12

Langston Hughes was not only revered for his astonishing poetry, but also for his influence on a variety of art forms. His Harlem was a place to find profound beauty and wisdom, and his aesthetic legacy lives on in this glowing tribute. Here, Hughes's poetry has been assembled and adorned with wise, simple, vivid art to describe his life and work. Also look for Alice Walker's *Langston Hughes: American Poet*.

The Real McCoy:
The Life of an African-American Inventor
Written by Wendy Towle, Illustrated by Wil Clay
Blue Ribbon, $5.99, 32 pages
First published in 1993
Ages 6–10

Elijah McCoy was an engineer and inventor. He was also the son of escaped slaves. His steadfast professional determination in the face of racial prejudice gives us a clue as to the derivation of the popular phrase "the real McCoy." You'll also enjoy *Dear Benjamin Banneker* by Andrea Davis Pinkney, the story of a freed slave and gifted mathematician who corresponded with Thomas Jefferson.

Richard Wright and the Library Card
Written by William Miller, Illustrated by R. Gregory Christie
Lee & Low, $6.95, 32 pages
First published in 1997
Ages 6–12

While Wright became one of the most venerated writers of his day, racial segregation hindered his early efforts. He was not permitted to use the non-integrated local library and pretended to be borrowing books for his white employer. You'll want to strongly encourage children to read this fictionalized episode, not only for its portrayal of the injustice of Jim Crow laws but also for its accessible picture book format and enduring message. Miller is also the author of *The Bus Ride* (detailed in "Story Books").

Through My Eyes
Written by Ruby Bridges
Scholastic, $16.95, 63 pages
First published in 1999
Ages 8–12

Bridges recalls her experiences as the first black child to be admitted to a public school in New Orleans. Vividly recollecting the protests that accompanied her arrival at school, Ruby wasn't aware that the turmoil was "all about the color of my skin." Another excellent portrayal of this accidental civil rights hero is *The Story of Ruby Bridges* by Robert Coles.

America

1621: A New Look at Thanksgiving
Written by Catherine O'Neill Grace and Margaret M. Bruchac, Photographs by Susse Brimberg and Cotton Coulson
National Geographic, $17.95, 47 pages
First published in 2001
Ages 6–12

This provocative book could easily be nicknamed "Thanksgiving: Behind the Myth." It reveals the probable political motivation and resulting turmoil behind the more romantic view of the fall festivities. There are useful facts about the Plymouth Plantation and colonization that sheds new light on the holiday, without diminishing its importance. For children in the early elementary grades, this title can be paired with *Giving Thanks: A Native American Good Morning Message* and *The Story of Thanksgiving* by Robert Merrill Bartlett.

Chapter Five

Children of the Dust Bowl:
The True Story of the School at Weedpatch
Written by Jerry Stanley
Crown, $9.95, 85 pages
First published in 1992
Ages 11–15

An excellent contribution to a topic that is often included in middle school curriculum, the stories featured here would also provide a wonderful extension to a reading of *The Grapes of Wrath* by John Steinbeck, for older students, and *Out of the Dust* by Karen Hesse (see "Chapter Books"), for middle readers. The plight of migrant workers during their attempted escape to California from the destruction of the Dust Bowl and their subsequent internment in labor camps makes for a highly personalized and compelling story.

A Child's Alaska
Written by Claire Rudolf Murphy
Alaska Northwest, $16.95, 47 pages
First published in 1994
Ages 5–9

Exploring the wildlife, terrain, and population of Alaska, this book features breathtaking photography and succinct text that will intrigue both children and adults. Search high and low for *Children of the Midnight Sun: Young Native Voices of Alaska* by Tricia Brown and the crucial ecological questions raised in *After the Spill: The Exxon Valdez Disaster Then and Now* by Sandra Markle.

The City by the Bay
Written by Tricia Brown, Illustrated by Elisa Kleven
Chronicle, $6.95, 26 pages
First published in 1993
Ages 5–9

Many people have left their heart there, and for good reason. The sights and sounds of San Francisco—cable cars, the Golden Gate Bridge, Lombard Street, the Japanese Tea Garden—are paid due tribute in this energetic picture book.

Nonfiction • America

The Flag We Love
Written by Pam Muñoz Ryan, Illustrated by Ralph Masiello
Charlesbridge, $16.95, 32 pages
First published in 1996
Ages 6–10

Flag facts and lore comprise this ode to our symbol of unity. The Stars and Stripes are duly saluted through patriotic images of high-flying flags in schoolyards, on monuments, and above baseball fields. Forever may it wave! *Flag Lore of All Nations* by Whitney Smith provides an interesting expansion beyond American shores.

Full Steam Ahead:
The Race to Build a Transcontinental Railroad
Written by Rhoda Blumberg
National Geographic, $18.95, 159 pages
First published in 1996
Ages 10 and up

Blumberg manages to capture a great amount of detail in this very readable account. A feat of unparalleled engineering, the building of the railroad reads like a suspense novel complete with crooked politicians, horrendous conditions, and Wild West drama. For an engaging fictional account, look for *The Iron Dragon Never Sleeps* by Stephen Krensky.

Gettysburg Address
Written by Abraham Lincoln
Houghton Mifflin, $6.95, 32 pages
First published in 1995
Ages 7–12

The oft-quoted groundbreaking speech is featured in its entirety, accompanied by graceful, subtle illustrations. Younger readers shouldn't miss *Just a Few Words, Mr. Lincoln: The Story of the Gettysburg Address* by Jean Fritz.

Chapter Five

Give Me Liberty:
The Story of the Declaration of Independence
Written by Russell Freedman
Holiday House, $12.95, 90 pages
First published in 2000
Ages 10–15

An accomplished historian and compelling storyteller, Freedman begins his account with the Boston Tea Party, guides readers through the formation of the Continental Congress, and moves onto the signing of the Declaration of Independence. Colonial life and revolutionary drama is richly explored through newspaper clippings and letters. This is a truly remarkable book and an essential accompaniment to middle school early American history curriculum.

Growing Up in Coal Country
Written by Susan Campbell Bartoletti
Houghton Mifflin, $7.95, 127 pages
First published in 1997
Ages 9–14

Archival photographs and personal accounts combine to create a interesting and seldom explored glimpse into the lives of children living and working in the coal mining towns of late-nineteenth-century Pennsylvania.

History of Us Series
Written by Joy Hakim
Oxford University Press, $154.95, 11 volume boxed set
First published in 1994
Ages 9 and up

A well-rounded and highly readable look at history's important events—organized both thematically and chronologically—this series is a must for history buffs. There's a lot of information about daily life in each era examined and pertinent questions to encourage further investigation. The volumes are available separately as well.

Nonfiction • America

Liberty

Written and Illustrated by Lynn Curlee
Atheneum, $18.00, 48 pages
First published in 2000
Ages 9–12

Ask any American about their favorite symbol of freedom, and you're likely to hear about Lady Liberty. This elegant book follows her journey, from creation by a young French sculptor, through her construction by a now-famous architect named Eiffel, and onto her travels to preside over New York City's harbor. She's been a sight for the sore eyes of immigrants and a constant reminder of our unity. Curlee pays her deserved homage. Also look for *Rushmore*, by the same author.

My New York

Written and Illustrated by Kathy Jakobsen
Little, $17.95, 36 pages
First published in 1993
Ages 5–10

The fact that Manhattan's skyline (but not its spirit!) was tragically diminished in 2001 is perhaps reason enough to seek this loving tribute to the Big Apple. Jakobsen's folk art representations pay affectionate attention to the sights and sounds of New York, including the Central Park Zoo, the Statue of Liberty, Chinatown, and, of course, F.A.O. Schwartz.

Remember Pearl Harbor: American and Japanese Survivors Tell Their Stories

Written by Allen B. Thomas
National Geographic, $17.95, 57 pages
First published in 2001
Ages 11 and up

The "day that will live in infamy" is given a human face through the testimonials of Japanese pilots, American soldiers, and medical personnel. The representation of both Japanese and American survivors sets this book on an unbiased footing, providing a neutral perspective that is necessary to view this dramatic event with the benefit of hindsight knowledge.

Chapter Five

So, You Want to Be President?

Written by Judith St. George, Illustrated by David Small
Philomel, $17.99, 52 pages
First published in 2000
Ages 6–10

This recent **Caldecott Medal** winner has a lot to say about "the good" and "the bad" things about being President. Offering a host of information by way of anecdotes, quips, and trivia, kids will want to learn more about life in the White House. There are lively stories from the oval office in *The Buck Stops Here: The Presidents of the United States* by Alice Provensen.

We Were There, Too!
Young People in U.S. History

parent's
guide
choice award

Written by Phillip Hoose
Farrar Straus Giroux, $26.00, 264 pages
First published in 2001
Ages 9–14

Now here's an ingenious way for kids to relate to historical events: through the eyes of other kids! These are the stories of both famous and lesser-known youngsters who made their mark on (or bore witness to) crucial episodes in history. From Diego Bermudez who sailed with Columbus, to contemporary environmental crusader Kory Johnson, there are colorful lessons to be learned from their profound experiences. It's due to the wide appeal of this concept that book series such as *The American Girls* and *American Diaries* (see "Chapter Books") have become so immensely popular.

What's the Deal? Jefferson, Napoleon, and the Louisiana Purchase

Written by Rhoda Blumberg
National Geographic, $18.95, 144 pages
First published in 1998
Ages 10–14

A true turning point in America's expansion, this thorough and savvy look at the key players and decisions involved in the Louisiana Purchase is a dramatic read. Blumberg includes a Q&A section that covers incisive "what if" questions.

Nonfiction • Ancient Civilizations

Who Said That? Famous Americans Speak
Written by Robert Burleigh, Illustrated by David Catrow
Henry Holt, $16.95, 45 pages
First published in 1997
Ages 8–12

Words of wisdom from some of America's most illustrious individuals including Martin Luther King Jr., Benjamin Franklin, Sojourner Truth, and Marilyn Monroe can be found in this collection of terrific talkers. It's amazing how many contemporary quotes are attributed to their speeches.

Ancient Civilizations—Archaeology

1,000 Years Ago on Planet Earth
Written by Collard B. Sneed III, Illustrated by Jonathan Hunt
Houghton Mifflin, $15.00, 32 pages
First published in 1999
Ages 7–12

What was happening on our fine planet a millennium ago? Well, modern religion, government, and culture were beginning to take root across Europe, Asia, India, and the Middle East. Readers will be surprised to learn how many crucial seeds of contemporary society can be traced so far back and will begin to see modern history from the beginning of its chronology.

The 5,000-Year-Old Puzzle:
Solving a Mystery of Ancient Egypt
Written by Claudia Logan, Illustrated by Melissa Sweet
Farrar, Straus & Giroux, $17.00, 48 pages
First published in 2002
Ages 8–12

In 1924, a young boy named Will Hunt travels with his family to witness the archaeological excavation at Giza. There's electric excitement in the air, but the enthusiasts will have to be patient; it will take nearly a year before the tomb can be opened. In the meantime, Will sends postcards home, writes in his journal, and takes photographs of the historical event he is witnessing, all of which combine to create a thrilling narrative for young readers.

Chapter Five

The Ancient City: Life in Classical Athens and Rome
Written by Peter Connolly, Illustrated by Hazel Dodge
Oxford University Press, $35.00, 256 pages
First published in 1998
Ages 12 and up

Temples, public buildings, and homes are magnificently re-created, and daily life in ancient Athens and Rome is explored in vivid detail, illustrating how the roots of many aspects of modern society can be traced back to the classical citizens. This is an exceptional source of information for students. Middle grade readers will also enjoy *The Greek News* by Anton Powell.

Dig This! How Archaeologists Uncover Our Past
Written by Michael Avi-Yonah
Runestone, $23.93, 96 pages
First published in 1993
Ages 9–14

From the *Buried Worlds* series comes this glimpse into the lives and work of archaeologists. There's information about excavation methods, famous discoveries, and what we've learned about ancient civilizations through this exciting work.

Gladiator
Written by Richard Watkins
Sandpiper, $7.95, 80 pages
First published in 1997
Ages 8–12

Kids may not have seen the Hollywood version, but the lives of gladiators provide a heroic, and often gruesome, glimpse into a unique aspect of life in Ancient Rome. Champion gladiators were heralded as heroes, but Watkins's investigation does not glorify the idea of public death as a spectator sport.

Animals

All about Deer
Written and Illustrated by Jim Arnosky
Scholastic, $5.99, 32 pages
First published in 1996
Ages 5–9

Through vivid illustrations and clear text, Arnosky relates important facts about the different species of deer, their life cycle, and mating habits. The end papers provide additional facts, making this title an excellent choice for children in the early- and middle-elementary grades. Also by Jim Arnosky, *All about Frogs*; *All about Owls*; *All about Turkeys*; and *All about Turtles*, among others.

And So They Build
Written and Illustrated by Bert Kitchen
Candlewick, $5.99, 26 pages
First published in 1993
Ages 4–8

Wonderfully detailed illustrations bring to life the building habits of a variety of animals. Why and how do beavers build dams? Where does a harvest mouse find shelter? These questions and more are found in this delightful book.

Cat
Written by Juliet Clutton-Brock
Dorling Kindersley, $15.95, 63 pages
First published in 1991
Ages 8–13

The ultra popular *Eyewitness Books* are hard to miss, and for good reason. They're widely regarded as excellent choices for curious readers seeking information about science and history. There's hardly a topic that hasn't been covered, so ask your favorite librarian or bookseller to point you in *Eyewitness's* colorful direction. In this volume, there are ample facts about the behavior and characteristics of both wild and domestic cats. Other volumes on animals include *Amphibian*; *Bird*; *Butterfly and Moth*; *Dinosaur*; *Dog*; *Elephant*; *Fish*; and *Horse* among many others. There's also a series suitable for early-elementary–aged children called *Eyewitness Juniors*. Titles in this series typically begin with "Amazing," for example, *Amazing Animal Babies*.

Chapter Five

The Chimpanzees I Love: Saving Their World and Ours

parent's
guide
choice award

Written by Jane Goodall
Scholastic, $17.95, 80 pages
First published in 2001
Ages 7–12

Having conducted groundbreaking studies with chimpanzees for 40 years, Goodall has become a true heartfelt hero among animal activists. Amazing facts about chimps' human-like emotions and their ability to learn sign language will captivate readers. Color photographs enliven Goodall's selfless devotion, from her years in Tanzania through her current focus on raising awareness about the plight of chimps in captivity. There's no doubt that kids will want to visit her Web site and become involved. Jane Goodall is a remarkable role model.

Home at Last: A Song of Migration

Written by April Pulley Sayre, Illustrated by Alix Berenzy
Henry Holt, $16.95, 34 pages
First published in 1998
Ages 5–9

The lengths taken by many animal species to complete their migratory destiny are certainly astounding. Led by their heightened sense of smell, salmon will swim for hundreds of miles to return home. The Arctic tern flies more than 12,000 miles, while whales and lobsters seem to "march" in formation toward their destination. All of which makes for astonishing reading from a very talented author/illustrator team. And don't miss April Pulley Sayre's *If You Should Hear a Honey Guide* (in "Story Books").

Koko's Kitten

Written by Francine Patterson
Scholastic, $4.99, 32 pages
First published in 1985
Ages 5–10

You may have seen video footage of Patterson's incredible relationship with Koko the gorilla. Working diligently together for many years, the gorilla built an impressive sign language vocabulary. In this irresistible story, Koko communicates her desire for a pet kitten. When the young cat arrives, Koko takes enormous pride and pleasure in her care, even bestowing the name "All Ball" on the kitty. When All Ball is killed after being hit by a truck, Koko expresses

Nonfiction • Animals

her grief and an amazing understanding of the concept of death. It's a book that shouldn't be missed for many reasons, including the expansion of our perception of mammal's abilities and emotions, as well as the happy ending when Koko is given another kitten to love. And look for *Koko-Love! Conversations with a Signing Gorilla*.

Peterson First Guide to Reptiles and Amphibians
Written by Roger Conant, Robert C. Stebbins, and Joseph T. Collins
Houghton Mifflin, $5.95, 128 pages
First published in 1999
Ages 8–13

Peterson Guides have long set the standard for high quality nature guides and *Peterson First Guides* are excellent choices for budding naturalists. Here, the authors teach readers to become backyard explorers, highlighting the characteristics and habitats of frogs, snakes, turtles, lizards, and more. Also in this series (all beginning with *Peterson First Guide to*) *Astronomy*; *Birds*; *Butterflies and Moths*; *Caterpillars*; *Clouds and Weather*; *Dinosaurs*; *Fishes*; *Insects*; *Mammals*; *Rocks and Minerals*; *Seashores*; *Forests*; and *Wildflowers*.

Safari
Written and Illustrated by Robert Bateman
Little Brown, $17.95, 32 pages
First published in 1998
Ages 8–12

The author, an acclaimed wildlife artist, takes readers on a thrilling visual trek through the lives and landscapes of twelve African animals. Sure to ignite excitement about wild animals and the challenges of living within the often harsh African terrain, children in the early- and middle-elementary grades will want to read this book in conjunction with any school study of Africa or endangered species.

Snakes
Written by Seymour Simon
HarperCollins, $6.95, 28 pages
First published in 1992
Ages 6–10

Did you know that you are more likely to be struck by lightning than bitten by a snake? Seymour Simon debunks many myths about snakes while providing photographs that are not for the fainthearted. In other words, kids will be completely glued to this book.

Chapter Five

Architecture

Brooklyn Bridge

Written and Illustrated by Lynn Curlee
Atheneum, $18.00, 35 pages
First published in 2001
Ages 8–12

The Brooklyn Bridge is sometimes referred to as the eighth wonder of the world, and this magnificent book will leave both children and adults wide-eyed with awe. After the original architect died suddenly, the massive project was passed to his son. Diagrams, cross-sections, and a dramatic narrative guide the reader through the fascinating building process.

Building Big

Written and Illustrated by David Macaulay
Houghton Mifflin, $30.00, 192 pages
First published in 2000
Ages 9 and up

**parent's
guide**
choice award

A companion to the PBS series of the same name, this is a book that will provide hours of amazement and wonder. From Ancient Rome to modern Manhattan, the inner workings of buildings, bridges, tunnels, and monuments are dramatically described through Macaulay's marvelous trademark cross-section detail. Also by David Macaulay, *Castle; Cathedral; Pyramid; Underground;* and *The New Way Things Work* (see "Science"), all of which are equally remarkable.

Art

The American Eye:
Eleven Artists of the Twentieth Century

Written by Jan Greenberg, Illustrated by Sandra Jordan
Delacorte, $22.50, 120 pages
First published in 1995
Ages 10 and up

Artistic movements are linked to social and historical change in this wonderful collection. Young adults will enjoy the colorful biographical detail of artists such as Andy Warhol and Edward Hopper. With easily understood interpretations of paintings, sculpture, and mixed media, this is a book that will be treasured through adulthood.

Nonfiction • Art

A Caldecott Celebration:
Six Artists Share Their Paths to the Caldecott Medal
Written by Leonard S. Marcus
Walker & Co., $18.95, 49 pages
First published in 1998
Ages 6–12

If ever a book were to engage the artistic impulses of young readers, it's this one. Profiling Caldecott Medal winners such as Robert McCloskey (*Make Way for Ducklings*), David Wiesner (*Tuesday*), and Chris Van Allsburg (*Jumanji*), appreciation for the art of illustration will certainly be enhanced after reading this terrific book.

A Child's Book of Play in Art: Great Pictures, Great Fun
Written by Lucy Micklethwait
Dorling Kindersley, $16.95, 45 pages
First published in 1996
Ages 5–9

The author deftly combines an introduction to basic art concepts with an interactive sequence of games and play-acting opportunities that truly makes art a living, breathing experience for children. Adults will appreciate the fine quality of the full color reproductions.

Chuck Close, Up Close
Written by Jan Greenberg
DK Ink, $10.95, 48 pages
First published in 2000
Ages 8–12

Who wouldn't be amazed by Chuck Close's intensely unique paintings? His trademark technique of integrating thousands of small images into a large portrait is an endless source of amazement. The fact that Close is paralyzed provokes additional wonder at the integrity and scope of his work, as well as the strength of the human spirit.

Chapter Five

Claude Monet: Sunshine and Waterlillies
Written by True Kelley
Grossett & Dunlap, $5.99, 32 pages
First published in 2001
Ages 7–10

Part of the *Smart About Art* series, this imaginative biography unfolds as a pretend book report by a young girl. The questions raised through her investigation of Monet are excellent models for biographical study while simultaneously shedding light on the life and work of the famous Impressionist painter. Other titles in the series include *Edgar Degas: Paintings That Dance*; *Henri Matisse: Drawing with Scissors*; and *Vincent Van Gogh: Sunflowers and Swirly Stars*.

Michelangelo
Written by Diane Stanley
HarperCollins, $15.95, 48 pages
First published in 2000
Ages 9–15

Diane Stanley's talents as a biographer are evident in this superbly crafted book. Most of Michelangelo's best known works are his large scale commissions (think Sistine Chapel), and Stanley's portrayal of his struggle to please his patrons is engrossing. Also by Stanley, *Leonardo Da Vinci*; *Good Queen Bess: The Story of Elizabeth I of England*; *Peter the Great*; *Cleopatra*; and *Joan of Arc*.

My Name Is Georgia: A Portrait
Written and Illustrated by Jeanette Winter
Silver Whistle, $16.00, 32 pages
First published in 1998
Ages 6–11

This powerful picture book portrayal of Georgia O'Keefe will please early- and middle elementary-aged children. Determined from childhood to become an artist, O'Keefe's work accounts for some of the most recognizable in American painting. Winter's own illustrations perfectly capture the mood of the artist's recurring motifs.

Nonfiction • Art

The Nine-Ton Cat: Behind the Scenes at an Art Museum

Written by Peggy Thomson, Illustrated by Barbara Moore and Carol Eron
Houghton Mifflin, $14.95, 96 pages
First published in 1997
Ages 8–14

You won't want to miss this rare glimpse into the inner workings of a museum. A great deal of preparation is involved in the planning of exhibits, development of educational programs, and storage of priceless works of art. The National Gallery of Art in Washington, D.C. provides the setting, and this is your backstage pass!

Norman Rockwell: Storyteller with a Brush

Written by Beverly Gherman
Atheneum, $19.95, 57 pages
First published in 2000
Ages 9–14

Best known for his prolific contributions to the *Saturday Evening Post*, Rockwell's paintings became a nostalgic symbol of American life. Gherman traces the artist's childhood and development of his signature style while addressing both the admiration and criticism that he received throughout his lengthy career.

Painters of the Caves

Written by Patricia Lauber
National Geographic, $17.95, 48 pages
First published in 1998
Ages 9–14

From the dawn of human culture comes the dawn of art, and this expose on cave painting is a real eye-opener. This is truly the most logical place to begin any discussion of art history. The book includes reproductions of the famous cave paintings at Lascaux and Chauvet, and raises questions about the motivations and experiences of primitive painters.

Chapter Five

The Picture That Mom Drew

Written and Illustrated by Kathy Mallat
Walker and Co., $14.95, 24 pages
First published in 1997
Ages 6–10

Using an effective "this is the house that Jack built" motif, Mallat introduces the basic vocabulary, principles, and processes of art. As two young girls and their mother discuss the elements—line, shading, color—of painting and drawing, a beautiful portrait emerges.

Rembrandt

Written by Gary Schwartz
Abrams, $19.95, 92 pages
First published in 1992
Ages 11–14

An artful contribution to the *First Impressions* series, the life and work of the Dutch master is depicted through anecdotes, social context, and more than 50 luminous color illustrations. There's no academic jargon here, just an enchanting look at the life of a genius. Similar in style and layout, the series also includes *Andrew Wyeth*; *Edgar Degas*; *Frank Lloyd Wright*; *Leonardo Da Vinci*; *Mary Cassatt*; *Michelangelo*; *Pablo Picasso*; and *Pierre Auguste Renoir*.

Vincent Van Gogh: Portrait of an Artist

Written by Jan Greenberg and Sandra Jordan
Delacorte, $14.95, 132 pages
First published in 2001
Ages 11–15

Treating Van Gogh's work with insight and sensitivity, the authors shed light on the work of one of the world's most renowned painters, as well as his intriguing personal history and emotional demons. Included are letters to and from his beloved brother and patron, Theo, further clarifying Vincent's artistic vision.

Biographies

Abigail Adams: Witness to a Revolution
Written by Natalie S. Bober
Atheneum, $18.00, 248 pages
First published in 1995
Ages 11 and up

Abigail Adams was a prolific correspondent. After all, she spent years apart from her husband, John Adams, and their family during the revolutionary years of America's independence. Her story is told through information gleaned from the many letters she wrote. While women were discouraged from participating in political discourse, Abigail lived by her own rules.

The Abracadabra Kid: A Writer's Life
Written by Sid Fleischman
Beech Tree, $4.95, 194 pages
First published in 1996
Ages 10 and up

A truly charming memoir by the **Newbery Award**–winning author. With both hilarious and touching moments, this is a great choice for kids looking for a book report subject that classmates are unlikely to choose. Fleischman's story will be of special interest to aspiring writers.

Across America on an Emigrant Train
Written by Jim Murphy
Clarion, $18.00, 150 pages
First published in 1993
Ages 11–14

Using excerpts from his diaries, the 1879 travels of Robert Louis Stevenson are amazingly reconstructed, providing biographical information that reads like a suspense novel. Particularly interesting are Stevenson's impressions of traveling by train during the early years of the transcontinental railroad.

Chapter Five

The Amazing Life of Benjamin Franklin
Written by James Cross Giblin
Scholastic, $17.95, 48 pages
First published in 2000
Ages 8–12

A highly accessible biography of one of history's most important contributors, Giblin details Franklin's early career as a printer's apprentice through his later years as an inventor, politician, and statesman. With abundant illustrations and an appropriate level of biographical detail, this is a great choice for children in the mid- to late-elementary school grades. Other quality biographies by Giblin include *Charles A. Lindbergh: A Human Hero*; *George Washington: A Picture Book Biography*; and *Thomas Jefferson: A Picture Book Biography*. For a unique perspective on Franklin's wisdom, ask for *The Hatmaker's Sign: A Story by Benjamin Franklin* by Candace Fleming.

Anne Frank, Beyond the Diary: A Photographic Remembrance
Written by Ruud van der Rol, Illustrated by Rian Verhoeven
Puffin, $10.99, 113 pages
First published in 1995
Ages 10 and up

Children's lives are forever changed after reading Anne Frank's journal entries. (See *The Diary of a Young Girl: The Definitive Edition* in Juvenile Fiction/Chapter Books.) This photographic exploration of the young writer is certain to further interest. Maps and interviews contribute to a brilliant depiction of Anne as an adolescent, history maker, and tragic symbol of a devastating time in history.

Bard of Avon: The Story of William Shakespeare
Written by Diane Stanley, Illustrated by Peter Vennema
Mulberry, $5.95, 45 pages
First published in 1992
Ages 8–12

Exploring the tragedy and comedy in the life of the world famous playwright, there are some startling revelations here and a lot of fascinating biographical information. Also by this talented author/illustrator team, the biographies of *Leonardo Da Vinci*; *Cleopatra*; and *Charles Dickens*. For further insight into the Bard, look for *Shakespeare: His Work & His World* by Michael Rosen as well as *William Shakespeare and the Globe* by Aliki.

Nonfiction • Biographies

Bull's Eye: A Photobiography of Annie Oakley
Written by Sue Macy
National Geographic, $17.95, 64 pages
First published in 2001
Ages 9–14

The woman behind the legend is revealed in this enthralling volume. Childhood hardships and an early aptitude for marksmanship begin the tale. After a while, thousands of people were traveling to see Annie perform in Buffalo Bill's Wild West Show. Facts are separated from common fiction through photographs, show programs, and a useful chronology.

The Dalai Lama: A Biography of the Tibetan Spiritual and Political Leader
Written by Demi
Henry Holt, $18.95, 32 pages
First published in 1998
Ages 9–14

Beginning with a letter from the Dalai Lama, explaining his concern about the political climate in Tibet, this visually rich biography explores the life and mission of the now exiled leader. The fundamentals of Buddhism are also explained. While the picture book format may be surprising to middle grade readers, this beautifully illustrated tribute is a perfect source of information about a fascinating man. For more information, look for *Dalai Lama, My Son: A Mother's Story* by Diki Tsering, the mother of the Dalai Lama.

Duke Ellington: The Piano Prince and His Orchestra
Written by Andrea Davis Pinkney, Illustrated by Brian J. Pinkney
Hyperion, $15.95, 32 pages
First published in 1998
Ages 5–10

This **Caldecott Honor** book will swing its way into the hearts of readers. The Pinkneys' tuneful text and illustrations perfectly match the rhythm of its Jazz Age story, which explores the life of Ellington, a true musical pioneer.

Chapter Five

Eleanor
Written by Barbara Cooney
Picture Puffins, $6.99, 40 pages
First published in 1996
Ages 7–10

While some children may be aware of the remarkable achievements of Eleanor Roosevelt, few know about her life prior to becoming First Lady. A painful childhood and coming-of-age at a British boarding school are honestly examined in this picture biography. Equally impressive, though intended for young adults, is *Eleanor Roosevelt: A Life of Discovery* by Russell Freedman. *A Letter to Mrs. Roosevelt* by Coco C. Deyoung is a highly enjoyable fictionalized account.

The Greatest: Muhammad Ali
Written by Walter Dean Myers
Scholastic, $4.99, 192 pages
First published in 2000
Ages 10 and up

Separating the private side from the public persona of one of the world's most famous and alluring figures, Myers masterfully paints a frank portrait of Ali. Born Cassius Clay, the young boxer's determination was evident from an early age, despite his upbringing in a segregated society. Myers pays fitting tribute to Ali's contributions as a larger-than-life legend.

Handel, Who Knew What He Liked
Written and Illustrated by M. T. Anderson
Candlewick, $16.99, unpaged
First published in 2001
Ages 7–12

His parents hoped he would become a lawyer, but Handel persevered, secretly practicing on the clavichord and honing his musical intuition. He would eventually create some of the most famous classical compositions including "Water Music" and "Messiah." Handel's rise to fame, complete with pitfalls and royal drama, is an enormously engaging story, even for young readers who are unfamiliar with his work.

Nonfiction • Biographies

Helen Keller: Rebellious Spirit
Written by Laurie Lawlor
Holiday House, $22.95, 168 pages
First published in 2001
Ages 9–14

When the time comes to write a book report (and the time will come!) about this most compelling symbol of strength and spirit, Lawlor's biography is an excellent source of information and inspiration. As a modern icon, Keller's triumphs are well documented. Plentiful photographs and insight into her relationships add additional intrigue.

Joan of Arc
Written by Josephine Poole, Illustrated by Angela Barrett
Dragonfly, $6.99, 34 pages
First published in 1998
Ages 8–12

The woman known as Saint Joan began her life as a farmer's daughter in the 15th century. After hearing voices, Joan began her mission to lead the French to victory in the Hundred Years' War. Poole emphasizes from the start that this is a true story, and Barrett's glorious illustrations—with tapestries, costumes, and paintings—add a mystical quality to Joan of Arc's legendary life. Diane Stanley's *Joan of Arc* is another excellent biographical rendering.

Leonardo Da Vinci for Kids: His Life and Ideas
Written by Janis Herbert
Chicago Review, $16.95, 90 pages
First published in 1999
Ages 8–13

Leonardo was truly a Renaissance man, and Herbert's clever biography depicts not only his many artistic endeavors, but his forays into science, philosophy, and invention as well. There are several intriguing projects to try, from growing an herb garden to making a kite.

Chapter Five

Martha Graham: A Dancer's Life
Written by Russell Freedman
Clarion, $18.00, 175 pages
First published in 1998
Ages 12 and up

The startlingly original choreography of Martha Graham is linked to the political and social climate of the early- to mid-twentieth century in this dynamic biography. Graham's creative accomplishments are thrilling to behold, and Freedman's discussion of her passionate political convictions paint the portrait of a true pioneer.

Martin's Big Words:
The Life of Dr. Martin Luther King Jr.

**parent's
guide**
choice award

Written by Doreen Rappaport
Jump at the Sun, $15.99, 34 pages
First published in 2001
Ages 6–11

In this stunning picture book tribute to the civil rights leader, King's message rings loud and clear throughout its pages. Its plentiful photographs, plus drawn and collage illustrations, bring King's work to life for younger readers, while older children will be drawn in by the power of King's words. All of which earned this title both a **Caldecott Honor** and a **Coretta Scott King Honor**. Also look for *Martin Luther King, Jr.* by Rosemary L. Bray.

Sadako
Written by Eleanor Coerr, Illustrated by Ed Young
Putnam, $6.99, 48 pages
First published in 1993
Ages 6–10

A picture book version of *Sadako and the Thousand Paper Cranes* (see "Juvenile Fiction/Chapter Books") intended for slightly younger readers. This is the moving story of Sadako Sasaki, a young girl who, after being diagnosed with post-Hiroshima Leukemia, is compelled to create 1,000 paper cranes, a symbol of hope and healing.

Nonfiction • Biographies

Satchel Paige

Written by Lesa Cline–Ransome, Illustrated by James E. Ransome
Simon & Schuster, $16.00, 36 pages
First published in 2000
Ages 6–10

The legend of this larger-than-life baseball hero is energetically captured by this author/illustrator duo. Paige was the first black pitcher in the major leagues and the first black player to be inducted into the Baseball Hall of Fame. Sports fans will be immediately drawn into this affecting tribute.

Savion: My Life in Tap

Written by Savion Glover
HarperCollins, $19.95, 79 pages
First published in 2000
Ages 9–14

"Fuh-duh-BAP!" is the jubilant sound of Glover's fancy footwork in this memoir. Glover first saw his name in the lights of Broadway at age eleven and proceeded to dazzle audiences with his dance performances and Tony Award–winning choreography. Glover pays repeated homage to his hoofing heroes, and it's quite likely that he will become a hero himself after your child reads his story.

Sebastian: A Book about Bach

Written and Illustrated by Jeanette Winter
Browndeer, $16.00, 40 pages
First published in 1999
Ages 6–10

Similar in style and scope to *My Name Is Georgia* (see under "Art"), this is a picture book biography that soars. Winter poetically describes the genius behind Bach's compositions and uses vividly colored brushstrokes to illuminate his musical moods.

Chapter Five

Sitting Bull and His World
Written by Albert Marrin
Dutton, $27.50, 246 pages
First published in 2000
Ages 11–17

Though often portrayed as a villain, Marrin's depiction of the Sioux leader is far more sympathetic. Rituals and ceremony are explained as a tool used to shed light on Sitting Bull's legacy and the continuing strife between Native Americans and whites.

Starry Messenger: Galileo Galilei
Written and Illustrated by Peter Sis
Farrar Straus Giroux, $5.95, 33 pages
First published in 1996
Ages 7–12

Acclaimed author Peter Sis charts Galileo's remarkable scientific career, celebrating his advancements during a time of plague and church censorship. Exquisite drawings, paintings, and maps complete the picture.

Careers

Career Ideas for Kids Who Like Animals and Nature
Written by Diane Lindsey Reeves
Facts On File, $12.95, 183 pages
First published in 2000
Ages 9–14

Does a trip to the zoo make your child starry eyed? Does she claim to want to be a veterinarian when she grows up? Well, there are a lot of career options for animal lovers including zoologist and animal trainer. This book will set children on the right career path. And if she changes her mind there are always *Career Ideas for Kids Who Like Talking*; *Career Ideas for Kids Who Like Art*; *Career Ideas for Kids Who Like Science*; *Career Ideas for Kids Who Like Sports*; and *Career Ideas for Kids Who Like Computers*.

Nonfiction • Cooking

I Want to Be a Chef
Written by Stephanie Maze, Illustrated by Annie Griffiths Belt
Harcourt, $9.00, 47 pages
First published in 1999
Ages 8–12

Peeking into the kitchens of fine restaurants across the country, the author introduces readers to the many opportunities for food lovers. Jobs including prep cook, pastry maker, as well as head chef are explained, as is the schooling required for each culinary career. This series also includes *I Want to Be a Dancer*; *I Want to Be a Doctor*; *I Want to Be a Fashion Designer*; *I Want to Be a Firefighter*; *I Want to Be a Pilot*; and *I Want to Be a Teacher*, among others.

Cooking And Food

American Heart Association Kids' Cookbook
Written by Mary Winston
Random House, $16.00, 127 pages
First published in 1993
Ages 8–14

A standout collection of simple and healthy recipes for kids, backed by the research of the American Heart Association. An extensive index and glossary are included. Also look for *The Children's Quick and Easy Cookbook* by Angela Wilkes.

It's Disgusting and We Ate It! True Food Facts from Around the World and Throughout History
Written by James Solheim, Illustrated by Eric Brace
Aladdin, $6.99, 37 pages
First published in 1998
Ages 6–10

Departing from the familiar burger and fries diet to which so many American children have become accustomed, here we find tasty treats in the way of spiders, maggots, seaweed, and soup made from birds' nests. Considered delicacies in exotic locale, these fun (and sometimes frightful) foods are real eye-openers about how cultural differences are often determined by what is found in any group's immediate natural surroundings.

Chapter Five

Pretend Soup and Other Real Recipes

Written by Mollie Katzen and Ann Henderson
Tricycle, $16.95, 95 pages
First published in 1994
Ages 6–10

Many grown-ups have delighted in Mollie Katzen's sumptuous recipes from the *Moosewood Cookbook*. Now her fine fare is served kid style, with dishes including noodle soup, quesadillas, and zucchini moons. While adult supervision is required during the preparation of many of these meals, Katzen and Henderson emphasize the importance of enjoying the process of cooking, rather than focusing too heavily on creating a perfect end result.

Crafts

Berry Smudges and Leaf Prints:
Finding and Making Colors from Nature

Written by Ellen B. Senisi
Dutton, $16.99, 40 pages
First published in 2001
Ages 7–12

Here's a unique and earthy approach to crafts. Children use objects found in the great outdoors of their own backyards (or more exotic spots) to create personal works of art including collages and beautiful dyed fabrics. There's interesting information about the effects of colors in nature and our responses to what we see around us when we step outside.

Easy Origami

Written by Dokutotei Nakano
Puffin, $6.99, 64 pages
First published in 1994
Ages 6–12

Origami is an exciting art form with a rich history, but its forms are often complex. This guide is a great introduction, detailing the steps required to make beautiful folded paper objects such as boats, snakes, swans, and, of course, paper cranes. More advanced folders will want to look for *Fantasy Origami* by Duy Nguyen.

Nonfiction • Crafts

Jumbo Book of Easy Crafts
Written by Judy Ann Sadler
Kids Can Press, $14.95, 208 pages
First published in 2001
Ages 5–10

Using easy-to-find materials—beans, magazines, popsicle sticks, glitter—there are countless crafts to be made. Why not make a paper lantern or a button bouquet? There are even simple instructions for making musical instruments from household objects. This book will cheerfully guide children through years of crafty inspiration. You'll also enjoy Loo-Loo, Boo, and *Art You Can Do* by Denis Roche.

Kids Knitting
Written by Melanie Falick
Artisan, $17.95, 127 pages
First published in 1998
Ages 7–14

Knitting is not just for grandmas anymore! In fact, you now find people knitting in the hippest Manhattan cafes. To get in on this crafty trend and become involved in a hobby that will last a lifetime, kids will want to check out this colorful guide that includes step-by-step instructions for cozy projects such as hats, scarves... even backpacks!

Look What You Can Make with Paper Bags
Written by Judy Burke, Illustrated by Hank Schneider
Boyds Mill Press, $5.95, 48 pages
First published in 1999
Ages 5–9

Crafts projects with an ecologically sound basis: Why not create fun crafts using discarded household items? Also in the series *Look What You Can Make with Egg Cartons* and *Look What You Can Make with Boxes*.

Chapter Five

Dance—Theater

Break a Leg!: The Kids' Guide to Acting and Stagecraft
Written by Lise Friedman
Workman, $14.95, 222 pages
First published in 2002
Ages 8–12

Shining the spotlight on the actor's craft, this guide includes essential tips for overcoming stage fright, memorizing scripts, breathing exercises and body language. There's also an intriguing look at the behind-the-scenes work of makeup artists, set designers, and other careers in the theater.

Dance
Written by Bill T. Jones and Susan Kuklin, Photographs by Susan Kuklin
Hyperion, $14.95, 32 pages
First published in 1998
Ages 6–10

An exuberant introduction to dance and an alternative to the more predominant material that focuses on the classical traditions of ballet. Jones's soaring moves are splendidly captured by Kuklin's camera in this picture book that's suited to early elementary-aged children.

Step-by-Step Ballet Class: The Official Illustrated Guide
Written by Antoinette Sibley
Contemporary, $14.95, 144 pages
First published in 1994
Ages 8–12

Addressing everything from proper shoes and attire to finding a good dance school and preparing for examinations, this book is based on the formal program at England's Royal Academy of Dancing. The thrilling photographs will be especially inspirational to hopeful ballet dancers. Also look for *My Ballet Book* by Kate Castle.

Nonfiction • Ecology

Ecology—Environmentalism—Earth Day

Common Ground: The Water, Earth, and Air We Share
Written and Illustrated by Molly Bang
Blue Sky Press, $12.95, 36 pages
First published in 1997
Ages 6–10

Appreciation and respect for our natural resources is at the core of this pointed parable, as it repeatedly emphasizes the importance of conservation. The message is made imminently clear to young readers who will revisit this story time and again. Children will remember Bang's knack for storytelling and illustration from her picture books including *When Sophie Gets Angry, Really Really Angry* (see "Picture Books").

Compost Critters
Written and Photographed by Bianca Lavies
Dutton, $15.99, 32 pages
First published in 1993
Ages 8–12

There's a miniature world of environmentalism alive and well in your own backyard. Lavies, a former National Geographic photographer, introduces the ecological efforts of insects and microscopic bacteria as they work to change household refuse into fertilizer. Even the smallest critters are photographed in all their glory.

The Drop in My Drink: The Story of Water on Our Planet
Written by Meredith Hooper
Viking, $16.99, 30 pages
First published in 1998
Ages 7–11

Hooper traces the journey of one drop of water from prehistoric origins through its arrival at the modern day faucet. Children will be fascinated by this concept as earth's chronology is accessibly examined. For more on this subject, dive into *A Drop of Water: A Book of Science and Wonder* by Walter Wick.

Chapter Five

Recycle! A Handbook for Kids
Written and Illustrated by Gail Gibbons
Little Brown, $6.95, 32 pages
First published in 1992
Ages 6–10

Imparting the importance of ecologically sound habits, this guide takes kids through the process of recycling. The author explains what happens to discarded bottles, newspapers, and other household items. A great tool for explaining how to turn everyday into Earth Day.

Explorers

Black Whiteness: Admiral Byrd Alone in the Antarctic
Written by Robert Burleigh, Illustrated by Walter Lyon Krudop
Simon & Schuster, $16.00, 40 pages
First published in 1998
Ages 7–12

Admiral Richard Byrd began an unprecedented journey in 1934, testing the limits of human endurance, as he made a home in an underground Antarctic shelter. From there he recorded his observations before becoming severely ill. Burleigh's sparse prose matches the haunting tone of Byrd's own solitary reflections, and readers are given a very immediate sense of the incredibly harsh conditions of an Antarctic winter.

Land Ho! Fifty Glorious Years in the Age of Exploration with 12 Important Explorers
Written by Nancy Winslow Parker
HarperCollins, $15.95, 28 pages
First published in 2001
Ages 8–12

Introducing the lives of adventurers such as Christopher Columbus, Amerigo Vespucci, Juan Rodriguez Cabrillo, and Ponce de Leon, the author gives readers a glimpse into the global importance of their travels. The cartoon illustrations make this book very accessible for young readers, while older children with a penchant for adventure will be thrilled by the maps and amazing facts. For a unique perspective on the New World pursuits of famous explorers, look for *Explor-A-Maze* by Robert Snedden. *Talking with Adventurers* by Pat Cummings and Linda Cummings features more contemporary groundbreakers.

Nonfiction • Family Issues

Lewis and Clark: Explorers of the American West
Written by Steven Kroll, Illustrated by Richard Williams
Holiday House, $6.95, 32 pages
First published in 1994
Ages 5–9

Beginning with the terms and conditions surrounding the Louisiana Purchase, Kroll and Williams portray the uncharted American landscape as an unsullied and boundless territory while making no bones about the immediately tumultuous relationship between Native Americans and white explorers. Gail Langer Karwoski offers a fresh perspective on the story of the famous traveling duo in *Seaman: The Dog Who Explored the West with Lewis & Clark*.

The Top of the World: Climbing Mount Everest
Written by Steve Jenkins
Houghton Mifflin, $6.95, 32 pages
First published in 1999
Ages 6–12

Not only has the author created an exquisitely illustrated tribute to Everest, he also sets forth a history of attempts to scale its heights and provides insight into the motivation behind those who are drawn to dangerous adventure. There's important detail about mountain climbing equipment and the conditions that climbers often face. At the same time, Jenkins uses Everest as a metaphor for the human predilection for conquering nature's most forbidding monuments.

Family Issues

Dinosaur's Divorce: A Guide for Changing Families
Written by Marc Brown and Laurene Krasny Brown, Illustrated by Marc Brown
Joy Street Books, $7.95, 31 pages
First published in 1986
Ages 4–8

The Browns use affable dinosaur characters to encourage discussion about divorce and related topics such as stepparents, visitation, and single parents. This is a child-centered book, highly useful for helping children through the confusion and sadness they may feel during a divorce. Marc Brown is the creator of the *Arthur* series (the popular aardvark), detailed in Easy Readers. Older children will benefit from *The Divorce Helpbook for Kids* by Cynthia Macgregor.

Chapter Five

Let's Talk about Drug Abuse
Written by Anna Kreiner
The Rosen Pub, $17.25, 24 pages
First published in 1996
Ages 6–10

Difficult discussions are made easier through the informative guides in the *Let's Talk* series. While your early elementary school child may seem far from danger, it's hardly inappropriate to raise the subject in a gentle, yet firm manner. Photographs depict a culturally diverse group of children and adults, while answering questions such as "what are drugs" and "why some drugs are illegal." Other timely topics include *Let's Talk about Alcohol Abuse*; *Let's Talk about Adoption*; *Let's Talk about Being Overweight*; *Let's Talk about Dyslexia*; *Let's Talk about Foster Homes*; *Let's Talk about Going to the Hospital*; and *Let's Talk about Smoking* among others.

Your Body Belongs to You
Written by Cornelia Maude Spelman
Albert Whitman, $13.95, 24 pages
First published in 1997
Ages 4–8

An age-appropriate forum for conversations with young children about sexual abuse, this book gently distinguishes between "good touching" and "bad touching" while advising parents to trust their child's instincts regarding unwanted contact by adults.

Games And Hobbies

Chess: From First Moves to Checkmate
Written by Daniel King
Kingfisher, $16.95, 64 pages
First published in 2001
Ages 9–14

Guaranteed to bring out the inner Bobby Fisher in your child, International Grandmaster Daniel King provides a history of chess as well as an accessible introduction to the strategies of the game. Other worthy introductions to the game include *Chess for Kids* by Michael Baseman.

Nonfiction • Games

The Kids' Campfire Book
Written by Jane Drake
Kids Can Press, $9.95, 128 pages
First published in 1998
Ages 8–12

With adult assistance, a campfire is a sure bet for a good time. Take this book along and you'll find plenty of ideas for songs, games and, of course, ghost stories. There are also useful safety tips and advice designed to turn everyone into intrepid campers. S'more anyone?

Marbles: 101 Ways to Play
Written by Joanna Cole, Illustrated by Stephanie Calmenson,
Michael Street, and Alan Tiegreen
Beech Tree, $8.95, 127 pages
First published in 1998
Ages 6–12

It's an old-fashioned game that can provide hours of enjoyment for even the most sophisticated kids. Hand over your marble collection and introduce games such as Old Bowler and Chinese Marbles. You'll find tips for shooting strategy and updated versions of familiar activities to perform with those colorful little globes.

So Many Dynamos: And Other Palindromes
Written by Jon Agee
Farrar Strauss Giroux, $6.95, 79 pages
First published in 1994
Ages 7–12

Palindromes are words or phrases that read the same forwards and backwards. They're also a ponderous source of amusement for kids. The black and white cartoons add further folly to the word play and captions such as "Snot or Protons" will surely become favorite catch phrases. Follow up with *Go Hang a Salami! I'm a Lasagna Hog!* also by Agee.

**The Best
Children's Literature**
A Parent's Guide

Chapter Five

Geography And Maps

Me on the Map
Written by Joan Sweeney, Illustrated by Annette Cable
Dragonfly, $6.99, 32 pages
First published in 1996
Ages 5–9

A superb introduction to maps, as well as an eye-opening perspective on our tiny but vital place in the world, a young girl begins by mapping her own bedroom and expands ever outward. A logical progression from this title would be the incredible *Mapping the World* by Sylvia A. Johnson.

The Scrambled States of America
Written and Illustrated by Laurie Keller
Henry Holt, $6.95, 40 pages
First published in 1999
Ages 5–9

parent's
guide
choice award

A highly imaginative blend of giggles and geography, Keller takes kids on a swift ride across the U.S.A. There's an amusing story line here, as each state wakes up and greets the day in its own unique way and, of course, within its own time zones. Young readers will quickly learn to identify each state on the map and the special contributions it makes to the big blended picture of America.

Grief And Loss

Part of Me Died Too:
Stories of Creative Survival among Bereaved Children
Written by Virginia Fry
Dutton, $19.99, 218 pages
First published in 1995
Ages 9–15

Using the artwork and stories of bereaved children, Fry provides a medium by which to discuss the process of grief and healing. The impact of each loss upon these children is devastatingly clear, and the book is, at times, very sad. However, children in similar situations will surely benefit from learning that there are many valid ways to deal with loss. Other helpful books include *Lost and Found: A Kids' Book for Living through Loss* by Marc Gellman; *Let's Talk About When a Parent Dies* by Elizabeth Weitzman; and *You and a Death in Your Family* by Antoine Wilson.

Health—Human Body— Human Sexuality

How the Body Works: 100 Ways Parents and Children Can Share the Miracle of the Human Body

Written by Steve Parker
Reader's Digest, $24.00, 192 pages
First published in 1994
Ages 8–14

Your kids are bound to have questions about their bodies, and this upbeat guide will provide a lot of age-appropriate answers. Vivid photographs add to the appeal of this interactive and helpful book. Younger readers will want to look for *The Magic School Bus: Inside the Human Body* by Joanna Cole (this series is listed in "Easy Readers").

How You Were Born

Written by Joanna Cole, Photographs by Margaret Miller
Mulberry, $6.95, 48 pages
First published in 1994
Ages 4–8

Joanna Cole has a wonderful touch for enlivening content areas such as science and history for children. (It's no wonder her *Magic School Bus* series is so successful.) Here, she narrates a photo essay that explains the process of conception through birth. The descriptions are candid, yet age-appropriate, and there's a lot of affection in the delivery of the text.

I'm Tougher Than Asthma

Written by Alden R. Carter, Illustrated by Siri M. Carter, Photographs by Dan Young
Albert Whitman, $6.95, 32 pages
First published in 1996
Ages 5–9

One of the most common childhood maladies, asthma affects millions of kids and their families. This book, narrated by a young girl named Siri (the author's daughter), shows how to monitor and treat the symptoms and causes of asthma. Most of all, it emphasizes that kids with asthma can lead happy, healthy, active lives! There's also *I'm Tougher Than Diabetes*.

Chapter Five

It's Perfectly Normal: A Book about Changing Bodies, Growing Up, Sex, and Sexual Health

Written by Robie H. Harris, Illustrated by Michael Emberley
Candlewick, $10.99, 89 pages
First published in 1994
Ages 10–14

An appropriate amount of informative detail and affectionate reassurance add to this guide's appeal as a great accompaniment to family discussions about sexuality and growing up. There's some serious subject matter here including STD's, abortion, and birth control, but its treatment is consistently well-suited to the book's intended adolescent audience. Younger readers should opt for *It's So Amazing!* described below.

It's So Amazing! A Book about Eggs, Sperm, Birth, Babies, and Families

Written by Robie H. Harris, Illustrated by Michael Emberley
Candlewick, $21.99, 81 pages
First published in 1999
Ages 6–12

If Harris and Emberley's book, *It's Perfectly Normal* (see above) doesn't quite fit the bill for younger children, here's a perfect source of information for the elementary school set. A lighthearted cast of late model birds and bees provide charming explanations for even the most bashful of curious children. Topics such as puberty, pregnancy, and sexual orientation are addressed in a gentle manner.

Hispanic Heritage

Family Pictures (Cuadros de Familia)

Written and Illustrated by Carmen Lomas Garza
Children's Book Press, $7.95, 30 pages
First published in 1993
Ages 6–10

Hispanic family and community are celebrated in this effervescent bilingual picture book. With evident nostalgia and affection, the author gives a vivid view of her own childhood in Texas near the Mexican border. A perfect choice for illuminating cultural diversity within America, this beautifully illustrated story will be a feast for your family's eyes. Follow up with *In My Family (En Mi Familia)*.

Nonfiction • Holidays

Fiesta USA
Written by George Ancona
Lodestar, $17.99, 48 pages
First published in 1995
Ages 5–10

Four Latino-American celebrations are featured here, as Mexican-Americans in San Francisco don skeleton costumes to observe El Dia de los Muertos (Day of the Dead). In New York, La Fiesta de los Reyes Magos (Three Kings' Day) gets underway twelve days after Christmas. With ample visual fun, this book is a great way to join in the festivities that so many Hispanic-American children celebrate.

Holidays And World Religions

A Calendar of Festivals
Written by Cherry Gilchrist
Barefoot, $18.95, 80 pages
First published in 1998
Ages 6–12

This lively collection uses legends and folk tales from a number of different cultural traditions to explain the customs associated with various familiar and lesser known holidays, including Kwanzaa, Christmas, Purim, Tanabata, and Vesak. You'll want to consult this terrific resource throughout the calendar year. Also seek *Kids Around the World Celebrate! The Best Feasts and Festivals from Many Lands* by Lynda Jones.

Celebrating Chinese New Year
Written by Diane Hoyt-Goldsmith, Photographs by Lawrence Migdale
Holiday House, $6.99, 32 pages
First published in 1999
Ages 5–9

All of the customary elements of celebrating the Chinese New Year are observed by Ryan and his family, as they head to the market to gather food for the festive meal, attend a parade, and pay tribute to his ancestors. The vivid photographs invite readers into the center of the excitement. Also look for *Celebrating Hanukkah*; *Celebrating Kwanzaa*; *Celebrating Passover*; and *Celebrating Ramadan*.

Chapter Five

Christmas Around the World
Written by Mary D. Lankford
Mulberry Books, $5.95, 47 pages
First published in 1995
Ages 6–10

A spirited look at how Christmas is celebrated in 12 different countries including Greece, Australia, and Ethiopia. How do children's visions of Santa vary around the globe? What are the origins of various holiday traditions and superstitions? You'll find the colorful answers and an array of easy Christmas craft projects in this dynamic book. As the winter holidays approach, don't miss *Let's Celebrate Christmas* by Peter Roop; *More Christmas Ornaments Kids Can Make* by Kathy Ross; *The Story of Christmas* by Barbara Cooney; and *The Night Before Christmas* by Clement Clarke Moore.

Dance, Sing, Remember:
A Celebration of Jewish Holidays
Written by Leslie Kimmelman
HarperCollins, $18.95, 34 pages
First published in 2000
Ages 5–10

There are many richly textured books about the observance of Jewish holidays—Passover, Hanukkah, Yom Kippur—and the traditions associated with them. Kimmelman's collection, however, is perfectly targeted in terms of age appropriateness and includes just the right blend of information, stories, lore, games, and songs. Also look for *Milk and Honey: A Year of Jewish Holidays* by Jane Yolen and *On Rosh Hashanah and Yom Kippur* by Cathy Goldberg Fishman. Slightly older readers will also enjoy *The Day the Rabbi Disappeared: Jewish Holiday Tales of Magic* by Howard Schwartz.

On Mardi Gras Day
Written by Fatima Shaik, Illustrated by Floyd Cooper
Dial, $16.99, 32 pages
First published in 1999
Ages 5–10

The golds, greens, and purples of Mardi Gras leap off of the pages in this Cajun celebration. You'll see parade floats and fancy feasts and learn about the origins of this bustling jubilee, with a fine focus on the rich traditions of the Mardi Gras Indians and the African-American Zulu parade.

Nonfiction • Holidays

Ramadan
Written by Suhaib Hamid Ghazi, Illustrated by Omar Rayyan
Holiday House, $6.95, 32 pages
First published in 1996
Ages 5–9

Intended as an explanation for non-Muslim children of the holy month of Ramadan. There's useful information about the tenets of Islam as well as the fasting and prayer that accompanies Ramadan's observance. Using a picture book format and a child's perspective, this book is an excellent choice for illuminating the rituals and worship practices of a major world religion.

The Story of Thanksgiving
Written by Robert Merrill Bartlett
HarperCollins, $14.95, 34 pages
First published in 2001
Ages 5–9

An updated version of the 1965 classic, this staple of holiday reading now includes a more enlightened perspective of the events surrounding the first Thanksgiving and the role of the Native Americans who had settled before the arrival of the Pilgrims. A recipe for pumpkin muffins is included as are the lyrics and music for "Over the River and Through the Woods" to round out a celebration of the joyful yet humbling holiday. Pair this title with *Thanksgiving Is* by Louise Borden; *Let's Celebrate Thanksgiving* by Peter Roop; and the lovely *Molly's Pilgrim* by Barbara Cohen (see "Story Books").

Witches, Pumpkins, and Grinning Ghosts: The Story of the Halloween Symbols
Written by Edna Barth
Clarion, $16.00, 96 pages
First published in 1996
Ages 6–10

How did toothy pumpkins become associated with Halloween? Why do children wear costumes and go "trick or treating?" You'll find out as the origins of spooky symbols and sweet treats are detailed. For more ghoulish glee, look for *The Big Book of Halloween: Creative & Creepy Projects for Revelers of All Ages* by Laura Dover Doran; *Boo! It's Halloween* by Wendy Watson; *The Halloween Book* by Jane Bull; and *The Halloween House* by Erica Silverman.

Chapter Five

Holocaust

After the Holocaust
Written by Howard Greenfield
Greenwillow, $18.95, 146 pages
First published in 2001
Ages 12 and up

An emotional account of concentration camp survivors and their lives after liberation. With photographs and a suggested reading list, this collection provides crucial closure to Holocaust studies.

I Never Saw Another Butterfly: Children's Drawings and Poems from Terezin Concentration Camp, 1942-1944
Written by Hana Volavkova
Schocken, $17.50, 106 pages
First published in 1994
Ages 10 and up

The heart-wrenching realities of the Holocaust are made abundantly clear through this collection of art from the youngest concentration camp victims. While more than 15,000 children were imprisoned at Terezin, only 100 survived. Teachers and parents will want to introduce this book as a way of viewing the Holocaust through the eyes of its children. Pair this title with *Tell Them We Remember: The Story of the Holocaust* by Susan D. Bachrach.

In My Hands: Memories of a Holocaust Rescuer
Written by Irene Gut Opdyke
Knopf, $12.00, 276 pages
First published in 1999
Ages 12 and up

When the Nazis invaded Poland, Irene Gut was only 17-years-old. Eventually forced to work as a waitress for Nazi officials, Irene began to leave food for people in the nearby Jewish ghetto. Her bravery and selflessness throughout the ensuing war years is remarkable. The fact that her efforts began when she was a teenager will make her story even more compelling to middle and high school readers. Middle school readers will also want to find *No Pretty Pictures: A Child of War* by Anita Lobel.

Immigration

How I Became An American
Written by Karin Gundisch
Cricket Books, $15.95, 120 pages
First published in 2001
Ages 9–12

An example of excellent historical fiction, this mock-memoir tells the story of Johann and his family during their emigration from a small village in Austria-Hungary to the United States. Their difficult voyage and poignant adjustment to life in America provide an intimate view of the immigrant experience. Be sure to look for *When Jessie Came Across the Sea* by Amy Hest.

Immigrants
Written by Martin Sandler
HarperTrophy, $10.95, 92 pages
First published in 1995
Ages 9–14

Archival photographs, posters, and memorabilia illuminate the immigrant experience in America from 1870 through 1920. From their voyage at sea and arrival at Ellis Island, to living and working in the U.S., there is a lot to learn about the hopes and fears of the immigrants,

Insects

The Big Bug Book
Written by Margery Facklam
Little Brown, $16.95, 32 pages
First published in 1994
Ages 6–11

Ever seen a Madagascar hissing cockroach? What about a Goliath beetle? A Wetapunga? These are but a few of the creepy yet captivating insects you'll find in this guide. The illustrations are amazing and are likely to encourage backyard exploration and a growing appreciation for the value and role of insects in nature. Still feeling buggy? Try Facklam's *Creepy, Crawly Caterpillars* for a close-up look at the process of metamorphosis. Also look for *About Insects: A Guide for Children* by Cathryn Sill.

Chapter Five

Bright Beetle

Written and Illustrated by Rick Chrustowski
Henry Holt, $15.95, 32 pages
First published in 2000
Ages 4–8

Ladybugs are the "beetle" in question, and readers get an up close and personal look at their life cycle, feeding habits, and predators. Widely regarded as a "friendly" bug, kids will delight in the cheerful illustrations and fascinating facts. Also seek *Face-to-Face with the Ladybug* by Valerie Tracqui.

An Extraordinary Life: The Story of a Monarch Butterfly

Written by Laurence Pringle
Orchard, $7.95, 64 pages
First published in 1997
Ages 9–12

The migration of Monarch butterflies from New England to Mexico is an astonishing feat of nature. This stunning book follows the journey of an individual butterfly named Danaus, detailing the trials—from bad weather to predators—and triumphs of this beautiful species. For more amazement, look for *Butterfly Story* by Anca Hariton.

Thinking about Ants

Written by Barbara Brenner, Illustrated by Carol Schwartz
Mondo, $4.95, 32 pages
First published in 1996
Ages 5–9

Just what makes that little old ant think he can move a rubber tree plant? Viewing life from the ground up, this introduction to ants will inspire many wide-eyed moments of wonder. There are basic facts about diet and habitat, but did you know that an average ant can transport several times its own weight in food? High hopes, indeed. Don't miss *Ant Cities* by Arthur Dorros and *Army Ant Parade* by April Pulley Sayre.

Inventions

Brainstorm! The Stories of Twenty American Kid Inventors

Written by Tom Tucker, Illustrated by Richard Loehle
Sunburst, $6.95, 150 pages
First published in 1995
Ages 9–13

Out of the mouths... and minds... of babes comes some of history's most interesting inventions. It was 15-year-old Chester Greenwood who is warmly credited with making the first earmuffs. There's also 7-year-old Maurice Scales who created a device that prevents children from getting their fingers caught in doors. Could your kid be next on the patent pending list? Get further inspiration from *Girls Think of Everything: Ingenious Inventions by Women* by Catherine Thimmesh; *How to Enter and Win an Invention Contest* by Ed Sobey; and *The Kids' Invention Book* by Arlene Erlbach.

Mistakes That Worked

Written by Charlotte Foltz Jones
Doubleday, $11.95, 78 pages
First published in 1994
Ages 8–14

What do Velcro and penicillin have in common? They were both invented entirely by fortunate accident. Jones provides fun anecdotes and facts about the origins of items that we use everyday. Also see the companion volume *Accidents May Happen: Fifty Inventions Discovered by Mistake*. And for more scientific happenstance, check out *Lucky Science: Accidental Discoveries from Gravity to Velcro* (see under "Science").

Chapter Five

Libraries And Research

Library: From Ancient Scrolls to the World Wide Web
Written by John Malam
Peter Bedrick, $16.95, 32 pages
First published in 2000
Ages 9–13

In the hallowed halls of the public library, there's a lot more than meets the eye. Readers of this special book are treated to a tour of a modern library, including explanations of circulation, children's services, a bookmobile, and multimedia collections as well as efforts toward conservation. A history of the public library is also included. Middle elementary curriculum often includes a study of the library, and this book provides perfect accompaniment.

The New York Public Library Kids' Guide to Research
Written by Deborah Heiligman
Scholastic Reference, $8.95, 134 pages
First published in 1998
Ages 9–14

With tips for finding information through encyclopedias, reference materials, and the Internet, kids are shown how to access the wide world of information. Especially useful for late-elementary and middle school projects, the research methods gleaned from this guide will serve students through college.

Homework Busters:
How to Use the Internet for A+ Grades
Written by Bill Thompson
Sterling Publishing, $9.95, 48 pages
First published in 2001
Ages 9–14

For both beginners and more advanced surfers, the author provides homework help for the millennium. Young researchers will find tips for accessing information, warnings about Internet security, and easy steps for acing every assignment. There are also ideas for online fun (after the homework is completed, of course) in the "Chilling Out" segments. Also, check your search engine for *Homework Help for Kids on the Net* by Lisa Trumbauer.

Math

Dazzling Division:
Games and Activities that Make Math Easy and Fun
Written by Lynette Long
John Wiley & Sons, $12.95, 122 pages
First published in 2000
Ages 8–12

For those of us who need a bit of extra stimulation when it comes to understanding number theory, this guide is a great place to start. You'll find games, puzzles, and alternative ways of viewing the processes involved in division. Because this book and its companion volumes offer so much in the way of hands-on activities, they are excellent choices for children with dyscalculia or other learning differences. Also look for *Fabulous Fractions*; *Marvelous Multiplication*; and *Measurement Mania*.

Janice Van Cleave's Play and Find Out about Math
Written by Janice Van Cleave
John Wiley & Sons, $30.00, 122 pages
First published in 1997
Ages 6–10

A leader in the creation of lively curriculum-based activity books, Ms. Van Cleave's *Play and Find Out* series also includes books about science, bugs, nature, and the human body. (They are all titled *Janice Van Cleave's Play and Find Out About...*) Here we find projects that shed new light on mathematical concepts. You'll create a paper chain to learn about length and patterns, for example. Search for other books by this clever author.

Medieval Era—Knights

Knights in Shining Armor
Written and Illustrated by Gail Gibbons
Little Brown, $5.95, 32 pages
First published in 1995
Ages 5–9

It took a lot more than mettle to become a knight, and Gibbons takes readers on a fascinating journey back to medieval times. There's information about castles, weapons, and tournaments, and an introduction to famous knights of lore such as Sir Gawain and the members of King Arthur's Round Table. With fine illustrations and insight, your kids will be royally thrilled. Also look for *Arms and Armor* by Michele Byam.

Chapter Five

The Making of a Knight:
How Sir James Earned His Armor
Written and Illustrated by Patrick O'Brien
Charlesbridge, $6.95, 32 pages
First published in 1998
Ages 6–12

Beginning his lifelong quest as a page at age seven, Sir James became a squire and, after demonstrating the requisite skills and bravery in battle, achieved the status of knight. His world of kings, queens, chivalry, and the occasional dragon will entrance readers of all ages. For more legendary bravado, be certain to seek *Saint George and the Dragon* by Trina Schart Hyman and *In the Time of Knights: The Real-Life Story of History's Greatest Knight* by Shelley Tanaka.

Medieval Life
Written by Andrew Langley
Dorling Kindersley, $15.95, 63 pages
First published in 2000
Ages 8–12

DK's trademark use of vivid photography brings the Middle Ages to life for young readers. Relevant historical background is provided as well as a captivating glimpse into everyday life, religion, clothing, and royalty. *The Encyclopedia of the Middle Ages* from Puffin Books is an excellent source of detailed facts about this era.

Money And Finance

If You Made a Million
Written by David M. Schwartz
Lothrop, $5.95, 40 pages
First published in 1989
Ages 7–11

While your child might want to hold off on cracking open the piggy bank, Schwartz offers sound advice for young financiers and future bankers. Basic and more sophisticated math concepts are introduced through discussion and visual aids, while economic matters such as savings, interest, and mortgages are explained. This book is a sound investment. Math wizardry abounds in David Schwartz' *How Much Is a Million?*

Nonfiction • Music

Money, Money, Money: The Meaning of the Art and Symbols on United States Paper Currency
Written by Nancy Parker
HarperCollins, $16.95, 32 pages
First published in 1995
Ages 9–13

Open your purse and take a good look at a dollar bill. There's a lot of patriotic symbolism to be found there. This is an interesting take on American history and an outstanding guide to the elements of currency.

Neale S. Godfrey's Ultimate Kids' Money Book
Written by Neale S. Godfrey
Simon & Schuster, $19.00, 122 pages
First published in 1998
Ages 8–13

Godfrey effortlessly anticipates kids' questions about currency, credit cards, taxes, and much more through her enjoyable vignettes and trivia. More than just a guide to financial vocabulary, there are ample opportunities for kids to speculate on different money-related questions in her "Penny for Your Thoughts" segments.

Music

The Beatles
Written by Mike Venezia
Children's Press, $6.95, 32 pages
First published in 1996
Ages 7–12

An apt addition to the *Getting to Know the World's Greatest Composers* series, kids receive an essential education on how the world was forever changed by the music of John, Paul, George, and Ringo. Bring this book home and help create a whole new generation of fans.

**The Best
Children's Literature**
A Parent's Guide

Chapter Five

Shake, Rattle and Roll: The Founders of Rock & Roll
Written by Holly George-Warren
Houghton Mifflin, $15.00, 30 pages
First published in 2001
Ages 8–13

Despite what some of today's young pop fans might say, rock and roll did not begin with N'Sync. This collective biography introduces such melody makers as Elvis Presley, Buddy Holly, James Brown, and Bo Diddley. The power of rock music as the force behind (and the reflection of) social change is also noted in this entertaining book.

Shout, Sister, Shout:
Ten Girl Singers Who Shaped a Century
Written by Roxane Orgill
McElderry, $18.00, 148 pages
First published in 2001
Ages 10–16

Shout they do... and they sing pretty well too. Orgill's enthusiasm for her subjects is as contagious as a catchy song. Featuring Bessie Smith, Judy Garland, Joan Baez, Lucinda Williams, and pop revolutionary, Madonna. You may be buying your daughter a guitar for her next birthday.

The Story of the Incredible Orchestra: An Introduction
to Musical Instruments and the Symphony Orchestra
Written and Illustrated by Bruce Koscielniak
Houghton Mifflin, $15.00, 32 pages
First published in 2000
Ages 6–10

This musical journey begins with a jaunty description of instruments and symphonies from bygone eras, including the Baroque and Romantic Periods, and continues toward an exploration of more modern symphonic sounds. Particularly interesting is the evolution of certain instruments. For example, did you know that the early version of an oboe was called a shawm? Open this book and strike up the band!

Mythology And Legends

Atlantis: The Legend of the Lost City
Written and Illustrated by Christina Balit
Henry Holt, $16.95, 28 pages
First published in 2000
Ages 5–9

Plato's legend of Atlantis is beautifully portrayed by Balit's enchanting illustrations and clear text. What happened when Poseidon fell in love with Cleito? Well, the rest is history... or myth. Read on with *Atlantis: The Lost Continent?* by Andrew Donkin and *Buried Blueprints: Maps and Sketches of Lost Worlds and Mysterious Places* by Albert Lorenz.

D'Aulaires' Book of Greek Myths
Written and Illustrated by Ingri and Edgar Parin d'Aulaire
Picture Yearling, $15.99, 192 pages
First published in 1962
Ages 5–9

Long the standard in myth adaptations for children, this is an accessible source of information and wonder about the gods and goddesses of Ancient Greece. Young readers may also want to look for *The Gods and Goddesses of Olympus* by Aliki and *Greek Myths* by Geraldine Mccaughrean.

The Gods and Goddesses of Ancient Egypt
Written by Leonard Everett Fisher
Holiday House, $6.95, 34 pages
First published in 1997
Ages 8–12

Sure, there were Ra and Isis, but did you know about Seshat and Horus? Fisher's depictions read like an engrossing novel, complete with romance and treachery. Young readers will be given a new perspective on Ancient Egypt as these legends come alive. A wonderful accompaniment to late-elementary studies of ancient civilizations, and a great choice for children who show early interest in mythology.

Chapter Five

Native American

Giving Thanks:
A Native American Good Morning Message
Written by Jake Swamp, Illustrated by Erwin Printup Jr.
Lee & Low, $5.95, 24 pages
First published in 1995
Ages 5–10

Derived from a Mohawk tradition of giving thanks for the earth, water, air, animals, and spiritual protectors, this lovely book imparts the simple message of expressing gratitude as a daily practice.

How We Saw the World:
Nine Native Stories of the Way Things Began
Written by C.J. Taylor
Tundra Books, $9.99, 32 pages
First published in 1993
Ages 6–10

Nine enchanting Native American legends are featured, including the Algonquin tale of how Niagara Falls was formed and the Kiowa story of the first tornado. There's also information about each tribe, creating a stirring vision of the beliefs of North America's earliest residents.

Thirteen Moons on a Turtle's Back
Written by Joseph Bruchac
Paperstar, $6.99, 32 pages
First published in 1992
Ages 5–10

The special significance of the moon cycle in many Native American traditions is illuminated by 13 stunning poems, all of which are illustrated with glorious oil paintings. Also look for *When the Moon Is Full: A Lunar Year* by Penny Pollack.

Poetry

Brown Angels: An Album of Picture and Verse
Written and Illustrated by Walter Dean Myers
Greenwillow, $6.95, 40 pages
First published in 1996
Ages 5–12

Myers has crafted a truly artful book that joins together lovely archival photographs of African-American children with equally atmospheric verse. The collection resembles a handcrafted heirloom album, certain to be gazed upon for years to come. Walter Dean Myers is the author of *Harlem* (see under African-American in this chapter); *Fallen Angels*; and *Hoops* among many fine others. You'll also enjoy *In Daddy's Arms I am Tall: African Americans Celebrating Fathers* by Javaka Steptoe.

The Gargoyle on the Roof
Written by Jack Prelutsky, Illustrated by Peter Sis
Greenwillow, $16.00, 39 pages
First published in 1999
Ages 6–12

This haunting collection of spooky poems featuring vampires, trolls, and gremlins will please not only poetry lovers, but also ghost story devotees. The amusing verse is told in first person (or first monster, as it were), so kids get a ghoulish glimpse of life on the other side. Peter Sis's illustrations are delightfully frightful but not too scary. Other wonderful poetry collections by Jack Prelutsky include *The Dragons Are Singing Tonight*; *The Frogs Wore Red Suspenders*; *The New Kid on the Block*; *A Pizza the Size of the Sun*; and *Something Big Has Been Here.*

Joyful Noise: Poems for Two Voices
Written by Paul Fleischman, Illustrated by Eric Beddows
HarperTrophy, $5.95, 44 pages
First published in 1988
Ages 8–12

There has rarely been a more charming collection of poetry than you'll find in this widely admired book. The verse focuses on the lives of insects, told from their perspective. Engaging readers in the most secret joys and fears of insects can be a risky proposition, but Paul Fleischman carries it off with a perfect tone and astounding grace. You'll want to look for other books by this gifted author including *Bull Run*; *Seedfolks*; and *Weslandia*. Young adults will adore his newest novel, entitled *Seek.*

Chapter Five

Jump Back, Honey: The Poems of Paul Laurence Dunbar
Written by Paul Laurence Dunbar, Illustrated by Andrea Davis Pinkney and
Ashley Bryan
Jump at the Sun, $16.99, 32 pages
First published in 1999

A star-studded array of illustrators celebrate the words of turn-of-the-20th century poet, Dunbar, in this wonderful collection. Proud poems such as "Dawn" and "Little Brown Baby" are accompanied by fittingly glowing illustrations by Ashley Bryan, Jerry Pinkney, and Faith Ringgold among others.

A Light in the Attic
Written and Illustrated by Shel Silverstein
HarperCollins, $17.95, 167 pages
First published in 1981
Ages 6–12

Sentimental favorite Silverstein (see *The Giving Tree* in Story Books) brought light to the lives of millions of children with this enduring classic, an affectionate collection of humorous verse and drawings. Each poem addresses common childhood themes that ring familiar bells for kids and nostalgic ones for grown-ups. You'll also adore *Falling Up* and *Where the Sidewalk Ends*.

A Poke in the I
Written by Paul B. Janeczko, Illustrated by Chris Raschka
Candlewick, $15.99, 35 pages
First published in 2001
Ages 5–12

The playful visual presentation of fonts and letter shapes share center stage with the content of Janeczko's clever verse, combining into a sensory extravaganza. Check out the double page spread of "Tennis Anyone," which invites readers to follow the text as though they were watching a match. Chris Raschka's illustrations never disappoint, and his talent is in top form here.

Nonfiction • Pre-Historic

A Visit to William Blake's Inn:
Poems for Innocent and Experienced Travelers
Written by Nancy Willard, Illustrated by Alice and Martin Provensen
Harcourt, $7.00, 44 pages
First published in 1981
Ages 6–12

Winning the triple crown of literary awards, this exceptional collection earned a **National Book Award**, a **Newbery Medal**, and a **Caldecott Honor**. It centers on an imaginary inn owned by William Blake, where a host of unforgettable characters reside and lively adventures unfold. Complete with Alice and Martin Provensen's elegant illustrations, this book is a must-read for all poetry lovers.

Prehistoric—Paleontology— Dinosaurs

Asteroid Impact
Written and Illustrated by Douglas Henderson
Dial, $16.99, 40 pages
First published in 2000
Ages 7–11

What caused the demise of dinosaurs and ancient reptiles? Well, many respected scientists cite a trillion-ton asteroid that hit the earth 65 million years ago. The idea of the impact is amazing enough, but Henderson's astounding illustrations add to the allure of this pre-historic account. Be sure to consult the question and answer segment at the back of the book.

Beyond the Dinosaurs!: Sky Dragons, Sea Monsters, Mega-Mammals and Other Prehistoric Beasts
Written by Howard Zimmerman
Atheneum, $18.00, 64 pages
First published in 2001
Ages 6–10

When your kids finally get their fill of T-Rexes and Brontosauruses, it's time to move on to the high flying, muck dwelling, and otherwise incredible pre-historic creatures featured in this spirited book. There are facts and theories about habitats, predators, and size. The Quetzalcoatlus is especially impressive, with a wingspan equaling the size of a small airplane!

Chapter Five

Gigantic! How Big Were the Dinosaurs?
Written and Illustrated by Patrick O'Brien
Henry Holt, $15.95, 32 pages
First published in 1999
Ages 5–9

The title certainly gives readers a clue, but the marvelous text and illustrations drive the point home, as the sizes of pre-historic creatures are paired with modern machines. There are familiar dinosaurs and other lesser known land and water beasts to amaze and astound all readers. This is a perfectly executed book that grabs the attention of dino-devotees while exploring the concept of relative size.

The Mystery of the Mammoth Bones and How It Was Solved
Written by James Cross Giblin
HarperCollins, $15.95, 97 pages
First published in 1999
Ages 8–12

When Charles Wilson Peale discovered the skeletons of two pre-historic mammoths in 1801, the field of paleontology was forever changed. His dramatic story is the subject of this terrific and suspenseful portrayal.

Science (General)

Hidden Worlds:
Looking Through a Scientist's Microscope
Written by Stephen Kramer
Houghton Mifflin, $16.00, 57 pages
First published in 2001
Ages 8–13

While their tiny size may be hard to fathom, this up-close and personal look at microorganisms and microscopic plant parts is one amazing adventure. Kramer, a scientist, uses a microscope that magnifies objects up to one million times, and discusses how the study of animal and plant cells can lead to breakthroughs in the cure of disease.

Nonfiction • Science (General)

Let's Read and Find Out Science Series
Various authors
HarperCollins, $4.95 per title
Ages 5–10

Exploring scientific subject matter from crickets to dinosaurs, earthquakes to space exploration, the picture books in this series are great choices for early readers. Look for them in the science section of your local bookstore or library. For every curious child, there's a topic, including: *Air Is All Around You; Animals in Winter; Be a Friend to Trees; Follow the Water from Brook to Ocean; Floating in Space; Germs Make Me Sick!; Hear Your Heart; Is There Life in Outer Space?; Sleep Is for Everyone; What Color Is Camoflage?*... and many more!

Incredible Comparisons
Written by Russell Ash
DK, $19.95, 63 pages
First published in 1996
Ages 8–14

The gloriously detailed illustrations, including a few intricate foldouts, provide a clear sense of relative size, weight, and speed in an array of objects. Fans of David Macaulay's *The New Way Things Work* (detailed in this chapter) will be dazzled, and kids (as well as their parents) with an affinity for scientific investigation will find this book quite useful.

Lucky Science:
Accidental Discoveries from Gravity to Velcro
Written by Royston M. Roberts
John Wiley, $12.95, 110 pages
First published in 1994
Ages 9–14

From gravity to silly putty, did you know that many famous discoveries happened entirely by accident? With parent-assisted experiments, upper-elementary and middle school-aged kids are encouraged to consider the process of scientific inquiry. Also see *Mistakes That Worked* by Charlotte Foltz Jones (in this chapter, see under "Inventions").

Chapter Five

The New Way Things Work
Written and Illustrated by David Macaulay
Houghton Mifflin, $35.00, 400 pages
First published in 1998
Ages 10 and up
An astounding union of science and art, Macaulay's attention to detail ignites a spark of inquisitive excitement in all readers. This is a revised edition of the original 1988 version, with enhanced illustrations and an added emphasis on the "Digital Domain." Truly a perfect gift, especially for recent grads with a penchant for technology.

Stephen Biesty's Incredible Cross Sections
Written by Richard Platt, Illustrated by Stephen Biesty
Knopf, $19.95, 48 pages
First published in 1992
Ages 6–12
Intricately detailed drawings show the inner workings and assembly of objects and edifices, from the space shuttle to a medieval castle. The cutaway illustrations will keep readers glued, while the fascinating text will encourage further investigation. Incredible, yes, and unforgettable, too!

Sign Language
The Handmade Alphabet
Written and Illustrated by Laura Rankin
Puffin, $6.99, 32 pages
First published in 1996
Ages 5–12
The American Sign Language alphabet is lovingly taught through lifelike colored pencil drawings, depicting the hand signs for each letter. Also look for *Handsigns: A Sign Language Alphabet* by Kathleen Fain.

You Can Learn Sign Language!
More Than 300 Words in Pictures
Written by Jackie Kramer
Troll, $4.95, 38 pages
First published in 2000
Ages 6–12
Photos and illustrations depict the hand shapes for a variety of objects and ideas, beginning with the alphabet and numbers and proceeding through emotions, food, school, and other familiar categories. Instructions for creating each sign are clearly explained and demonstrated.

Social Responsibility—Volunteerism

Guns: What You Should Know
Written by Rachel Ellenberg Schulson, Illustrated by Mary Jones
Albert Whitman, $5.95, 24 pages
First published in 1997
Ages 5–9

Through its picture book format, important information about the dangers of improper gun usage is detailed. The author explains that while children frequently see gun-toting heroes on TV and in the movies, in real life (and in the wrong hands) guns can cause serious harm or death.

The Kid's Guide to Social Action:
Over 500 Service Ideas for Young People
Written by Barbara A. Lewis
Free Spirit, $18.95, 211 pages
First published in 1998
Ages 10–16

If you're looking for ways to impart the concept of social responsibility and activism to your pre-adolescent or teenager, look no further. Complete with dozens of do-able projects such as waste cleanup and youth rights canvassing, this guide might even inspire your child to enlist her friends and classmates in various campaigns. At the very least, kids will be encouraged to begin examining their own priorities as they relate to a greater good.

Space

Adventure in Space: The Flight to Fix the Hubble
Written by Elaine Scott, Illustrated by Margaret Miller
Hyperion, $7.95, 64 pages
First published in 1995
Ages 8–12

The Hubble was in trouble! Featuring astounding photography and first-hand accounts, the attempts of seven astronauts to repair the Hubble telescope are documented. A perfect accompaniment to late-elementary and early-middle school space studies. Also look for *Space Exploration* by Carole Scott.

Chapter Five

Postcards from Pluto: A Tour of the Solar System
Written and Illustrated by Loreen Leedy
Holiday House, $6.95, 32 pages
First published in 1993
Ages 5–9

Here's a great blast off into space for the early elementary grades, as Dr. Quasar leads six young explorers to each planet. Perfect for beginning readers who enjoyed *The Magic School Bus* series as well as for any child with astronaut ambitions.

See the Stars: Your First Guide to the Night Sky
Written by Ken Croswell
Boyds Mills, $16.95, 32 pages
First published in 2000
Ages 7–12

Young astronomers will be gazing at the heavens with new enthusiasm after reading this lovely guidebook. The constellations are vividly illustrated and explained, and as the author turns readers' attention skyward, she explains the best times of the month and year to view the heavenly star shapes. Next, be sure to point your telescope toward *Stargazers* by Gail Gibbons.

Sports—Exercise

All About Soccer
Written by George Sullivan
Putnam, $15.99, 122 pages
First published in 2001
Ages 8–12

A favorite game worldwide, it's likely that your child will be eager to get into the action. You'll find clear explanations of skills, drills, rules, and strategy here, as well as a history of World Cup and Olympic competition. There's a nice balance of focus on both men and women players and a glossary of soccer organizations, too! Also look for *Starting Soccer* by Helen Edom and *My Soccer Book* by Gail Gibbons.

Nonfiction • Sports

Baseball ABC
Written by Florence Cassen Mayers
Abrams, $12.95, 40 pages
First published in 1994
Ages 6–12

A sophisticated alphabet book for sports lovers, this is a great gift selection. Baseball trivia, memorabilia, lore and legend make this unique book a real crowd pleaser. Fans will want to look for *The Story of Baseball* by Lawrence S. Ritter.

Casey at the Bat:
A Ballad of the Republic Sung in the Year 1888
Written by Ernest Thayer, Illustrated by Christopher Bing
Handprint, $17.95, 30 pages
First published in 2000
Ages 4–9

Thayer's oft-quoted poem has been given a fantastic visual treatment through Bing's clever illustrations. The book resembles a treasured scrapbook with aged newspaper clippings, vintage baseball cards, and game tickets. This is a wonderfully rendered tribute to a favorite American pastime.

Children's Book of Yoga: Games &
Exercises Mimic Plants & Animals & Objects
Written by Thia Luby
Clear Light, $14.95, 96 pages
First published in 1998
Ages 4–12

Drawing inspiration from objects and animals found in nature, the author clearly presents dozens of poses, for beginners and more advanced young yogis. There are color photos of children in various yogic positions accompanied by lovely pictures of the object being mimicked. Namaste.

Chapter Five

Dirt on Their Skirts: The Story of the Young Woman Who Won the World Championship
Written by Doreen Rappaport and Lyndall Callan, Illustrations by E. B. Lewis
Dial Books, $16.99, 32 pages
First published in 2000
Ages 5–9

It's the Racine Belles battling the Rockford Peaches for the All American Girls Professional Baseball League championship of 1946. The score is tied at 0 and the thrill of the game is exuberantly captured. There's even information about the real players and leagues of the teams of this era; an important salute to some terrific female athletes.

For the Love of the Game: Michael Jordan and Me
Written by Eloise Greenfield
HarperCollins, $6.95, 32 pages
First published in 1997
Ages 5–9

For the millions of kids who aspire to "be like Mike," here's a fitting tribute and an inspiring story. There's more here than meets the eye. At once, it's the story of Jordan's rocket ride to sports fame and fortune, while imparting a message about working hard to follow a dream. Jordan devotees will want to read *Just Like Mike* by Gail Herman and *Michael Jordan: A Life above the Rim* by Robert Lipsyte.

McGwire and Sosa: A Season to Remember
Written by James Preller
Aladdin, $5.99, 32 pages
First published in 1998
Ages 6–10

The summer of 1998 was surely one for the record books, and one that may have contributed to your child's budding enthusiasm for the game of baseball. Shining stars Sammy Sosa and Mark McGwire's stellar season is documented in this engaging book.

The Official Book of Figure Skating
Simon & Schuster Editions, $30.00, 266 pages
First published in 1998
Ages 8 and up

Authorized by the United States Figure Skating Association and featuring an introduction by Peggy Fleming, this comprehensive book includes profiles of famous skaters and legendary Olympic moments while also offering information about technique, creating routines, and fitness for young skaters. Further illuminating the high-flying leaps and soaring spins is *This Is Figure Skating* by Margaret Blackstone.

Olympics!

Written by B.G. Hennessy, Illustrated by Michael Chesworth
Puffin, $5.99, 32 pages
First published in 2000
Ages 5–10

It's the thrill of victory and the agony of defeat, as readers are swept into the excitement of the winter and summer games. Through an excellent history of the modern Olympics and its array of competitive activities, legendary athletes and winning moments are brought to life.

Swimming

Written by Rick Cross
Dorling Kindersly, $9.95, 45 pages
First published in 2000
Ages 7–12

An Olympic gold medallist introduces young readers to the basics of swimming, including training methods, different strokes, and water safety. This book is a revised edition of *The Young Swimmer*, part of a series from DK that also includes *The Young Martial Arts Enthusiast* and *The Young Ice Skater*.

Women

100 Most Important Women of the 20th Century

Written by Kevin Markey
Meredith Books, $34.95, 192 pages
First published in 1998
Ages 10 and up

With enough biographic material to endure years of book reports, this collection of profiles includes activists, writers, politicians, artists, scientists, athletes, and other fascinating females.

The Best
Children's Literature
A Parent's Guide

Chapter Five

Extraordinary Explorers: Women of the World
Written by Rebecca Stetoff
Oxford University Press, $12.95, 151 pages
First published in 1992
Ages 10 and up

Focusing on the 19th and 20th century travels of such fearless females as Mary Kingsley, Alexandra Day-Neel, Isabella Bishop, and Fanny Workman, the author provides archival photos and maps to enliven the important contributions of each adventurer.

World Cultures

Dia's Story Cloth:
The Hmong People's Journey of Freedom
Written by Dia Cha, Illustrated by Chue Cha and Nhia Thao Cha
Lee & Low, $6.95, 24 pages
First published in 1996
Ages 6–12

A story cloth is an artful tradition of the Hmong people of Laos. Here, Dia recounts the story of her family's history through her beautiful heirloom, beginning with her ancestors fleeing China, though their years in a Thai refugee camp, and onto their immigration to America. Double-page spreads show the cloth in all its glory and additional text provides background information about Hmong culture and history.

In Search of the Spirit:
The Living National Treasures of Japan
Written by Sheila Hamanaka
Morrow Junior Books, $16.00, 48 pages
First published in 1999
Ages 10 and up

In Japan, artisans are deemed "living national treasures" and this stunning book presents the work of six of them, including a basket weaver, a puppeteer, and a traditional actor. The rich heritage of Japanese crafts and culture is abundantly clear, as is the power of the creative spirit.

Nonfiction • Writers

If the World Were a Village: A Book about the World's People
parent's guide
choice award

Written by David J. Smith
Kids Can Press, $15.95, 32 pages
First published in 2002
Ages 7–12

There are more than six billion people in the world, but Smith's book shrinks the population down to a kid-friendly village of 100 residents. The idea here is to help children understand the wide world of global citizens and their many differences and similarities on a smaller scale. For example, out of the 100 villagers, only 5 are from the United States, and only 24 people have enough food to eat. It's an intriguing concept, certain to provoke discussion.

Sami and the Time of Troubles

Written by Florence Parry Heide and Judith Heide Gilliland, Illustrated by Ted Lewin
Clarion, $6.95, 33 pages
First published in 1992
Ages 6–10

Though it was written ten years ago, this book seems sadly current. A young boy dodges bombs and lives with constant fear of impending violence in his homeland of Beirut, Lebanon. Thought provoking and immediate, readers are given an important perspective—that of a child—of life in a war torn land.

Writers And Writing

How Writers Work: Finding a Process That Works for You

Written by Ralph Fletcher
HarperTrophy, $4.95, 114 pages
First published in 2000
Ages 9–13

For kids who want a glimpse inside the writer's life, here's more than a sneak peak. With tips on brainstorming, proofreading, and publishing, Fletcher sets the writing record straight: good writing requires inspiration and hard work. And search the bookstore or library shelves for *Author: A True Story* by Helen Lester.

Chapter Five

Messages in the Mailbox: How to Write a Letter
Written by Loreen Leedy
Holiday House, $16.95, 32 pages
First published in 1991
Ages 7–10

Okay, so we live in a world of e-mail and telecommunications. But Leedy's introduction to letter writing is likely to revive a lost art. Graceful messages about thank you notes, fan mail, invitations, business letters and envelope addressing are cleverly conveyed. Correspondence is an important skill. Why not encourage your child to find a pen pal?

What Do Authors Do?
Written and Illustrated by Eileen Christelow
Clarion, $5.95, 32 pages
First published in 1997
Ages 6–10

How do authors get ideas? How do books get published? Such worthy questions are addressed in Christelow's lighthearted look at the inspiration and perspiration of writers. You'll also want to look for the companion for this book of books, *What Do Illustrators Do?* for insight into the creation of picture books. For further reading on writing, there's *If You Were a Writer* by Joan Lowry Nixon.

What's Your Story?
A Young Person's Guide to Writing Fiction
Written by Marion Dane Bauer
Clarion, $6.95, 134 pages
First published in 1992
Ages 9–14

You'll find instruction, inspiration, and downright good advice from a Newbery Honor recipient in this useful guide. Using anecdotes and wit, Bauer details the elements of finely crafted fiction including keeping a journal, character and plot development, revision, and the role of an editor. As your pre-adolescent's ink starts flowing, you'll want to look for Bauer's follow up, *Our Stories: A Fiction Workshop for Young Authors*.

Chapter Six
Juvenile Fiction/Chapter Books

Once children are able to read relatively smoothly, without the frequent halting for decoding words and new vocabulary that accompanies earlier stages, it's time to graduate to the astonishing and diverse collection of literature found in Chapter Books and Juvenile Fiction. Within this wide and ever-growing selection are tenured favorites like *Alice's Adventures in Wonderland*, *Charlie and the Chocolate Factory*, and *Little House in the Big Woods* as well as more contemporary classics such as *Bridge to Terabithia* and *From the Mixed-Up Files of Mrs. Basil E. Frankweiler*. Some of the newest titles described in this chapter have seen tremendous popularity and acclaim, including *Maniac Magee*, *Because of Winn Dixie* and though it goes without saying, *Harry Potter and the Sorcerer's Stone*. You'll find tales of brave adventure, comedic escapade, dramatic realism, and magical fantasy that represent a broad spectrum of cultural traditions and ethnic experiences. There is truly something for every elementary school-aged reader.

Chapter Six

As is the case with Easy Readers, series books play a large role in the reading lives of middle grade children. The breadth and scope of these series is mind boggling, with an approximate 400 children's series available at any given time (see Let's Talk About... Series Books, page TK), and parents will want to continue to help their children select books that will become fast favorites while encouraging the discovery of fine novels and nonfiction. Kids will continue to read and re-read the books that are most appealing to them, and this is a truly typical behavior. It's the comfort of the familiar that prompts the repeated re-reading of preferred stories in children and even some adults!

Once again, the recommended age ranges provided are merely a guideline. You know, and your children know, better than anyone what they are ready to read. There's a very wide span of age-appropriate books in this chapter, from the stories of Beverly Cleary, including *Ramona the Pest*, that are more likely to please kids in the early elementary grades to more dramatic novels such as *Walk Two Moons* by Sharon Creech, which is probably best understood by children in the upper-elementary and middle school grades. And remember, chapter books are great for reading aloud, too!

Abel's Island
Written by William Steig
Farrar Straus Giroux, $4.95, 117 pages
First published in 1985
Ages 7–11

Abel is a very genteel mouse with a big problem. He becomes stranded on an uninhabited island! His strength and resources are challenged as he struggles to survive and return home. Children will certainly remember Steig's story books including *The Amazing Bone; Brave Irene; Doctor De Soto; Sylvester and the Magic Pebble* (see "Story Books"); and *Pete's a Pizza* (in "Picture Books") as well as many others. Many of Steig's stories are available in Spanish and as audio adaptations.

Juvenile Fiction/Chapter Books

Afternoon of the Elves
Written by Janet Taylor Lisle
Paperstar, $4.99, 122 pages
First published in 1989
Ages 10–14

Imagination becomes the basis for an unlikely friendship in this wonderful **Newbery Honor** recipient. Sara-Kate has a difficult home life and few friends. Her neighbor, Hillary, is lured by the "elf village" constructed by Sara-Kate in her backyard and becomes intrigued by the lonesome girl's elaborate stories about her personal life. Will their friendship survive the truth? Other enchanting fiction by Lisle includes *The Art of Keeping Cool*; *Forest*; and *The Lost Flower Children*.

Alan and Naomi
Written by Myron Levoy
HarperTrophy, $4.95, 192 pages
First published in 1977
Ages 10–14

A lovely story of star-crossed friendship set in New York City during World War II. Alan meets Naomi after she moves into the apartment building where he lives. She has clearly been traumatized by what she has seen in wartime France but slowly begins to open up to Alan.

Alice's Adventures in Wonderland
Written by Lewis Carroll
Aladdin, $3.99, 150 pages
First published in 1865
Ages 8–12

Children are certainly familiar with the Hollywood version of Lewis Carroll's magical tale, but the original story far exceeds the film in terms of sheer delight. Originally written as a gift for a young girl named Alice Liddell, Carroll's story quickly became legendary. This is due, of course, to its dream-like, almost hallucinatory plot, not oft seen in 19th century children's literature. Following the hurried White Rabbit down the rabbit hole, Alice encounters the Cheshire Cat, the Queen of Hearts, and a spectacular land of adventure that would indelibly impact the course of children's literature as well as popular culture. The fun and fantasy continues with *Through the Looking Glass and What Alice Found There*. Also by Lewis Carroll, the poetry of *Jabberwocky* and *The Hunting of the Snark*.

Chapter Six

Did You Know?

Lewis Carroll was a pseudonym for Charles Lutwidge Dodgson, a serious and reserved English mathematician. After **Alice's Adventures in Wonderland** became increasingly popular, Dodgson refused, for a period of time, to admit that he was responsible for the book's creation. Imagine that!

All-of-a-Kind Family

Written by Sidney Taylor, Illustrated by Helen John

Dell, $5.50, 188 pages

First published in 1951

Ages 8–13

There's much for both children and parents to love in this story of five sisters growing up in Manhattan's Lower East Side during the early years of the 20th century. There is a poignant spirit of family devotion, Jewish tradition, and homegrown fun amongst the members of their loving family. In the meantime, it also paints a colorful picture of city life in the early 1900s. An excellent audio adaptation is available from Listen & Live Audio. Sequels include *All-Of-A-Kind Family Downtown*; *All-Of-A-Kind Family Uptown*; *Ella of All-Of-A-Kind Family*; and *More of All-Of-A-Kind Family*.

Amber Was Brave, Essie Was Smart: The Story of Amber and Essie Told Here in Poems and Pictures

Written and Illustrated by Vera B. Williams

Greenwillow, $15.95, 32 pages

First published in 2001

Ages 8–12

You won't want to miss this uniquely rendered story, with narrative taking the form of verse and pictures. The two title sisters have some difficult burdens to bear; their father is in prison and their mother is constantly working. Yet, they find comfort in creativity and in each other's company. This is an eloquent tribute to sisterhood that will appeal to all girls, especially those who seek alternative forms of fiction.

Juvenile Fiction/Chapter Books

American Diaries Series
Written by Kathleen Duey
Aladdin, $4.50 per volume, 120–150 pages
First published in 1997
Ages 8–13

Here's a series that leaves many moms wishing something similar had existed during their girlhoods. Each volume relates the story of a young girl living in various eras and witnessing historic events. There's *Agnes May Gleason: Walsenburg, Colorado, 1933* (Great Depression); *Amelina Carrett: Bayou Grand Coeur, Louisiana, 1863* (Civil War); *Francesca Vigilucci: Washington, D.C., 1913* (women's rights); and *Nell Dunne: Ellis Island, 1904* (immigration) among other clever characters. A fine introduction to American history through the eyes of a child, especially for readers who enjoy fictionalized journals. Admirers of this series are likely to enjoy *A Gathering of Days: A New England Girl's Journal, 1830-32* by Joan Blos.

Dear Diary....
What's the reason for the popularity and influence of children's books written in the form of journal entries or letters? Such novels give kids the feeling of taking a sneak peek at a character's most intimate thoughts, a very appealing notion. What's more, these fictionalized reflections often inspire readers to record their own joys, fears and longings in a diary or to take up the lost art of letter writing by beginning a pen pal correspondence.

American Girl Series
Various authors
Pleasant Company, $5.95 per volume, 40–70 pages
First published in 1988
Ages 7–11

Another girlish glimpse at history (and merchandising phenomenon) can be found between the covers of the many volumes of this series. The adventures of each character address everyday life and historical themes during the era in which they lived. Characters include *Addy* (slavery); *Felicity* (Revolutionary War); *Josephina* (19th century Mexican immigration); *Kirsten* (pioneer life); *Kit* (Great Depression); *Molly* (World War II); and *Samantha* (turn of the 20th century Manhattan). For each character, there are at least four books, taking them through the seasons, and the titles are consistent. For example, there's *Meet Felicity*; *Changes for Felicity*; *Felicity Learns a Lesson*; *Felicity's Surprise* and so forth for the other characters.

Chapter Six

Amos Fortune, Free Man

Written by Elizabeth Yates, Illustrated by Nora S. Unwin
Dutton, $15.99, 181 pages
First published in 1967
Ages 10–14

Amos Fortune was an 18th century African prince who was captured and sold into slavery at the age of fifteen. After being transported to America, he worked as a slave for more than forty years before buying his freedom at the age of sixty. Elizabeth Yates's poignant rendering of his story earned a **Newbery Medal** and has served as an essential document of the brutal injustices of slavery.

Anastasia Krupnik

Written by Lois Lowry, Illustrated by Diane de Groat
Dell, $4.99, 113 pages
First published in 1979
Ages 9–12

Ten year-old Anastasia lives in a suburb of Boston and is quite clever and always entertaining. It's the adept portrayal of her fears, foibles, and daily adventures that makes this title a perennial favorite for upper-elementary school readers. Also available in Spanish. Sequels take our protagonist through junior high school in *Anastasia at Your Service*; *Anastasia, Ask Your Analyst*; *Anastasia On Her Own*; and *Anastasia and Her Chosen Career*. Also by Lowry, *The Giver* and *Number the Stars* (both detailed in this chapter).

...And Now Miguel

Written by Joseph Krumgold, Illustrated by Jean Charlot
HarperTrophy, $5.95, 245 pages
First published in 1953
Ages 9–14

After Miguel celebrates his twelfth birthday, he expresses his wish to join his family during their shepherding expedition to New Mexico's Sangre de Cristo Mountains. Krumgold beautifully captures both the atmosphere and charged emotions in this coming-of-age story that received the **Newbery Medal** nearly fifty years ago. Also by Krumgold is *Onion John* (detailed in this chapter).

Juvenile Fiction/Chapter Books

Anne of Green Gables
Written by L.M. Montgomery
Bantam, $4.99, 308 pages
First published in 1908
Ages 9–13

After being sent to live with foster parents on Prince Edward Island, Anne Shirley begins to have an often unintentional, yet always profound, impact on everyone around her. Lucy Maud Montgomery's stories have enchanted her mostly female audience for generations, as girls follow Anne through adulthood in *Anne of Avonlea*; *Anne of the Island*; *Anne of Windy Poplars*; *Anne's House of Dreams*; and *Anne of Ingleside*.

Are You There, God? It's Me, Margaret
Written by Judy Blume
Dell, $5.50, 149 pages
First published in 1970
Ages 10–14

Ask any pre-adolescent girl in America about her favorite books and you're likely to hear about Judy Blume. Addressing the questions and issues that accompany puberty, Blume deftly weaves a story that continues to feel contemporary 30 years after its publication. In this book, one of Blume's best-selling titles, Margaret shares the woes and wonders of adolescence with a new group of girlfriends. Also by Judy Blume, *Starring Sally J. Freedman as Herself* (in this chapter); *Blubber*; *Deenie*; *Here's to You, Rachel Robinson*; *Iggie's House*; *It's Not the End of the World*; *Just as Long as We're Together*; *Then Again Maybe I Won't*; and *Tiger Eyes*. Younger readers (ages 7–11) will adore *Tales of a Fourth Grade Nothing* (in this chapter) and its sequels, as well as *Otherwise Known as Sheila the Great* and *Freckle Juice*.

Featured Author: Judy Blume

Striking a resonant chord with her readers since the early 1970s, Judy Blume writes about the honest-to-goodness issues that universally effect children and young adults. Entertaining, often amusing, and always topical, Blume's books have addressed puberty, divorce, scoliosis, obesity, friendship, death, sibling rivalry, sexual awakening, religion, and racial prejudice. While her early work was sometimes criticized for introducing subject matter that was, at the time, considered off-limits, very few children's writers have matched her long-term success and popularity. Clearly her books provide a comforting mirror into which young readers peer and discover that they are not alone.

Chapter Six

Artemis Fowl
Written by Eoin Colfer
Hyperion, $6.99, 277 pages
First published in 2001
Ages 9–13

The title character is a twelve-year-old mastermind. He devises a get-rich-quick scheme that involves the kidnapping of a fairy named Holly Short for a ransom of gold. Artemis, however, underestimates the powers of his sprightly captive's family and friends, who quickly enlist the help of the LEPrecon Unit to rescue her. From there, an action packed fantasy drama unfolds, as a team of trolls, goblins, dwarfs, and satyrs are dispatched on a rescue mission like no other. There's a lot of humor and techno-wizardry in this tall tale that will surely please sci-fi fans while drawing many new readers into the fantasy fold.

The Ballad of Lucy Whipple
Written by Karen Cushman
HarperTrophy, $5.99, 218 pages
First published in 1996
Ages 9–13

After her father's death, Lucy and her family travel west from their home in Massachusetts, heading toward the Gold Rush dreams of California. Lonesome and homesick, Lucy feels ill at ease in her wild new surroundings. Yet, as the story follows a period of growth and self-discovery, Lucy decides to stay in California even as her family plans to move with her mother's new husband to the Sandwich Islands. The portrayal of California as the land of opportunity combined with Lucy's coming of age is especially effective. For more historical fiction set during this era, look for *Bandit's Moon* by Sid Fleischman. Other books by Karen Cushman include *Catherine; Called Birdy* (a young adult novel); *Matilda Bone*; and *The Midwife's Apprentice*.

Juvenile Fiction/Chapter Books

Baseball in April and Other Stories
Written by Gary Soto
Harcourt, $6.00, 111 pages
First published in 1990
Ages 9–12

Set in California, a group of Mexican-American youths are torn between the cultural heritage that has shaped their parents' experiences and the allure of popular American pastimes. This is a short story collection that will appeal to all middle-grade readers, especially those who face issues involved in cultural assimilation. Also available in Spanish as *Beisbol en Abril y Otros Historias*. Gary Soto is the author of other stories with Hispanic-American settings including *Taking Sides*; *Pacific Crossing*; and *Buried Onions* (ages twelve and up), as well as wonderfully amusing tales for younger readers such as *Chato's Kitchen* (see "Story Books").

Because of Winn-Dixie
Written by Kate DiCamillo
Candlewick, $5.99, 182 pages
First published in 2000
Ages 9–13

parent's
guide
choice award

The love of a new pet helps to heal the heart of a young motherless girl. India Opal Buloni and her dad are new arrivals in a small Florida town. She rescues a dog at the local grocery store and names him in tribute to the place of her good fortune... Winn-Dixie. Soon, Opal and the big pup meet a variety of eccentric characters while she works up the courage to ask her father some long overdue questions. Memorable, touching, and truly wonderful.

Ben and Me
Written and Illustrated by Robert Lawson
Little Brown, $5.95, 113 pages
First published in 1939
Ages 8–12

In this charming story, Ben Franklin's confidante is a mouse named Amos. After making a home in Ben's hat, Amos provides humorous commentary on the life and work of the famous history maker. Also look for *The Hatmaker's Sign: A Story by Benjamin Franklin* by Candace Fleming.

Chapter Six

The BFG
Written by Roald Dahl, Illustrated by Quentin Blake
Puffin, $5.99, 207 pages
First published in 1982
Ages 7–11

And now for something completely different. From the brilliant mind of Roald Dahl comes this good-natured but pointed story of a BFG (Big Friendly Giant) who kidnaps a young orphan named Sophie. The BFG has the best of intentions, bottling good dreams for children and devising a plan to save the world. Also by Dahl, *Charlie and the Chocolate Factory* (in this chapter); *Danny, Champion of the World*; *James and the Giant Peach* (also in this chapter); and *Matilda*, among others.

Big Red
Written by Jim Kjelgaard, Illustrated by Carl Pfeuffer
Bantam, $5.50, 218 pages
First published in 1956
Ages 9–13

Having long since earned its classic status, this story of a boy and his dog rarely fails to bring a tear to even the most stoic readers' eyes. The son of a trapper and his champion Irish setter face brave adventure and impending maturity together. Its sequels are *Irish Red* and *Outlaw Red*.

Black Beauty
Written by Anna Sewell
Aladdin, $3.99, 210 pages
First published in 1877
Ages 9–14

Black Beauty is a horse story like no other, tracing the life story of a glorious equine from pampered colt to London carriage horse to a far less glorious occupation as a mistreated cab puller. Of course, there's a powerful message about the beauty of nature and humankind's sporadic respect for animals. All in all, the timeless effect of this story is flawless. It's a story that has been cherished by millions and will continue to draw readers in the new millennium.

Juvenile Fiction/Chapter Books

The Black Bull of Norroway: A Scottish Tale
Written and Illustrated by Charlotte Huck
Greenwillow, $15.95, 40 pages
First published in 2001
Ages 7–11

While this is a difficult book to classify, its appeal will be evident for all upper-elementary-aged children. Peggy Ann will only marry when she falls in love... even if it's with the monstrous Black Bull of Norroway? This handsome volume will revitalize children's interest in folk and fairy tales, or may serve as a wonderful introduction to the more sophisticated stories in this genre.

Black Stallion
Written by Walter Farley
Random House, $5.99, 187 pages
First published in 1941
Ages 9–14

An unforgettable story of a boy and a wild horse, this book has been a stand out in juvenile fiction for years. Animal lovers will be especially moved, and should place this classic at the top of their must-read list. What's more exciting than a good old-fashioned horse story? Sequels, of course! Look for *The Black Stallion and Satan*; *The Black Stallion Returns*; *The Black Stallion's Filly*; and *The Black Stallion's Shadow*.

Blister
Written by Susan Shreve
Arthur A. Levine, $15.95, 153 pages
First published in 2001
Ages 9–13

After the stillbirth of a baby sister leaves her family traumatized, Alyssa seeks solace in the shade of the backyard willow tree. Soon, however, she responds to her family's depression by taking on a new image, and a new name... Blister. She dons flashy clothes and a new attitude in an attempt to be accepted by the popular fifth grade crowd. She also takes vengeful steps toward her father, whose departure seems responsible for Blister's personality crisis. Susan Shreve treats her subjects and the harsh realities of family struggles with profound respect, and has created a work of realism that is destined for classic status. Also by this author *The Flunking of Joshua T. Bates*; *Goodbye, Amanda the Good*; and *Jonah, the Whale*.

Chapter Six

Parent/Child Review: Blister

The Parent: Colleen, Age 49, Hair Stylist

The Child: Lilianne, Age 10, Tap Dancer

Lilianne says: "I think everyone should read this book even though it's sad and difficult. I mean, the girl tries to make her life better but she's not really doing the right things to help herself. I wanted her to talk to her father instead of doing mean things, but I guess she was taking it out on him."

Colleen says: "I was really impressed with the writing and also impressed with how much Lilianne got out of the story. I wasn't really aware that she was up to reading this level of fiction."

The Book of Three

Written by Lloyd Alexander

Dell, $5.99, 224 pages

First published in 1964

Ages 9–14

The first volume in a series that includes *The Black Cauldron*, this story is set in the land of Prydain, a mythical place that strongly resembles Wales. It concerns a pig keeper named Taran who longs to see a brave battle like his hero Prince Gwydion. Indeed, Taran will ward off the evil Horned King and restore peace to Prydain before tale's end. This is a wonderful fantasy sequence that doesn't take itself too seriously, as Alexander injects humor at every turn. Other titles in the series include *The Castle of Llyr*; *Taran Wanderer*; and *The High King*.

The Borrowers

Written by Mary Norton, Illustrated by Beth and Joe Krush

Harcourt, $6.00, 180 pages

First published in 1953

Ages 7–11

This venerated classic is a lively fantasy involving a group of little people who make their home under the kitchen floor of an old country house. Follow their adventures in *The Borrowers Afield*; *The Borrowers Afloat*; *The Borrowers Aloft*; and *The Borrowers Avenged*.

Juvenile Fiction/Chapter Books

The Boxcar Children Series

Written by Gertrude Chandler Warner, Illustrated by L. Kate Deal
Albert Whitman, $3.95 per volume, 110–150 pages
First published in 1942
Ages 7–10

In the first installment, four young orphans take up residence in the boxcar of an old train. From there, they solve mysteries with an old-fashioned flair that continues to attract new generations of readers. With dozens of volumes available in this series, your middle-grade readers have a lot to anticipate.

Let's Talk about... Series Books

Children's book series are an ever-growing phenomenon, often based on pop culture icons and sustained by merchandising fury and word of mouth. Some parents feel that their children spend too much time reading series that are somewhat ephemeral and not quite up to the literary high bar that has been set by so many children's writers. It's true that some series may seem "flimsy" or "not worthwhile" at first glance, but it's important to allow children access to their favorite reading material, regardless of the fact that it may not be award-winning literature. The fact is, books in series invite children to become well acquainted and involved with a set of characters and circumstances. Kids, then, become invested in continuing to read each sequential book, and it's hard to begrudge that! Nonetheless, trying to encourage children to blend more highly regarded books with their preferred diet of chilling, silly, fashionable, and ultimately entertaining series books can't hurt. In the meantime, here are a few current chapter books, juvenile fiction, and nonfiction series that are worth a second look:

- Amazing Days of Abby Hayes
- American Girls
- Dear America
- Extraordinary People
- Hank the Cowdog
- History Mysteries
- Junie B. Jones
- Matt Christopher Sports Stories
- Nate the Great
- A Series of Unfortunate Events
- American Diaries
- Captain Underpants
- Dinotopia
- Eyewitness Books
- Hardy Boys
- In Their Own Words
- Magic Tree House
- Nancy Drew
- Royal Diaries

Chapter Six

Bridge to Terabithia

Written by Katherine Paterson, Illustrated by Donna Diamond
HarperCollins, $5.99, 128 pages
First published in 1977
Ages 10–14

Beauty, grace, and a little bit of magic are the hallmarks of this wise story of friendship and tragic loss. Jess is lonely in his rural surroundings until he befriends Leslie, a bright and creative young girl who moves into the neighborhood. Together they create a special forest hideaway called Terabithia, which becomes the unfortunate site of Leslie's accidental death. Certain to provoke important questions about life and death, this **Newbery Medal** winner will be treasured by both children and adults. Katherine Paterson is the author of *The Great Gilly Hopkins* (in this chapter); *Jacob Have I Loved*; and *Lyddie*, as well as the classic *The Tale of the Mandarin Ducks* (see "Story Books").

Bud, Not Buddy

Written by Christopher Paul Curtis
Yearling, $5.95, 245 pages
First published in 1999
Ages 10–14

**parent's
guide**
choice award

After being shuffled through several unhappy foster home placements during the Great Depression, ten-year-old Bud Caldwell runs away to seek his long-absent father. Believing that his dad is a noted jazz musician and club owner, Bud heads for Grand Rapids, Michigan, encountering some shady characters and hazy truths along the way. As with his wonderful *The Watsons Go to Birmingham—1963* (detailed in this chapter), Curtis's story is a masterly mix of humor and pain, earning it a **Newbery Medal** and a great deal of deserved notoriety.

Let's Talk about... Difficult Issues

Parents often worry that their children will read books with subject matter that is too mature for them. Generally speaking, children won't read books that they're not ready for. However, some of today's popular juvenile fiction does raise questions about sex, illness, death, abuse, drugs, and other social issues. It's important that parents and caregivers are standing by to provide answers and reassurance. If kids have concerns or feel confused about what they've read, they'll be relieved to know that all topics are open for discussion. Conversely, if your child has personally faced some of the issues mentioned above, the introduction of thoughtful children's novels can go a long way in gaining understanding and mirroring their own experiences.

Juvenile Fiction/Chapter Books

Caddie Woodlawn

Written by Carol Ryrie Brink, Illustrated by Trina Schart Hyman
Aladdin, $5.99, 275 pages
First published in 1935
Ages 9–13

Growing up with her six siblings on the plains of 19th century Wisconsin, Caddie's pioneer adventures made her a forerunner in the category of strong female literary characters. Fans of *Little House on the Prairie* and *Anne of Green Gables* will want to make a connection with Caddie in this **Newbery Medal** winning novel.

Call It Courage

Written by Armstrong Perry
Macmillan, $4.99, 116 pages
First published in 1939
Ages 9–14

Mafatu has feared the sea since his mother drowned in the South Pacific. The son of the Great Chief of Hikeru, Mafatu proves his courage and conquers his fear. A timeless classic, Perry's adventure story earned a **Newbery Medal**.

The Cat Ate My Gymsuit

Written by Paula Danziger
Puffin, $4.99, 147 pages
First published in 1974
Ages 10–14

Now combined in one volume with its sequel, *There's a Bat in Bunk Five*, Marcy Lewis is a spokesperson for all frustrated teens. She dreads gym class, is misunderstood by her strict father, and is self-conscious about her weight. It takes a caring and somewhat unconventional teacher to help Marcy see the light at the end of the teenage tunnel. Teen readers will also enjoy *Goodbye, Amanda the Good* by Susan Shreve. Paula Danziger is the author of *Amber Brown Is Not a Crayon* (in "Easy Readers") and its sequels.

Chapter Six

Charlie and the Chocolate Factory
Written by Roald Dahl, Illustrated by Quentin Blake
Puffin, $5.99, 155 pages
First published in 1963
Ages 9–12

After the elusive and prized golden tickets are found, several delightfully horrid children are granted the honor of touring Willie Wonka's amazing and mysterious chocolate factory. Ah, then there's Charlie Bucket. He just wants an opportunity to glimpse a world beyond his own impoverished home and tell his grandparents about the glorious ride! You'll want to follow his deserved good fortune in *Charlie and the Great Glass Elevator*. Roald Dahl is also the author of *The BFG* (in this chapter); *The Enormous Crocodile*; *James and the Giant Peach* (in this chapter); *Matilda*; and *The Witches*. Also look for his remarkable memoirs, *Boy: Tales of Childhood* and *Going Solo*.

Did You Know?
Literary academics have speculated about Dahl's infamous work, **Charlie and the Chocolate Factory**, even theorizing that the children represent the Seven Deadly Sins. Charlie's a sure bet for the pride category!

Charlotte's Web
Written by E. B. White, Illustrated by Garth Williams
Harper & Row, $6.95, 184 pages
First published in 1952
Ages 8–12

Salutations! Wilbur gives new meaning to the phrase "prize pig" after his life is spared with the help of some fearless females. First there's Fawn, a young girl who pleads with her farmer father to let her care for the piglet. Later, a spider named Charlotte, who has a way with words, gives Wilbur a new lease on life by weaving inspiring messages into her web. The barnyard banter is especially entertaining as the nature of the different animals provides White with an opportunity for gentle social commentary. Your child is likely to be assigned a reading of this **Newbery Honor** book in elementary school. What a perfect opportunity for parents to share in the many joys of this wonderful story. Also look for the big heart of *Stuart Little* as well as *The Trumpet of the Swan* (both detailed in this chapter).

Juvenile Fiction/Chapter Books

Chocolate Fever

Written by Robert Kimmel Smith, Illustrated by Gioia Fiammenghi
Dell, $4.50, 93 pages
First published in 1978
Ages 8–12

Henry loves chocolate and who can blame him? But after eating one morsel too many, he breaks out in mysterious brown bumps... yep, chocolate fever! His affliction helps him foil some criminals and learn a little bit about himself. There's a lesson about over-indulgence here, but mostly it's a far-fetched and funny tale. Also by this author, *Bobby Baseball* and *The War with Grandpa*.

The Color of My Words

Written by Lynn Joseph
HarperTrophy, $4.95, 138 pages
First published in 2000
Ages 9–13

Ana Rosa lives in the Dominican Republic and dreams of becoming a writer. She spends her days writing poetry and prose and, in doing so, introduces readers to her family and to her private world. When the young girl learns that her neighborhood will be demolished in order to build a tourist resort, she participates in a protest and witnesses a violent struggle that culminates in the death of her older brother. The form and content of this new novel is inventive, compelling, and quite memorable. Lynn Joseph is also the author of *A Wave in Her Pocket: Stories from Trinidad*.

The Cricket in Times Square

Written by George Selden, Illustrated by Garth Williams
Dell, $5.99, 149 pages
First published in 1960
Ages 8–12

The rather blasé residents of Manhattan are aflutter, Tucker Mouse and Harry Cat included. There's a new creature in their midst and he's making a mysterious sound. It's only Chester Cricket, of course, who made the unfortunate mistake of traveling via picnic basket from his happy Connecticut home to the Big Apple. It's going to take a while for Chester to acclimate to his new surroundings, but his melodic chirping may be the ticket to musical fame! A sheer delight and staple of children's reading lists, there's little doubt that your child will adore this story. Also look for *Chester Cricket's New Home*; *Chester Cricket's Pigeon Ride*; *Harry Kitten and Tucker Mouse*; and *Tucker's Countryside*.

Chapter Six

The Dark Is Rising
Written by Susan Cooper
Aladdin, $4.99, 244 pages
First published in 1973
Ages 10–14

Though Will is sometimes overshadowed by his siblings, an elusive stranger informs him that, as the "last of the old ones," he is the guardian of good who holds many powerful talents. This intriguing **Newbery Honor** recipient is the second in the *Dark is Rising Sequence*. Other titles include *The Grey King; Over Sea, Under Stone; Greenwitch; Silver on the Tree*; and *Seaward*, all of which will whet your child's appetite for fantasy adventure. Also by Susan Cooper, *The Boggart*.

Dave at Night
Written by Gail Carson Levine
HarperTrophy, $5.95, 281 pages
First published in 1999
Ages 9–13

Set against the backdrop of the Harlem Renaissance, this beguiling story centers on a young orphan named Dave who each night escapes the confines of the Hebrew Home for Boys to peer into the starlit world of Upper Manhattan. Dave is befriended by a colorful cast of characters, and he soon rubs elbows with some of the era's renowned artists, musicians, and authors. Eventually, he summons his resources to protest the orphanage's squalid living conditions. It's an affecting mix of realism and creativity from an author who is best known for fine works of fantasy such as *Ella Enchanted* (in this chapter); *The Princess Test*; and *The Fairy's Mistake*.

Dear America Series
Various authors
Scholastic, $10.95 per volume, 150–200 pages each
First published in 1996
Ages 9–13

Similar in content and scope to the *American Diaries* series (in this chapter), historical events are viewed through the fictional journal entries of curious children. The series covers a lot of ground and uses historical settings to great effect in not only exposing events and the lives of history makers, but also focusing on the positive outlooks of their young narrators. The series includes *The Winter of the Red Snow: The Revolutionary War Diary of Abigail Jane Stewart, Valley Forge, Pennsylvania, 1777*; and *When Will This Cruel War Be Over?: The Civil War Diary of Emma Simpson, Gordonsville, Virginia, 1864*; and *Picture of Freedom: The Diary of Clotee, A Slave Girl, Belmont Plantation, Virginia, 1859* among others.

Juvenile Fiction/Chapter Books

Dear Mr. Henshaw
Written by Beverly Cleary, Illustrated by Paul O. Zelinsky
HarperTrophy, $5.95, 133 pages
First published in 1983
Ages 8–12

With her knack for realistic depictions of childhood emotions and thoughts, Cleary created this outstanding novel for middle-grade readers. Written as a series of letters, ten-year-old Leigh Botts openly expresses his feelings about his parents' divorce and being the new kid in school. Its affecting sequel is *Strider*. Cleary became a literary celebrity with *Ramona the Pest* and its sequels (detailed in this chapter), as well as *Henry Huggins*; *Ellen Tebbits*; *Henry and Beezus*; *The Mouse and the Motorcycle* (in "Easy Readers"); *Muggie Maggie*; *Ribsy*; and *Runaway Ralph* among others.

Featured Author: Beverly Cleary

Raised on an Oregon farm, Beverly Cleary was not very interested in books as a young child. From that awkward start, she went on to create some of the most wonderfully memorable children's stories ever written. It's apparent that Cleary has profound respect for the simple pleasures of childhood. Her famous protagonists romp, cavort, and wonder. They also make mischief and often have realistic concerns. Her characters spring to life and become fast friends with their readers, who always seem to return for more.

The Devil's Arithmetic
Written by Jane Yolen
Puffin, $5.99, 170 pages
First published in 1990
Ages 10–13

Hannah is annoyed and befuddled by her family's insistence on observing various Jewish traditions. Her outlook, however, is greatly altered after she travels back in time to Nazi occupied Poland. There, she witnesses her ancestors struggle to preserve their heritage and health during the Holocaust.

The Best
Children's Literature
A Parent's Guide

Chapter Six

The Diary of a Young Girl: The Definitive Edition

parent's
guide
choice award

Written by Anne Frank, edited by Otto H. Frank and
Mirjam Pressler, translated by Susan Massotty
Anchor Books, $12.95, 340 pages
First published in 1996 (original diaries published in 1947)
Ages 10 and up

It's impossible to find anyone who after reading Anne Frank's journal
entries is not overwhelmingly moved. Now, the entirety of her diaries is available, including excerpts previously omitted due to Otto Frank's (Anne's father,
the only family survivor of the Holocaust) protective initial editing. These
reintroduced segments allude to Anne's awakening sexuality and growing
frustrations, and are dramatically important to the tragic story of this unwitting symbol of the devastating losses associated with the Holocaust. Also look
for *Anne Frank, Beyond the Diary: A Photographic Remembrance* by Ruud van
der Rol (in "Nonfiction").

The Doll People

Written by Ann M. Martin
Hyperion, $15.99, 256 pages
First published in 2000
Ages 8–13

Just what do dolls do when the kids aren't looking? It's an intriguing
premise, the hidden life of dolls, and Martin sets readers up for an entertaining mystery. Annabelle is a member of a venerated English doll family
who prowls her dollhouse at night. She decides to search the world beyond
the threshold of her miniature front door. You see, she's looking for clues
about the unsolved disappearance of her Auntie Sarah. And when new modern
Funcraft dolls move in, Annabelle enlists the help of Tiffany, a doll of about
the same age. It's all wonderfully offbeat and perfectly rendered. Ann M.
Martin is the author of the mega-popular series *The Babysitter's Club* and is
a co-author of *P.S. Longer Letter Later* (in this chapter).

Juvenile Fiction/Chapter Books

Dragonwings
Written by Laurence Yep
HarperTrophy, $6.95, 317 pages
First published in 1975
Ages 10–15

In the early years of the twentieth century, as the world gets its first glimpse of air travel, a young Chinese immigrant helps his father create their own flying machine. There's a prequel entitled *Dragon's Gate*. Often based on his own experiences, Yep's depictions of immigrant life in San Francisco ring true. Other books include *Dream Soul*; *The Imp That Ate My Homework*; *The Magic Paintbrush*; and *Ribbons*.

The Egypt Game
Written by Zilpha Keatley Snyder, Illustrated by Alton Raible
Dell, $5.99, 215 pages
First published in 1967
Ages 9–14

April and Melanie are fascinated by ancient Egypt. After using an abandoned lot to stage an elaborate re-creation of the ancient civilization, they become involved in a truly dangerous situation. This is a thrilling and imaginative novel that earned a **Newbery Honor**. Its sequel is *The Gypsy Game*. Also by Snyder, *Gib Rides Home*; *The Headless Cupid*; *Spyhole Secrets*; and *The Witches of Worm*.

Ella Enchanted
Written by Gail Carson Levine
HarperTrophy, $5.95, 232 pages
First published in 1997
Ages 9–13

A winning version of the classic Cinderella story, this updated fairy tale will certainly enchant fantasy fans. A spell has been cast on poor Ella, causing her to obey every command. With ogres, giants, fairy godmothers, and wicked stepsisters, this funny debut is a true delight and a **Newbery Honor** recipient. Also look for *Dave at Night* (detailed in this chapter); *The Princess Tales*; *The Fairy's Mistake*; and for younger readers, the splendid *Betsy Who Cried Wolf* (detailed in "Story Books").

**The Best
Children's Literature**
A Parent's Guide

Chapter Six

Encyclopedia Brown Series
Written by Donald J. Sobol, Illustrated by Leonard Shortall
Bantam, $4.50 per volume, 70–120 pages
First published in 1963
Ages 8–12

Leroy Brown is a veritable encyclopedia of facts, thus the nickname bestowed on him by his father. A mastermind in mysterious matters big and small, young Leroy outwits any criminal who may be lurking in his hometown of Idaville. Got a mystery buff at home? This series is a great introduction to the genre. There are twenty or more volumes currently in print including *Encyclopedia Brown and the Case of the Mysterious Handprints*; *Encyclopedia Brown and the Case of the Disgusting Sneakers*; *Encyclopedia Brown and the Case of the Slippery Salamander*; and *Encyclopedia Brown, Boy Detective*.

Esperanza Rising
Written by Pam Muñoz Ryan
Scholastic, $4.99, 262 pages
First published in 2002
Ages 9–13

After thirteen-year-old Esperanza's father is murdered, she and her mother are forced to leave the privileged comforts of home for the opportunities that await them in California. This wonderful novel explores the effects of the Great Depression from the perspective of Mexican-American migrant workers. Interestingly, the author based much of the story on the experiences of her own grandmother. Pam Muñoz Ryan is the gifted author of a host of books including *Amelia and Eleanor Go for a Ride* (see "Story Books"); *The Flag We Love* (see "Nonfiction"); and *Riding Freedom*.

Everything on a Waffle
Written by Polly Horvath
Farrar Straus Giroux, $16.00, 149 pages
First published in 2001
Ages 9–13

Eleven-year-old Primrose Squarp is certain that her parents will return to her, despite the fact that everyone is convinced they were lost at sea. Life in her small Canadian fishing town is full of wacky characters, bittersweet promise, and an awful lot of waffles. Horvath's unique recipe for storytelling earned a **Newbery Honor** in 2002.

Juvenile Fiction/Chapter Books

Freak the Mighty
Written by Rodman Philbrick
Scholastic, $4.99, 169 pages
First published in 1993
Ages 9–14

The beauty of an unlikely and mutually beneficial friendship is at the heart of this unique novel. Oversized and lumbering Maxwell Kane is learning disabled and the victim of a disastrous home life. Kevin, otherwise known as "Freak," is intellectually gifted, but has a birth defect that caused his growth to be stunted. Together they form an unbeatable collaboration aptly called "Freak the Mighty" and use their collective power to outsmart bullies. When tragic events befall the pair, the lessons that they have taught each other are apparent.

From the Mixed-Up Files of Mrs. Basil E. Frankweiler
Written by E.L. Konigsburg
Aladdin, $5.50, 162 pages
First published in 1967
Ages 9–13

Twelve-year-old Claudia Kincaid is looking for a change of scenery. Bored with life in the suburbs, she hatches a plan to escape to a place full of history, grandeur, and beauty: The Metropolitan Museum of Art. With brother Jamie in tow, she sets up camp at the museum, avoiding the night guards and becoming enthralled by a beautiful statue with a mysterious past. It's the title character, a previous owner of said statue, who provides Claudia with ample reason to find her way home. Read this book and subsequent visits to Manhattan's great house of art and artifact will never be the same. Konigsburg is the author of *The View from Saturday* (in this chapter).

A Girl Called Al
Written by Constance C. Greene, Illustrated by Byron Barton
Viking, $5.99, 127 pages
First published in 1969
Ages 9–13

Al is short for Alexandra. She extols the virtues of being a nonconformist and demonstrates the value of friendship to her best pal, a narrator who remains nameless. The two girls form a special bond with the superintendent of their Manhattan apartment building, sharing life's joys and concerns, and learning a lot about loyalty. Sadly, the equally enjoyable sequels are out of print. They're worth a good search through the library stacks or out of print book searching service. Look for *I Know You, Al; Your Old Pal, Al; Al(exandra) the Great*; and *Just Plain Al*. Greene is also the author of *Beat the Turtle Drum*.

Chapter Six

The Giver
Written by Lois Lowry
Laurel Leaf, $6.50, 180 pages
First published in 1993
Ages 10–14

This **Newbery Medal** winner truly shows Lowry's versatility as a children's writer. While *Anastasia Krupnik* and *Number the Stars* (both detailed in this chapter) are based in realistic fiction, *The Giver* is very much a work of science fiction. Twelve-year-old Jonas becomes the bearer of memories that are shared with another individual in his futuristic community, but slowly comes to recognize the dangerous truth surrounding him. Admirers of this story will likely adore *A Wrinkle in Time* and its sequels (in this chapter) by Madeline L'Engle.

The Golden Compass: His Dark Materials, Book One
Written by Philip Pullman
Del Rey, $6.99, 351 pages
First published in 1996
Ages 11 and up

Here is fantasy fiction at its finest, to be devoured by middle-grade readers, teenagers, and adults alike. The world that Lyra Belacqua inhabits bears little resemblance to our own. People are accompanied at all times by personal daemons, animal beings that reflect the soul of their human counterpart. Lyra and her daemon witness a startling assassination plot and are drawn into a series of events that will compel the most earthbound readers. The stunning sequels are *The Subtle Knife* and *The Amber Spyglass*. Outside of this series, Pullman has penned *Count Karlstein* and *I Was a Rat!* among others.

The Graduation of Jake Moon
Written by Barbara Park
Aladdin, $4.99, 115 pages
First published in 2000
Ages 9–13

Jake learns a hard and fast lesson about life's unexpected perils after his beloved grandfather, Skelly, begins to slowly succumb to Alzheimer's Disease. Accepting responsibility for Skelly's care takes its toll on Jake's relationships, and he struggles to come to terms with the caregiver role reversal that occurs between his grandfather and himself. Barbara Park's treatment of difficult subjects is masterful and is again in evidence in *Mick Harte Was Here* (in this chapter).

Juvenile Fiction/Chapter Books

The Great Gilly Hopkins
Written by Katherine Paterson
HarperCollins, $5.95, 148 pages
First published in 1978
Ages 9–13

Hardened and cynical from years of being tossed between foster homes, Gilly clings to the hope that her mother will return to rescue her. She refuses to form attachments and quickly becomes known as difficult and abrasive, yet quite clever. When she is sent to live with the rather eccentric Trotter family, she devises a plan for escape. Circumstances, however, lead Gilly to value the hard-won relationships she has formed with her newest foster family. Clearly these are not lightweight themes, but Paterson draws her protagonist with such loving care that readers cannot help but be forever in her thrall. This story is the recipient of a **Newbery Honor**. Also look for *Missing Girls* by Lois Metzger. Katherine Paterson is also the author of *The Bridge to Terabithia* (in this chapter); *Jacob Have I Loved*; and *Lyddie* among others.

The Great Good Thing
Written by Roderick Townley
Atheneum, $17.00, 216 pages
First published in 2001
Ages 9–14

A new and thoughtful twist on fantasy is not easy to come by, but you'll find it between the pages of this enchanting book. In fact, the story centers on a fairytale princess named Sylvie who has resided within the confines of a book for 80 years. She refuses to submit to her "happy ending" destiny until she sets out to accomplish a "Great Good Thing." Meanwhile, outside the world of her storybook existence, the tome she calls home is threatened by fire. She begins to make contact with the book's reader, a young girl named Claire (the granddaughter of the book's first reader) in order to ensure her existence and the alteration of her fairy tale outcome. This interplay between the fairytale characters and their readers is marvelously imaginative, and young readers will not soon forget it!

Bethany, Age 11, says: "**The Great Good Thing** is one of my favorite books of all times. The author is so smart to think of it. I mean, it's so cool that there are characters inside a book and then characters inside the book in that book, and they get to meet each other. It's so cool. My friend's name is Claire like the girl in the book and she loves the book, too."

Chapter Six

Harriet the Spy
Written by Louise Fitzhugh
Yearling, $5.99, 300 pages
First published in 1964
Ages 9–13

Journalistic integrity is one thing but friendship is quite another, as young Harriet quickly discovers. After deciding to keep an uncompromisingly honest record of her school observances, Harriet misplaces her journal. She's then faced with her classmates' reactions to her rather blunt descriptions. Written nearly 40 years ago, this story remains fresh and immensely enjoyable. Its sequel is *The Long Secret*. Fitzhugh is also the author of *Nobody's Family Is Going to Change* (in this chapter).

Harry Potter and the Sorcerer's Stone

parent's
guide
choice award

Written by J. K. Rowling
Scholastic, $6.99, 384 pages
First published in 1998
Ages 9–99

He needs no introduction and his name carries a lot of literary clout. He's the boy wizard, Harry Potter, who after spending miserably orphaned years in the care of an evil aunt and uncle, finds himself whisked away to the wondrous hallowed halls of Hogwarts Academy. That's where the fun really begins because Harry, having only recently discovered his magical status, meets amazing beings (human and otherwise), witnesses astounding acts of wizardry, makes loyal friends, and tests out his own powers. And that's just the first volume! The revered Rowling intends to take Harry through seven years of school so there are three highly anticipated volumes yet to come. For now, however, readers cling to *Harry Potter and the Chamber of Secrets*; *Harry Potter and the Prizoner of Azkaban*; and *Harry Potter and the Goblet of Fire*. Audio versions from Listening Library feature the terrific narration of Jim Dale, and the books are available in a multitude of world languages so kids from Alabama to Zaire are joined in a worthy and wonderful fan club.

Juvenile Fiction/Chapter Books

Why Harry Potter Is a Great Teacher

It's been a long time since kids were overheard in the playground pretending to be characters from a book, but young wizard Harry Potter and his creator J.K. Rowling have changed all that. The books' influence cannot be overstated, as they have not only drawn millions of readers, reluctant and otherwise, they have duly demonstrated that fun can come from reading great books. Three cheers for Harry!

Hatchet

Written by Gary Paulsen
Aladdin, $5.99, 195 pages
First published in 1987
Ages 10–14

Aboard a single engine plane on a trip to visit his father, thirteen-year-old Brian must safely land the craft after the pilot dies of a heart attack. He must then brave the direst of circumstances, left alone in the Canadian wilderness for 56 days. Stark and finely honed narrative follows Brian's struggle, as he summons the courage to survive. Following this striking drama are *The River*; *Brian's Winter*; and *Brian's Return*.

Heaven Eyes

Written by David Almond
Delacorte, $15.95, 233 pages
First published in 2001
Ages 10–14

The acclaimed author of *Kit's Wilderness* and *Skellig* brings us a surreal story complete with deftly drawn characters and dark secrets. Three orphans begin a mysterious journey to freedom and meet a young girl with webbed fingers and toes named Heaven Eyes along with her shadowy companion, Grandpa. Their dreamlike travels shed light on lessons about fear, friendship, love, and grief.

Chapter Six

The Hobbit
Written by J. R. R. Tolkien
Del Rey, $6.99, 304 pages
First published in 1937
Ages 10 and up

As the film versions of the *Lord of the Rings* series ignite excitement amongst a new generation, the amazing and complex literary world created by J.R.R. Tolkien continues to entrance new readers. Perhaps the best-known and most widely read introduction to fantasy fiction, *The Hobbit* and its companion volumes are likely to become the most influential source of inspiration for further fantasy reading amongst your middle-grade and teenaged readers. After all, millions of *Harry Potter* fans have recognized the standard set by Tolkien, gravitating to his thrilling stories with renewed enthusiasm. By way of introduction, Bilbo and Frodo are small creatures called Hobbits who must face dragons, dark lords, and the pervasive power of a missing ring. Readers proceed through *The Hobbit*, *The Fellowship of the Ring*, *The Two Towers*, and *The Return of the King*. All four books are available as a boxed set from Ballantine Books. Upon completion, a logical progression for enraptured fantasy fans would be to begin *The Chronicles of Narnia* series (see under *The Lion, the Witch and the Wardrobe* in this chapter) by C. S. Lewis.

Holes
Written by Louis Sachar
Yearling, $6.50, 233 pages
First published in 1998
Ages 10–14

Camp Green Lake may sound inviting, but there are no happy campers there. In fact, there's no lake. It's a detention facility for delinquent boys who must spend their days digging holes as part of their punishment. For Stanley Yelnats (note the palindrome), the camp seemed a viable alternative to jail. Never mind that his conviction is based on a stunning case of mistaken identity that seems to affirm his family's longstanding history of misfortune. When Stanley and his fellow detainees discover the real reason for their incessant digging, Sachar's talent as a satirist is unearthed. There's a terrific audio version available from Listening Library. If your pre-teen reader enjoyed this book, look for *The Maze* by Will Hobbs and *Nine Man Tree* by Robert Newton Peck. Other books by Louis Sachar include the farcical *Marvin Redpost* series and *Wayside School* series (see under *Sideways Stories From Wayside School* in this chapter).

Kalil, Age 12 says: "We read **Holes** during summer reading at the library and it was so crazy. I couldn't believe it. I read a lot of books and this one is totally nuts... but really good. I wonder if there are really places like that where they make you do useless things like dig holes, or where there are bad adults doing mysterious things."

Juvenile Fiction/Chapter Books

Homeless Bird

Written by Gloria Whelan
HarperTrophy, $5.95, 186 pages
First published in 2000
Ages 10–14

Thirteen-year-old Koly, raised in India, will soon marry a man she's never met. Her arranged marriage forces her to leave the comfort and security of home to live in the presence of strangers, including her new husband who is terminally ill. Though her journey seems terribly harrowing, Koly finds hope after meeting a generous widow and embarking on a new and completely unforeseen future. Details of Indian culture and tradition make for especially compelling reading. Also by this author *Once on This Island*; *The Indian School*; and *Miranda's Last Stand*.

The House of Dies Drear

Written by Virginia Hamilton
Aladdin, $5.99, 279 pages
First published in 1968
Ages 10–14

With masterful storytelling skill, Virginia Hamilton weaves this thrilling tale of thirteen-year-old Thomas and his family as they move into a house that was a former junction on the Underground Railroad. Buoyed by rumors that the house is haunted, Thomas finds a maze of subterranean passageways and discovers important truths about the plight of slaves who sought liberty at any cost. Look for the sequel, *The Mystery of Drear House*. Intrigued readers will also enjoy *Stealing Freedom* by Elisa Lynn Carbone. Other middle-grade and young-adult novels by Hamilton include *Bluish*; *Cousins*; *M.C. Higgins the Great*; *The Planet of Junior Brown* (in this chapter); and *Sweet Whispers, Brother Rush*.

Featured Author: Virginia Hamilton

Few children's authors have garnered as much critical acclaim as Virginia Hamilton. She's the recipient of the Newbery Medal and the National Book Award among others, and consistently receives rave reviews for her novels. Focusing largely on different African–American perspectives and experiences, Hamilton has a magical storytelling style. Her feel for atmosphere and dialogue make even her contemporary stories seem like the finest folk legends. The dark issues of slavery, death, and homelessness have received Virginia Hamilton's graceful treatment. She often weaves elements of fantasy into her stories while always retaining believability and the utmost honor.

Chapter Six

The House with a Clock in Its Walls
Written by John Bellairs, Illustrated by Edward Gorey
Puffin, $5.99, 179 pages
First published in 1973
Ages 8–12

A boy goes to live with his oddly magical uncle in a mysterious mansion. There's a clock hidden in the walls... but what does the ticking signify? Edward Gorey's illustrations add good old-fashioned spooky appeal to the timeless (or timeful) tale. Also look for *The Figure in the Shadows* and *The Letter, the Witch, and the Ring*.

How to Be a Real Person (in Just One Day)
Written by Sally Warner
Knopf, $15.95, 123 pages
First published in 2001
Ages 10–14

A young girl's attempts to reconcile her mother's mental illness with the idea of being a "real person" is at the heart of this sensitive and honest novel. Kara begins to make lists that reflect her observations of "normal" life, deciding that "if you do everything perfectly, you feel more real." Kara's struggle is quite real and readers will immediately identify with her plight, as well as her appropriate adolescent responses. Sally Warner is also the author of *Bad Girl Blues*; *Finding Hattie*; and *Totally Confidential*.

How to Eat Fried Worms
Written by Thomas Rockwell, Illustrated by Emily Arnold McCully
Dell, $4.99, 116 pages
First published in 1973
Ages 8–13

With giggling and grossed-out readers dating back to 1973, this story is a study in culinary kookiness. Fancying himself a risk taker, Billy accepts a bet to eat fifteen worms in as many days and proceeds to prove that worms are the latest in continental cuisine. There's a terrific audio adaptation available from Listening Library. The sequels are *How to Fight a Girl* and *How to Get Fabulously Rich*. These titles can be tastily paired with *Beetles Lightly Toasted* by Phyllis Reynolds Naylor.

Juvenile Fiction/Chapter Books

Hush
Written by Jacqueline Woodson
Putnam, $15.99, 181 pages
First published in 2002
Ages 10–14

Toswiah's family enters the witness protection program after her father testifies against two white cops who shot and killed a young black boy. Forced to change her name and leave her home, the new Evie Thomas witnesses the gradual disintegration of her family. The novel is masterfully told through a variation of present and past perspectives as the young girl slowly comes to reconcile her new existence and the "what if's" of her old life. Jacqueline Woodson is the truly talented author of *Miracle's Boys*; *The Other Side* (in "Story Books"); and *I Hadn't Meant to Tell You This*.

In the Year of the Boar and Jackie Robinson
Written by Bette Bao Lord, Illustrated by Marc Simont
HarperTrophy, $5.99, 169 pages
First published in 1984
Ages 9–13

Brooklyn, 1947 provides the setting for this lovely story of a young Chinese immigrant and her immersion into American culture. It's baseball, namely the famous Dodgers, that catches her fancy. The book's title and its adept narrative suggest the struggle between retaining one's cultural heritage while being lured by the magnetic pull of assimilation. Mark Simont's affectionate illustrations add a wonderfully wry and atmospheric touch.

The Incredible Journey
Written by Sheila Burnford
Bantam, $4.99, 145 pages
First published in 1961
Ages 9–14

A book with popularity that knows no boundaries, this is the story of three house pets—a Labrador retriever, a bull terrier, and a Siamese cat—that brave the hazards of the vast Canadian wilderness to find their way back home. Incredible indeed, and a perfect introduction to the genre of adventure fiction that includes such esteemed works as *Call of the Wild* and other books by Jack London.

Chapter Six

The Indian in the Cupboard
Written by Lynne Reid Banks, Illustrated by Brock Cole
Avon, $5.99, 181 pages
First published in 1981
Ages 8–12

Omri's birthday looks as though it will be a bit disappointing. His brother couldn't afford a gift and presented him with an old bathroom cupboard. After his mother finds the key, however, a world of enchanting imagination and childhood fantasy opens before his eyes. You see, the cupboard can transform favorite toys into living, breathing beings! A plastic toy Indian comes to life first, giving new meaning to the term "action figure." The lively sequels are *The Return of the Indian*; *The Secret of the Indian*; *The Mystery of the Cupboard*; and *The Key to the Indian*. Lynne Reid Banks is also the author of *I, Houdini*.

Island of the Blue Dolphins
Written by Scott O'Dell
Dell, $6.50, 184 pages
First published in 1960
Ages 9–14

Maintaining its well-deserved position on all recommended reading lists for children, this haunting **Newbery Medal** winning story of survival grasps readers' attention and leaves an indelible impression. It's the story of a girl who must rely on courage and determined resourcefulness after being abandoned on an uninhabited island for 18 years. Karana learns to find food and shelter while retaining a serene composure that becomes as important as any survival skill. Scott O'Dell is the acclaimed author of *The Black Pearl*; *My Name Is Not Angelica*; *Sing Down the Moon* (in this chapter); and *Zia*.

Parent/Child Review: Island of the Blue Dolphins

The Parent: Milt, Age 44, Editor

The Child: Josh, Age 11, Comic Book Collector

Josh says: "We read this for school and at first I didn't like it... I didn't believe it. But then I got sucked in. I'd probably die after three days on an island."

Milt says: "I haven't read a kid's novel for years and I sat down and read this one straight through without getting up. It was awesome, to use Josh's favorite word."

Juvenile Fiction/Chapter Books

James and the Giant Peach

Written by Roald Dahl, Illustrated by Quentin Blake
Puffin, $5.99, 146 pages
First published in 1961
Ages 8–12

A tragic accident involving a rhinoceros claimed the lives of James' parents. Sent to live with two rather unsavory aunts, James's misery seems unbearable until a chance meeting with a mystical old fellow provides a fruitful escape. A sprinkling of magic crystals allows James to climb inside a giant peach where he meets an unforgettable array of multi-legged characters including Grasshopper and Miss Spider. Be sure to pluck this literary gem from the library or bookstore shelves. Roald Dahl is the celebrated author of *The BFG* and *Charlie and the Chocolate Factory* (both in this chapter) as well as *Danny The Champion of the World*; *George's Marvelous Medicine*; *Matilda* and other favorites.

Joey Pigza Swallowed the Key

Written by Jack Gantos
HarperTrophy, $5.95, 153 pages
First published in 1998
Ages 9–14

parent's
guide
choice award

Joey Pigza has ADHD and a host of unresolved difficulties at home. He is immediately recognizable as the child whose baffling behavior leads classmates to treat him as a scapegoat. The book is told in the first person, as Joey invites readers to examine his erratic conduct, which is sometimes amusing but often startling. In the hands of a less talented writer, such subject matter may seem a bit lurid. Gantos, however, does not exploit his troubled character, but allows him to be viewed as the unwitting vehicle for a disturbing condition. As a result, readers become gradually sympathetic to the plight of Joey and his millions of real-life counterparts, as they begin to redefine the concept of "normal" behavior. *Joey Pigza Loses Control*, the very satisfying sequel, is a **Newbery Honor** book.

Chapter Six

Johnny Tremain
Written by Esther Forbes
Yearling, $5.99, 256 pages
First published in 1943
Ages 10–14

Readers are not only treated to a daring adventure story in this **Newbery Medal** winning classic, they also receive a timeless message about the personal tragedies that accompany war. Johnny works as an apprentice to a silversmith when a series of dark events leads him to become irrevocably involved in the dangerous drama of the Revolutionary War. This book has wide audience appeal, read by upper-elementary-grade children as well as older adolescents.

Julie of the Wolves
Written by Jean Craighead George
HarperTrophy, $5.99, 170 pages
First published in 1972
Ages 9–13

Here's a truly remarkable and engrossing survival story. Julie runs away from an unhappy young marriage and becomes lost in the frozen Alaskan tundra. After quietly observing the habits of a family of wolves, she gradually becomes accepted as a member of the pack. The wolves' behavior is fascinating, and George's sense of suspense is perfectly paced in this **Newbery Medal** winning book. The drama continues in *Julie* and *Julie's Wolf Pack*. Jean Craighead George is also the author of *My Side of the Mountain* (in this chapter) as well as a delightful assortment of animal story books and nonfiction for young readers.

The Last of the Really Great Whangdoodles
Written by Julie Andrews Edwards
HarperTrophy, $5.95, 277 pages
First published in 1989
Ages 8–12

What exactly is a whangdoodle, you ask? It's a wise yet highly endangered species, once considered the most generous and kind beings on earth (or someplace like it). In the land where the last of these special creatures resides, you'll find whimsical Flukes and Whiffle Birds. A determined Professor Savant and three wide-eyed children set out on a campaign to raise awareness about the plight of the whangdoodle, leading them on an amazing journey. Fans of Roald Dahl will not want to miss this triumphant tale by Julie Andrews Edwards (yes, she of *The Sound of Music*).

Juvenile Fiction/Chapter Books

The Lion, the Witch, and the Wardrobe

Written by C. S. Lewis
HarperTrophy, $8.95, 189 pages
First published in 1950
Ages 10 and up

In the first book of the highly heralded *Chronicles of Narnia* series, four children discover that a mysterious wardrobe is the portal to a magical world. Sibling group Lucy, Peter, Edmund, and Susan waste no time in immersing themselves in adventure as they enter Narnia and help rid the land of the White Witch and her dangerous clan. Aslan is the brave lion that risks his own life to save the children. The dramatic fantasy continues with *Prince Caspian*; *The Voyage of the Dawn Treader*; *The Silver Chair*; *The Horse and His Boy*; *The Magician's Nephew*; and *The Last Battle*.

Little House in the Big Woods

Written by Laura Ingalls Wilder, Illustrated by Garth Williams
HarperTrophy, $6.99, 238 pages
First published in 1932
Ages 8–12

While children of the 1970s became well acquainted with Laura Ingalls Wilder through the popular television series (a loose interpretation, some would say), her books have delighted readers for nearly seventy years. Documenting life with her pioneer family, Laura provided a slice-of-life picture of the Midwest in the late nineteenth century. Her stories have attracted a largely female audience, but boys are pleasantly surprised by some of the rough and tumble adventure elements, as well as the details of daily life as a pioneer. The series continues with *Little House on the Prairie*; *On the Banks of Plum Creek*; *By the Shores of Silver Lake*; *The Long Winter*; *Little Town on the Prairie*; and *Those Happy Golden Years*, which takes Laura into adulthood and marriage.

Did You Know?

Laura Ingalls Wilder didn't publish her first book, **Little House in the Big Woods**, until she was 65 years old!

Chapter Six

A Little Princess

Written by Frances Hodgson Burnett, Illustrated by Tasha Tudor
HarperTrophy, $5.99, 245 pages
First published in 1963
Ages 8–12

Sara Crewe endures life at Miss Minchen's boarding school by pretending she's a princess. When she enrolled as the privileged daughter of a wealthy man, she was welcomed with open arms by the greedy headmistress. After Sara's beloved papa's wartime disappearance, however, she is viewed as a charity case and forced to withstand repeated humiliations. But even when series of misunderstandings occur that seem to cast doubt on the little girl's chances for future happiness, her optimism lives on and brightens the lives of her schoolmates. Tasha Tudor's black and white illustrations are a lovely complement to this treasured story. Frances Hodgson Burnett is also the author of *The Secret Garden* (in this chapter).

Little Women

Written by Louisa May Alcott
Puffin, $6.99, 669 pages
First published in 1868
Ages 9 and up

Not only is this tender story a literary classic, it is also a wonderful introduction to adult fiction for younger readers. Meg, Jo, Beth, and Amy are the March sisters, each possessing her own set of values, virtues, and hopes. Yet their story, based largely on Alcott's own Civil War era girlhood, speaks volumes about the devotion of family. Their beloved Marmee provides loving sustenance as the young women suffer from poverty, the wartime absence of their father, and sweet Beth's chronic illness. Also look for *Jo's Boys; Little Men;* and *Rose in Bloom.*

Parent/Child Review: Little Women

The Parent: Celia, Age 50, Pharmacist
The Child: Mosey, Age 13, Horseback Rider
Mosey says: "We read this book for school and then I saw the movie with Kirsten Dunst in it, even though my mom says that's not the best version of it. Anyway, it's a great book, you know, and everyone should read it... not just girls!"
Celia says: "It was so great to reread this book and to talk about it with Mosey. I can't believe how well I remember the story. I guess it stays with you."

Juvenile Fiction/Chapter Books

A Long Way from Chicago
Written by Richard Peck
Puffin, $5.99, 148 pages
First published in 1998
Ages 9–13

Grandma Dowdel is not your typical grandparent, and that's why Joe and Mary Alice Dowdel eagerly anticipate their yearly visit to her home in a small Illinois town. You see, Grandma has strong opinions about the folks in her community and isn't afraid to tell a little lie (or a rather large one) to effect change, or just to eliminate the things that irk her. She certainly entertains her grandkids with her antics and, along the way, helps both her good and bad neighbors get what she feels they deserve. It's a hilarious trip by multi-faceted author, Richard Peck. *A Year Down Yonder* is the equally enjoyable sequel. Also look for *Lost in Cyberspace*; *The Last Safe Place on Earth*; and *Strays Like Us*.

Love That Dog
Written by Sharon Creech
HarperCollins, $14.95, 86 pages
First published in 2001
Ages 8–12

Jack is skeptical about the value of poetry until his own free-verse journal entries and a newfound (and deserved!) admiration for the work of Walter Dean Myers allow him to see the light. Jack's observations are delightful and allow Creech to create a narrative that will especially appeal to children who seek creative forms of fiction. Also by this author, *Ruby Holler*; *Walk Two Moons* (in this chapter); and *The Wanderer*.

M. C. Higgins, the Great
Written by Virginia Hamilton
Aladdin, $4.99, 278 pages
First published in 1974
Ages 11–14

Young M.C. surveys his family's property and worries about the approach of a slag heap from the local strip-mining efforts. The effects of this run-off could destroy his land, and M.C. must choose to fight for his home or convince his mother to leave. It's another award winning effort for Virginia Hamilton who was awarded the **Newbery Medal** and the **National Book Award** for this novel. Also look for *The House of Dies Drear* and *The Planet of Junior Brown* (both in this chapter).

Chapter Six

Maniac Magee
Written by Jerry Spinelli
Little Brown, $5.95, 184 pages
First published in 1990
Ages 9–13

   A powerful modern folk tale unfolds as Jeffrey Lionel Magee faces racism and closed-mindedness in a small town. That Jeffrey is a "maniac" is the commonly held position of the town folk. Fact is, the boy was a white runaway who was taken in by a black family in Two Mills, Pennsylvania, until pressure from the community forced him to continue his search for home. In the meantime, "Maniac" Magee outruns every race, outhits every ball, and outwits the bigoted citizens of Two Mills after crossing the dividing line between the town's white and black neighborhoods. To say that Spinelli has a way with words would be a vast understatement, and this **Newbery Medal** winning story has ample charm, energy, and moral drama. Jerry Spinelli is the author of *Crash*; *The Library Card*; *Loser*; *Stargirl*; and *Wringer*.

Mick Harte Was Here
Written by Barbara Park
Bullseye, $4.99, 89 pages
First published in 1995
Ages 8–12

parent's
guide
choice award

   Thirteen-year-old Phoebe confronts her grief and shock after a bicycle accident kills her brother. There are unresolved feelings and a number of "what if's," due to the fact that young Mick was not wearing a helmet. Park's masterful treatment rings true, as Phoebe and her family face the anger and sadness that accompany loss. Especially poignant is Phoebe's affectionate portrayal of her brother as her best friend, a revelation that deepens the powerful emotions of this poised story. Also by this author, *The Graduation of Jake Moon* (in this chapter); *Skinnybones*; and the *Junie B. Jones* series.

Juvenile Fiction/Chapter Books

Midnight Magic
Written by Avi
Scholastic, $4.99, 249 pages
First published in 1999
Ages 10–14

This medieval whodunit takes place in a grand Italian kingdom where young Fabrizio is the servant of Mangus the Magician. A ghost sighting threatens to postpone the wedding of the king's daughter to the loathsome Count Scarazoni. That's when Fabrizio proves his mettle, summoning up courage and bravery to uncover an insidious line of deception. Surprises await readers as the story draws to a close. Avi is the prolific author of *Perloo the Bold*; *The True Confessions of Charlotte Doyle*; and *Don't You Know There's a War On?*

Missing May
Written by Cynthia Rylant
Dell, $5.50, 89 pages
First published in 1992
Ages 10–14

Summer has lived with her beloved Aunt May and Uncle Ob for half of her life, since she was six-years-old. Faced with overwhelming grief upon her aunt's death, Summer worries about her bereaved uncle's state of mind. An unlikely friendship with a boy from school presents a glimmer of hope, as Summer and Ob face their loss by attempting to make contact with May's loving spirit. Cynthia Rylant is the gifted and prolific author of dozens of children's books including the *Henry and Mudge* series (in "Easy Readers") and *A Fine White Dust*. For picture and story books by Rylant, consult the Author Index.

Misty of Chincoteague
Written by Marguerite Henry, Illustrated by Wesley Dennis
Aladdin, $4.99, 173 pages
First published in 1947
Ages 9–13

An ethereal story that plucks readers' heartstrings like a favorite folk song, Marguerite Henry's classic book is set on a small island where a band of wild ponies run free. A young boy and girl become fascinated by an elusive mare named Phantom. However, it's a colt named Misty who gives the greatest gift, as the children become gradually aware of the perils associated with taking wild animals into captivity. There are several sequels, including *Misty's Twilight*; *Sea Star: Orphan of Chincoteague*; and *Stormy: Misty's Foal*. Other horse stories by Henry include *King of the Wind* and *Brighty of the Grand Canyon*.

Chapter Six

Morning Girl
Written by Michael Dorris
Hyperion, $4.99, 74 pages
First published in 1992
Ages 8–12

Set in the Bahamas in 1492, a young Taino girl named Morning Girl and her brother Star Boy take turns telling their story. Both children raise questions about their identity and impending adulthood. When Morning Girl welcomes visitors who arrive by canoe, readers are treated to a bit of historical fiction. Those visitors are Christopher Columbus and his crew.

Mrs. Frisby and the Rats of Nimh
Written by Robert C. O'Brien, Illustrated by Zena Bernstein
Aladdin, $5.50, 233 pages
First published in 1971
Ages 8–12

A **Newbery Medal** recipient, this story's evergreen popularity is perhaps based on its fanciful plot. In order to save her ailing son, Mrs. Frisby (a mouse) must turn to the secretive and highly intelligent society of rats that live beneath the rosebush. Their relationship becomes mutually beneficial; as the widow mouse helps the rats to form a civilization of their own design. You see, the rats had been bred as part of scientific investigation at NIMH—The National Institute of Mental Health—thus explaining their wisdom and resourcefulness.

My Side of the Mountain
Written and Illustrated by Jean Craighead George
Puffin, $5.99, 177 pages
First published in 1959
Ages 9–13

Setting the highest standards for children's adventure fiction, Jean Craighead George crafted this fine story of a young boy who, bored with life in New York City, runs away to live in the wilderness of the Catskill Mountains. He builds a tree house, befriends a falcon, braves the elements, and realizes his dream of freedom. Also by this author, *Julie of the Wolves* (in this chapter). Pleased readers will also enjoy *Island of the Blue Dolphins* by Scott O'Dell and *The Incredible Journey* by Sheila Burnford.

Juvenile Fiction/Chapter Books

National Velvet
Written by Enid Bagnold
Avon Camelot, $4.95, 265 pages
First published in 1935
Ages 9–14

Velvet Brown is a fourteen-year-old equestrian who, with steadfast determination, tries to turn a wild horse into a champion. She's got her heart set on victory at the Grand National steeplechase. It's a thrilling ride filled with tender adolescent emotion and nail-gnawing drama.

Nim's Island
Written by Wendy Orr
Knopf, $14.95, 125 pages
First published in 2001
Ages 8–13

Creating the most modern of survival stories, while paying homage to *The Swiss Family Robinson*, Orr tells the tale of Nim and her father who have been stranded (by choice) on an otherwise uninhabited island. Their isolation doesn't bother Nim a bit, as her island home is a high-tech shelter, complete with e-mail and a cellular phone. When their tropical utopia is threatened by inclement weather and—gasp!—tourists, Nim begins corresponding with an author of adventure novels to seek advice. Thoroughly entertaining, Orr's puckish satire is a twenty-first-century gem. Also by this author, *Peeling the Onion* (ages eleven and up).

Nobody's Family Is Going to Change
Written and Illustrated by Louise Fitzhugh
Farrar Straus Giroux, $5.95, 221 pages
First published in 1974
Ages 9–14

Eleven-year-old Emma wants to be a lawyer, despite (and perhaps because of) her father's prejudicial stance that women should not pursue careers in law. Meanwhile, her younger brother dreams of becoming a dancer like his Uncle Dipsey. There are certainly issues of sexism and stereotypes here, but mostly it's a compelling drama with characters and family dynamics that feel quite familiar and real. Fitzhugh is also the author of *Harriet the Spy* (in this chapter).

Chapter Six

Number the Stars
Written by Lois Lowry
Dell Yearling, $5.99, 137 pages
First published in 1989
Ages 9–13

Witnessing the Nazi invasion of Copenhagen in 1943, ten-year-old Annemarie Johansen goes to great lengths to protect her best friend, a Jewish girl named Ellen Rosen. The Nazis' effort to evacuate the Danish Jews to concentration camps, and the heroic response by many Christian families is at the heart of this beautiful and haunting novel, a **Newbery Medal** winner. Also look for *Good Night, Maman* by Norma Fox Mazer. Lois Lowry is the gifted author of *Anastasia Krupnik* and its sequels as well as *The Giver* (both in this chapter).

One-Eyed Cat
Written by Paula Fox
Aladdin, $4.99, 216 pages
First published in 1984
Ages 9–12

After Ned Willis takes a single shot with a forbidden rifle from the attic, he becomes overcome with guilt and shame. His feelings are made worse by the sudden appearance of a one-eyed cat whose injury, Ned suspects, must have been caused by his irresponsible behavior. Paula Fox's sensitive portrayal and pared prose earned a Newbery Honor for this story. She is also the author of *The Slave Dancer* (in this chapter); *Monkey Island*; and *A Place Apart*.

Onion John
Written by Joseph Krumgold, Illustrated by Symeon Shimin
HarperTrophy, $5.99, 248 pages
First published in 1959
Ages 9–14

The title character is a recent immigrant who's largely misunderstood. Twelve-year-old Andy becomes friends with Onion John and helps him build a house. Sadly, Andy's father unintentionally offends the man by trying to change his way of life. Also by Krumgold is *...And Now Miguel* (in this chapter).

Juvenile Fiction/Chapter Books

Our Only May Amelia

Written by Jennifer L. Holm
HarperTrophy, $5.95, 253 pages
First published in 1999
Ages 10–13

May Amelia despairs of becoming a "Proper Young Lady." She's the only girl in a sibling group of eight, and much prefers overalls to the unenviable dresses that everyone seems to foist upon her. Set in late-nineteenth-century Oregon, this lively story will appeal to fans of Laura Ingalls Wilder. An excellent debut from author Holm, and a **Newbery Honor** book, too.

Out of the Dust

**parent's
guide**
choice award

Written by Karen Hesse
Apple, $4.99, 227 pages
First published in 1997
Ages 10–15

Written in spare free verse, fourteen-year-old Billie Jo offers a haunting slice of life in Oklahoma during the Dust Bowl in this **Newbery Medal**–winning book. No one can escape the pervasive dust, which covers everyone and everything in a grim thick coat. And aside from the daily challenges of poverty, drought, and her father's illness, Billie Jo's mother is killed in a horrific accident for which the young girl bears much of the blame. There's a lot to admire in this deftly written novel, which will appeal to upper-elementary and young adult readers who seek alternative forms of fiction. The story also puts a very human face on the realities of life during the Dust Bowl and Great Depression. Karen Hesse is the author of *Letters from Rifka; The Music of Dolphins; Phoenix Rising*; and *Witness* (in this chapter).

Amelia, Age 14, says: "I just read **Out of the Dust** and it's a special book. At first I was confused by the way it's written but as you get into the story, it's hard to put down. Billie Jo feels so guilty about her mother dying, but her father is responsible also. You wonder what happens to Billie Jo after the book ends."

Chapter Six

Paddle to the Sea
Written and Illustrated by Holling Clancy Holling
Houghton Mifflin, $11.95, 63 pages
First published in 1941
Ages 9–12

This gloriously illustrated **Caldecott Honor** recipient is no simple story book. It's the tale of an Indian boy who places a toy Indian in a tiny carved canoe that will take him from the Great Lakes to the Atlantic Ocean. The panoramic scenery is breathtaking, and the book will prove especially compelling to children who are making a transition from story books and easy readers to chapter books.

P.S. Longer Letter Later: A Novel in Letters
Written by Paula Danziger and Ann M. Martin
Apple, $4.99, 234 pages
First published in 1998
Ages 9–13

Enlivened by the co-authors' close friendship, this novel in letters is warm, witty, and very entertaining. Tara Starr's letters (written by Danziger) are answered by her best friend Elizabeth (written by Martin). Their friendship survives pre-teen trials and is described in colorful, giggly vocabulary. When Tara moves away, their correspondence begins in earnest. The two girls' different personalities are defined by their various likes and dislikes, a charming observation of adolescence, and readers truly believe that the friendship will see them through to old age. Paula Danziger is the author of *The Cat Ate My Gymsuit* (in this chapter). Ann M. Martin penned the popular *Babysitter's Club* series.

The Phantom Tollbooth
Written by Norman Juster, Illustrated by Jules Feiffer
Random House, $5.99, 255 pages
First published in 1961
Ages 8–12

Milo drives his electric car through a pretend tollbooth and enters a place where numbers and odd logic are the law of the land. The wordplay is phenomenal, especially as a fanciful cast of characters is introduced, including the Doctor of Dissonance and Kakofonous A. Dischord. A staple on the children's literature roster for many years, fans of Ronald Dahl and Dr. Seuss will surely want to accompany Milo to the Kingdom of Wisdom and beyond.

Juvenile Fiction/Chapter Books

The Pinballs
Written by Betsy Byars
HarperTrophy, $5.99, 136 pages
First published in 1977
Ages 10–13

Abandoned and broken, Carlie, Harvey, and Thomas J. are three unrelated children who are placed in the same foster home. Carlie bemoans her fate as a "pinball;" she feels she's being "bounced from bumper to bumper." Yet, in their newest home, the three gradually become friends and begin to take control of their futures. Betsy Byars is the author of *The Summer of the Swans* (in this chapter) as well as *Beans on the Roof* and *The Midnight Fox* among others.

Pippi Longstocking
Written by Astrid Lindgren, Translated by Florence Lamborn
Illustrated by Louis S. Glanzman
Puffin, $4.99, 160 pages
First published in 1950
Ages 8–12

There are few mischievous messes that Pippi can't make. She lives alone with a monkey in a small Swedish village. Her daily activities are the envy of children everywhere, since Pippi's routine consists of fun, fun, and more fun. She's a pigtailed imp with a heart of gold, and she won't soon be forgotten. Her sequels include *Pippi in the South Seas*; *Pippi Goes on Board*; and *Pippi on the Run*. There are also a few illustrated Pippi story books for younger readers.

The Planet of Junior Brown
Written by Virginia Hamilton
Aladdin, $4.99, 210 pages
First published in 1971
Ages 10–14

Buddy and Junior live very different lives but become fast friends in this **Newbery Honor** book. Buddy lives on the streets and is involved in a hidden network of homeless kids. Junior is a gifted pianist. He's also overweight and overprotected by his mother. After Junior begins regularly skipping school, the two become nearly inseparable, helping each other bear their different burdens. Other wonderful stories by Virginia Hamilton include *The House of Dies Drear*; *M.C. Higgins the Great* (both in this chapter); *Zeely*; and *Sweet Whispers, Brother Rush*.

Chapter Six

Ramona the Pest

Written by Beverly Cleary, Illustrated by Louis Darling
Avon, $5.99, 192 pages
First published in 1968
Ages 7–10

Ramona Quimby is about to begin kindergarten, but don't let her young age fool you. Her constant curiosity, persistence, frustrations, and general zest for living make her an appealing literary character for all ages. It's Beverly Cleary's magical way with plot and personality that has allowed her to maintain her spot among the very upper echelons of children's authors. For more on Ramona, look for *Beezus and Ramona; Ramona Quimby, Age 8; Ramona and Her Father; Ramona and Her Mother;* and *Ramona Forever.*

Redwall

Written by Brian Jacques
Berkeley, $6.99, 333 pages
First published in 1987
Ages 9–15

From the deepest trenches of the animal underworld comes this exceptional story about a mouse monastery that is being threatened by an evil rat named Cluny. It's young mouse Matthias who, though a meek novice, vows to recover the stolen sword of Martin the Warrior and save the mouse kingdom. There are some gory moments but, all in all, the effect will please *Lord of the Rings* fans while drawing new readers into its continuing series that includes *Mattimeo; Mariel of Redwall; Salmandastron; The Bellmaker; Martin the Warrior; Outcast of Redwall; The Great Redwall Feast; The Pearls of Lutra; Marlfox; The Legend of Luke; Lord Brocktree;* and *Taggerung: A Tale from Redwall.*

Roll of Thunder, Hear My Cry

Written by Mildred Taylor
Puffin, $5.99, 276 pages
First published in 1976
Ages 10–14

This important **Newbery Medal** recipient remains in the hearts and minds of all its readers. Set in the Depression era South, the novel is based largely on the author's own childhood. It's the story of an African-American family who continuously faces prejudice and the threat of racist violence. Young Cassie clings to her close-knit family in the face of danger as well as to the ideals of entitlement. A prequel called *The Land* was released in 2001 and earned a **Coretta Scott King Award** for Mildred Taylor.

Juvenile Fiction/Chapter Books

Sarah, Plain and Tall
Written by Patricia Maclachlan
HarperTrophy, $4.99, 58 pages
First published in 1985
Ages 9–13

A masterpiece of American literature for children, this beautifully written **Newbery Medal** winning story unfolds as two motherless children become acquainted with their new mother, a mail order bride who had responded to their father's newspaper ad. The children are immediately smitten with Sarah who tells tales about her life by the sea in Maine. When it becomes clear that Sarah is homesick, the young siblings fear they will lose her but, instead, accompany her on a trip back home. *Skylark* and *Caleb's Story* are the stunning sequels.

The Secret Garden
Written by Frances Hodgson Burnett, Illustrated by Tasha Tudor
HarperTrophy, $5.99, 358 pages
First published in 1912
Ages 8–12

Mary Lennox is a jaded and somewhat sullen child who is sent to live with her guardian in an old English manor. Mary and her ailing cousin, Colin, discover a magical hidden garden that not only seems to restore Colin's health, it also replenishes the children's spirit. Make no mistake, this is a story worth many times its weight in gold. Tasha Tudor's illustrations add a glowing charm to the Victorian scenery. Frances Hodgson Burnett is also the author of *The Little Princess* (in this chapter).

The Secret of the Old Clock (Nancy Drew Mysteries, Vol. 1)
Written by Carolyn Keene
Price Stern Sloane, $5.99, 180 pages
First published in 1930
Ages 8–12

Okay, the Nancy Drew stories may seem a bit outdated, even kitschy. However, even as readers chortle at our heroine's perpetual naiveté, they continue to ask for this series. Perhaps it's *because* of Nancy's innocence that new generations of readers are drawn to her. Whatever the case may be, you may want to unpack your old volumes and see if your daughter wants to give them a whirl. Chances are, you'll soon be engaged in conversation about Nancy's various pursuits and even find yourself cracking open a book or two with nostalgic glee. The old faithful yellow bound hardcovers are still available, so check the library or bookstore for missing volumes.

Chapter Six

A Series of Unfortunate Events
Written by Lemony Snicket, Illustrated by Brett Helquist
HarperTrophy, $10.99 per volume, 150–200 pages each
First published in 1999
Ages 8–12

The Baudelaire children are the masters of Murphy's Law. They seemed destined to live a life of perpetual problems, conundrums, and mishaps. In the first volume, aptly titled *The Bad Beginning*, we find the orphaned Violet, Klaus, and Sunny in the the hands of the evil Count Olaf. These are somewhat dark stories that are not for the fainthearted, but children everywhere are gobbling them up with vigor. Maybe it's the characters' persistent distress that allows kids to see their own dilemmas as not so bad after all. The series continues with *The Reptile Room; The Wide Window; The Miserable Mill; The Austere Academy; The Ersatz Elevator; The Vile Village;* and *The Hostile Hospital.*

Shiloh
Written by Phyllis Reynolds Naylor
Aladdin, $5.50, 137 pages
First published in 1991
Ages 9–12

Marty is an eleven-year-old boy who lives in the mountains and becomes smitten by a runaway dog named Shiloh. Marty does everything in his power to protect the pup when it becomes clear that his owner is abusing him. He hides Shiloh in the woods and takes drastic measures to prevent his family from returning the dog to the evil Judd Travers. The themes of love and loyalty versus the power of the law are explored in this finely crafted **Newbery Honor** novel that has wide appeal. Follow up with *Saving Shiloh* and *Shiloh Season.*

Sideways Stories from Wayside School
Written by Louis Sachar, Illustrated by Julie Brinckloe
Avon, $4.99, 124 pages
First published in 1985
Ages 8–11

With effervescent wit and wacky wisdom, Louis Sachar weaves hilarious yarns about a school that was accidentally built on its side! One story is sillier than the next as the children from the thirtieth floor classroom engage in antics that impart gentle morals and a lot of fun. Additional titles include *Wayside School Is Falling Down; Sideways Arithmetic from Wayside School;* and *Wayside School Gets a Little Stranger.*

Juvenile Fiction/Chapter Books

Sign of the Beaver

Written by Elizabeth George Speare
Dell, $5.50, 135 pages
First published in 1984
Ages 9–13

After being left alone to guard his pioneer family's home, Matt soon discovers that life in the wilderness is a constant struggle. When he meets a Native American man and his grandson, Attean, an agreement is struck. Matt will teach Attean to read in exchange for some invaluable survival tips. Children who enjoyed *Julie of the Wolves* and *My Side of the Mountain* will certainly be enthralled by this **Newbery Honor** recipient. Also by this author *The Witch of Blackbird Pond* and *The Bronze Bow*.

Sing Down the Moon

Written by Scott O'Dell
Dell, $5.99, 124 pages
First published in 1970
Ages 10–13

Two Navajo teenagers, Bright Morning and Running Bird, contentedly watch their sheep when they are suddenly attacked and taken as prisoners by slavers. The year is 1864, when soldiers forced the Navajos to march to Fort Sumner. The story is an important and haunting historical document, told from a Native American perspective. Scott O'Dell is the author of *Island of the Blue Dolphins* (in this chapter).

A Single Shard

Written by Linda Sue Park
Clarion, $15.00, 152 pages
First published in 2001
Ages 10–14

Hunger and homelessness are the startling themes of this new novel set in twelfth-century Korea and twelve-year-old Tree-ear knows about both. As an orphan, he finds shelter with his disabled guardian Crane-man under a bridge and forages through garbage for food. When a fine potter named Min entrusts the transport of a priceless piece of art to Tree-ear's care, the young boy must summon all of his strength to prove himself worthy of the task. It's a fine work with quiet insistence that will touch all readers. This novel was the **Newbery Medal** recipient in 2002. Linda Sue Park is the author of *The Kite Fighters* and *Seesaw Girl*.

Chapter Six

The Slave Dancer

Written by Paula Fox
Dell, $5.99, 152 pages
First published in 1973
Ages 10–14

Upon being kidnapped by slave traders, a young boy named Jessie is forced to play music during the captured slaves "exercise" periods during their sea journey. It's a horrible fate that agonizes Jessie in this emotional and captivating **Newbery Medal** winning story. Also by this author *One-Eyed Cat* (in this chapter), *A Place Apart*, and *Monkey Island*.

Sounder

Written by William H. Armstrong, Illustrated by James Barkley
HarperTrophy, $5.99, 116 pages
First published in 1969
Ages 10–14

This **Newbery Medal** winning classic exposes the lives of a family of African-American sharecroppers whose lives are tragically changed by a single episode. After the father is jailed for stealing a hog, his son must bear the burden of responsibility and earn enough money to support his family. Sounder, their devoted dog, is a symbol of loyalty and strength and even after he is wounded, the family perseveres. *Sour Land* is the affecting sequel.

Starring Sally J. Friedman as Herself

Written by Judy Blume
Dell, $5.50, 298 pages
First published in 1977
Ages 9–13

As the story opens, Sally's neighbors are celebrating the end of World War II. A couple of years later, ten-year-old Sally and her family have moved to Miami Beach, but the young girl is a bit confused and frightened by the wartime stories she has heard. She even comes to believe that Adolf Hitler is alive and well and living in Miami! Sally's imagination is the star of the novel, as she fancies herself a future movie star and begins to take notice of the boys in her midst. Though historical fiction is something of a departure for Blume, this novel is clearly based on her own girlhood experiences. Other books by this mega-bestselling author include *Are You There God? It's Me, Margaret* and *Tales of a Fourth Grade Nothing* (both in this chapter) as well as *It's Not the End of the World*; *Deenie*; *Blubber*; and *Here's to You, Rachel Robinson*.

Juvenile Fiction/Chapter Books

Strawberry Girl

Written and Illustrated by Lois Lenski
HarperTrophy, $5.99, 194 pages
First published in 1945
Ages 9–13

Birdie Boyer upholds her family's longstanding vocation of strawberry picking in Florida's lake country. Besides a constant battle with unpredictable crops and sporadic fires, the Boyers also endure the persistent hostility of their neighbors. Meanwhile, Birdie dreams of getting a proper education and playing the organ. A **Newbery Medal** winner, the novel features terrific and atmospheric use of regional dialect.

Stuart Little

Written by E.B. White, Illustrations by Garth Williams
HarperTrophy, $5.99, 131 pages
First published in 1945
Ages 8–12

If your child didn't have the opportunity to read this adorable story before viewing the Hollywood film version, there's no better time than the present. The second child of the very human Little family is a very well-mannered white mouse. The Littles love and care for young Stuart, though Snowball the cat never quite takes to him. Stuart embarks on a cross-country trip to visit an old friend, a bird who once visited the Littles' Manhattan garden. Along the way he sees America, finds himself in a few precarious scrapes, and gains a whole lot of confidence. It is a truly wonderful tale, as one would expect from the adored author of *Charlotte's Web* and *The Trumpet of the Swan* (both in this chapter).

Parent/Child Review: Stuart Little

The Parent: Karen, Age 38, Attorney
The Child: Sarah, Age 10, Sticker Collector
Sarah says: "When we decided to read this for your book I thought it would be babyish but it's not. It's better than the movie because the movie makes it seem like everyone is really rich. It's funny that they don't ask 'Why is our son a mouse?'
Karen says: "Good question. I guess good stories can get away with things like that. I read this book when I was young and it's just as wonderful now."

Chapter Six

The Summer of the Swans
Written by Betsy Byars
Puffin, $5.99, 142 pages
First published in 1970
Ages 10–13

On an otherwise ordinary summer evening, Sara's mentally retarded younger brother, Charlie, gets lost. Earlier in the day, she had taken him to view the beautiful swans that resided on a nearby lake, and Charlie, clearly smitten with the graceful birds, decided to revisit the lake alone. An agonizing search ensues as Sara grapples with her role in the event and her feelings for her younger brother. Other lovely titles by Betsy Byars include *The Pinballs* (in this chapter) and *Midnight Fox.*

Tales of a Fourth Grade Nothing
Written by Judy Blume
Dell, $4.99, 120 pages
First published in 1972
Ages 7–10

Little brother Fudge is the bane of Peter Hatcher's existence. Everyone else seems perpetually bemused by Fudge's typical two-year-old antics, but Peter wonders if life will ever return to normal. The final straw comes when Peter's beloved pet turtle disappears. With funny family dynamics and realistic kid feelings, Judy Blume's books have marked the pinnacle of popular children's fiction for years. The must-read sequels include *Superfudge; Fudge-A-Mania;* and, at the time of this guide's publication, a new addition to the family is expected, entitled *Double Fudge. Otherwise Known as Sheila the Great* tells the related tale of Peter's scandalously self-confident neighbor. Other books by Judy Blume include *Are You There God? It's Me, Margaret* and *Starring Sally J. Friedman as Herself* (both in this chapter) as well as *Blubber; Iggie's House;* and *Freckle Juice.* Slightly older children will enjoy *It's Not the End of the World; Then Again Maybe I Won't; Deenie;* and *Here's to You, Rachel Robinson.*

Juvenile Fiction/Chapter Books

Time Warp Trio Series
Written by Jon Scieszka
Puffin, $4.99 per volume, 50–80 pages each
First published in 1991
Ages 8–11

Time travel has never been so zany, and in the hands of spoof-master Scieszka, satirical sci-fi will never be the same. In the first volume, *Knights of the Kitchen Table*, young Joe and his pals are given a book that transports them to medieval times and the land of King Arthur and Lancelot. The boys become unwitting heroes, with the author's ever-plucky wit dropping frequent historical allusions and providing readers with smiles at every action packed turn. Further titles in this series include *The Not-So-Jolly Roger*; *The Good, the Bad, and the Goofy*; *Your Mother Was a Neanderthal*; *2095*; *Tut, Tut*; *Summer Reading Is Killing Me!*; *It's All Greek to Me*; *See You Later, Gladiator*; *Sam Samurai*; and *Hey Kid, Want to Buy a Bridge?*

Treasure Island
Written by Robert Louis Stevenson
Aladdin, $3.99, 339 pages
First published in 1883
Ages 10 and up

Editions of the classic swashbuckling adventure tale abound, with several publishers producing abridged, illustrated versions. Some of these volumes are handsome and useful, as the original version may skew toward a slightly older reader. However, it's worth giving the whole book a shot, as Stevenson's mastery of the adventure genre involves his reverent descriptions of the island, some of which are cut in the shortened volumes. And once kids get a glimpse of Long John Silver, their view of villainous characters will never be the same. Robert Louis Stevenson is the famous author of *Kidnapped* and *A Child's Garden of Verses*.

Chapter Six

The Trumpet of the Swan
Written by E. B. White, Illustrated by Fred Marcellino
HarperTrophy, $6.50, 251 pages
First published in 1970
Ages 8–12

Louis is a trumpeter swan without a voice, but he's determined to toot his own horn. He learns to communicate via a stolen trumpet and receives reading and writing lessons from a boy named Sam. Now he's a bird with a purpose, and he soon wins the heart of his true love, a swan named Serena. White's mastery of anthropomorphism is apparent in all his books, and Louis is a character that will proudly stand alongside Charlotte (of *Charlotte's Web*) and Stuart Little.

Tuck Everlasting
Written by Natalie Babbitt
Farrar Strauss Giroux, $5.95, 139 pages
First published in 1975
Ages 9–13

A magical, mysterious, and highly compelling story unfolds as Winnie Foster unlocks the secret of the Tuck family's immortality. At the same time, an ill-intentioned stranger hatches a plan to exploit the source of eternal life... a fountain of youth hidden in the forest. Winnie risks her life to protect her new friends, but the reward requires a great deal of thought about the meaning of life and death. The issues are pretty weighty, but the book is a true gem. Natalie Babbitt is also the author of *The Search for Delicious*; *Knee Knock Rise*; and *The Eyes of the Amaryllis*.

The Twenty-One Balloons
Written by William Pene du Bois
Puffin, $5.99, 179 pages
First published in 1947
Ages 7–11

Professor William Waterman Sherman embarks on an around-the-world hot air balloon journey in 1883, only to find himself tossed into the middle of the Pacific Ocean. When he finally makes it to land, on the sumptuous and rather strange island of Krakatoa, he is in awe of the people he meets. They all appear to be extravagantly wealthy and, what's more, they share a secret about a hidden diamond mine located on the island. From there, the adventure escalates. It's a **Newbery Medal** winner that is great to read aloud or alone.

Juvenile Fiction/Chapter Books

The View from Saturday
Written by E. L. Konigsburg
Aladdin, $4.99, 163 pages
First published in 1996
Ages 10–14

 With intertwining storylines and meticulous attention to detail, this is an exceptionally well-crafted novel for children. The story concerns four sixth grade students who are chosen to compete in an Academic Bowl competition. These aren't your typical honor students, and part of the charm of the story is uncovering why they were chosen. Each of the four kids—Nadia, Julian, Ethan, and Noah—adds an intriguing piece of the dramatic puzzle. Konigsburg is the outstanding author of *From the Mixed-Up Files of Mrs. Basil E. Frankweiler* (in this chapter).

Parent/Child Review: The View From Saturday
The Parent: Maggie, Age 35, Skating Instructor
The Child: Abby, Age 13, Olympic Hopeful

Abby says: "I'm happy I got to read this book 'cause I never heard of it. I liked it a lot and will probably read it again. I do that a lot when I like a book. There are parts that I didn't totally understand, I can't remember now, but I read it instead of doing homework for three nights in a row."

Maggie says: "Oh, really? That's okay, I guess. I really liked the book, too. It's better than anything I've read in a long time!"

Walk Two Moons
Written by Sharon Creech
HarperTrophy, $6.50, 280 pages
First published in 1994
Ages 9–12

parent's
guide
choice award

 Sal Hiddle's life is undergoing a lot of changes. Her mother has embarked upon a "spiritual journey," leaving the thirteen-year-old and her father behind. After moving to Ohio, Sal meets Phoebe Winterbottom whose life experiences parallel many of Sal's own. During a six-day car trip with her grandparents, designed to trace the steps of her errant mother, Sal relates Phoebe's story. Creech's novel is enlivened by this layering of stories that reflect and sustain each other. It's a terrific technique, that weaves together the connected, and ultimately diverging, stories of each girl as they each seek resolution. Sharon Creech is also the author of *Love That Dog* (in this chapter); *Chasing Redbird*; *Ruby Holler*; and *The Wanderer*.

Chapter Six

The Watsons Go to Birmingham—1963
Written by Christopher Paul Curtis
Laurel Leaf, $5.99, 210 pages
First published in 1995
Ages 10–14

Set before the stirring backdrop of the Civil Rights Movement, Curtis tells the tale of Kenny Watson and his family as they drive south from their home in Michigan toward Birmingham, Alabama. Kenny's older brother, Byron, has been the cause of concern recently, and the boys' parents decide that time spent with their strict southern grandmother will help the older boy. When Kenny's baby sister narrowly escapes a church bombing, the startling effects of racist violence are brought to the foreground, and very close to home for the Watsons. The author skillfully mixes some humorous moments related to the kids' sibling rivalry and family dynamics with actual events. His use of a political setting is never heavy-handed, but provides a thoughtful boundary in which a child's view of the American social landscape expands. This book is a **Newbery Honor** recipient and **Coretta Scott King Honor** book. Curtis is also the author of *Bud, Not Buddy* (in this chapter).

The Westing Game
Written by Ellen Raskin
Puffin, $5.99, 216 pages
First published in 1978
Ages 10–14

In this **Newbery Medal**–winning mystery novel, sixteen potential heirs of a recently deceased millionaire gather to solve a crime and collect their reward. The diverse group of players (and indeed this novel reads like a suspenseful Broadway whodunit) must uncover the cause of their benefactor's demise before cashing in.

Where the Red Fern Grows
Written by Wilson Rawls
Yearling, $5.99, 313 pages
First published in 1961
Ages 9–12

Here's a wonderful novel, set during the Great Depression, about a boy and his two dogs. Billy Colman lives in the Ozark Mountains and saves his money to purchase two coonhounds. After diligently training the dogs—Old Dan and Little Ann—to be champion raccoon hunters, they win the grand prize in an annual contest. The adventure and emotion doesn't end there, however. Billy endures danger and eventual grief, and realizes the meaning of Native American lore about the spiritual properties of the wild red fern.

Juvenile Fiction/Chapter Books

The Whipping Boy

Written by Sid Fleischman, Illustrated by Peter Sis
Troll, $4.95, 90 pages
First published in 1986
Ages 9–12

Prince Brat gives new meaning to his name, but it's forbidden to wallop a prince. Thus the need for a whipping boy who can bear the punishment for his master's misbehavior. The Prince and the boy, named Jemmy, one day decide to take leave of the kingdom and become involved in an uproarious comedy of errors. Soon enough, they become friends. A whirlwind, high-flying comedic fairy tale.

The Wind in the Willows

Written by Kenneth Grahame, Illustrated by Ernest H. Shepard
Aladdin, $3.99, 305 pages
First published in 1908
Ages 7–12

Featuring Shepard's supremely ethereal illustrations, Grahame's enchanting story deserves a prized spot on every bookshelf. Set alongside a gentle river, the stories revolve around four animal inhabitants: Toad, Rat, Mole, and Badger. There's a glowing grace and charm to these stories that truly sets them apart, and each characterization seems perfect. While Grahame's book is set as an old-fashioned tale, it's likely that readers will be partaking of its joys for centuries.

Winnie the Pooh

Written by A. A. Milne, Illustrated by Ernest H. Shepard
Puffin, $4.99, 161 pages
First published in 1926
Ages 5–11

While Winnie the Pooh, as an oft-franchised entity, is immensely appealing to preschoolers, the book in which he makes his first appearance continues to be enjoyed by older readers. Nothing represents cozy storytelling quite as well as tales told from Pooh Corner. It's Christopher Robin's imaginary conversations and playful collaborations with Pooh, Piglet, Eeyore, and Tigger, too, that continue to charm and delight. And though Pooh may not seem like the brightest of bears, he spouts wisdom that rivals the great philosophers. A single volume collection, *The Complete Tales of Winnie the Pooh*, features unabridged versions of all the stories.

Chapter Six

The Witch of Blackbird Pond

Written by Elizabeth George Speare
Dell, $5.99, 223 pages
First published in 1958
Ages 10–13

The year is 1687, and Kit Tyler has recently moved from her home in Barbados to Connecticut to live with relatives. She comes to form a deep resentment for the Puritan restrictions that rule the land and befriends a lonely old woman. The problem is, her new friend has been labeled a witch by the Puritan community, and Kit is soon immersed in a dangerous drama that involves standing trial for witchcraft. It's a marvelous and suspenseful novel and **Newbery Medal** winner. Also by this author, *The Sign of the Beaver* (in this chapter).

Let's Talk about... Historical Fiction

If your child wants to know more about a particular historical episode or era that she's studying in school or simply curious about, historical fiction can often fit the bill. Novels set within the context of an important event can enliven and put a human face on social studies themes. Check the subject index for titles that match your child's interest.

Witness

Written by Karen Hesse
Scholastic, $16.95, 161 pages
First published in 2001
Ages 9–14

In her second novel written entirely in free verse, Karen Hesse sets her startling tale in a small Vermont town circa 1924. As the Klu Klux Klan establishes a foothold amongst the community, we are provided with the divergent accounts of 11 witnesses from different races and creeds. More than just an examination of hatred and sympathy, this book is a glowing example that the use of interesting storytelling conventions—alternate voices and poetic verse—can result in a powerful and glorious novel. And don't miss Hesse's *Out of the Dust* (in this chapter).

Juvenile Fiction/Chapter Books

The Wonderful Wizard of Oz

Written by Frank Baum, Illustrated by W. W. Denslow
Knopf, $12.95, 208 pages
First published in 1900
Ages 7–13

Children tend to think of Dorothy from Kansas as a pigtailed Judy Garland in a blue-checkered smock dress. Such is the power of Hollywood. When introduced to the original book, however, young readers are often surprised. While the story and its sequels are somewhat different, they are also full of imaginative characters and scenarios that don't appear in the film. In any event, the Land of Oz is a magical literary world that takes everyone in its thrall. *The Wonderful Wizard of Oz: A Commemorative Pop-Up* (Little Simon Publishers) is an elaborate and enjoyable anniversary edition. Also look for *The Marvelous Land of Oz*; *Ozma of Oz*; and *Glinda of Oz*.

A Wrinkle in Time

Written by Madeleine L'Engle
Dell, $6.50, 190 pages
First published in 1962
Ages 9–13

If you ask a group of thirty-something Americans in the early part of the new millennium about their favorite childhood books, you're likely to hear a great deal about this one. It's a science-fiction story with a loving heart and obvious appeal. The story involves a somewhat awkward girl named Meg and her younger brother Charles who, in the company of Mrs. Whatsit, Mrs. Which, and Mrs. Who, set off on a whirlwind mission to save their father from IT. What is IT, you ask? It's certainly worth reading this marvelous tale to find out! Sequels include *A Wind in the Door* and *A Swiftly Tilting Planet*. Other wonderful novels by Madeleine L'Engle include the realistic fiction series of *Meet the Austins*; *The Moon by Night*; and *A Ring of Endless Light*. Also look for *Troubling a Star* and *Camilla*.

Chapter Six

The Yearling
Written by Marjorie Kinnan Rawlings, Illustrated by Edward Shenton
Aladdin, $5.95, 428 pages
First published in 1938
Ages 10–15

A more tender, touching story is hard to find. Young Jody is a boy who lives in rural Florida. He is faced with a heart-wrenching decision that involves trying to save the life of a fawn he's raised as his own. Also look for the hardcover edition from Simon & Schuster that features illustrations by N. C. Wyeth.

Indices

INDEX
By Title

The Best
Children's Literature
A Parent's Guide

INDEX

The Best Children's Literature

A Parent's Guide

INDEX

INDEX

INDEX

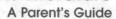

The Best Children's Literature
A Parent's Guide

INDEX

INDEX

By Author

The Best
Children's Literature
A Parent's Guide

INDEX

INDEX

INDEX

The Best
Children's Literature
A Parent's Guide

INDEX

The Best Children's Literature
A Parent's Guide

INDEX

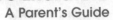

The Best
Children's Literature
A Parent's Guide

INDEX

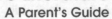

INDEX

INDEX

INDEX

INDEX

INDEX

The Best
Children's Literature
A Parent's Guide

INDEX

The Best
Children's Literature
A Parent's Guide

INDEX

INDEX

The Best
Children's Literature
A Parent's Guide

Awards

Newbery Medal Winners 1922–2002

- *A Single Shard* by Linda Sue Park
- *A Year Down Yonder* by Richard Peck
- *Bud, Not Buddy* by Christopher Paul Curtis
- *Holes* by Louis Sachar
- *Out of the Dust* by Karen Hesse
- *The View from Saturday* by E. L. Konigsburg
- *The Midwife's Apprentice* by Karen Cushman
- *Walk Two Moons* by Sharon Creech
- *The Giver* by Lois Lowry
- *Missing May* by Cynthia Rylant
- *Shiloh* by Phyllis Reynolds Naylor
- *Maniac Magee* by Jerry Spinelli
- *Number the Stars* by Lois Lowry
- *Joyful Noise: Poems for Two Voices* by Paul Fleischman
- *Lincoln: A Photobiography* by Russell Freedman
- *The Whipping Boy* by Sid Fleischman
- *Sarah, Plain and Tall* by Patricia MacLachlan
- *The Hero and the Crown* by Robin McKinley
- *Dear Mr. Henshaw* by Beverly Cleary
- *Dicey's Song* by Cynthia Voigt
- *A Visit to William Blake's Inn: Poems for Innocent and Experienced Travelers* by Nancy Willard
- *Jacob Have I Loved* by Katherine Paterson
- *A Gathering of Days: A New England Girl's Journal, 1830-1832* by Joan W. Blos
- *The Westing Game* by Ellen Raskin
- *Bridge to Terabithia* by Katherine Paterson
- *Roll of Thunder, Hear My Cry* by Mildred D. Taylor
- *The Grey King* by Susan Cooper
- *M. C. Higgins, the Great* by Virginia Hamilton
- *The Slave Dancer* by Paula Fox
- *Julie of the Wolves* by Jean Craighead George
- *Mrs. Frisby and the Rats of NIMH* by Robert C. O'Brien
- *Summer of the Swans* by Betsy Byars
- *Sounder* by William H. Armstrong
- *The High King* by Lloyd Alexander
- *From the Mixed-Up Files of Mrs. Basil E. Frankweiler* by E. L. Konigsburg
- *Up a Road Slowly* by Irene Hunt
- *I, Juan de Pareja* by Elizabeth Borton de Trevino
- *Shadow of a Bull* by Maia Wojciechowska
- *It's Like This, Cat* by Emily Neville
- *A Wrinkle in Time* by Madeleine L'Engle
- *The Bronze Bow* by Elizabeth George Speare
- *Island of the Blue Dolphins* by Scott O'Dell
- *Onion John* by Joseph Krumgold
- *The Witch of Blackbird Pond* by Elizabeth George Speare
- *Rifles for Watie* by Harold Keith
- *Miracles on Maple Hill* by Virginia Sorenson
- *Carry On, Mr. Bowditch* by Jean Lee Latham
- *The Wheel on the School* by Meindert DeJong
- *...And Now Miguel* by Joseph Krumgold
- *Secret of the Andes* by Ann Nolan Clark
- *Ginger Pye* by Eleanor Estes
- *Amos Fortune, Free Man* by Elizabeth Yates
- *The Door in the Wall* by Marguerite de Angeli
- *King of the Wind* by Marguerite Henry
- *The Twenty-One Balloons* by William Pène du Bois
- *Miss Hickory* by Carolyn Sherwin Bailey
- *Strawberry Girl* by Lois Lenski
- *Rabbit Hill* by Robert Lawson
- *Johnny Tremain* by Esther Forbes
- *Adam of the Road* by Elizabeth Janet Gray
- *The Matchlock Gun* by Walter Edmonds
- *Call It Courage* by Armstrong Sperry
- *Daniel Boone* by James Daugherty
- *Thimble Summer* by Elizabeth Enright
- *The White Stag* by Kate Seredy
- *Roller Skates* by Ruth Sawyer
- *Caddie Woodlawn* by Carol Ryrie Brink
- *Dobry* by Monica Shannon
- *Invincible Louisa: The Story of the Author of Little Women* by Cornelia Meigs
- *Young Fu of the Upper Yangtze* by Elizabeth Lewis
- *Waterless Mountain* by Laura Adams Armer
- *The Cat Who Went to Heaven* by Elizabeth Coatsworth
- *Hitty, Her First Hundred Years* by Rachel Field
- *The Trumpeter of Krakow* by Eric P. Kelly
- *Gay Neck, the Story of a Pigeon* by Dhan Gopal Mukerji
- *Smoky, the Cowhorse* by Will James
- *Shen of the Sea* by Arthur Bowie Chrisman
- *Tales from Silver Lands* by Charles Finger
- *The Dark Frigate* by Charles Hawes
- *The Voyages of Doctor Dolittle* by Hugh Lofting
- *The Story of Mankind* by Hendrik Willem van Loon

Awards

Caldecott Medal Winners 1938–2002

- *The Three Pigs* by David Wiesner
- *So You Want to Be President?* Illustrated by David Small, Written by Judith St. George
- *Joseph Had a Little Overcoat* by Simms Taback
- *Snowflake Bentley* Illustrated by Mary Azarian, Written by Jacqueline Briggs Martin
- *Rapunzel* by Paul O. Zelinsky
- *Golem* by David Wisniewski
- *Officer Buckle and Gloria* by Peggy Rathmann
- *Smoky Night* Illustrated by David Diaz, Written by Eve Bunting
- *Grandfather's Journey by Allen Say,* Edited by Walter Lorraine
- *Mirette on the High Wire* by Emily Arnold McCully
- *Tuesday* by David Wiesner
- *Black and White* by David Macaulay
- *Lon Po Po: A Red-Riding Hood* Story from China by Ed Young
- *Song and Dance Man* Illustrated by Stephen Gammell, Written by Karen Ackerman
- *Owl Moon* Illustrated by John Schoenherr, Written by Jane Yolen
- *Hey, Al,* Illustrated by Richard Egielski, Written by Arthur Yorinks
- *The Polar Express* by Chris Van Allsburg
- *Saint George and the Dragon* Illustrated by Trina Schart Hyman, Retold by Margaret Hodges
- *The Glorious Flight: Across the Channel with Louis Bleriot* by Alice & Martin Provensen
- *Shadow* Translated and Illustrated by Marcia Brown, Original Text in French by Blaise Cendrars
- *Jumanji* by Chris Van
- *Fables* by Arnold Lobel
- *Ox-Cart Man* Illustrated by Barbara Cooney, Written by Donald Hall
- *The Girl Who Loved Wild Horses* by Paul Goble
- *Noah's Ark* by Peter Spier
- *Ashanti to Zulu: African Traditions* Illustrated by Leo & Diane Dillon, Written by Margaret Musgrove
- *Why Mosquitoes Buzz in People's Ears* Illustrated by Leo & Diane Dillon, Retold by Verna Aardema
- *Arrow to the Sun* by Gerald McDermott
- *Duffy and the Devil* Illustrated by Margot Zemach, Retold by Harve Zemach
- *The Funny Little Woman* Illustrated by Blair Lent, Retold by Arlene Mosel
- *One Fine Day* Retold and Illustrated by Nonny Hogrogian
- *A Story A Story* Retold and Illustrated by Gail E. Haley
- *Sylvester and the Magic Pebble* by William Steig
- *The Fool of the World and the Flying Ship* Illustrated by Uri Shulevitz, Retold by Arthur Ransome
- *Drummer Hoff* Illustrated by Ed Emberley, Adapted by Barbara Emberley
- *Sam, Bangs & Moonshine* by Evaline Ness
- *Always Room for One More* Illustrated by Nonny Hogrogian, Written by Sorche Nic Leodhas
- *May I Bring a Friend?* Illustrated by Beni Montresor, Written by Beatrice Schenk de Regniers
- *Where the Wild Things Are* by Maurice Sendak
- *The Snowy Day* by Ezra Jack Keats
- *Once a Mouse* Retold and Illustrated by Marcia Brown
- *Baboushka and the Three Kings* Illustrated by Nicolas Sidjakov, Written by Ruth Robbins
- *Nine Days to Christmas* Illustrated by Marie Hall Ets, Written by Marie Hall Ets and Aurora Labastida
- *Chanticleer and the Fox* Illustrated by Barbara Cooney, Adapted from Chaucer's *Canterbury Tales* by Barbara Cooney
- *Time of Wonder* by Robert McCloskey
- *A Tree Is Nice* Illustrated by Marc Simont, Written by Janice Udry
- *Frog Went A-Courtin'* Illustrated by Feodor Rojankovsky, Retold by John Langstaff
- *Cinderella, or the Little Glass Slipper* Illustrated by Marcia Brown, Translated from Charles Perrault by Marcia Brown
- *Madeline's Rescue* by Ludwig Bemelmans
- *The Biggest Bear* by Lynd Ward
- *Finders Keepers* Illustrated by Nicolas, Written by Will
- *The Egg Tree* by Katherine Milhous
- *Song of the Swallows* by Leo Politi
- *The Big Snow* by Berta & Elmer Hader

Awards

- *White Snow, Bright Snow*
  Illustrated by Roger Duvoisin,
  Written by Alvin Tresselt

- *The Little Island*
  Illustrated by Leonard Weisgard,
  Written by Golden MacDonald

- *The Rooster Crows* by Maude & Miska Petersham

- *Prayer for a Child*
  Illustrated by Elizabeth Orton Jones,
  Written by Rachel Field

- *Many Moons*
  Illustrated by Louis Slobodkin,
  Written by James Thurber

- *The Little House* by Virginia Lee Burton

- *Make Way for Ducklings* by Robert McCloskey

- *They Were Strong and Good* by Robert Lawson

- *Abraham Lincoln* by Ingri & Edgar Parin d'Aulaire

- *Mei Li* by Thomas Handforth

- *Animals of the Bible, A Picture Book*
  Illustrated by Dorothy P. Lathrop,
  Text Selected by Helen Dean Fish